And suddenly spider
the frozen to the unfr
and glittering in an in
well, sparkling as if they'd been dipped in sugar.

And the day went dark. Not as if there were clouds,
but as if someone had interposed a filter between
Earth and the sun, leaching away the light.

Eric Banyon had faced Nightflyers, the Unseleighe
Sidhe, the Wild Hunt. He'd riddled with a dragon.
He'd traveled through parts of Underhill that were
a close approximation of Hell.

None of it had prepared him for this.

He was surrounded by grief—drowning in it. Sheer
anguish beat him to his knees. He couldn't tell if it
was his own or someone else's. Pain—loss—devastating
bereavement bordering on madness.

Shield!

He barely forced his shields into place—*a sloppy
discordant wail of clarinets*—when whatever had come
to his call changed tactics. Now he was at the center
of a physical, not an emotional storm, though he could
still sense the grief that lay beneath the attack.

He found himself at the center of a hurricane, but
blood, not rain, was born upon the arctic wind. It
glittered pinkly, freezing as it dashed itself against his
shields, but Eric found time to strengthen them now—
mellow wail of horns—and they stood firm against the
assault as he staggered to his feet again.

What had come against him? What in heaven's
name had he summoned? Was *this* what Jaycie was
running from?

Mad Maudlin

Mercedes Lackey
Rosemary Edghill

Mad Maudlin

This is a work of fiction. All the characters and events portrayed in this book are fictional, and any resemblance to real people or incidents is purely coincidental.

A Baen Books Original

Baen Publishing Enterprises
P.O. Box 1403
Riverdale, NY 10471
www.baen.com

ISBN: 0-7434-9905-0

Cover art by Stephen Hickman

First paperback printing, May 2005

Library of Congress Cataloging-in-Publication Number 2003012128

Distributed by Simon & Schuster
1230 Avenue of the Americas
New York, NY 10020

Typeset by Bell Road Press, Sherwood, OR
Production & design by Windhaven Press, Auburn, NH (www.windhaven.com)
Printed in the United States of America

CONTENTS

PROLOGUE:

THE STRAYAWAY CHILD

She had once thought that all the lands of Underhill were as familiar to her as the bounds of her own Domain, but the realms Rionne ferch Rianten now rode through were known to her only through the tales of Court Bards and the descriptions in the oldest books in her liege-lord's library. She was certain of only one thing about them: if she were caught here, she would be slain outright, without the privilege of fair combat, of trial, of Challenge. These were the realms of the Great Enemy, and Rionne slunk through them as a thief in the night, her every breath a prayer to Danu that her passage would go unnoticed. Each Gate she managed to pass unchallenged was both a gift and a curse, for even as it sped her on her journey, it meant that Jachiel had gone before her, deeper into peril, though he had as yet no more than a child's magic to call upon.

Jachiel. Each thought of him endangered was like a blow to the heart, filling her with the strong emotion that was the Sidhe's greatest danger. But she had accepted the *geas* willingly. Jachiel ap Gabrevys was a prince, and a prince's son, and his father's Court was beset by enemies. That much she had known from the moment he had been given into her hands at his Naming, she to be mother and father to him both, for his Lady Mother was untimely slain in the Chaos Lands defending their realm, and the Lord Prince his father had no time for mewling infants. As the boy had grown toward adulthood, she had faced the day when she must give up some of his care to those others who had stood up at his Naming, those who would teach him the arts of war, of sorcery, of music, and of torture. Those arts would make him strong. He would have less need of her strong arm to protect him, and that was good; she could look to the day when she could seek Healing for the bond that had grown up between them, for passions so intense were not meant to be among their kind. When Jachiel was an adult, and the term of her Oath was run, she would seek, as she was bound to, a Court far from this, so that the memory of him would fade into simple friendship, nothing more. But until that day she had sworn herself his Protector, his shield against all the world's ills.

And she had failed him.

How not? Why else had he fled from her? For it must be that—no enemy could penetrate his father's Court, subvert Prince Gabrevys' Mages and Knights to carry off the young Prince. Only Jachiel himself could have borne himself away from Prince Gabrevys' Domain.

And Rionne must find him, wherever he was.

She had told no one of the young Prince's disappearance. Any Ruler's Court was a place of shadow and intrigue: what could not be done by force might well have been done by trickery, and it would place a weapon in the Enemy's hand to let him know he had succeeded. No. She had summoned up her elvenhound and elvensteed and followed her charge as quickly as she could. Let the Court think they had gone together, and think nothing more. Prince Gabrevys was away, as he so often was, and no one else would have any right to summon the young Prince into their presence. Only Jachiel's Lady Mother would have had that right, she who had been dead these many years.

If she had lived—if she had not died fighting monsters in the formless lands—would it have made any difference?

No! It is I who am his Protector! Mine is the responsibility for his safety, until the day he can guard himself!

And so she would guard him.

The Domain she rode through was green and pleasant, its boundaries firm with long definition and the work of many generations of Elven Mages. It lay in endless twilight, a parkland with no strollers, perfectly groomed and perfectly lovely—perfectly insipid, but then, that was the hallmark of the Enemy. And this made her move faster; now he was in lands that were firmly in the Enemy's hands. She followed Jachiel's trail as swiftly as she could, but no matter how fast she rode, no matter the spells of Tracking and Finding that she unloosed, he was always before her. The Gate that was her current goal lay only a short distance ahead, and as she approached it, Rionne's heart sank. Always the Gates led outward and upward, toward the

World Above and the lands of Mortal Men, a place Rionne had never been.

It was a place filled with danger unimaginable—with poisons that could destroy the Sidhefolk, with metal that could burn away both magic and life, and with worse than these: with strange temptations that could destroy both sanity and grace. Her great-grandmother had been the last of her direct Line to walk among the Mortalkin, in the days before the High Court had summoned all the Princes of the Land to Council, to determine whether the Children of Danu would yet live among the Children of Earth.

Woe betide the High King for that summons! For— so song and legend had it—before that Council there had been no Dark Court and no Light, and the High King and the Queen of Air and Darkness had shared one throne and one bed. But the Princes of the Air could not agree to quit the treacherous pleasures of the World Above, even to save themselves. Instead of agreement, there had been war. Some, like Rionne's folk, had gone Underhill at once. Some had stayed. The Council had ended in strife and disarray, without a ruling being handed down, and from that moment, Oberon and Morrigan had ruled two separate Courts, the High King took himself a new Queen, and the Children of Danu were at war among themselves.

All for Earthborn whose bones were now less than dust upon the wind, so brief were their lives. Yet how enchanting, how dangerous they must be, to destroy so many Sidhe lives and noble houses!

Rionne hoped she would never see one.

As she approached the Gate, her every instinct cried warning, and she slowed, approaching warily. It was impossible that the Enemy would leave a Gate in their Domain unguarded.

Farras growled, his hackles rising. She had raised

and trained the elvenhound herself, and knew his senses were keener than her own. She reined in her 'steed, loosening her sword in its sheath. Aeldana was tired; she must conserve the elvensteed's strength as much as possible, for at any moment she might face the need to fight or flee. She had pushed Aeldana hard in her search for Jachiel, but she had not dared to claim hospitality from any of Prince Gabrevys' allies, lest the fact that Jachiel was not with her be discovered. Any delay on her quest could prove disastrous to her charge—she must find him!

With a flicker of light, the warrior guarding the Gate dropped the *glamourie* shielding her.

"Halt!" she said. "Who goes there?"

Without hesitation, Rionne set Farras on.

The 'hound struck the defending Sidhe like a bolt of silent thunder, slamming her armored body to the grass. She hadn't been expecting an immediate attack. Good. It would buy Rionne the time she needed.

It was an unequal match, war-hound against armored foe. Farras could not win, but Rionne knew that the Enemy would show him no mercy because of that. And she could not stay to save him. Her mission was more important. She must set love against love and choose the greater, though it wounded a heart already broken. She spurred Aeldana forward.

There! She could plainly see Jachiel's mark still on the Gate. Her way was clear. She keyed the Gate, turning in her saddle just in time to see the enemy warrior drag a dagger from its sheath and plunge it into Farras' side.

Thrusting the 'hound's dying body aside, the Enemy ran forward, drawing her sword. But Rionne was faster. Aeldana leapt through the Gate, and Rionne used a hoarded levin-bolt to scramble the Gate's settings behind her.

They went on, two now instead of three, and she no longer had any doubt of Jachiel's destination.

The World Above—the deadly and treacherous human lands.

My heart, my heart . . . what are you seeking there? Rionne mourned wildly. But then she shook her head, smiling grimly at her own foolishness. Undoubtedly she would find out.

If she lived to reach the deadly lands of the Sons and Daughters of Adam.

And lived past reaching them.

CHAPTER ONE:

THE FAIRIES' LAMENTATION

The children huddled in the meager protection of the doorway on the Lower East Side across from the homeless shelter. They passed around hoarded cigarettes and drank from bottles of Coca-Cola swaddled in brown paper bags in imitation of their elders. None of them was older than eight or ten, but their faces were already hard and set, the legacy of a life spent on the street.

Monday was just another day if you didn't have anywhere else to be. School was something to be avoided. Too many awkward questions, too many meddling adults wanting you to get with the program—or into a program. Only a few of them were enrolled anyway. Enrollment required a home address, or a fixed address, and none of them had homes to go to. Not really. In the wake of the unfathomable disaster that had struck New York a year ago, the city's social services had been stressed even further than before. People who had been marginally able to cope before the disaster were no longer able to manage, and those who had fallen through the cracks were being buried beneath the avalanche of lives falling through what were no longer mere cracks, but canyons in the system. New York these days, as many social commentators had said, was one large enclave of post traumatic stress disorder, and, as always, it was the children who were the invisible and largely-unnoticed victims.

For these kids as for many others, home was a single room occupancy or a bed in a shelter, if they still had a family. If not, it was whatever refuge they could find out of the chill November wind. And every one of them already knew that refuge came at a price.

Most of them were dressed in hand-me-downs and cast-offs, worn, dirty, nothing quite the right size, nothing quite warm enough for the cold November day. When clothes were so hard to come by, it was better to get something you could keep as long as possible, and not have to give up because it had gotten too small—though one boy in the group was wearing a new well-fitting leather jacket over a hoodie. The jacket was shiny and cheap, the thin leather already starting to craze and crack, but even so, it marked him out as someone with more resources than his peers. All of them kept a wary eye out for adults, ready to run if they were challenged, but the few pedestrians paid no particular attention to the cluster of young street kids.

"Where you been, Elio?" a very small child piped up—impossible to tell if it was a girl or a boy.

"Yeah—you got girlfriend?" Definitely a boy, this one, elbowing the kid in the jacket with a sly look.

Another about the same age, with an even more knowing look. "Nah—Elio's got a *boy*friend!"

"He give you that mad jacket?" asked a third, with great interest, perhaps wondering if it was worth going that way himself.

"Cut it out, guys!" Elio hunched his shoulders, pulling his hood up over his head and leaning against the side of the building. He stared down at the ground.

"I seen her."

"Seen her? Seen who?" the little kid asked, not getting the hint.

"I seen *her*." Elio's dark face was pinched and pale, and so terrified that it was utterly blank. "*La Llorona.*"

There was a moment of confused silence, as if his listeners wanted to ridicule him, but didn't quite dare. Finally another boy—darker-skinned than Elio—stepped forward.

"Yo, dog, you can't be just saying her name out like that."

"I seen her," Elio repeated, looking up into the other boy's face, sharply, his eyes dull and hopeless. "She's real."

"Then you gotta say," the other boy said. "That's the rule."

Elio took a deep breath. His face twisted, as if he wanted to cry, but when he spoke, his voice was flat.

"I was over at my uncle Esai's place. He had his crew there, and there was like a dozen pizzas, and everything, and he said I could eat as much as I wanted, and he let me watch 'toons on his big-ass television, and gave me a beer and everything."

Murmurs of derision and veiled disbelief greeted

this part of the narrative, but nobody challenged it openly. They wanted to hear the rest, the part about *La Llorona.*

"And he had to go out on, you know, his business, but he said I could stay, on account of Mama was working late, and everybody was still being nice to me 'cause Julio got whacked last month. So I fell asleep on the couch, but in the middle of the night I woke up, on account of beer makes you pee, and I went into the bathroom, and . . . there she was, in the mirror."

Elio's voice dropped to a whisper and his listeners drew in closer.

None of them noticed the older boy around the corner of the building. He'd been loitering, waiting for them to leave before going into the homeless shelter across the street, not wanting to be noticed—the oldest of them might be a good six or seven years younger than he was, but there were at least eight of them, and he knew several of them carried knives. Not good odds if they decided to mug him, and with that many of them, they could swarm him and cut anything off him that they wanted.

And besides, the story interested him. . . .

Elio's voice, thin and shaky, just carried to where he was skulking. "She was all blue, and wearing this floaty stuff, like curtains, and it was all blowing around her, like in the movies when there's a ghost. And she was crying, only it was all black, like blood, and *she didn't have any eyes.*"

The other children backed away now, as if suddenly afraid that the boy in the leather jacket had become dangerous to know. There was a moment of frozen silence, and then they all started talking at once, their voices low and urgent, creating a babble out of which a few shrill phrases emerged.

"Why'd you look?"

"Why'd you tell us?"

"You shouldn't have looked in the mirror."

"If you didn't see her, you'd be okay."

Then the oldest boy, demanding. "If you seen her, how come you still alive, Elio? Everybody know if you see the Crying Woman, you going to die."

No one laughed.

"I guess it too soon," Elio said, shaking his head, in a voice utterly without hope. "I guess I am going to die, just like Julio. She just waitin'."

"Maybe . . . maybe she didn't see you, dog."

The oldest boy smacked the other across the back of the head, and now *his* voice shook with fear. "You dumb or somethin'? Of course she see him! She in the mirror, ain't she? And once Bloody Mary see your face, you gonna die, you know that. She gonna find E. wherever he go, track him down an' drag him down to Hell. She a demon. She got *powers*. Once she see you, ain't no escape."

From his hiding place around the corner of the building, Magnus watched as the boy Elio tried to put a brave face on things, and failed. He hugged himself tightly, his heart beating in fear, watching the other boy. Bloody Mary—*La Llorona*—the Crying Woman. Now he had a name for the woman he'd seen.

It should have been easy to make fun of what he'd overheard. Just little kids telling each other ghost stories. Just urban legends, after all. School-yard tales.

But it wasn't quite so funny when you'd seen her yourself.

And if what the rest of what they said was true . . .

Elio ran off down the street, hitting out angrily at his friends. They followed at a little distance, still subdued, and watching him the way that cats watched one of their number that was dying—wary, and frightened, and a little in awe. It was easy to see what was uppermost in their minds. *It wasn't me. Thank God, it wasn't me.*

Magnus moved cautiously away from the building in the opposite direction, his intention to visit the shelter forgotten.

Bloody Mary. He winced. It was like that story he remembered from when he was a little kid, that if you went into the school bathroom alone on a Friday and stood with your back to the mirror and chanted "Bloody Mary" three times and turned around really quick, you'd see a horrible demon face in the mirror.

And . . . something . . . would happen. He forgot what it was supposed to have been. Something terrible. Maybe there was a movie about it, too.

Only this was real, because he'd seen her, with his own two eyes.

Last week he'd gone out walking alone. Ace hated it when he did that, but he didn't care. He didn't have any money, and who was going to bother him except to mug him? And except for the raggedy kids that didn't have enough clothes to keep warm, nobody wanted what he had.

She always worried that he was going to get dragged into a big black car for a "date," but with his chestnut hair, green eyes, and choirboy looks, Magnus had learned how to deal with *that* sort of thing a long time ago. Besides, people looking for rentboys cruised under the West Side Highway or down on the Strip, not up in the Bowery, so he figured his virtue was pretty safe. And it wasn't like Ace needed help to watch Jaycie. Jaycie slept most of the time, anyway.

It'd been late, maybe two or three in the morning. He'd done gone out just to do it, just because he could, because there was nobody around these days telling him to do this, do that, be good, behave. Besides, he'd wanted to be alone. It was pretty noisy back at The Place at night. Most of the kids were up and out, but if they were there, they wanted to party, whether or not they had anything to party with.

And he'd seen her—the woman Elio had talked about.

He'd been all alone on the street—or he'd thought he'd been.

Then all of a sudden *she* stepped out from between two parked cars, right in front of him.

Tall. Fashion-model tall. And somehow he could see her clearly, even though it was dark and there weren't any lights on the side street. She hadn't been glowing or anything; it was just that somehow she was bright enough to see even in the dark. Pale blue draperies flowing around her, rising and settling, constantly in motion, even though there hadn't been much wind. Black tears flowing down her face out of two black holes where eyes should have been, and he'd been so freaked, because she'd just *appeared*, out of nowhere, that he'd barely had time to start getting really frightened when she vanished again.

He hadn't stayed to look around. He might have been in New York for only about three weeks, but he wasn't an idiot. He'd beat feet back to The Place, and by the time he'd gotten there, the snapshot image of what he'd seen—kind of like the Blue Fairy on crack—had fully developed in his head: tall, willowy, eyeless, weeping tears of black blood.

He didn't know where she'd come from, or where she'd gone, and he didn't care, just as long as he never saw her again.

And to tell the truth, even now he didn't want to admit, even to himself, how scary she was. In

seventeen years of disappointing experiences, Magnus
had learned that the best way to handle things he
didn't like was silence. If you didn't talk about things
you didn't like, you could pretend they hadn't happened, and sooner or later, it was almost like they
never had. So he hadn't said anything to anyone
about what he'd seen, not even Ace. And he hadn't
gone out alone again late at night, either.

But now these kids said one of them had seen her
too, and they'd all seemed to know about her.

Right. He had to think about this, right now, real
hard, before he scared himself into holing up in The
Place and never coming out. Did that really mean what
he'd seen had been no-shit real? Or had the whole
thing been a goof staged for his benefit?

Magnus considered the idea carefully. No. They
hadn't known he was there, so they hadn't been putting it on for his benefit—and how could they possibly
have known what he'd seen? Besides, they'd been *little*
kids, half his age—and kids that age weren't that good
at acting—not that kind of acting, anyway. The oldest
of them couldn't have been more than ten. And he
didn't even know them. Okay. They hadn't seen him
and even if they'd seen him, they didn't know him.
Why should they bother to ring his chimes?

That only left the other explanation. The worse
one.

She was something *real*.

And—if the rest of what those runt losers said was
true, too—she was going to find him and kill him,
because he'd seen her and she'd seen him.

Bloody Mary.

Magnus shivered, heading for home—or what passed
for home these days. Even at its worst, it was still
better than the one he'd left.

Even if it was going to kill him.

At least when it did, it would kill him on his own terms.

The Jacob Riis Shelter in Lower Manhattan occupied what had been—a century before—an upper-middle-class home in what had then been a well-to-do residential district.

Times had changed.

Now, suitably renovated—though too long ago, on the slenderest of shoestrings—the aging brownstone did the best it could with what it had to provide: beds, hot meals, and counseling to an ever-shifting population of the city's poor and homeless. These days, that was a precarious interlocking web of grant money, city stipends, and private donations, less every year, though sometimes there was still a little money for "extras"—the things that shelter director Serafina Macunado knew weren't extras, but necessities, if they were to bring any light and hope into the lives of their youngest clients. Color, creative play, laughter, music.

Hosea Songmaker shrugged Jeanette's strap higher on his shoulder and smiled down at the circle of children who surrounded him. Some of them—those who had been here longest—smiled shyly back. The others regarded him with expressions ranging from shocked blankness to outright suspicion.

For the last six months, Hosea had been spending four days a week here, providing "music therapy" to the shelter's children, a simple enough task for an Apprentice Bard, and one that required no more credential than his New York City busker's license and a willingness to help. The director insisted on paying him—he made sure that it was a pittance, the minimum he could get away with and still be taken seriously. He enjoyed working with the children, and—since the previous autumn—had found his skills especially needed.

Paul and Toni were handling most of his training as a Guardian, and Hosea had been frankly surprised to find out how little there was: becoming a Guardian seemed to be pretty much a matter of "sink or swim." His lessons with Eric made a lot more sense, to his way of thinking—after all, he'd come East looking for someone to teach him the music magic in the first place. Eric took those responsibilities seriously, and Hosea felt he was making progress there. Well, Eric said he was, and one Bard couldn't lie to another, even if it had been in Eric Banyon's nature to lie to anyone. Which it wasn't, not unless there was a lot of call to lie, or the need to lie, and besides, they were both Bards, and Bards *had* to be honest with each other.

But this Guardian business was enough to scare a man blue, when it wasn't downright confusing, and Eric couldn't help him there. Haunted subways with phantom trains, were-coyotes in Central Park, stuff in the storm sewers that was a *lot* stranger than the alligators and giant rats in the urban legends, rogue gargoyles, that cursed opera up at Lincoln Center haunted by the ghost of its composer . . . Hosea'd begun to wonder why *anybody* would want to live in New York.

He'd barely begun to settle in to his dual duties as Guardian and Bard last autumn when the disaster had hit New York. Two numbers and a slash; say 9/11 and that was all you had to say these days. It had changed everything in ways that no one could have imagined before that morning. From now on, there was Before, and there was After.

It was not only the shock, the pain, and the trauma,

the sudden senseless deaths of so many that hurt the soul of the city and the nation; it was the need for everyone to fight their way past the knee-jerk flash of hatred and the lust for revenge to an understanding that what was needed was not just an end to this, here, but an end to anything like this, everywhere, for all time. That was the aftermath. Going on. Living day to day in a world where all the rules seemed to have changed. Living in a world where the illusion of safety—and it had never been more than that, not really—had been brutally ripped away, a kind of innocence destroyed forever. Living in a city where every breath of air for months and months carried the stink of burning in it, having to run air filters for most of a year, having every air conditioner within a mile of Ground Zero break in the first couple of weeks on account of all the crud in the air; and where, for the psychically sensitive, every moment of every day was awash with tears enough to fill an ocean.

But . . .

Each day of After brought a small triumph for the city—the Thanksgiving Day parade, held right on schedule; the Christmas Tree Lighting at Rockefeller Center; the July Fourth fireworks display. Every day of business as usual in the months that followed was a triumph for New York and a defiance of the forces of darkness and destruction.

The healing was slow, but healing there was, and Hosea, working at the shelter with the most damaged of the city's residents, saw it clearly. The spirit of New York was as indomitable as the green of the Spring. Nature went on, no matter how cruel the storms of Winter. Life would go on. Everything was changed, but they would all go on.

But lately, here at the shelter, Hosea was hearing things that disturbed him: small, subtle things,

too vague to be even called rumors, from the most
unlikely of sources.

The children.

"What shall Ah play?" he asked them, his broad
Ozark drawl bringing giggles from all but the most
withdrawn. After a moment, one of the boldest children offered a suggestion—it was, as usual, a current
hip-hop hit.

As always—it was a practiced routine by now—he
only got a few bars into the melody before getting
it hopelessly tangled up in something else. This time
he chose the Muppets' "Rainbow Connection," slipping back and forth between the two tunes as if they
were two warring radio signals. Finally he stopped
and grinned at the children.

"What's that you say, Jeanette? You don't like that
song?" Hosea asked, cocking his head toward the
banjo and strumming its strings lightly.

:I said, these rugrats have no imagination,: Jeanette
answered acidly.

Hosea pretended not to hear. Though he talked
to his instrument for the children's benefit, only
he knew that the spirit that inhabited it could hear
him—and answer.

Jeanette Campbell had been an outlaw chemist,
creator of the drug T-6/157—known as T-stroke—that
had been responsible for hundreds of deaths in the
city last spring before she'd been dragged off Underhill
to serve the Unseleighe Sidhe Aerune mac Audelaine.
Poisoned by her own creation, and faced with the
choice between dying and going to Hell or staying in
the world to try to make amends somehow for the
wrongs she'd done, she'd elected to be bonded to
Hosea's banjo until she had made reparations for the
damage she had done in life—in effect, haunting it.

"You want me to play something else, Jeanette? Well,

Ah guess Ah'll let you pick the song, then." And he segued back into "Rainbow Connection" again, by now with all the children sitting forward, and with some of them clapping enthusiastically.

Before they had come to Jacob Riis, many of his audience had never heard a live performer, unless it was a street-corner, trash-can drummer or a rapper. Hosea fascinated them, and music was a way of bringing even the most withdrawn children out of themselves, encouraging them to talk about their troubles. For the next hour, he played for them— simple songs, weaving a tiny thread of Bardic magic into them, small spells of joy and hope, encouraging the children to sing along, until all but the hardest to reach were participating.

It was little enough that he could do for them. The shelter was not a permanent home—it couldn't be, with so many in need of its services. No one was allowed to stay at Jacob Riis for longer than two weeks now. The shelter was only a waystation, while the overworked staff frantically tried to find permanent accommodations for those who came to them, though that wasn't easy these days. Fortunately there was no limitation on its drop-in services, other than space and money. The shelter fed hundreds every day, for as long as the supplies held out, and was frequently the only place the city's burgeoning homeless population could go to get a shower, clean clothing, and even rudimentary medical attention.

Sometimes "his" children came back for weeks, sometimes even for a month or two, giving Hosea time to learn their names, and start to form friendships with them. But in the end, they always disappeared. Sometimes Serafina could tell him where they'd gone, but more often she'd only shrug wordlessly and turn away.

"Try not to care too much," she'd told him when she'd hired him. "It will only break your heart."

❖   ❖   ❖

Music Therapy ended, and the children were herded off to Art Therapy—the grant-approved name for an hour spent with paints and crayons. One little girl hung back. Her name was Angelica. Hosea guessed that she was about four, but she wasn't sure herself.

She'd been here for a month now, in defiance of all the shelter's policies, but there was simply no place to send her. Her mother had begged them to keep her. The woman's name was Erika, Hosea remembered. No one had seen Erika for a week and a half. Next week Serafina was going to have to go to Child Protective Services and get them to take Angelica away. Serafina had done all she could, hoping Erika would come back, hoping they could get her into a program that would let her keep her daughter; hoping that Erika wouldn't simply come back and take her baby back out onto the streets.

Angelica's drawings were . . . disturbing.

Not in the way some of the other children's were, when they drew pictures that were obviously portrayals of violence or abuse at home, depictions of gang shootings, or worse. Angelica's were different. As if she was trying to set down on paper something that she'd seen, but as if that something were so far out of the ordinary that a four-year-old couldn't manage to share it.

"Would you like to hold mah banjo?" Hosea said, still sitting on the floor, running his hand lightly over the strings to make them shiver.

:Don't let her near me, you troglodyte!:

Angelica came shyly forward, reaching out to pluck at one of the silver strings with a chubby baby hand.

"Sometimes she sounds like that," Angelica confided. "When she's the Blue Lady." She ducked her head. "I'm not supposed to tell you," she whispered confidentially. "Cause you're a grownup."

"Ah'm not so growed-up as all that," Hosea said, willing a thin thread of Bardic magic—what he'd always called his *shine,* before he'd met a real Bard—out to enfold the little girl. He needed to hear more about this, and he suspected he didn't have much time.

He'd started hearing hints of what he thought of as Blue Lady stories a few months ago, but he suspected they'd been going on for a lot longer than that. They were stories the youngest children told each other when they thought the adults couldn't hear, but there wasn't much privacy in a shelter crammed to overflowing. The Stories were things the children shared to give themselves hope in a world where all hope was dead. Slowly, from bits and whispered pieces, Hosea had started piecing the whole larger story together.

"They're a Secret," Angelica told him sternly, kneeling beside him. "They're the Secret Stories."

Hosea—over Jeanette's protests—slipped the strap of the banjo over his head and settled the instrument in Angelica's arms. She cradled it like a doll.

"But you wasn't going to tell me anything secret," he coaxed. "You was jest going to tell me about how the Blue Lady sounds like ol' Jeanette here."

"When she's nice," Angelica agreed. "Because sometimes she still is, almost like if you know her Secret Name. Bloody Mary is bad. It says on television. She makes girls her slaves, or to be in gangs. But sometimes, one in a thousand girls with no home is a Special One. When Bloody Mary comes to take her to Hell, the girl is so smart and brave that Bloody Mary disappears and the Blue Lady comes, and the Special One can protect all the other kids from Bloody Mary. Since I don't have a home anymore, do you think maybe I'm a Special One, Hosea?" Angelica looked wistful. "Like Buffy on television?"

"Ah think yore purty special, Angie," Hosea said softly. "Can you tell me the Secret Name?"

"Nobody knows—" Angelica began.

Just then Serafina came in. "Oh there you are! Run along, Angie—it's time to go draw pictures, okay?"

Sighing in disappointment, Hosea got to his feet and took his banjo back from Angelica. The little girl ran off into the other room.

"I just got off the phone with Child Welfare," Serafina said with a grimace. "They asked if we could keep her one more night. They'll be sending a caseworker down for her in the morning."

Hosea nodded. He'd known it was inevitable, but that didn't mean he had to like it. "What's going to happen to her?" He knew he shouldn't ask, but he couldn't help himself.

"We always hope for the best," Serafina said, her voice colorless. "She's a sweet kid. If she's placed with a good family. If her mother shows up again and releases her for adoption. If." Serafina shrugged. "Come on. I'll sign your voucher so you can get out of here. Unless you want to hang around and wash dishes?"

It was cold but clear—last winter had been mild, but this year seemed determined to make up for it—and Hosea decided to walk home. He wanted the exercise, and few people would bother a man his size, even in this neighborhood. Besides, he could use the walk to get Angelica's story—the Secret Stories—clear in his head.

Only the youngest children told them, and only to each other, though Hosea had managed to overhear quite a lot. He'd never heard them from any child older than twelve, and the boys seemed to concentrate on a different aspect of the Stories than the girls did.

All their tales spoke of a grim and frightening world—though no worse, Hosea imagined, than the one they themselves lived in.

In the Stories, God was dead, or gone away somewhere. Once he'd lived in Heaven in a beautiful palace of blue-moon marble, until on Christmas night a horde of demons led by Bloody Mary had come over the wall and smashed his palace to dust. Now Heaven was gone, and God was missing in action.

The reason that adults didn't know this had happened was because TV news had kept it secret, but word had gotten out, brought to the children themselves by their dead relatives. Now Earth itself was the battleground. Here angels fought in God's absence, defending His last Earthly strongholds from demonic attacks. The demons' gateways into the human world were mirrors, abandoned appliances, dumpsters, and SUVs with black windows. The demons' stronghold was a place called "Ghost Town," where the dead lived.

The dead figured more frequently in the childrens' tales than angels—dead relatives who paid them visits to warn of trouble, or to give them information to help them survive on the streets. Since Heaven was gone, the good dead had no place to move on to, but that didn't worry the children. In the Secret Stories, the good dead joined the angels in hidden military camps, fighting the ongoing war against the demon armies. They encouraged the children to study hard, and to be brave and strong and not get sucked into the gangs, so that when they died, they could be good soldiers too, and fight against the gangs who did the demons' work. Every child knew that the gangs belonged to Bloody Mary and worked for the demons.

Bloody Mary, the children's particular enemy, was feared even by the demons, even though she had led the assault on Heaven. As far as Hosea could tell, she took special joy in the destruction of children—they said she crooned with joy when a child was murdered. All the children knew that once Bloody Mary had seen them, they were marked for death. All knew that Bloody Mary could enter the heart of whoever a child trusted most, causing that person to betray them to the demons and their human helpers. It did not occur to most of the children Hosea met through the shelter to seek out adult help or protection, for adults had failed all of them—and in some cases, more than failed them—and they no longer trusted the adult world. Adults were the enemy, the predators—or at the very best, fellow victims. The best of the children wanted to grow up to be strong enough to protect themselves, and the rest . . . well, the rest of them hoped to grow large enough and strong enough to become predators themselves. For them, it was better to get into the gangs and serve the enemy—the demons—because at least in the gangs, you had some protection from the real world, and as for the other, well, if you served Bloody Mary, she wouldn't come looking for you.

The girls told a special story about Bloody Mary as well, about how Bloody Mary could invade the souls of girls, making them become her slaves; drug addicts and whores for the gang members. As soon as a girl-child down here on the mean streets could walk, she knew just what the girls in the thongs and fishnets, the high heels and miniskirts were peddling. And she knew that one day it was likely that someone would be making her peddle the same commodity—and in the Secret Stories, that someone was Bloody Mary.

And now Hosea knew—thanks to Angelica—about the Special One—the one girl in a thousand who could resist Bloody Mary, making the Blue Lady appear instead.

Hosea knew that the Blue Lady was the homeless children's chief ally, a beautiful angel with pale blue skin who lived "in the ocean." She loved the children as much as Bloody Mary hated them, and often spoke to them, giving them messages of love and reassurance, but the demons had rendered her powerless with a spell. Only if her true name were known could she regain her full power and defeat Bloody Mary forever.

And Angelica said that nobody knew it anymore.

Well, here's a fine kettle o' fish, Hosea grumbled to himself. The Secret Stories might be just that, and known in their entirety only to the very youngest, but even the gangs believed in Bloody Mary. Just the other day, Serafina had told him about an execution down by the river, where the body of the victim had been left on top of a pile of broken mirror glass. According to the children, mirrors were demon gateways, but they were particularly special to Bloody Mary, who often appeared in them, and possibly came through them.

The execution—had it been an offering . . . ?

Or had Bloody Mary come to claim one of her own?

It didn't take a rocket scientist to see that the little'uns weren't just creating stories to make sense of their lives. They were doing more than that. As a Guardian and a Bard-in-Training, Hosea knew perfectly well that nightmares could step out into the Real World if sufficient belief energy was poured into them. From Eric, Hosea knew that the elves thought that creativity was the human form of magic—elves didn't have it, and thought it was as amazing and mysterious as most humans thought magic was. In

the right—or wrong—hands, there was a very fine
line between creativity and magic, and kids, especially desperate kids like the ones that filled Jacob
Riis at the moment, were just bursting with creative
energy and, more to the point, *belief*. And if a lot
of them had been believing in the same thing for
a long time—long enough to create the elaborate
tales that Hosea had overheard and pieced together
over the last several months—they might have even
managed to create what Paul Kern called a *mythago*,
a spirit form which had actual independent objec-
tive reality.

So Bloody Mary might be out there, walking around
loose. Somewhere. And acting according to her created nature, as a sort of urban-techno Lilith: a night-
stalking child predator.

Hosea considered the matter, turning it over in his
mind. The trouble with being a Bard *and* a Guardian was that sometimes it was difficult to make up
your mind whose business a particular kind of jinx or
hoodoo was. But after a while, he decided to bring
the matter to Eric first. It wasn't actually a problem.
Not yet. He wasn't *sure* Bloody Mary was "real." The
gangs could just be aware of her legend, playing on
it to scare their enemies—and, in the way of kids
everywhere, each other. And with a little Bardic
tweaking, he might be able to nip that in the bud.
Remove Bloody Mary's power to frighten, and nobody
would use her to frighten anyone.

Easier said than done.

The little'uns stories were so dark, so bleak. Even
the Blue Lady, their only hope, didn't have any real
power to help them. But maybe he and Eric could
put their heads together and find a way to steer the
Secret Stories—just a little bit. Maybe between the
two of them, they could figure out a way to put a

little hope into the kids' world, a kind of hope that didn't involve being dead first.

It was surely worth a try.

This was the part that always made her nervous, heading back home carrying all this stuff and money besides, because if anybody started up with her, it would take her a minute or two to drop enough of it to be able to run, and a lot could happen in a minute or two. Lord Jesus knew she'd learned that already, to her sorrow and cost.

Ace winced, the way she always did when she heard herself taking the Savior's name in—well, in anything. When she'd lit out on Billy Fairchild and the Salvation Gospel Choir and Ministry, she'd sworn she was done with God, Jesus, and the Book. And with music most of all. If she never sang another note of music, it would be fine with her. The way Daddy'd always gone on about how what she could do having been sent to him from God . . . well, as much as he'd slung the Gospel, she'd never heard anything in it about God sending *anybody* the gifts of the Spirit just to make somebody else rich.

It'd been bad enough when she'd been a little girl, when Daddy'd had his salvation show, and they'd traveled on the big bus from town to town all through the hills, with Daddy pitching Gospel and Mama passing the hat, and her singing at the head of the choir from the time she was old enough to walk.

It'd been worse when they moved to Tulsa and Daddy'd gotten his television ministry: Billy Fairchild's Salvation Ministry and Gospel Choir. She'd been so scared to be up there in front of the cameras, even though he'd told her, "Heavenly Grace, you are the keystone of my Cathedral of the Airwaves." It had all sounded mighty fine, and they'd had a big house to live in with wall-to-wall carpets and a bathroom for each of them, and Mama had gotten a fur coat and Daddy'd gotten a big car.

And along the way there'd been more cars, and bigger houses, and she'd learned to hate it, and then to be afraid of it, but that hadn't been the worst of it. No, the worst was when Daddy Fairchild's new bad friend had showed up from somewhere. Gabriel Horn. And if Gabriel Horn wasn't Mr. Splitfoot himself, it was Ace's opinion (she'd always hated the name "Heavenly Grace," and nobody in New York was ever going to hear of it, if she had any say in things), that he was a very close relation. When she'd left last year, Daddy Fairchild was talking about moving the Ministry from Tulsa to Atlantic City, New Jersey, to minister to the sinners right in the heart of their damnation to hear him tell it. And that was all Gabriel Horn's notion. She knew that for sure. Mama was perfectly happy in Tulsa, and Daddy'd been happy there too, until Mr. Horn had shown up.

And Heavenly Grace was still going to be the keystone of Daddy's new cathedral. Ace had realized then that she was never going to get out—was never going to be *let* to get out. That Daddy and Gabriel Horn were going to use her and what she could do to keep the money coming in forever, and as much as both of them talked about Jesus and the poor, she'd never seen the money going anywhere but Fairchild Ministries, Inc.

So she'd left. She'd hit the road and kept moving, always north and east. She guessed that New York was about as far from Jesus and Tulsa as it was possible to get, and maybe Daddy would give up on Atlantic City once his little "keystone" was gone.

She was almost back to The Place now. Once she was off the street and out of sight, she'd be as safe

as safety came these days. Even all bundled up and
with a hat pulled way down over her hair, she knew
she didn't look right to be around here: too white and
too womanly, and here and now, both those things
were bad. She wished she wasn't *pretty*—she'd had
to move on pretty damned quick because of it more
than once, and here, it was just like having a target
painted on your back—a big sign that said FRESH
MEAT: COME AND GET IT.

Not that it had been any better when she'd been
a baby. Nobody'd ever looked at her *that* way, but
what they'd done had almost been worse. Daddy's
Little Angel, he'd called her, just like Mary in Heaven.
They'd used to sell pictures of her on the Salvation
Gospel Hour, until she'd felt like a doll, a *thing*,
something anybody could buy for five dollars and put
up on their wall next to Jesus and Elvis and John F.
Kennedy. Sometimes she'd used to wonder if she was
real at all, or just something Daddy'd bought from
the same place he bought all those boxes of white
Bibles with his picture inside, and the robes for the
choir, and the big cross he stood in front of when he
preached once the money started coming in.

She wondered what Daddy would think if he could
see his heavenly angel now.

*Better not think of that while you should be watch-
ing the street, or you'll be a heavenly angel double
quick,* she told herself sternly.

She checked to make sure the block was deserted,
and went around the side of the building, down the
little alley, climbing up the fire escape to the open
second-floor window. It was hard work with the heavy
backpack and several full grocery bags, but she managed. She'd had a lot of practice since she'd found
The Place last summer.

Everybody knew about The Place, she guessed, even

the police, but as long as all the ground-floor doors stayed chained shut and the windows stayed closed, and there weren't any lights showing upstairs, it was safe enough. At least, no one was going to hassle the kids living here.

Until something bigger and stronger chased them all out.

She went up the stairs, carefully avoiding the holes in the treads and trying not to step on the garbage and trash that littered them. She was just as glad it was almost as cold in here as it was outside; that way the place didn't smell so bad—not like it had when it was warmer. It wasn't like they had indoor plumbing or anything, and none of them was old enough to rent a room anywhere, even if they could come up with the money. Apartments in New York cost as much as a whole house back in Tulsa, it seemed like.

She reached the fourth floor and looked around. Most of the interior walls had been torn down long ago. All that remained were the support beams of the large interior space. When the building had been condemned, the glass had been removed from the windows facing the street and replaced with large pieces of sheetrock as a defense against vandals. The kids themselves had covered the ones at the sides with sheets of cardboard scavenged from the subway, so that it was always dark now, except for the little light provided by candles and battery-powered lanterns.

The building's new tenants had also covered the walls with posters—stolen from the subways mostly—but nobody wanted to put up things they cared about too much. People were always stealing from each other, and anything you really cared about, you kept with you all the time.

Ace was pretty sure they wouldn't steal from her and risk being cut off from the shopping—and the handouts that went with it—but she knew too much about human nature to test the theory. Most of them—all of them probably, except for Magnus and Jaycie—were hooked on drugs, and would do anything to get the money for them.

She sighed, shaking her head. It was because of the street life, she knew that. The other girls were always urging her to come out with them at night, to meet their "boyfriends," to go on "dates." Ace had no intention of doing any such thing, but that meant she had to be very careful. She had to watch where she went, and who she was with—and what she ate and drank, especially here. She didn't begrudge the need for caution. It was the price of freedom.

And she knew Daddy and Mr. Horn must be looking for her. It'd been months, but she knew they wouldn't give up. Sometimes she wondered which one of them was looking harder. Daddy would be missing his heavenly meal ticket, but she hadn't liked the way Mr. Horn had looked at her, no, not at all.

Well, if she could be careful for long enough, it wouldn't matter. She'd be seventeen in a few months. That meant all she had to do was hide out for another year, and she'd be free. Eighteen was a legal adult. After that, there was no way anyone could drag her back. She wasn't afraid of work. She'd get a job—scrubbing floors, waiting tables, something. She'd save up her money, and then—

College. Just the way she'd always dreamed. She'd finish high school, get her diploma, get the rest of her schooling, and then nobody could stop her, nobody could touch her, ever again.

And she'd never have to sing another note.

As she walked into the center of the room—neutral territory—and set down the shopping bags, shrugging

off the backpack with a sigh of relief, the inhabitants
of The Place began coming over to her. There were
about a dozen of them living here, and this early
in the day, everyone was here—except Magnus, she
noticed, taking a quick glance around. Everybody
had their own space, with mattresses (of a sort) and
blankets, and the edges of their area marked off in
playground chalk on the dusty splintery floor. Some
even had lamps and tables—whatever they could
scavenge off the streets and get inside. You'd lose
everything if you had to run, but at some point the
need to have something that looked like a home
outweighed caution.

Sometimes I feel just like Wendy in Peter Pan, Ace
thought with a sigh. It had been one of her favorite
stories, until she'd realized what Wendy must have
gone through taking care of the Lost Boys.

Quickly, she handed out her purchases—batteries,
paper towels, candy (a lot of candy), bottled water,
condoms. Nothing she couldn't buy legally, and she'd
bought all of it. She'd told them all her rules at the
beginning: she wouldn't steal, and she wouldn't lie
about her age to buy booze or cigarettes. If they
had money, they had to pay for what they wanted.
If they lied about not having money when they did,
she'd know. And they couldn't bring their friends
around for handouts, because the money would only
stretch so far.

It had worked pretty well, so far. And thanks to
Jaycie, there was always enough money so that nobody
starved. Being the one in charge of the money gave
her enough power to set a few rules, and to protect
Jaycie, though she wasn't sure how long that could last.
If Magnus hadn't shown up like manna from heaven
just when he did, her system would all have fallen
apart. But that boy was as touchy as a wolverine with

a toothache, and you just had to look at him to know you didn't want to mess with him.

Once she'd distributed the purchases—she shopped as often as she dared, about three times a week—the others went away again. Ace picked up the backpack once more—still half full—and went over to the corner she shared with Magnus and Jaycie.

He was curled up—asleep, as usual—with only the top of his hat showing at the top of the battered old sleeping bag. She watched until she was sure she could see the rise and fall of breathing, then sat down on her own sleeping bag to wait for Magnus to come back.

Neither of them knew anything much about Jaycie (other than that he had really long black hair and really green eyes) including his last name or where he came from—but then, neither of them knew that about each other, either. She thought his parents might be Scandinavian, because his skin was really pale, but he didn't have any kind of an accent. She also thought he might be sick, because he slept a lot of the time. Too much of the time, in fact.

He'd been here when she'd first found The Place last summer. He'd always seemed to have money—quite a lot of money, in fact. It hadn't taken her long to realize that the other kids picked on him and stole it from him like he was some kind of ATM, and that Jaycie didn't fight back.

She'd put a stop to that real quick.

But she'd known that wasn't a real solution. There was no way Jaycie would be let to just *keep* all that money when they knew he had it, and the fact of the matter was, he didn't really seem to want it, or know what to do with it. The important thing was to keep fights from starting—and the second most important thing was to keep everybody from getting their hands on wads of cash, because, well, they never used it for the things they really needed. Like food.

She'd gotten the idea of using it for the good of *all* of them, within certain strict guidelines, providing Jaycie was left completely alone. It worked for a while, but she didn't think she could have made it stick if Magnus hadn't shown up and backed her.

The weird thing was, as she'd quickly come to realize, was that Jaycie *always* seemed to have money, no matter what.

'Cause I'll be switched if I know where you get it, Ace thought, looking down at him. *I never see you go out—so if you* do *go out, you sure aren't out long enough to* earn *it. And I don't think you're stealing it. Who'd be afraid of you? A high wind'd blow you away, and you never eat much of anything but those sodas of yours, and that awful Baker's chocolate....*

It was a couple of hours later by the time Magnus reached The Place. He went inside cautiously, listening for sounds from upstairs. Everything was quiet, except for the sound of music played low and some conversation. It was a good day then. He hated it when there were fights, and it seemed like there was always something to fight about, especially things like clothes, makeup, batteries, CDs . . . and cigarettes, booze, and drugs, though it was easier for kids their age to get their hands on grass, lady, or crack than a bottle of Mad Dog or a carton of Marlboros.

Magnus shuddered. Drugs and alcohol didn't tempt him. He'd gotten drunk. Once. And long before he'd come here. There was something frightening about being out of control, about being in a condition where anybody could do whatever they wanted to with you and there was nothing you could do about it. He even hated *sleeping*, but there wasn't much he could do about that. Everybody had to sleep.

He reached the fourth floor and looked around. It was late afternoon. Everybody was up; he could tell by the number of candles that were lit. It gave Magnus a kind of creepy feeling, like living in a bombed church. Sometimes he thought it was cool; there was a kind of surrealness about it, as if he was living in an old war movie; he half expected to hear the tanks and the shells any moment. But right now it just irritated him. Why did they try to make it look like home when they knew they were just going to have to leave it all behind when they had to move on? Because eventually they would; sooner or later, one of the gangs would decide they needed The Place as a crack house, or the city would make the landlord tear it down, and they'd have to find somewhere else, probably on five minutes' notice.

He hadn't gotten to that point yet, the point of pretending he had a real home when he didn't. Everything he had was in a big backpack that was chained to a pipe in the wall with a tamper-proof bike lock. He knew the others could get into it if they were willing to rip it up, but this way they couldn't just take stuff without him knowing. And he didn't think they wanted to rip it up and piss him off, not with Ace and Jaycie to watch his back. And if they did, he wouldn't lose too much. Just some clothes, and his sticks.

Maybe it was stupid to pay that much money for a couple of pieces of wood, but he'd wanted them—wanted what they meant, what they represented, the freedom to do music *his* way, not the approved way. And the balance was so perfect; he knew that the moment he got them in his hands. A pair of Greg Bissonette signature sticks, extra heavy, the best hickory—clear-coated, which was a little disappointing, but it was the feel that counted, not what color they were stained.

His folks had been ticked when he'd spent his birthday money on them instead of on clothes or something they approved of. But a drummer needed good sticks. And he didn't have enough money for a drum kit, not that they would've let him bring it into the house anyway, or practice on anything but the piano. He hated the piano. He'd tried to get an electronic drum kit, but the good ones were all expensive, and his parents had kept him purposefully short of cash. He got everything he *needed*, and often things that he *wanted*—or that his parents said he wanted—so what did he need money for? Or a car, or a drivers' license, or—

Or, well, anything that would give him the freedom just about every other kid he knew had.

That was all over with. He didn't know what was going to happen now, but he knew he was never going to see Mr. and Mrs. My-Son-The-Artiste again. He hoped they thought he was dead, not that they'd care much. Well, maybe they would, because their ticket to Fortune and Fame was gone along with him. But that was all they'd care about. They'd have been happier with a robot than a kid.

Ace was already waiting there, sitting on her bag next to Jaycie. He felt a flash of relief; he knew it was dangerous for her to go out. He walked over, trying to look as if he didn't care.

"Hi," she said. "Did you find out about the showers?"

Magnus felt a simultaneous flash of guilt and irritation. The reason he'd gone down to Jacob Riis today was to find out if it would be safe for them to go there to take showers, or if they'd be busted: held to be sent home to their parents by a bunch of busybody social workers. But when he'd heard the street kids talking about *La Llorona*, he'd completely forgotten about it.

"Never mind," Ace said hastily. "I got your stuff."

Magnus felt his mouth start to water. "I'll wake up Jace."

He knelt beside the sleeping bag as Ace dug around in the backpack, bringing out the rest of her day's purchases.

"Jace? Hey, Jaycie? Time to rise and shine, guy." Magnus shook the sleeping bundle gently and stepped quickly back. You had to be careful how you woke Jaycie up. Sometimes he woke up screaming and flailing, and that upset everybody.

There was a pause, and then the contents of the sleeping bag began to shift. At last it began to move, and finally, with a sound of zippers, Jaycie sat up, pulling his cap—only the top layer; he wore several at once—firmly down over his ears and all the way down to the bridge of his nose.

Jaycie dressed like the original Homeless Person, in Magnus' opinion, though at least he didn't smell bad. Magnus had no idea how many layers of clothing Jaycie wore, since he'd never seen him remove any of them, but there had to be at least three or four sweaters under that battered Army jacket, and at least two or three layers of sweatpants below. Hell, the guy didn't even take off his *shoes* at night.

He was skinny enough, though, from what Magnus could see from his hands and wrists and throat, and as pale as a vampire, if there were such things. He had long hair like a Goth, too, though most of the time it stayed tucked under his jacket.

He smiled wistfully at Magnus, blinking the sleep out of his eyes, and Magnus, as always, felt a moment of pure *hate* for whoever had driven Jaycie out of his

home and made him cry and scream the way he did
sometimes. For a moment, Magnus allowed himself to
live in a fantasy world where the three of them—him
and Ace and Jaycie—had a place where they could
all live together. Somewhere that they didn't have to
hide. Somewhere with plumbing, and electricity, and
Internet access where they could all be safe and warm
and do what they wanted to do. . . .

"Did you go to the markets?" Jaycie asked hopefully of Ace.

"Yeah, I went shopping. I got your stuff," Ace said,
handing him a wrapped bar of cooking chocolate.

Jaycie tore off the wrapper eagerly, and began gnawing at the thick block of bitter unsweetened candy.

"I can't understand how you can eat that stuff," Ace
said, as she always did. "It tastes horrible."

"It's better," Jaycie said simply. "Oh. Here." He
held out his hand.

In it was a crumpled wad of bills that would choke
a very healthy horse. Magnus swore under his breath
and grabbed it—quick, before anyone else in the room
saw—and stuffed it quickly into his pocket. They could
take it out and count it later.

Ace pretended to pay no attention. That was the way
to keep a secret, both of them had learned. Pretend
nothing was going on, and most of the time people
would believe it. She pulled the rest of the backpack's
contents out and arranged them on her own sleeping
bag: a bag of fast-food hamburgers, two six-packs of
Coke, a quart of milk for her (Ace hated soda and
wouldn't drink it if she had a choice), and a box of
Oreos. She passed a burger to Magnus.

By the time she and Magnus had worked their way
through the hamburgers and milk, Jaycie had finished
two cans of Coke (it was warm, but he didn't seem
to mind) and most of the block of chocolate. Sighing

contentedly, he wormed his way back down into his sleeping bag and went back to sleep.

"That's nothing like a balanced diet," Ace complained to the empty air.

"Who are you, his mother?" Magnus gibed.

"Closest thing he has, right here," Ace shot back without missing a beat. "And . . . I worry about him," she added, dropping her voice, though they both knew from experience that Jaycie would neither hear nor care that they were talking about him. There was something very *strange* about Jaycie, even by the loose standards of the street. Sometimes they'd speculated that he'd run away from some weird strict religious commune.

"Yeah, I worry about him," she repeated. "Like the money, you know?"

"Oh." Reminded, Magnus dug into his pocket, his body shielding the action from any watchers. They huddled together, as if they were necking, while they let just enough light show on the wad to make out the numbers. Carefully, they counted the wadded bills.

"Four hundred dollars," Ace said, managing to sound upset and frightened and disgusted all at once. "Where do you suppose he gets it?"

Magnus shrugged. He had no clue. He was just glad Jaycie *did* get it, wherever the source, because what he'd managed to bring with him when he bolted was long gone.

Ace frowned. "He's not mugging people," she said.

Magnus snorted and shook his head, unable to believe in that any more than she could.

"If he's turning tricks . . ." Ignoring Magnus' look of revulsion, she plunged on. "He could get sick. Or sicker, but this sleeping all the time, it doesn't look like AIDS to me, you know, like what Cleto probably had. I've tried to get him to go to one of the clinics, but he won't. And if he's sleeping all the time, when would he be going out and, well, *working*, if you know what I mean?"

Magnus made a face of disgusted acceptance, though he knew Ace was right. If you survived on the street, you sold your body or you joined a gang and did other things. And if you joined a gang, you had a clubhouse to live in, not a place like this. He'd even heard some of the girls talking wistfully about hooking up with a pimp, because a pimp would move them into a real apartment—one that they'd share with half a dozen other girls of his string, true, but . . .

"So where *is* he getting the money?" Magnus asked. It was the same conversation they had every time Jaycie came up with another wad of money, but somehow the question was like a sore tooth. You just couldn't stop poking at it.

Ace shrugged. "Maybe the Tooth Fairy's leaving it under his pillow. If she is, I sure wish she'd leave some stuff for me, like a valid New York State driver's license that says I'm twenty-one."

"You could rent an apartment then, if you had enough money," Magnus said, willing to play along, though even with a forged driver's license, Ace didn't look anything near twenty-one. He guessed she might even be a year or two younger than he was, though she'd never said.

Still, this was one of their favorite games. Ace sighed wistfully. "Take a shower, wash my hair. Have furniture . . ."

"A kick-ass kit, just like Rick Allen—"

"A television with all the channels—"

"Internet access—" That was what Magnus missed most, since half the time his parents hadn't known what he was doing on his computer, and what they didn't know, they didn't bother to forbid—or block. He'd spent hours on the *Modern Drummer* site, downloading clips and learning all he could. Someday—someday he was going to have a band. And it was *not* going to have a piano in it.

"A refrigerator and a stove," Ace said yearningly.

Magnus winced inwardly. Today the game wasn't going very well. He hated to see her like this. Ace was so strong; hard as nails, and ready to cut your throat if you looked crosswise at her. But sometimes she got a look on her face that made Magnus want to protect her almost as much as he wanted to protect Jaycie.

He'd never say so, of course. She'd kill him.

"Coffee any time you wanted it," Magnus said coaxingly, trying to make her feel better. It was what Ace talked about most, especially now that the days were so cold. She grinned at him.

"A bathroom and a door that locks," they finished in chorus.

Ace looked longing and vulnerable for just another moment, then the look was replaced with the determined one Magnus knew so well. "We'll have those things again. And on our own terms. You can bet the farm on it."

CHAPTER TWO:

THE DOGS AMONG THE BUSHES

The "Reverend" Billy Fairchild (the title, like most of his other honors, was self-conferred) had risen up out of backwoods obscurity and touring tent-show revivals due to one fortunate circumstance: his beautiful blue-eyed daughter.

Heavenly Grace had been on stage from the very beginning—carried by her mother as a babe in arms, then toddling on alone as soon as she could walk. She'd always been a musical child, singing before she could talk, and if there was one day in his entire life that Reverend Billy had cause to bless, it was the day he got the idea to have her sing with the Salvation Gospel Choir.

An unbiased observer (had there been one) might have said that it was really Donna Fairchild's idea, or even little Heavenly Grace's, but Billy knew that all the ideas for the Billy Fairchild Salvation Gospel show were actually his. Well, his and Jesus's, of course.

At any rate, Heavenly Grace—the Living Miracle and Pledge of God's Holy Love!—had come out to the front of the auditorium stage, dressed in her white Monkey Ward dress (the wishbook said it was a First Communion dress, but Billy Fairchild didn't hold with anything Catholic, and neither did his audience, because Lord knew, Jesus hadn't been any kind of a Catholic Roman) and looking like a little beauty contest bride or even Shirley Temple, and his heart had just swelled up with love. He had just known the collection plate would be extra full that day. She looked so pretty, it wouldn't have mattered if she'd sounded like a screech owl.

And then she'd opened up her mouth and sang, and the miracle had occurred.

Billy knew all about miracles. He'd been with Gospel shows in one form or another since his teens, and with a circus before that. A miracle was when the audience got up off its dead ass and put its hand on its wallet and came to Jesus, opening up those wallets so that Billy could go on doing the Lord's good work. He knew just about exactly how much there was going to be in the free-will love offering plates even before the audience sat down, just by eyeballing the crowd and figuring out how badly they needed to buy God's forgiveness, and how scared he could make them that they weren't going to get it without digging into the rent money.

But from the first time Heavenly Grace sang, all that changed. There was love in the air, and Billy was smart enough to know that the love wasn't for him, it was for that little girl with the golden curls and the golden voice. But when there was so much love going around, some of it just naturally slopped over onto him. And into the offering plates.

The take was a good twenty percent higher that day than he'd calculated. And it kept getting bigger. He had the sense to start the show with Heavenly Grace and keep her onstage as much as possible, and the audience just couldn't get enough of her and her singing. They opened their hearts and—more to the point—their wallets.

And Billy Fairchild never looked back.

By the time his daughter was six, he was able to put the traveling show behind him forever. He put down roots—bought a house in Tulsa—and Billy began building an empire.

At first it was guest appearances on other preachers' shows. Then a weekly half-hour of his own on a local cable channel. He'd worried at first that whatever gift Jesus had seen fit to give Heavenly Grace wouldn't work over the airwaves, but either it did, or once the studio audience got all worked up it didn't matter. He went to a weekly show, then to a daily show on a regular local channel, and at last to a syndicated national show airing six times a week, and along the way he built up Fairchild Ministries, Inc., doing God's Holy Work with pamphlets, books, CDs, documentaries, and recorded samplers of the Billy Fairchild Crusade.

But it all took time. And while he was building up his temple in this Godless Babylon, Heavenly Grace was growing up. She never lost her looks—thank Lord Jesus for that—but she was turning willful and mean-spirited, just when he needed her most. He had plans for Fairchild Ministries. There was room for expansion. America was crying out for good Christian leadership. A career in politics was not out of the question. He had an impeccable past. No breath of scandal had ever touched his family.

He'd been too modest, too self-effacing, to see that God was calling him to such a grand purpose. If not for Gabriel Horn, he would have spent the rest of his days crying out in the wilderness, hiding his light under a bushel basket. But Gabriel had a way of making everything seem so clear and right. It was only right for a daughter to submit her will to her father, for example, just as she would submit it to the Lord Jesus.

Gabriel had appeared to help Billy run the administrative side of things, just when Billy needed him most. He was a man of vision and insight. He'd seen ways to make the Ministry even bigger and more profitable, to reach out to more people, so that Billy could go on doing God's work. And he'd been right to remind Billy that Heavenly Grace was the keystone of the plan. Wasn't Billy's little girl the living proof of God's Holy Favor? God had sent Heavenly Grace and her divine gifts to Billy for a purpose. He meant for Billy to use her powers, not let them go to waste. When the girl was older, she'd thank him for his wise guidance through the troubling storms of adolescence, when Satan was at his most powerful. Once Billy had moved to a position of national prominence—so Gabriel counseled him—the child would understand the importance of his work, and submit her will to his in a proper Godly fashion. Why, all you had to do was to read the Scripture—the Old Testament, of course—to see where, over and over, God gave his command to children, especially girl-children, to submit their will to the will of their fathers. Fathers even had the right to have rebellious children put to death, not that he *would*, of course, but God gave that right, and no law of man could take it away.

Even Donna had agreed, but Donna Fairchild had always been a proper handmaid of the Lord.

The only person who hadn't seen the light had been Billy Fairchild's rebellious daughter. She had all kinds of ideas that weren't fit nor proper for a Godly child—college, and not even a proper place like Bob Jones University neither, but some state university or even an abode of pagans like UCLA. She didn't need college! She'd got all the education she needed, home-schooled by her mother! He'd told her so, in no uncertain terms, the same way he'd told her she didn't need a driver's license.

But the Devil had gotten into his child, somehow. Heavenly Grace had disappeared one day. Run off. Vanished.

At first Billy'd thought she might have been kidnapped. A man in his position, doing God's work, had enemies. He'd kept the police out of it, of course. Scandal was the last thing Fairchild Ministries needed. He'd hired some very discreet, very experienced professionals.

They'd found nothing. No ransom demand, no threatening letters had ever come, and slowly Billy had come to realize that his Heavenly Grace had committed the ultimate act of defiance: she'd *run away*.

He kept the professionals on the payroll. Gabriel had been a tower of strength. He'd sworn they'd find Billy's daughter, that they'd get her back. And meanwhile, her absence was easily explained: she was away at school—a good, God-fearing, private, Bible-based girls' school, away from all the temptations that the world posed for sensitive and vulnerable teenage girls.

It had to be done that way, Gabriel explained. It was important—for the future—that no breath of scandal be attached to her disappearance. There was Billy's future to think of. And Heavenly Grace's, of course. When she returned, their Prodigal Daughter,

undoubtedly sorrowful and repentant over the tribu-
lations she had caused them, naturally they would
want her to be able to slip right back into her old
life again without anyone knowing about her shame.
That would be what *she* would want, as well.

Donna had been the hardest to convince, but she
had doted on Gabriel Horn from day one, and finally
she had given in. Gabriel had sworn to her that he
would work day and night—over and above his duties
for the Ministry—to find her daughter and return her
to the fold of her family's love. Why, Gabriel had come
to think of her as his own little girl as well. . . .

What could have been a more convincing argument
than that? Nothing that Billy could think of.

Humans were really a constant source of
entertainment—when they didn't vex one half to
madness.

The being who—in this time and place—chose to
be known as Gabriel Horn closed the door to his
private apartment in the Fairchild Ministries Tower
and activated the wards that sealed the doors. No
human could pass them now.

With a sigh of relief, he dropped the *glamourie*
that he wore among humans. It was necessary, but
it was also rather demeaning to go about aping the
appearance of one's inferiors. And the *clothes*! Gabriel
shuddered. A second spell adjusted his garments
to something closer to his liking; he inspected the
embroidered velvet sleeve of his tunic critically, then
headed toward the liquor cabinet and poured himself
a large measure of a venerable single-malt Scotch.

Still, there were some things about the human world
that Gabriel liked quite well. He stood for a moment,
inhaling the complex scent and admiring the play of
light through the facets of the cut-crystal glass.

He had come to the World Above to entertain himself, for what else was a Prince of Underhill to do? If one could not enjoy the pleasures of war among one's own kind, the next best thing was to make trouble among the Mortalfolk, yet in these degenerate days that was a delicate proposition, for there were always spies of the Bright Court ready and willing to meddle where they weren't wanted, as if all Mortalfolk belonged solely to them.

Finding Billy Fairchild had been a stroke of luck—the pompous fool was so easily manipulated, and came ready-supplied with a coterie of foolish followers. But Gabriel would have taken him as a momentary pleasure—a quick scandal, and the destruction of his "Ministry"—if it had not been for the daughter.

The girl had Power. Gabriel had known it from the moment he'd first seen her. The Power to bend human hearts to her will any time she sang.

She hadn't known him for what he was, of course, but she'd known enough to fear him. He couldn't beguile her as he could her parents, but that made things all the sweeter, to Gabriel's mind. And so he had abandoned his plans for the quick destruction of Billy Fairchild, and settled down to a longer and ultimately more satisfying game. He would use the girl to give Billy *real* power—the power to make great trouble in the land. The one thing that was guaranteed to make trouble among the mortals was *religion*. Religion had caused more wars, more scandals, more pogroms, and more death and torture than any other aspect of humans' lives—save, perhaps, money. And even then, it was difficult to tell which caused the most havoc, for religion and money were inextricably tangled among the mortals.

And what could his high-nosed Bright Court cousins

do about *that?* They would never make war upon a
human child. And the girl *was* but a child, well under
the control of her parents. A pawn. Helpless. And
that was even if the Seleighe Sidhe realized that *he*
was the power behind Billy Fairchild's throne, which
they likely never would.

Later it had occurred to him that perhaps he could
even enchant the parents enough to make them give
him the girl. And then, with time, he would wear away
her will, and take her power for his own.

Or so he had thought, a year ago, as the Earthborn
reckoned time.

A flash of anger crossed Gabriel's face, and the
glass in his hand shattered. With an absent gesture,
he made the shards of crystal and the spilled liquor
vanish, turning away from the liquor cabinet.

But the girl had run. Against all prediction, against
all expectation, she had fled—and not all his spell-
craft had been able either to summon her back, or
determine her location.

Impossible.

A fact.

Gabriel began to pace the room, his scarlet cloak
belling out behind him. He was a Magus Major, a
Knight and Prince of Elfhame Bete Noir: as the
Unseleighe reckoned power, he was a mighty force
Underhill. There were only three possibilities that
would keep him from finding her.

One—that she was dead. And if she were dead, by
now his sorcerous allies ought to have brought him
some word of that, so while it was still a possibility,
it was a very unlikely one.

Two—that she had been found and taken Underhill
by the Enemy.

This was much more likely—he knew how much
his Bright Court cousins liked to meddle, especially

among Children of Power, and it was a possibility
he could never rule out. But Gabriel had spies in a
number of places, and there was always the possibility he would get word of her. And if he did . . . well,
then he could always arrange for her parents to beg
for her return. His Bright Court cousins were as
soft-headed as they were soft-hearted, and would
probably return her.

Of course, if she had fallen into the hands of some
other faction of the Dark Court . . .

Why, then, he would merely *take* her back, and she
would undoubtedly be so grateful to see him that she
would fall in with any plans he made.

The third—and most vexing—possibility was that
she had managed to flee to one of the blighted places
in the Mortal World where Sidhe magic simply didn't
work at all reliably. Unfortunately, there were more of
them every day. Seeking spells wouldn't work there,
in the lands where there was so much Cold Iron that
spellcasting, even when the mortals did their petty and
foolish spells, went awry. None of the Sidhe entered
such places without good reason. In fact, very few of
the Folk were even *able* to venture into such places at
all—and he did not command such numbers that he
could afford to search all such places in the world.

But even if the girl had gone to ground in one of
them, if she used her Gift, he would know. He knew
the signature of her magic, the scent and taste of it,
and if she practiced it anywhere in the World Above
or Underhill, he would know.

He stopped before a large cabinet on one wall of
his apartment. It was an antique Chinese apothecary
cabinet, filled with many tiny drawers. He opened the
one he sought unerringly and took out a small silver
casket. From it he removed a silver ring wrapped
with a single strand of long blonde hair.

Hers. And by all the magical Laws of Consanguinity, still a part of her.

He turned away from the cabinet and gestured. A patch of air began to ripple, darkening and solidifying until it gleamed as dark as any mirror, hanging before him in the air. He touched the ring to the mirror, but—as so many times before—nothing happened.

Hide if you can. Flee if you will. But you can only escape me for a time, Heavenly Grace Fairchild. And when you fall into my hands again, you will be mine forever.

With a gesture he banished the black mirror. Slipping the ring onto his finger, he walked over to the desk. There was much to do to prepare the world for the coming of Billy Fairchild.

CHAPTER THREE:

~~AWAY~~ WE GO AGAIN

This had been his last class before the Thanksgiving break, and why all the odd gods of scheduling had put it on a Monday was going to have to remain a mystery, because nobody he'd been able to ask had been able to explain things to Eric's satisfaction.

Even with all the makeups and takeover classes he'd had to do to compensate for missed coursework and failed exams (he'd been off saving the world, but sometimes the best excuses were the ones you couldn't use), he was finally going to do it. After an almost twenty-year interregnum, Eric Banyon was finally going to graduate from the Juilliard School of Music this spring.

And what then?

What did he want to do with his life here in the World Above?

He'd already rejected one life—that of a Human Bard at the Elven Courts of Underhill—and come back to finish Juilliard, just to see if he could. Well, it turned out he could. With his Juilliard degree, he could now get a legitimate high-class professional music gig just about anywhere, but that really wouldn't fit the life that had grown up around him in the last couple of years, and the need he'd discovered to be ready to deal with Evil when it showed up and had to be fought.

It sounded awfully melodramatic when he put it that way—as if he might have a cape and tights hanging in his closet—and as a matter of fact, he did, since they were common articles of apparel Underhill, where he still made frequent visits—but how else was he supposed to describe things like Threshold and Aerune, or Perenor, or the powers behind the Poseidon Project? Cranky? Bad-mannered? Socially unacceptable? No. They were Evil. Each of them, in their own ways, had been out to hurt or kill a large number of people for nothing more than their own personal gain, and if there was a better definition of Evil, Eric hadn't found it yet.

He wasn't going to waste his time on the differently social who just needed a little time to work out their personal adjustments. They might be really loud and hurt a lot of feelings, and maybe even leave a few bruises behind, but nobody was going to die. And for the average run-of-the-mill villain who killed by accident or design, there were a whole lot of people and agencies better trained than Eric was to take them down. Call 911, leak information to the FBI, but don't ring up Call-A-Bard.

But they couldn't go after people like Aerune. When people like that showed up (and if someone like Aerune *never* showed up again, Eric would be just as glad), even finding out about them was a job in itself, let alone stopping them. The police, the FBI, the CIA, even the Marines weren't the right people to call when someone like that appeared on the scene.

Which still left the question: what *was* he going to do with his life? Because while taking out weird villains might be a mission, and a necessary job, it was hardly a career. You couldn't tell when or where—or if—those kinds of problems were going to happen, for one thing. What did you do with the rest of your time? Even Batman had a social life. Sort of.

Though Eric could spend the rest of his life living off *kenned* gold with the best wishes of Prince Arvin of Elfhame Misthold—who was, as the Seleighe Sidhe understood things, his patron—that wouldn't satisfy him either. He'd discovered in himself a need to be useful, odd as that would have seemed to him at twenty.

So what was he going to *do* after he left Juilliard, in between bouts of saving the world? Which—he devoutly hoped—might never need to happen again.

In front of Lincoln Center, he caught the bus and, after a series of transfers, reached Museum Mile.

It was like stepping into another world. Even though the Upper West Side, where Juilliard was, could hardly be said to be an area of New York lacking in money and class, Museum Mile was so different that by rights there ought to be a high wall around it. Museum Mile was old money, Edith Wharton money, and it showed. Even in an unseasonably cold November, everything was still green, and the air positively reeked of the kind of wealth that had nannies and live-in servants, that summered on Fire Island or Martha's Vineyard, that took its limousines for walks and thought that shopping at Bloomingdale's was slumming. Apartments in these buildings almost *never* came up for sale—they were handed down through the generations, like the Renoirs and Monets and the Limoges services for forty-eight.

His shrink lived up here.

Eric had seriously resisted the whole idea of professional counseling for too long. His parents had dragged him to far too many of them when he'd been a child, and he'd quickly realized that every single one of those professional "helpers" had been interested in only one thing: getting inside his head and turning him inside out, to get a handle on what would control him. And once they did, no matter what they said, no matter how many times they promised they'd keep everything confidential, they'd take back whatever they found to his parents to use against him.

Bitter much? Eric thought with a rueful smile.

This time, he'd nearly drowned in his own problems before he'd been willing to admit that they were bigger than he was. But the fact that he'd been seriously considering going back to drinking—had been standing outside a liquor store last September with money in his pocket, thinking about walking in the door—had finally scared him enough to take the problem to Hosea.

Hosea had listened and come back with a name and address. Eric had been furious—terrified, he was willing to admit now. But Hosea had been just plain stubborn. Eric had asked for help. This was help, the Ozark Bard had said implacably. What would it cost him to simply go and *see* the woman? He'd faced Nightflyers and Unseleighe Lords, after all.

Eric hadn't been willing—hadn't been able, really—to explain. So he'd gone, sure that all he'd find when he arrived would be one more clueless psychotherapist, probably with a specialization in substance abuse, telling him things he already knew too well.

But this time, it had turned out to be a whole different gig.

For one thing, *he* was paying the shrink. For another, there were no secrets, because Oriana Dunaway was a magician herself, though Eric knew little more about her than that.

"You don't need to know about me, Eric, or about what I do," she'd told him at their first meeting. *"All you need to know is that you can trust me. And that whatever you tell me, no matter how unbelievable it is by the standards of the Worldlings, I will believe that it is so, though I may require an explanation of it, should it lie outside my own experience. And so, shall we begin?"*

He was a Bard. He knew the truth when he heard it. Together, the two of them had begun to try to make sense of a life that had been twisted and damaged long before the events of last autumn. He slowly came to realize that he had to get his head straight before trying to get on with his life, lest the past reach out and drag him under when he least expected it. He was a Bard, gifted with the power to make or mar. He *had* to be able to use it wisely. Sanely. Because, if he couldn't get his own psyche in order, as the power within him grew stronger, so would it find the weakest places in him.

And to his surprise, Oriana's specialty was *not* substance abuse at all, but the problems of magicians, Talents, and nonhumans living in the World Above. That much she had been willing to tell him, though she would not otherwise discuss her patients.

"And I tell you this because it is important for you to know that you are not alone, either in your strengths or your weaknesses, Eric. It is a small community—often it is not a community at all—but you are not unique."

❖   ❖   ❖

He reached the door of her building—after almost a year of Mondays, the doorman knew him by sight—and went inside. He passed through the exquisitely tasteful lobby—it had always rather reminded Eric of a high-class mortuary, with its dark heavy furniture, gilt mirrors, and oriental carpets over parquet marble floors. All that was missing were the vases of funereal lilies; fortunately the flowers here ran to something more cheerful. Shrugging his gig bag higher onto his shoulder, he went down the hall to the bank of elevators.

If the lobby was a mortuary, then the elevators were surely top of the line sarcophagi, all highly polished, heavily ornamented bronze, lined with more mirrors, so the building's inhabitants could give themselves one last once-over before hitting the street. The infinite number of reflected Erics always made him faintly uneasy; he stared fixedly at the doors as the car made its leisurely way to his floor.

The doors opened. He stepped out onto the thick carpet of the corridor and headed down the hall. Right on time. Maybe even a minute or two early. He opened the door into Oriana's apartment.

As always, the wards she had set tingled faintly over his skin when he crossed the threshold. They were a necessary part of her work, given the people she saw. It wouldn't do to disturb any of the other tenants of the building with anything that happened in her sessions, or leave any psychic detritus lying around from one appointment to contaminate the next.

What would have been the foyer if Oriana had not chosen to see her patients in her own home had been set up as a waiting room. There were a couple of comfortable couches and a low coffee table, covered with the sort of bland, inoffensive, upscale magazines that filled any professional's waiting room, occupying the space now. Eric picked up a copy of *Architectural Digest* and sat down.

A few moments later, Oriana's previous patient walked out. Eric had seen him a few times, but had never spoken to him. He didn't even know his name. He was a spare, slender man, closer to fifty than to forty. His dark hair was several weeks late (always! How did he manage it?) for a haircut, shot with early silver, and his eyes were a curious light amber color, nearly gold, making Eric wonder if he might be one of Oriana's nonhuman patients. He was dressed for Wall Street, in a completely unremarkable business suit that would blend in anywhere in New York. The only thing at all out of the ordinary about his appearance was the scarab pendant in bright blue *faience* that hung from a silver chain about his neck, resting against the sober institutional necktie. He nodded slightly to Eric, recognizing him as well, then walked out.

Oriana poked her head through the inner door a moment later.

"Ah, good. You're here. A moment, please." She withdrew.

Eric occupied himself until her return looking at pictures of gold faucets and hand-painted French porcelain bathroom sinks, not to mention Jacuzzis big enough to seat the entire Elven High Court, and made a mental note to give Kory and Beth a subscription to this thing. The elves could find *some* way to get this stuff shipped Underhill, and both his friends were bonkers for bathroom gadgets of every kind. Hell, actually all things considered, the elves could probably make every bit of it. If they hadn't already—hadn't Kory said something about there being an Elven casino in Vegas?

Still, the last time he'd been on a visit, all that he'd

seen was an old claw-foot bathtub (okay, it was solid alabaster, but still) straight out of a Victorian mansion. Most of the time the Underhill crowd seemed to go for hot springs in grottos—nice for atmosphere, but not exactly Jacuzzis. *I'll be remembered throughout history as the man who brought modern plumbing to Underhill.*

A few moments later Oriana was back. "I'm ready for you now."

Eric got up and followed her down the hall to her study.

The room was small and intimate and even more heavily shielded than the rest of the apartment. The walls were fully paneled in red pecan, and folding shutters covered the windows. Eric preferred them closed, and so Oriana always shut them before he arrived.

Between the shuttered windows was a range of shallow shelves, on which were a variety of enticing knickknacks for nervous patients to fidget with: glass globes, small toys, seashells, ornamental boxes—the sort of souvenirs any traveler might acquire. There was a chair for Oriana, with a small table beside it that held a clock, her notepad, and a box of Kleenex. There was a wastebasket, and a dimmable torchiere in the corner to provide light if the shutters were closed. Aside from that, the only furniture in the room was a large grey couch—"a non-directive couch," she'd said once, making a rare joke, "as you may sit, lie, sprawl upon it. Whatever you like. The couch does not care. And neither do I."

As always when he arrived, the room held a strong indefinable spicy smell. It seemed to fade during his session—though whether it faded, or whether he got used to it, was something Eric had never quite decided.

He took his place on the couch. Oriana followed him in, closing the door behind him, and seated herself in the chair, picking up her pad and pen and waiting for him to begin.

She was somewhere in her late sixties, Eric supposed, one of those lucky blondes whose hair simply went silver with age. She was wearing an expensive, nubbly, cowl-neck sweater in ash-taupe shades that flattered her complexion—nobody who had spent any time at all Underhill could help having a good eye for clothes—paired with a pencil-thin tweed skirt and designer pumps. She looked like a psychiatrist in a movie, down to the half-glasses she wore on a chain around her neck, and he was pretty sure that she consciously dressed to play up the image.

"Do I pass muster?" she asked.

Eric grinned, refusing to feel guilty for checking her out.

"And how are you feeling this week?" she asked, prodding him to begin their session.

"I'm realizing that I have decisions to make," Eric admitted. "I graduate in the Spring. I *could* just coast. The money's there. But it feels dishonest."

"Good," Oriana said noncommittally.

"I know that I want to do *something*. Something worthwhile. But I know that whatever it is, it has to be something that will leave me the freedom to do the things that need to be done—as a Bard. And those things show up on awfully short notice."

Oriana pursed her lips, and absently tapped once on her notebook with her pencil. "Yes, they do. And they're things that can't always be explained to Worldlings, even when they find themselves involved. And, reasonably enough, you don't want to put yourself into a position where you might have to let someone down who depended on you, or hurt their feelings, even if that were necessary for the greater good."

Eric nodded ruefully. "And I know there has to be a way to do both—to do something meaningful and still have that freedom . . ."

For a few minutes he discussed all the various alternatives he'd considered—going back on the RenFaire circuit; playing solo freelance gigs in the New York area; finding work as a session musician; working as a tutor. All of them sounded attractive as he spoke of them, and all of them would give him the freedom he needed.

Oriana raised her hand, silencing him.

"Eric, I am not a placement counselor at Juilliard. I have no interest in your future employment opportunities. You're blowing smoke at me. Stop it, and tell me what's bothering you."

Eric sighed, feeling guilty and relieved all at once.

"I have no idea what I'm going to do when I graduate," he admitted. "I try to feel drawn to some particular course of action, but I don't. There must be something that's right—but I just can't see it. Am I ever going to be able to see it?"

Oriana took a moment to page through her notes.

"Eric, you've been coming to me for almost a year now. And you've made a great deal of progress in dealing with your emotional baggage in that time. But you're still holding back. Oh, not consciously. But let's review your background a bit.

"You were born with the gift of Bardic magic, into a family that had no understanding of your Talent and no idea of what magic is. Since Bardic magic is linked to music, you presented as a musical prodigy. Since your parents were ambitious, they perhaps placed too much pressure on you to excel in an arena that was not entirely suited to your actual Gifts. Yes, you're a talented musician, perhaps even a gifted one, but talent and Talent are two very different things, and young magicians should not be forced into the public eye. However, what's done is done.

"When your Talents made an explicit presentation of themselves at puberty, you began seeing Otherrealm creatures, which were drawn by your magic. Naturally, you had no idea of what was occurring. Your parents were . . . not supportive, insisting that you continue with your course of studies. Eventually, you had what amounted to a nervous breakdown upon seeing the Nightflyers at your recital at age eighteen."

"I ran away from home," Eric said sourly.

"Certainly we could see it in those terms," Oriana said, looking up from her notes. "It is equally valid to suggest that you ran *toward* your own self-preservation in the only way you knew to do it. However, you continued to make bad life choices. You became an alcoholic, a drug abuser, and a drifter, in an attempt to shut out your perception of the Otherworld."

Eric winced. It was an accurate, if very unflattering, assessment of his life before he'd met Kory.

"When you met Korendil and were forced by circumstances both to acknowledge and to take up the use of your magical Gifts, a great deal changed for you. For one thing, you received external validation of your world view—in layman's terms, you discovered you *weren't* crazy, and never had been. You received proper magical training from an Elven Bard. You acquired a replacement family, one that loves and supports you. You terminated your addictive and avoidance behaviors, which is a very important step in the healing process.

"But the damaged child created during the first

eighteen years of your life, when our first perceptions and assumptions about the nature of the world are being formed, is still within you, and *he* is not lightly set aside. You have acknowledged in our previous sessions that your parents saw you less as a child to be nurtured than as an accessory to their own life-style: a trophy that would enhance their own consequence. A child derives his first image of self through his parents' image of him, and your parents, as you have told me on several occasions, never saw you as anything more than an object and a playing piece.

"I do not believe you will ever truly be able to understand what it is that you, Eric Banyon, actually want out of life, until you have fully externalized this image of yourself and set it aside once and for all."

"You mean I have to stop believing them?" Eric said.

Oriana nodded.

"But I don't!" he protested.

She said nothing, forcing Eric to think.

Was it true? He hated to think so. He hadn't thought about his parents—or his childhood—for years.

But, as she'd warned him, there were ways of not thinking about a thing that were just as poisonously obsessive as thinking about it constantly. From the moment he'd walked out of that concert hall with nothing more than his flute and the clothes on his back, he'd built a wall between himself and his past, one that he'd allowed nothing to breach. He bit his lip, feeling himself start to shake.

In silence, Oriana passed him the box of Kleenex.

"I hate this," Eric said thickly, around a wad of tissues.

"Nobody said this would be either easy or fun," she answered quietly. "We defend the damaged parts of ourselves fiercely. It takes courage to confront our scars, and bring the shadowed parts of our deepest selves into the light so that they can be healed. Until you no longer see yourself as an object and a playing piece, you will not be able to accurately identify what you are feeling *now*."

He hated it, but he knew she was right. Because an object couldn't feel. A playing piece couldn't make decisions. And he had to do both. Right now he didn't know *what* he felt about so many things—Aerete's death, Aerune's imprisonment, Jimmie's death, Jeanette's transfiguration—there was so much to think about and get straight in his mind before he could move on. And he had responsibilities. There was Hosea to teach, and Kayla to keep an eye on, just for two. He was managing both of those responsibilities adequately so far, but if there was one thing Eric knew about any situation, it was that nothing ever stayed the same. Things always got better . . . or worse. And if he didn't deal with this ticking time bomb in his past, he knew which direction he was going to put his money on. And he had his own future to plan for.

"I think we've made some progress today," Oriana said gently. "And now, our hour is up. Call me if you need me sooner, and we'll set something up. Otherwise, I'll see you next week."

Back home, Eric paced his apartment, a cup of tea in his hand. He felt restless and agitated, the way he always did after a particularly good—or bad—session with Oriana.

It was as if she'd opened a door in a wall, and things he hadn't thought about in years were boiling out. Sick, bad, frightening things.

But they had only as much power as he was willing to give them. Oriana had taught him that, had proved it to him over and over. Confront them; drag them into the light—painful as that was—and most of them would simply wither away.

He could do that now.

Inspiration struck, with a force that nearly made Eric drop his mug. So his past—his long-entombed image of his parents—was the root of his present problems, was it? Well, they'd just see about that. He'd confront his problem directly.

He'd confront his parents.

He'd been tying up all the loose ends of his life, hadn't he? Finishing up at Juilliard? Well, he'd been working his way backward to the beginning of his problems. That made sense, in a way. But now it was time to deal with the beginning.

Boston wasn't that far away—especially on his elvensteed Lady Day. He could get up there and back tomorrow, and it would be a good run for both of them.

Even though it had been twenty years by the world's time since he'd left, he was sure they were still in the same place. You didn't give up a house in Cambridge lightly, and they were both undoubtedly still at Harvard.

And if they had—unthinkably—moved, they wouldn't be that hard to find. Not with magic to help.

Determined on a course of action—if not in the least settled in his mind about it—Eric was about to go in search of another cup of tea when he heard a knock at his door.

He went to open it, without bothering to first perform the New York ritual dance of peering through the peephole. For that matter, his door had far fewer locks on it than the usual door in even the best neighborhoods. Eric lived in Guardian House, and the House had its own unique security systems.

Hosea was standing on the doorstep, which was pretty much whom Eric had expected to be there, given the time of day and day of the week it was. Everyone else he knew was either at their mundane jobs or in class.

"Come in," Eric said, stepping back. He knew Hosea wouldn't come around on a Monday unless it was for something important. Everyone who knew about his sessions with Oriana—and that was everyone close to him—knew to give him a little breathing room after them. Though from the look of him—Hosea was still dressed for the outside, and still had Jeanette slung over his shoulder—Hosea had come straight from the shelter with something serious on his mind.

"Tea?" Eric asked.

"If it's no trouble," Hosea said, and Eric went to get him a cup.

Hosea was sitting on the couch when Eric came back with two mugs of fresh tea. He was frowning at nothing, Jeanette propped against his knee, still in her case. Hosea was normally as sunny as a spring morning; this must be something bad, or at least pretty complicated.

The last thing in the world Eric wanted to do right now was think about somebody else's problems, but he forced himself to take a deep mental breath and turn his thoughts outward, away from his own troubles. Hosea was his apprentice. That meant Eric had responsibilities toward him.

Responsibilities. There was that word again. Life had been so much less complicated when he'd been irresponsible—

"Want to tell me about it?" he said, handing over the mug.

"It might be nothin' but a bag o' moonshine," Hosea said, after a long hesitation. "Ah don't rightly know."

*But whatever it is, it was important enough for
you to come by on a Monday, wasn't it?*

"Well, maybe we can figure it out together," Eric
said. "Right?"

Hosea grimaced, and took a deep breath, preparing
to begin. Slowly he explained to Eric all that he'd
pieced together about the Secret Stories that the
children in the shelter told—and that it wasn't just
the kids at Jacob Riis telling them, but children in
every shelter Hosea visited, and that *all* the children
seemed to know them. He explained about Bloody
Mary, and how belief in her extended far beyond
the very young children who believed in the Secret
Stories—that, in fact, Hosea feared she might almost
have an independent reality.

"So . . . one of the things Ah was wondering, Eric,
was . . . is that possible?"

Eric considered, choosing his words carefully.

"Well, I know that belief can compel magic—or a
creature of magic—to take a particular form. From
what little Master Dharniel told me about the way
humans and elves used to get along—or *not* get along,
more to the point—together in the old days—the
really old days—there used to be a whole school of
human magic, now mostly lost, that could actually
compel the Sidhe not only to appear, but to appear
in certain forms. That's one thing. But it's not too
likely that there's a Sidhe running around New York
that somebody's twisted into a knot. Too much Cold
Iron here—it weakens their magic, and makes it go
all funny. They'd have to be seriously crazy in the
first place—like Aerune was—to come here at all.
And the creatures of magic that *can* stand up to
Cold Iron aren't quite as vulnerable to the power of
human belief.

"The other possibility is, if there's a pool of untapped

power out there—and belief is power, if enough people believe hard enough, and you throw a few Talents into the mix—that much belief could take form and become what magicians call an Artificial Elemental."

"A *mythago*," Hosea said.

"You've been listening to Paul," Eric said with a faint grin. Paul Kern was the Guardians' researcher who, like Giles on *Buffy*, knew the pedigree and history of most of the Otherworldly threats the Guardians faced. "The label—ghost, *mythago*, Artificial Elemental—doesn't matter. What does matter is that as soon as it has any kind of a defined shape at all, it becomes a lot more efficient at absorbing belief energy and using it to define itself. It can begin to appear—manifest—and that, of course, encourages more and stronger belief, and sets up a whole feeding cycle. Hard to break, if it turns out to be something you don't happen to want around.

"So . . . yes, if your shelter kids are believing in something hard enough, it might start showing up. *Might*," Eric said firmly.

"Well . . . Ah'm not quite sure whether she is, or whether the gangs are jest ridin' on her coattails, so to speak. Either way, Ah'd like to do something about it. And it wouldn't hurt none to give the little'uns a hopeful spark in their lives," Hosea said thoughtfully.

"By making Bloody Mary a little less . . . bloody?" Eric suggested, thinking carefully. "That way she wouldn't be any more use to the gangs, and the children wouldn't have to be afraid of her any more. It would be a delicate task." He thought about it carefully. "In fact, it would be a *Bardic* sort of task. A perfect apprentice piece for you, in fact." Eric grinned wickedly, enjoying himself now as he thought the matter over more thoroughly.

"Why don't you write some songs—the kind that kids

would sing themselves—that shape the Bloody Mary story toward a happy sort of ending? When you've got some that you think will work, show them to me so I can approve them as your great and powerful Bardic Master. Then you can start sneaking them out into the shelters and let them work their way out among the kids on their own."

Hosea thought about it for a moment and then smiled slowly.

"Now that's a right sneaky plan, Master Bard. And if it works, Bloody Mary will dry up and blow away on her own, and maybe the little'uns'll be able to conjure themselves up a bit o' help now and then," Hosea said thoughtfully.

"It's worth a try," Eric agreed.

Hosea finished his tea and set the cup down. "If you don't mind mah bringin' it up, Eric, you look like a feller with more'n usual on your mind tonight," he said hesitantly.

"And here I thought I was doing such a great job of being the original Great Stone Face," Eric said, with a rueful sigh.

Hosea raised an eyebrow and said nothing.

"Yeah, well," Eric said after a pause. There wasn't any reason *not* to tell Hosea where he was going, and several good reasons to come clean. "You know I saw Oriana today . . . and, well, I just realized I've got some major unfinished personal business to take care of, and school's over for a few weeks, so . . . tomorrow I'm going to go up to Boston. To see my parents."

There was a silence while Hosea digested this. "Don't they think you're dead?" he asked at last.

"Probably," Eric admitted. "Think what a great surprise it will be for them when I show up, then."

The anger in his voice surprised even him. And there it was, out in the open: at least part of his reason for going was the desire, still not dealt with or satisfied, to balance the pain of his childhood with hurting his parents back. It was something he'd have to keep an eye on. He couldn't afford to act out of either anger or malice. No Bard could.

Hosea said nothing. Eric had never talked about his family before; Hosea knew nothing of his past before his time as a street musician. For his part, Eric knew that Hosea had never known his own parents; they'd died when he was very young, but he'd been raised by his grandparents with a great deal of love. Eric wondered if Hosea could even *imagine* having parents who didn't love you.

Hosea let the moment pass without further comment, and moved on to practical matters. "Won't seeing them be a tad awkward? Won't they expect you to look older'n you do?"

Eric frowned. That was a detail he *did* have to work out.

"I'm not actually sure I expect them to notice, frankly. And if they do, a little *glamourie* will take care of that while I'm there, and afterward, they'll remember seeing what they expected to see. I walked out on them when I was eighteen. That was almost twenty years ago by the World's time. If I'd stayed in the World Above all that time I'd be—let me see—about thirty-six or seven by now? I look like I'm still in my twenties, and there are days when I feel like I'm about a thousand years old. . . ." Eric shrugged.

"Ah guess Ah'm not the man to change yore mind," Hosea said, getting to his feet, "but . . . are you sure you know what you're doing?" he asked.

That's a question I ask myself every day. "No," Eric admitted. "But I still think it's something I have to do."

"Well then," Hosea said, and he still didn't sound

very certain about matters, "Ah guess Ah'll wish you good luck. And Ah'll see you when you get back?"

"Count on it," Eric said, feigning a cheerfulness he did not feel. "We'll go out and grab a couple of pizzas or something."

He wasn't all that surprised to receive another visitor as soon as it was fully dark. There was a tapping at the window, and then the sound of the casement being raised, and the clicking of stone hooves as his visitor clambered daintily over the sill.

"Eric me lad, are you quite sure you haven't lost the few marbles you still have rattling around in that pretty skull of yours?" Greystone said.

Greystone was an actual, genuine, medieval-style gargoyle, one of four that decorated the top of Guardian House. He had a fanged doglike face and curling horns, long apelike arms, and hindquarters like a satyr's, right down to the cloven hooves. Great bat wings lay against his back like furled umbrellas, and in defiance of all aerodynamic principles, they could actually be used for flight. Except for his big dark eyes, he was a uniform, textured grey all over, right down to the soot smudges and patches of lichen that came from being exposed to all the wind and weather of New York City since the day he'd been carved. And despite the fact that he lived and moved and talked, and certainly ate and drank with every evidence of enjoyment, Greystone, as his name implied, seemed to be made of solid stone. He'd been Eric's first friend in Guardian House, coming that first night to Eric's tentative Bardic request for a friend. And Greystone had been a good one ever since.

He was also an inveterate busybody, being privy to all the conversations that went on in Guardian House, as well as most of the surface thoughts of the inhabitants, though he never gossiped, and didn't abuse the privilege that went with his power.

"Pretty sure," Eric said. "Popcorn and a movie?" Both were good ways to distract Greystone, he'd found; though the gargoyle could *hear* any movie the inhabitants ran anywhere in Guardian House, until Eric had invited him inside on his first night here, Greystone had never had a chance to *watch* any of them, and the chance to see the movies at last that he'd only heard for so long fascinated him.

"If that's what you're offering, laddybuck, I'll be pleased to accept. But I'll choose the movie."

Pleased to have gotten off so easily from what had looked to be shaping up to be a stern lecture, Eric went off to pop some popcorn while Greystone inspected Eric's daily-growing DVD collection.

But Eric was not to escape so easily. Halfway through *The Thomas Crown Affair*, Greystone returned to the subject he wanted to discuss.

"And that lady alienist. What does she think of this daft notion of yours?"

Sometimes Greystone's terminology was decades out of date—intentionally so, Eric was sure. Psychiatrists hadn't been called "alienists" for at least eighty years. "I haven't mentioned it to her."

Greystone snorted. "Nae doot she'd think it a fine idea."

"Your accent's slipping. And as a matter of fact, she would," Eric said, mentally crossing his fingers. She'd said he needed to deal with the issues of his childhood. She hadn't necessarily said he should pay his parents a visit.

Greystone made a rude face, something the gargoyle's carven apelike face was wonderfully well designed to do. "The young! Have they no respect for tradition, then? It's cruising for a bruising, plain and simple—and you of all people, Underhill's Bard, should know that!"

Eric turned to Greystone, studying him in puzzlement. He knew that going home again—not that it had ever been home, not really—was fraught with hidden land mines, but Greystone seemed to have something specific in mind.

Greystone sighed, and seemed to resign himself to putting all his cards on the table and speaking plainly.

"Going home. Going back to your mortal family. Seeing your parents again, after a sojourn in Elven Lands. It never turns out well, at least according to all the old songs."

Eric regarded Greystone. *That* aspect of things hadn't occurred to him.

What if the old ballads were right?

CHAPTER FOUR:

THE JOB OF JOURNEYWORK

All the way here, his stomach had been telling him this was a mistake, but he'd come too far to back out now.

Maybe he wouldn't talk to them, though—at least not as himself. A little Bardic *glamourie* would be enough to ensure that they didn't recognize him—and it wasn't as if they were expecting to see him, after all. Like Hosea said, they thought he was dead.

Maybe just *seeing* them would be enough. Right now Eric was sure it would be *more* than enough. No matter how many times he told himself that they were nothing more than human beings—misguided human beings, to be sure—with absolutely no power over him, he was unable to shake the conviction that he was walking into a trap. That the moment he crossed the threshold of his old home, he'd find himself ensnared in the web of his childhood again, at the mercy of people that his subconscious insisted were monsters.

Well, that's what this little pleasure trip is all about, isn't it? To prove that none of that is true.

He found his old neighborhood without trouble. His parents had lived for as long as he could remember on the same spacious tree-lined street within walking distance of Harvard University. Everything had a refined and mannered elegance that set his teeth on edge; a self-satisfaction that bordered on smugness. It took a great deal of money to live comfortably in Cambridge, but it was the height of bad form to flaunt it in any way. These were houses—very large houses, of course, but certainly not mansions. They were set close together, and close to the street; Boston was a very old city, and its architecture reflected the fact. Volvo station wagons and the occasional chaste BMW were parked in the driveways and along the streets; nothing vulgar and flashy for the inhabitants of the People's Republic of Cambridge. Lady Day (not that she was vulgar or flashy!) stood out like a frog on a birthday cake.

Good, Eric thought with savage satisfaction.

The house looked just as he remembered it. There were two cars in the driveway; both unfamiliar, but that was only to be expected. He'd been gone for twenty years, after all. But maybe his parents weren't living here any more?

He supposed he'd better check.

He wheeled Lady Day in behind the second car parked in the driveway—there was *just* enough room to get her off the street—and swung off, pulling off his helmet and hooking it over the back. He patted her absently on the gas tank. "Be good," he told the elvensteed.

She flashed her lights in silent reply.

It was a little after two when he went up the steps and onto the porch, and only stubbornness kept him moving forward. For a moment he hoped he could give up, turn back—he could always try over at the university, after all; it was probably what he should have done in the first place—but no, the brass plate over the mailbox still said "BANYON."

He was in the right place after all.

He was about to leave anyway—going over to the university really *was* a better idea—when the front door opened, and Eric found himself staring at his mother.

She's old! was his first automatic shocked thought.

Fiona Sommerville Banyon stared at him without recognition, raising one well-manicured auburn eyebrow. She wore a cashmere twinset, tweed skirt, and pearls, his mother's uniform for as long as Eric could remember. Her chestnut hair was shoulder-length, carefully colored to mask any trace of grey.

"Thank you for coming," she said, opening the door wider and stepping back. "We're glad you could make it so quickly."

Feeling a growing sense of unreality, Eric opened the storm door and stepped inside. How could she have been expecting him? He hadn't known he'd be coming himself until yesterday.

Was this a trap? A trick? A spell?

Feeling tense and off-balance, Eric followed her inside, into the company parlor on the right. The music parlor was on the left; with an effort he kept himself from looking to see if the piano and the concert harp were still there.

They'd redecorated since he'd left. Some of the pieces, like Grandmother's antique sideboard and the long-case clock, were still there, though in different places than he remembered, but the couch and chairs were new.

And his father was there. Eric took a deep breath, willing his face to remain expressionless. He'd faced down Aerune mac Audelaine Lord of Death and Pain, and worse. He was *not* going to run from a college professor!

There was grey in Michael Banyon's hair now; distinguished silver wings at the temples, and Eric just bet that all the girls in his History of Music Arts classes just swooned over it. He advanced toward Eric, hand out.

They must think I'm someone else. I have got *to tell them who I am!*

But Michael Banyon didn't give him the chance.

"We're very grateful you were able to come on such short notice, Mr. Dorland. Our son is very important to us, and believe me, we will do *anything* to get him back."

He took Eric's hand and shook it firmly, in his strong musician's grip.

Now? Eric thought, stunned to silence. *They're looking for me* now? That made no sense at all. It had been twenty years, World time. And when he'd come back to live in the World Above, he'd covered his tracks very carefully—and Ria was doing a lot more to help. Certainly he was attending Juilliard as Eric Banyon, but it was a common enough name. And if his parents should have happened to hear about it, and connect that Eric Banyon with their vanished son, they wouldn't have needed to hire a private detective to find him. They'd just have gotten in a car and driven down.

"Would you like to see Magnus' room?" his mother said.

Magnus?

Suddenly Eric really did seriously wonder if he were under a spell, or if he'd fallen into a parallel universe. Or if this could somehow be the wrong house, despite the fact that he'd come to the right address, and these *were* his parents, twenty years older, and the name "Banyon" was still on the front door.

"Yes. Thank you." He managed to find his voice at last.

"You go ahead, Fi," his father said, sitting down on the couch. As usual, once he'd done the meet-and-greet, Michael Banyon thought his duties were discharged, Eric thought irritably. He followed Fiona Banyon up the stairs, to . . . *his* . . . old room.

But not his any longer. It, like the parlor, had been completely redecorated, and now bore a certain family resemblance (though without the black walls) to Kayla's apartment. It was obviously the room of a teenaged boy.

"We left it just the way it was when he . . . left," Mrs. Banyon said. "I don't know how many times I told him to take down those posters. Rock music! It's just noise. Not real music."

Eric looked around. He felt more comfortable here. At least this place looked completely different than everything he was used to.

"Why don't you tell me everything?" he said.

"But I told you—over the phone—"

"I'd like to hear it again," Eric said gently. "Sometimes the smallest details can be important." Such as what his parents were doing with a teenaged boy they were calling their son.

Fiona walked into the room and sat down. The bed had been made to Marine Corps standards.

"About a month ago—let me see, that would be, September 8th—I came home and Magnus wasn't

here. He was supposed to come straight home from
school; we'd grounded him because his psychologist
said he'd respond well to limits. I asked Connie—she
was our cook-housekeeper at the time—where he
was, and she said she hadn't seen him at all that day.
Naturally I fired her.

"We called the police. Michael even tried checking
his computer, but he'd, oh, formatted the hard disk
or something, and we couldn't get it to work. We
went to the police and filled out all the papers, and
they . . . well, frankly, I was very disappointed. We
were devastated, of course."

She didn't sound devastated, Eric thought cynically.
She sounded more annoyed than anything else. Of
course, his parents weren't big on emotional displays,
but he would have thought a missing child would
be worth *something*. A few tears at least, or some
evidence of sleepless nights?

"Mr. Dorland, I am terribly worried about my child.
Magnus is . . . special. He's a gifted and talented musician. Both Michael and I have a certain amount of
musical ability, but Magnus is a musical prodigy. He's
been giving performances since he was four. But as
you know, geniuses have certain . . . emotional problems,
and lately he'd become rather, well, moody and rebellious. It was bad enough when he started listening to
this rock music, but then he developed this obsession
about actually performing it, and that, of course, we
couldn't allow. Magnus is a pianist. He can't possibly
be allowed to debase his gifts.

"Of course he receives counseling, and naturally he
attends one of the best private schools in Boston."

"St. Augustine," Eric said. Of course it would be
St. Augustine.

Her eyes widened in surprise. "You know it?"

"It's my business to know things, Mrs. Banyon," Eric

said, covering his slip smoothly. He remembered St. Augustine, and not fondly: he'd gone there until he'd switched to Juilliard, and it had been several years of unmitigated hell.

"I've written a *very* stiff note to the headmaster there! What's the point of a private school if not to protect its students from unhealthy influences? But obviously Magnus fell in with a bad crowd there, because he's always been such a good little boy. . . ."

"And your son was how old, exactly?" Eric asked, sending out a thread of Bardic Magic to keep her from finding the question odd, to encourage her to tell him everything she knew, freely and without constraint. Whoever Dorland was, he obviously already knew the answers, and Eric wanted to know them too.

"He just turned seventeen in July," Mrs. Banyon said. "We'd wanted to send him to Juilliard, but he really needed more structure. Michael was thinking of a good boarding school, but . . . the music."

The music. It was always the music, wasn't it? You didn't think you could trust this kid in the big city, and if you locked him up somewhere, he wouldn't be around to feed your ego, would he? Eric took a deep breath, forcing his emotions down, away from the surface. He couldn't afford to show them. And he'd abandoned all idea of letting them know who he really was. Not now.

"Find him, Mr. Dorland. Bring him back. We'll put an end to this rock music nonsense. Magnus will study classical music, just like. . . ." She faltered to a stop, looking confused.

"Just like who, Mrs. Banyon?" Eric asked softly, strengthening the thread of magic in his words. "Do you have any other children? Any other family? Someone he might go to?"

"Oh no," Mrs. Banyon assured him, her eyes clear

and untroubled. "Magnus did have an older brother once. But Eric died before Magnus was born."

She got to her feet, looking around the room with distaste. "I suppose you'd like to stay here for a while and look around. I'll be downstairs if you need me for anything."

She walked out, leaving Eric alone.

Eric crossed the room and sat down at the desk, willing himself to be calm. He took several deep breaths, forcing serenity on himself as if he wrestled with a living enemy.

It was bad enough that he'd come here at all. That had been a stupid idea. But he knew now, it had been a bad choice made for a good reason, because if he hadn't done it, he would never have known that Magnus Banyon existed.

His brother.

I have a brother.

Not only was that unbelievable, it wasn't the worst part.

If my brother is seventeen—and add nine months gestation to that—then about how long was I gone for when they decided to wash their hands of me and start over?

Not long enough.

His parents had obviously learned nothing from ruining his life, and had in fact repeated their mistake line for line—another trophy child, another "prodigy." The only plus was that this time apparently they hadn't driven their son crazy, if reading between the lines was any clue. *This* son was no docile victim. He was a fighter, a discipline problem, a candidate for one of those boarding schools where the rich sent their children so they could be someone else's problem, safely out of sight, and controlled and confined so that any "unsuitable" tendencies could be eviscerated out of them.

And Magnus, who undoubtedly knew that, had run away before that could happen. And his parents had waited an entire month before bothering to apply their own resources to the hunt for him. Anything could have happened to him by now.

If anyone ever deserved full and proper punishment for their acts, it was Michael and Fiona Banyon. And Eric had the power to provide it in the last full measure. With a word, with a gesture . . .

Wait! Stop it! What are you thinking?

Eric forced himself to stop. Just . . . stop. He stepped back from his anger as Master Dharniel had taught him, as Eric was teaching Hosea, withdrawing himself from it until he stood outside it, until he could push it away from himself and set it aside. *If there is a proper day for this, then that day will come. But that day is not today.*

He could *not* think about this now. And he didn't really have the time. If the *real* Dorland showed up while he was here, there would be explanations to make that Eric didn't have the energy or control for just now. The barriers he had just erected were fragile. He dared not test them.

And his mother was right about one thing. Magnus had to be found—and *he* had to be the one to do it.

Before they did. The elves that were his friends, mentors, and role models made it part of their life's work—and they had very long lives—to rescue abused children from their abusers. If Eric's own life was anything to go by, the Banyons, Fiona and Michael, certainly fit that description. The fact that Magnus was his own blood, his own brother, just made it that much more important that he be rescued.

And—hidden?

Bet your sweet ass.

He got to his feet and quickly searched the room. There wasn't much in the way of personal items—no letters or diaries—and when he turned on the computer, he found that it had, indeed, been wiped, and there were no backup disks or copies of personal files anywhere. *Clever Magnus!* he found himself thinking in approval. *Smarter than I ever was at your age . . .*

Tucked in the back of a sock drawer he found a bus pass with a picture on it, and for the first time got a look at his brother.

The same auburn hair—they both got that from their mother. Worn long—to make him look like a Baby Mozart, Eric guessed sourly. Green eyes, at least the bus pass said so. Girlishly pretty—Eric winced in sympathy, remembering the fights he'd had to get into as a kid because of his own looks—but the mouth was set in a permanent smirk that indicated this kid was nothing but trouble. *Good for you, kid.*

Eric tucked the bus pass in his pocket and kept looking.

In another drawer, he found a hairbrush, with several strands of long auburn hair tangled among the bristles. Carefully, Eric teased several of them free, winding them around his finger, and tucked them into his wallet. With those, and a little magic, he'd be able to find Magnus quickly and easily.

If he was still alive.

Eric winced, fighting down fear.

A month on the streets alone. Not everybody was as smart and lucky as Kayla had been. As *he* had been, face it. Kids died on the streets, every day.

If that had happened . . .

Don't borrow trouble, Eric told himself firmly.

He went down the stairs, schooling his face to blankness.

"I think I have everything I need here," he said,

as the elder Banyons rose to their feet. "I'll be in touch." *When Hell freezes rock-solid.*

They walked him to the door. As he went down the steps, hearing the door close behind him, he realized there was one last thing he needed to do here.

Cover his tracks. It wouldn't do for them to tell Dorland he'd already been here when the man finally arrived, after all.

He turned back to the house, reaching out for his magic, feeling the music well up in him. He sighed a little with relief to have it come so easily, but the control he'd learned Underhill held firm after all, even rattled as he was. The song spilled through him, into the world; Eric pursed his lips and whistled a few notes of an old country air.

Forget. Forget I was ever here. Forget you spoke to me. Forget . . . forget . . . forget . . .

It was done. His parents wouldn't remember he'd been here, or that they'd spoken to him, or that they'd mistaken him for their Mr. Dorland. He swung his leg over Lady Day and backed out of the driveway, heading sedately down the street just as a sleek grey Mercedes with smoked windows pulled up in front of the Banyon house.

He didn't go far. Finding Magnus was the highest priority, and it couldn't wait. He headed over to Harvard, where there was a lot of open space where he could work undisturbed. Parking Lady Day and commanding her to make herself inconspicuous, Eric walked until he could put his back against a tree.

The weather was freezing, the wind promising more early snow. Eric saw very few people, and those he did see were bundled up and hurrying on their way to be elsewhere.

Fortunately, the campus was fairly deserted at this time of year. Thanksgiving break, everyone heading home to their families, all of the schools closed, only a few students left on campus.

He was starting here on the chance that Magnus was still somewhere in the Boston area. Eric couldn't afford to ignore any possibility. How far the boy had run depended on how much money he'd had, how lucky he'd been at hitching rides, and whether he had any friends in the area who would have taken him in and hidden him.

Eric reached into his wallet and took out the lock of hair, coiling it around his finger again. The old magics, the simple magics, were the strongest. According to the Doctrine of Contagion, objects that were once linked were linked forever, so a lock of hair, even though no longer physically attached to a person, was still a part of them.

Summoning up his flute of air, Eric closed his eyes and began to play, concentrating on the strands of hair wound around his finger. *Show me where you are. Alive or dead, show me where you are at this moment.*

Wistful songs, yearning songs—"She Moved Through The Fair," and "Greensleeves," and "Hame, Hame, Hame." On and on he played, searching outward, mile after mile.

At last, exhausted, he had to stop.

He'd found nothing.

Eric felt a combination of frustration and relief. Magnus wasn't here. Not in Boston, not anywhere near it. Neither alive nor dead.

That was something, anyway. He wasn't sure what, but something.

By the time Eric got back to New York again, he'd had far too much time to do nothing but think, and he was furious all over again. It wasn't enough that his parents had ruined his life. No, they'd thrown him away like a used paper cup—without even a decent period of mourning—and gotten themselves another child to ruin. And that hurt, actually—

It hurt more than he had expected it to. He'd always known he was just a trophy, a possession to them, but he had never thought of himself as disposable.

He'd always assumed they'd searched for him when he disappeared. Now he wondered if they ever had. He'd been eighteen, after all. A legal adult. Pretty hard to drag back and make jump through hoops again.

Not like Magnus.

He was shaking so hard he could barely hold on to the handlebars of the bike. Fortunately Lady Day could do all the driving, but he could feel the elvensteed's worry. He tried to send her reassuring thoughts, but he was so angry he could hardly think straight.

Get it together, Banyon. Before you do something really stupid.

Lady Day pulled up in the little parking lot behind Guardian House and stopped. It was already dark. Eric got off stiffly and checked his watch. Six o'clock.

He needed to talk to someone about this before he blew a gasket. Hosea would be a good place to start.

But when he went inside and tapped on Hosea's door, there was no answer. *Must be out,* Eric thought, feeling oddly disappointed.

Kayla? He rejected the idea. What he was feeling right now would probably fry the Healer in her tracks, and besides, she was too young for this.

Toni? Paul? José? Eric considered and rejected the idea. The other Guardians were friends, but, well, this was something too personal to discuss with them.

He went up to his own apartment and looked at the phone.

Was this something he needed to call Oriana about?

Eric thought the matter over carefully. Was his reluctance to call her reasonable, or was he hiding out because he'd done something really stupid and didn't want to get zinged for it? *Probably a little of both,* he decided. *I'll sleep on it, and I'll call her tomorrow during office hours and see if she thinks I need to come in before next Monday.*

Knowing she probably would.

How could something he hadn't known about this morning—that had been going along for years without him knowing about it—*hurt* so damned much? And he knew he had to get himself straightened out about it fast, because Magnus' problems wouldn't wait.

But there was someone here he could talk to now.

"Greystone?" he said aloud. "You want to come down?"

He went into the kitchen to put up the water for tea.

When he came back into the living room, Greystone had just finished climbing in through the window.

"Hola, boyo," the gargoyle said. "And how was Beantown?"

"I've got a baby brother," Eric said, torn between laughter and tears. He threw himself down on the couch. It all seemed utterly ridiculous when he said it aloud.

"It must have been some family reunion," Greystone said, easing himself into a chair. The leather creaked and groaned under the gargoyle's weight, but it held. It was Greystone's favorite chair. "Do you want to tell me all the gory details?"

"Not much of a family reunion," Eric said. "He's run

away from home. A month ago. I guess it's a family tradition. His name's Magnus."

"'Magnus Banyon.' Now *there's* a name to resonate through the halls of history," Greystone commented dryly. "And where is the little lad now?"

"I don't know!" Eric shouted, lunging to his feet again. "I don't know if he's alive, or— I looked all over Boston for him. He's not there. He's seventeen. They must have . . . they had him studying music, too. At St. Augustine. Another little *prodigy*," he said in disgust.

He began to pace back and forth, too worked up to sit still. "I went to see my parents. They thought I was this private detective they've hired, so they told me all about it. They left me alone in his room long enough for me to pick up some things to set the spell to find him with, but . . . that really isn't my kind of magic. I could have made a mistake. He *could* be there, somewhere. I might have missed him. He's been on the streets for a month. Anything could have happened to him. He's only seventeen—a baby!"

"Not so very much younger than you were when you hit the streets, laddybuck. You survived," Greystone reminded him quietly.

"Yes— And— But—" Eric sputtered. *But when I think of all the things I did in order to survive, and how I almost* didn't *survive . . .*

"And yon bairn has allies and friends, even if he doesn't know it yet," Greystone went on reasonably. "Powerful allies and powerful friends. So why don't you just go pick up that phone and call one of them? And by the by, your tea kettle's boiling."

It was a little after seven P.M., but Ria Llewellyn had no plans to leave for hours yet. There was work to do. There was always work to do. Glancing up from the top of her antique rosewood desk, she could look out through the glass walls of her office at the lights of the other buildings along the avenue where other New Yorkers were staying equally late. New York, as the saying went, is the City that Works.

And that suited Ria just fine.

The construction on the five floors of LlewellCo offices had finally been finished late last fall, including installing the new carpet for her penthouse suite—cream, with the red dragon of her corporate logo woven into the center. This spring, she'd finally finished the paperwork involved in shifting her power base to the East Coast, and turned LlewellCo West over to Jonathan as his own private sub-fief, a reward for many years of good and faithful service.

She'd gotten tired of fighting with the co-op board of her Park Avenue apartment and bought another one on Central Park South, buying the building first to make sure she wouldn't have any further trouble with the tenants' committee. The view of the Park was breathtaking; well worth the trouble of moving and redecorating, in Ria's opinion.

She guessed it was time to give up and admit she was just a New York City kind of girl. She'd been all over the world, spent a lot of time in most of the "great" cities, and never found one that fit her so well emotionally. And if that meant, as Eric often teased, that she was a clothes-obsessed workaholic, so be it. Somebody had to see that the work got done.

And there was always more work.

If—finally, slowly—LlewellCo was starting to take on the shape she envisioned for it, and not the shape that Perenor had given it, then that hardly meant her work was finished. Each problem solved only seemed to mean that two or three more sprang up. Dragon's teeth.

The Threshold disaster, for example. They were most of the way out from under the immediate consequences—though they'd still be battling cleanup on that one for years to come—but there was still the question of *who* all of Robert Lintel's clients had been. They had to be tracked down, each and every one of them, and nailed to the nearest barn door—if she had to build the barn herself.

And she couldn't think about Threshold without thinking about Aerune mac Audelaine. Aerune himself was dealt with, trapped in a magical labyrinth that Eric had gotten from a dragon named Chinthliss, so he was no longer a threat. But Aerune had been partners with a man named Parker Wheatley, who had ties to the government, and Wheatley remained a threat. Because Wheatley not only believed in elves, but thought (thanks to Aerune's manipulations) that they were out to destroy the human race. Wheatley had a little black budget operation called the Paranormal Defense Initiative that was out to get its hands on elves by any means possible, and—also thanks to Aerune—had its hands on a selection of techno toys that made that frighteningly possible.

They all—she, Eric, his Guardian friends—had been pretty sure that without Aerune's backing, Wheatley would just dry up and wither away, but that had been before the government had started making a major antiterrorism push. Now getting rid of Wheatley's Elven *padrone* might not be enough to get rid of the PDI.

And getting rid of a Washington insider wasn't something Eric could do, nor his little friends with their swords and spells, as much fun as they might be to spend a weekend Underhill with. This was something only Ria could do, and it was something that required delicate manipulation, and more than a little string-pulling in the political arena.

But thinking about that "weekend Underhill"—though it hadn't exactly been a weekend—turned her thoughts, as they so often turned when she was tired, to the peculiar ordeal the seven of them had shared when they had entered Aerune's mind: of actually experiencing what it had been like to live in a world millennia dead, when Sidhe had lived openly among humans as their guardians and caretakers.

Ria frowned. Fascinating and uncomfortable as it had been, it had raised more questions than it had answered.

Just what exactly *was* the relationship between Sidhe and humanity? Where and when did it start, and what was it *for*? Was it a good thing, or a bad thing, and should it be allowed to continue?

The phone rang.

Ria glanced at her phone. Anita was gone for the evening, and the switchboard routed everything to voicemail after 5:00, but the light that was flashing was for her private line. Very few people had that number.

She picked up the phone.

"Llewellyn."

"It's Eric."

He didn't sound as if he'd had a good day at all, and Eric's bad days tended to be bad for more people than just Eric. "What's wrong?" she asked sharply.

"Can I come over?" he asked, and that wasn't like Eric either. He teased, he fenced, he played with words; she shouldn't have gotten off without at least *one* gibe about him finding her here so late.

"Yes. I'll be here. I'll call down and make sure Security is expecting you."

The phone went dead in her ear. He'd hung up.

This must be something *truly* bad. And she couldn't

think of anything that he wouldn't at least *try* to prepare her for over the phone. *Not Hosea. I don't think I could stand it if anybody else died right now. Or Kayla—*

No. If something was wrong with Kayla, he'd have told her immediately. Or if Kayla was dead, and there was nothing to be done, he'd have come immediately and called her from downstairs.

But he'd sounded so rattled, so lost. . . .

At least she knew it wasn't family problems. Eric didn't *have* any family, if you didn't count the Misthold elves and Kentraine, and all of them were locked up safe Underhill. Baby Maeve even had her own personal bodyguard. If there was one set of people Eric didn't have to worry about, it was his family.

Ria stood it as long as she could, then gave up and began to pace. She had a fine large executive office—about the size of Eric's entire apartment— with plenty of room for pacing.

If she was worried about Eric, it was only because he was a friend.

She was *not* in love with Eric Banyon, she told herself firmly and not for the first time. Love was a very bad idea for their kind. It always ended badly. It made you want more than it was good for you to have. Loved him, *that* she'd admit to freely. Eric was a loveable man, and there'd been a bond between them from the first moment they'd met as adversaries, she as Perenor's pawn and he as the Sun-Descending Sidhe's last hope. That tie, strange and ill-starred as it was, had only strengthened through the years. She knew he felt it as much as she did.

Lovers, yes. Friends, always, or so she hoped.

But *in* love with him? No. Never. That would be madness.

Eric wouldn't know what to do with a real love affair—and, Ria suspected, neither would she.

Eric, what's wrong? If the world's hurt you, I— I'll tear it down around us both, I swear!

About twenty minutes after the call, there was a knock on the door. Ria opened it. Eric was standing there, next to one of the LlewellCo security guards.

"Thanks, George," he said, with the ghost of a grin. "I think I can find my way from here."

"You have a good evening, Mr. Banyon. Be sure to call when you're ready to come down."

"I'll remind him," Ria said. The guard touched his cap, and walked off.

Eric looked at her questioningly.

"New security measures," Ria said.

"You should just buy the building," Eric said. "Then you wouldn't be bothered."

"As a matter of fact, I *do* own the building; real estate is always a good investment. These *are* my security measures," Ria said with a little smile. "If you don't work here—and can't show an ID even if you do work here—you don't get above the lobby without an escort, no matter what time of day it is."

"Welcome to New York," Eric said with a sigh. He looked around the office as if he'd forgotten why he'd come.

There were deep shadows under his eyes, and an unfamiliar set to his mouth. No, Ria decided with an odd pang of recognition. A familiar one, but one she hadn't seen in years: it was that look of sullen anger the *old* Eric had worn, that look of always being on the verge of lashing out at something.

Eric walked over to the window and stood looking out, staring down into the city streets below. Chains of head- and taillights moved through the streets below like rivers of sluggish jewels.

"Tea? Coffee? Well, actually, I can't offer you either one now that Anita's gone home, but I'm sure there's something around here. But you didn't come over for a drink," Ria said.

Eric leaned against the glass, his back to her. She watched him force himself to relax, saw the effort it took.

"You know I've been seeing Dr. Dunaway for almost a year now, getting some stuff straightened out. It's been pretty useful. You know, you might think about trying it," he said, as if the thought had just occurred to him.

Ria laughed. She couldn't help it. "Eric, my dear, any daughter of Perenor's got over the need to talk to strangers a long time ago. And I'm sure that inviting me to seek psychiatric help is *not* what this is about."

"No." She watched as he took a deep breath, forcing himself to come to the point. "I came because I need help . . . to keep from killing somebody."

His voice was as tight as Hosea's banjo strings, and the over- and under-tones so complicated that even she couldn't make head or tail of them, other than for the fury in it. Anger was too tame a word, and fury, too, wasn't the right word for what she heard in him tonight. Call it rage. Carefully controlled rage, that was on the edge of slipping that careful control.

"Well," Ria walked over to her desk and sat on the edge, watching his back intently, "most people would say the opposite sort of help was more in my line."

"I don't . . . I can't keep from hating them. I'm trying, but . . . I can't," Eric said raggedly.

Ria walked over to him and put an arm around him, feeling the tension of the muscles beneath the

jacket, and led him firmly over to the couch, forcing
him to sit down. His face looked white and strained.
"Make sense," she commanded. "Now. Or I am going
to phone your very competent headshrinker and sit on
you myself until she gets here." She sat down beside
him and took both his hands. They were colder than
the November weather outside could account for.

"I've got a little brother." Eric's voice was forlorn.

She'd been prepared to hear horrors—tales of death,
dismemberment, terminal illness, coming apocalypse.
Eric's simple statement caught Ria completely off-
balance. She whooped with startled laughter.

"It isn't funny!" Eric snarled, but then the sense of
his own words seemed to penetrate, and his mouth
quirked up in a rueful grin, setting Ria off again.

She did her best to stop laughing, but it was
hard.

"Yes," she said, as gravely as she could manage,
"I can certainly see that a baby brother is a *great*
catastrophe." She took a deep breath, sobering further.
"Are you sure? How do you know?"

"I'm sure. I went to see my parents today."

That drove the last of the laughter from Ria's emotions. Of all of Eric's close circle of friends, she was
the one who knew the most about his childhood, and
that only because she'd stolen the memories from his
mind years before while she'd had him trapped and
besotted in one of Perenor's pocket domains.

"Why?" she asked bluntly.

"I realized they still had too much power in my life.
I'd never let go of the past, not really, just walled it
up and pretended it wasn't there. I thought confronting
them might help. It was probably a stupid idea."

"Reckless at least," Ria said calmly. "Did they recognize you?"

"They thought I was the private detective they'd hired

to find their son. Their *other* son. Their seventeen-year-old piano prodigy son Magnus, who ran away from home last month."

Ria could do the math as well as Eric could. Her eyelids flickered. Aloud she said only, "They took their sweet time hiring a specialist. Who?"

"Someone named Dorland." Eric's voice was flat, colorless beneath his iron control.

"I'll get on it, find out what I can about him. And do they remember you were there?"

"No," Eric said, his voice even. "I took care of it."

"That's my Bard," Ria said, kissing him gently on the forehead. "Now, where's Magnus?"

"I looked in Boston," Eric answered. "He wasn't there. Ria, how could they—"

"Because they're morons," Ria said matter-of-factly, cutting through Eric's rekindling anger with simple pragmatism. "Blind, stupid, selfish, ignorant *morons,* who have never taken a moment in their entire lives to think about anything but themselves and what they want. They aren't worth another minute of your time, now or ever. Eric, my—" she stopped herself before she could say the forbidden word, "—my friend, if they considered you disposable, how much more right have you got to think the same of them? Dispose of them; wad them up and throw them away. They're trash; they aren't worth a moment of heartache. But Magnus *is.* A runaway teenager—especially one as stubborn as a brother of yours is likely to be—oh yes, and don't forget one who's also likely to have the Bardic Gift, or at least leanings in that direction, since it runs in bloodlines—could be getting into all kinds of trouble out there, wherever he is. We should find him. Now."

Eric took a deep breath, accepting the truth of her words. "Okay. We find him."

"What have you tried so far?" Ria asked.

"A Finding spell, up in Boston." Eric dug around in his pockets. "Here's a picture of him. And here's a lock of his hair. He wasn't there, either dead or alive. But I was only able to search the immediate area."

Ria took the small card Eric handed her and studied the picture, then examined the lock of hair. "Cute kid. Plenty to go on here. Let me get what I need, and we'll try another kind of spell."

Ria walked out of the office, leaving Eric sitting on the couch, and went looking for what she needed. She came back a few minutes later with a shallow metal dish full of water, which she placed carefully on the large round glass-topped table in front of the couch.

"I am *not* getting water spots all over my leather-topped desk," she said firmly, noting Eric's quizzical glance.

"What are you doing?" Eric asked curiously. Bardic magic was one thing, and Elven magic tended to be constructs of pure energy, but Ria, being half-human, tended to rely sometimes on things that owed nothing to the Elven magic that Eric was familiar with. In fact, Ria had told him once that she was a sorceress, not any kind of a Sidhe Magus at all. . . .

"Scrying. Your brother's image should appear in this bowl of water, no matter where on Earth he is—and if he's been taken Underhill, we should at least get a hint of that from whatever images appear. The hard part will be seeing enough of the background to be able to pinpoint his location, but once I've got him, I should be able to move the image and look around a little. . . ."

She selected a single strand of hair out of the coil and floated it on top of the water, then breathed across the surface.

The water in the bowl went milky, then faded until it was as if they were staring down into a pool of mercury, though, oddly, the silvery surface reflected neither of their faces.

"What's it doing?" Eric whispered, unconsciously keeping his voice low.

"It's working," Ria said shortly. "Quiet."

Shapes appeared in the mirrored surface, familiar yet distorted, breaking apart and reforming almost too fast to be recognized. Eric caught the Port Authority Bus Terminal, Grand Central Station, the New York Public Library, the lobby of the Empire State Building. . . .

"New York," he said.

"He's here—and alive," Ria said. "Where is he? Show me!" she demanded of the magic.

The mercury darkened now to true black, with moving flecks of light that Eric guessed must be the lights of passing cars, or maybe streetlights. But it still kept up its frantic dance of images, moving from scene to scene too fast for either of the watchers to quite identify any of them.

Finally Ria gave up, passing her hand across the surface of the bowl. The liquid within faded to water once more.

"He's in Manhattan," Ria said.

"He's alive," Eric said, with relief. This morning, he hadn't known he had a brother. Tonight, he was weak with thankfulness that his brother was still alive. And he hadn't even had a chance to meet the boy yet!

Ria frowned down at the scrying bowl as though it were a personal enemy. "It should have worked better than that," she said.

"Bardic blood?" Eric suggested. It was the only thing he could think of.

"Shall we test the theory?" Ria said. "Give me a strand of your hair."

Eric wore his hair short these days, but he managed to yank a few strands loose. Ria coiled up the strand of Magnus' hair and returned it to Eric, then floated the short strands of Eric's hair on the surface of the bowl and repeated the spell. The water quickly darkened to silver and showed them Ria's office, with Eric sitting on the couch beside Ria.

"Not that, then," Eric said, puzzled.

"But something's interfering with the magic," Ria said. "Now what?"

"I guess I go after him the good old-fashioned way," Eric said. "He's a runaway, and I know he's in Manhattan. There aren't *that* many places he can be."

Ria made a face eloquent in its disbelief. "Why don't you ask Hosea about that sometime?" was all she said. "Eric, do you want some help? There are people who specialize in this sort of thing, you know. I can hire the best. They'll have contacts, experience. . . ."

Eric hesitated. Was he being stupid, wanting to do this by himself? But all his instincts said no.

"Just give me a few days. I'm not going to turn this into any kind of crusade. If I do need help, I'll ask for it. I'm not going to play games, Ria. Not with my . . . brother's . . . life. But . . . I feel almost like I already know him. And I *do* know his parents. He'll be expecting detectives. I did. And if he does have a trace of Bardic Gift—which might still be why your scrying spell didn't work—he'll recognize them through any disguise. If he gets frightened and runs again, to somewhere else, he could end up in even worse trouble than he's in now. I don't want to scare him, I just want to find him. But . . . what do I do then?" Eric smiled at her crookedly, and Ria reached out to ruffle his hair gently.

"Find him first. Keep him safe when you *do* find him. Sort out everything else after you've done those two things."

"I . . . thanks. You're a good friend."

"Well, don't let anyone hear you say that. You'll ruin my corporate shark image," Ria said lightly.

Eric got to his feet. "I guess I'd better be going. You're probably going to want to stay here and work all night."

"Somebody's got to," Ria said. She went over to the phone and punched a two-digit number. "George? Mr. Banyon's ready to come down now."

She set down the phone, and turned to give him a good once-over with her eyes. Maybe with more than her eyes. "Are you going to be all right tonight? Really all right?"

Eric smiled tiredly, not pretending to misunderstand what she meant. "Greystone's just waiting for me to get back. We're going to order in Thai and have a Bogart film festival. And I'll call Dr. Dunaway in the morning."

"That's my nice well-grounded Bard." She hesitated again. "Eric . . . just remember . . . if you *should* happen to see your parents again . . . or think about them . . . that you are what you are. So don't make any decisions that you'll regret before you've made up your mind what you really want to do."

Because the anger of a Bard can kill. Eric heard the words that Ria left unsaid. "I'll be good, Ria," he promised, kissing her lightly on the cheek.

There was a quiet tap on the door, and Eric opened it.

Walking out with George across the penthouse floor of the LlewellCo building—only one bank of elevators ran after five, and it was a long walk to get to them—Eric wondered whether all this could possibly be what Ria really wanted out of life.

And more to the point, could she afford to be such a public figure when she was going to live such an embarrassingly long time? True, she was only half-Elven, and would hardly have the millennium-and-more long lifespan of a full-blooded Sidhe, but even a couple of centuries would be awfully hard to explain. And as Chairman and CEO of LlewellCo, especially after the whole Threshold thing, she was incredibly well-known: on the cover of *Time*, *Newsweek*, and *Fortune* in the last year and a half just for starters. It would be hard for someone like that to just disappear from the public eye, even if she were willing to give up LlewellCo.

Money that does nothing but make more money. Call me an old hippie, but it just all seems . . . pointless, somehow, Eric thought, riding down in the high-speed elevator. *Nice, but pointless.*

"Have a good evening, Mr. Banyon," George said, as they reached the front door. Eric stepped out onto the street.

"You do the same, George," he said. The night air was raw and cold—unseasonably so—and he turned up the collar of his jacket.

He wondered where Magnus was, and what he was doing.

CHAPTER FIVE:

CHASE AROUND THE WINDMILL

Hosea had stopped by Eric's apartment when he'd gotten home from work at five, but Eric still wasn't back from his trip to Boston—or if he was, he wasn't home. Hosea sighed. He hoped it had gone well—or at least not too badly. Being on the outs with your kinfolk was a sorrowful thing, no matter what sort of people they were.

Not finding Eric in, he went on down to his own place.

He'd taken over Jimmie Youngblood's apartment after her death, inheriting not only her position as Guardian and her apartment in Guardian House, but everything she owned, for Jimmie'd had no living relatives by the time she died to pass her possessions to. Over the next several months, he'd helped Toni with the painful task of going through Jimmie's things, destroying personal papers, giving mementos to those who would value them, donating her clothing to charity. When they were done, the apartment was considerably emptier, but it still didn't feel like *his*.

Repainting helped. Jimmie'd favored cool blues and greens, colors that weren't to Hosea's taste. He'd felt a little guilty, repainting the place in warm creams and yellows—it had been Eric, surprisingly, who'd told him it was for the best.

"It's not a shrine. She's gone. It's your apartment now."

With the apartment repainted in more congenial colors, it had been easier to see what else should go. The large framed photos of wilderness scenes that Jimmie had decorated the living room with: beautiful, but not his style. He'd taken them along to one of the Basement Parties and given them away, along with a couple of the smaller pieces of furniture that just didn't seem to suit now.

And slowly, he'd begun to accumulate his own things to fill in the gaps. The long bookshelves that filled the front hall—emptied now of Jimmie's books on police procedure, forensic science, and criminal law—were beginning to fill with his own books, plus those of hers, mostly fiction and poetry, that he'd kept. The day after the Basement Party where he'd given away all the photographs, Tatiana had showed up at his door with a pair of Thomas Canty prints that she said needed a new home. He'd hung them over the couch, and they looked mighty fine there. Funny, that. When he'd come to New York, he hadn't known who Thomas Canty was, and though he'd admired the covers the man had done for science fiction and fantasy books, most of the books themselves hadn't been to his taste, so he'd never bothered with finding out who the artist was. Now, divorced from those books, he could admire the covers as artworks in their own right.

There had been other gifts along the way. Eric had given him a story-quilt—he used it to cover the couch, which had looked proper in a blue room but not in a yellow one—and Ria had presented him with a fine hard-rock maple rocking chair, just right for a man his size.

"It stands to reason that a man with a banjo needs a rocking chair," she'd said with a smile on the day she'd brought it. *"Please accept it as a housewarming gift. In New York, everyone's your neighbor."*

And he did have to admit that a rocking chair made any place seem a bit more like home.

After he'd showered and changed, Hosea thought about calling Eric again, and decided against it. Eric would call if he needed him, and more than likely he'd just want to be left alone. And to be perfectly fair about things, Hosea had his own plans for the evening.

For the past several months, Hosea had been seeing Caity Tambling, a children's book illustrator who lived on the floor below. He'd met her at one of the informal Basement Parties the inhabitants of the House threw every few weeks, and they'd taken to one another pretty quickly. Caity was a shy, soft-spoken young woman from the mountains of West Virginia, born and raised not too far from where Hosea had grown up, in fact. She had a mop of white-blonde hair that was constantly falling in her eyes, and was plump in a way that Hosea liked to see in a lady, though Caity had been doubtful, at first, in accepting his compliments.

He checked his watch, frowning at the time. She'd

said she'd meet him here, but it was already a quarter of six, and she'd been going to meet him at five-thirty. She'd probably sat down at her drawing board to do just one little thing and fallen in. Hosea grinned to himself. He'd better go down to her place and roust her out, or they'd never have time for dinner before the movie.

"Hosea!" Caity said, opening the door. She looked wide-eyed and jittery, and for a moment Hosea was sure she'd forgotten all about their date.

Her hair was scraped severely back from her head and pulled into a tight ponytail—not a particularly flattering style, as it made her face look very round. She was dressed in clothes he'd never seen her wear before: a stark black velour tunic top and pants that looked oddly like a uniform.

"If something's come up . . ." he said gently.

"No, no, no . . . come in. I was just—with a client. Last-minute thing. It ran later than I expected. Come on in. I need to change, then we'll go. Is that okay?"

"Of course it's okay," Hosea said reassuringly. "Take your time."

Caity skittered off toward the bedroom, and Hosea followed her in, locking the front door behind him. In a moment he heard the sound of running water.

Caity's apartment was a mirror image of his, but the living room had been set up entirely as a studio and workroom. The walls were covered with art in all stages of execution from concept sketches to proof pages and a few finished book covers. Most artists these days worked on computer, but Caity still worked on paper and canvas, converting her work to IRIS files only at the last step before she turned them in. She said the paper and pigments talked to her, and the computer didn't.

Her work was lovely—if her drawings were anything
like what Underhill looked like, Hosea was surprised
that Eric had ever wanted to leave. Plump graceful
unicorns with iridescent coats; small winged fairies
that still managed to be cheerful and dignified, not
sappy; forest brownies with all the happy innocence
of puppies . . . this was the Enchanted Forest without
its darkness, as was suitable for the young readers
who would see her works. She was known for her
whimsical animals as well. He looked at the titles of
some of the finished books on the shelf: *Strawberry
Tea*, *Earl Ferret Goes To Town*, *The Cat Who Sang
Opera*, *Tea With Mice*. . . .

Caity was a special lady, which was hardly surprising. Guardian House chose all its tenants. Not all
of them were magicians like Eric and the Guardians, but all of them were special in some way. All
of them had what Hosea's grandmother would have
called "a touch of the 'shine.'" Most of them were
artists in one way or another—either actual artists,
like Caity, or writers, dancers, musicians, poets and
the like, even if they had to work other jobs to
support their art. He wandered around the room
for a few minutes, revisiting favorite pieces. Most of
Caity's professional work was in colored inks and ink
wash, with a lot of fine linework, but occasionally
she would do a piece "just for me" and then she
would paint with brush and pigments. Some of these
were wildly abstract—Caity sometimes claimed that
nobody who couldn't draw a cow that looked like
a cow had any business doing nonrepresentational
work, but that sometimes it was fun to let go of
pure shape—some were representational, but almost
Expressionistic. None were framed.

The lights were on over her drawing table. He
wondered what she was working on now. He went over

and looked down. Pen and ink, a blur of colored lines, but so many lines, so much dense cross-hatching, that it almost looked like an engraving. He took a closer look, and frowned. If this was for a children's book, he'd hate to meet the children it was for.

At first he'd thought it was an abstract piece, a "just for me" piece, despite the medium. But her other abstracts were light and playful, in love with color and light, not this dark muddy thing. And the longer he stared at it, the more he seemed to see figures appearing out of the squalid blur of cross-hatching. Red-eyed, angry figures, with long wicked claws . . .

He looked away with a faint shudder of distaste. There was a sketchbook lying on top of the taboret beside the drawing table. With a faint sense of guilt—this was snooping, and he knew it—he picked it up and paged through it quickly.

More sketches, some obviously studies for the work on the table, others different, but with the same feel to them.

If this was a new direction for her art, he really didn't care for it.

And he wondered why she'd fibbed to him about where she'd been this afternoon, because unless she'd been meeting her client down at the local Catholic church—or some other place where they burned a lot of frankincense—she hadn't just come in from any business meeting. Her clothes and hair had reeked of the stuff. He knew the smell perfectly well from Toni's apartment. And he also knew that Caity wasn't herself any kind of a Catholic—most folk from her neck of the woods were some flavor of Baptist or Pentecostal, and he knew Caity well enough by now to know that she wasn't especially churchly.

Not my business, Hosea told himself firmly. *Less'n she makes it my business.* Guardians didn't interfere

in the affairs of ordinary folk unless asked for help.
Paul and Toni had dinned that into his head thoroughly. Guardians didn't meddle unasked, hard as it
might be to stand back and watch somebody head
down the greased road to Perdition while you did
nothing. The most a Guardian might do was offer
help—but if that help was rejected, there was an
end to it.

"Always remember this, Hosea," Toni had told him.
*"You can't save the whole world. You'll find you have
enough to do just trying to save the people who ask
you for help. And you won't always be able to save
even them."*

"All ready?" Caity asked brightly, coming out of the
back. She'd taken the time for a quick shower, and
to put on the blue dress he'd told her he especially
liked.

She saw him looking at the picture on the drawing
table, and the bright smile dimmed, just a little. "Oh,
that," she said, switching off the Tensor lamps over
the table. "I should have put that away. It's nothing,
really. Come on, we'll be late."

But Hosea, holding her coat for her as they prepared to leave, could not rid himself of the notion
that the painting on the table was just a little bit
more than "nothing."

The apartment was not what he intended to become
used to, the man known to his followers as Fafnir,
Master of Treasure, told himself. It was certainly
not as much as he deserved. But at least it was free,
courtesy of one of his so-called Inner Circle. They
fell all over themselves to give him things—money,
electronics, living space. It was funny; the more things
people handed over to you unasked, the smarter
they thought they were. And if they weren't yet . . .

sufficiently appreciative . . . well, he had plans to take care of that.

It wasn't much of an apartment—a small one-bedroom in an area that had been known in less-gentrified days as Hell's Kitchen—but at least he hadn't had to ask for it. To ask was an admission of weakness, and Fafnir had no intention of ever appearing weak. He'd dropped a few well-placed and properly subtle hints around the time that Andrew had gotten so pissy about him being behind on the rent, and Juliana had just offered it to him. That was the beauty of this whole deal. He never had to demean himself by asking for anything. That would ruin the whole aura of mastery.

The room was lit solely by dozens of white candles in glass jars that stood clustered on tables and along the walls, and the air was heavy with incense smoke from the three tall antique censers that burned in three corners of the room, constantly replenished by one of the Faithful. In fact, one of his minions was going around tending to the censers and candles at the moment. By now the ceiling had been tinted a shiny dark umber by the pounds of frankincense that they'd burned since they'd begun meeting here. The scent permeated the rugs, the drapes, the walls, everything in the room. His supervisor at work had complained about it once or twice, until he'd started keeping his work clothes in double layers of plastic bags in the back of the closet, and showering just before he left for work. That cut the smell, and he'd gotten no more complaints.

It was nice to be able to bank most of his salary. Nice to be able to afford to buy anything he wanted, and to make an occasional show of wealth to impress the sheep (of course they had no idea about the job. That wouldn't go at all well with his aura of mystery).

Nicer still to be able to get his Faithful to buy everything he needed or wanted, and have them urge him
to accept these gifts to aid him in his Work.

The best sort of cons were the ones in which the
mark fleeced himself.

It was Andrew who'd given him the first hint, back
when they'd still been friends, back when he'd still
just been plain Freddie Warwick. One night a few
years ago Andrew had gotten spectacularly drunk on
a bottle of Scotch a grateful client had given him for
getting him out of a tax mess—Andrew wasn't much
of a drinker—and had told Freddie about something
that had happened to him when he'd first come to
New York, when he'd sublet an apartment for a rent
that had seemed too good to be true.

It turned out—so Andrew had said—that it was.
The apartment was haunted by a succubus—a spirit
that drained the life-force of whoever slept there.
Andrew couldn't figure out what was wrong. Neither
could his doctors.

Fortunately, the computer consultant at Andrew's
office could. Paul Kern, Andrew had said his name
was. He'd figured out Andrew's problem, and gotten
rid of the succubus. Andrew had gone on to enjoy
one of the cheapest apartments in New York for
years, until the leaseholder finally figured out that if
he wasn't dead, it must be safe to evict him.

And while solving Andrew's problem, Paul had told
him a little about himself. Paul was a Guardian, someone
who protected people like Andrew from things like that
succubus. While he hadn't said much, Andrew had been
pretty impressed. Apparently this Paul Kern could do
some pretty amazing things, things just like Dr. Strange
in the comic books Andrew had read as a kid.

Andrew wasn't really forthcoming the next day once
he sobered up. He tried to pretend he'd just been

goofing, pulling his roommate's leg, and refused to talk about it any more. But Freddie had known better than to believe that. Andrew had about as much imagination as the average accountant. So Freddie had gone to a comic book store and bought a bunch of old Dr. Strange comic books.

If Paul Kern could do even half of what Dr. Stephen Strange, Master of the Mystic Arts, could do . . .

At first, it had all seemed completely unbelievable, but he applied Occam's Razor to the situation and finally decided to suspend his disbelief and assume that all of this psychic magic crap was real and investigate it as such.

He'd cruised the 'net, now that he knew there was something to look for, and found a few more references to Guardians. From that he picked up a few facts that Andrew had missed, or maybe hadn't known.

There was more than one, for example.

And when one died, another was created.

But most important, the more he found, the more certain he became that all this *was* real. There *were* Guardians, they had amazing abilities, and for that reason, they were working very hard to keep their existence a secret.

Now he had a new ambition. He wanted to become a Guardian. But he wouldn't waste his Guardian power going around saving losers like Andrew from demons. No. He'd do really cool things with it. And he would certainly not squander his time and effort on anyone but himself.

And he bet there were a lot of other people who felt the same way he did.

That was how he got his second idea.

His very own cult. But not a bunch of bottom-feeder losers, whose day jobs consisted of asking "Would you like fries with that?" No, *his* cult would be for the elite, or at least those with ambition and aspirations in that direction.

His Faithful gathered at his feet now, looking up at him expectantly: Juliana, and Neil, and Gregory; Luke, Vanessa, Quinn and Faith and Sarah. The flower of his searching, the cream of the crop. Well-to-do, well-educated, well-bred. Young, competitive, fast-tracked New Yorkers, looking for a little something more in their lives to help them make sense of it all, and just maybe, help them along to the fast track. And, down where it really mattered, not smart enough, not educated enough, and just a little too trusting to save themselves from people like him.

"Now, my Inner Circle, we have dismissed the Outer Circle to the mundane world. It is time to unveil the Eye of the Inner Planes," Fafnir said.

A sigh of expectation traveled around the circle of eight men and women who sat at his feet.

"Neil, it is your turn to fetch the Eye," he said.

Neil got to his feet and crossed the room, coming back with a large wooden box. He set it at Fafnir's feet. Fafnir opened it reverently.

Inside, on a bed of black velvet, lay a perfectly clear sphere of quartz crystal the size of a softball. It had cost over $7,000. Fafnir hadn't paid for it, of course. He had merely remarked idly that such an object would be the perfect vehicle to focus Inner Plane Energies for the Work of the group. And it had appeared, presented to him as a gift.

He lifted both the sphere and the tray out and set them on the floor. "See how it glows?" he said, knowing that everyone in the room would be willing to believe that they saw it glowing, though it was nothing more than the natural property of crystal and reflected candlelight, plus a little hypnotic suggestion.

"It feeds on your energy, storing it for its work. In

the presence of the False Guardians it would turn black and shatter. Once they are destroyed, you will see it glow so brightly you will be able to read print by it." The power of suggestion was a wonderful thing.

"And your powers will be restored to you," Gregory said, in a combination of reverence and awe, with just a hint, just a touch, of resentment—but not resentment aimed at Fafnir.

Fafnir smiled faintly and said nothing. He never claimed powers for himself, not explicitly. He let others do that for him. It was much more effective that way, he'd found.

"The False Guardians are very powerful," he said in warning tones. His voice became deeper, his words slower, as he retold the old story—the central myth of the Inner Circle—once again. "Their first act, upon seizing power, was to shackle the True Guardian, and render him powerless on this plane. They felt that humanity, deprived of its only remaining defender, would be easy prey."

At the familiar words, the eight sighed deeply, gazing raptly at Fafnir's face. Though he told this story openly and completely now, it had been months before he'd allowed them to know it, forcing them to piece it together out of hints and unfinished sentences, and even now he told it only in the third person. It made him sound so much more humble and self-effacing that way, so much more the innocent and noble victim.

"It did not occur to them that the True Guardian, even though mortally wounded, would seek out others with a spark of the latent Guardian power, would gather those potential defenders about him, would painstakingly impart what knowledge he still could to them, so that—when the time was right—he and his Inner Circle could rise up—together—and overthrow,

not only the False Guardians, but the shackles that
bound him. When the False Guardians are destroyed,
and their power restored to its rightful possessor, the
True Guardian shall be the founder of a new order
of Guardians, imparting his power to all his loyal
followers, so that all of them can take up the task of
protecting humanity from supernatural evil. . . ."

The storytelling ritual came to a close, and the
sheep sighed contentedly, not one of them seeing that
there were holes in his story that you could drive a
truck through. If the False Guardians were as evil
as all that, why wouldn't they simply *kill* the True
Guardian? Wouldn't that make a lot more sense than
leaving him around to cause the same kind of trouble
that Fafnir was causing now?

But they *wanted* to believe in his fairy tale, and
they weren't going to ask any questions that might
make it go away.

And when the False Guardians—oh, well, why
not be honest, if only in his own mind—when the
Guardians, or at least one of them, was destroyed,
wouldn't the closest suitable person become the next
Guardian? That was the way it went, according to the
Internet. The power passed from one Guardian to the
next. And he'd be the closest suitable person, right?
Because he'd be right there. And then *he'd* have the
Guardian power. And the rest of the Guardians just
better watch out then.

Along with the rest of New York.

"Now, friends, it is time to work. Let us gaze into
the Eye of the Inner Planes, and see what it tells us
about what we must do next. Breathe with me. . . ."

After a few moments of deep breathing and staring
into the stone, they were in a light trance, ready for
his suggestions of what *he* saw in the crystal. Not that
he ever actually saw anything, of course. Fafnir was

interested in molding his followers into a weapon for his wielding, not having actual visions.

He'd told them the truth, too, more or less. He had every intention of overthrowing the Guardians, and taking their power for his own. With the backing of both his Inner and Outer Circles—and what he was planning should be enough to arrange the wholehearted cooperation of both—he should be strong enough for that. He wasn't entirely a charlatan. He had some power of his own—as much as anybody could gain through rudimentary hypnosis. It wasn't much, but it gave him enough for him to know that he wanted more.

But as for the rest of it . . . there'd be no sharing, no founding a new order of Guardians. He called these witless dupes gathered at his feet his Inner Circle, and they certainly thought they were, but there was room for only one person in *his* Inner Circle, and that was Fafnir, Master of Treasure.

"Here, my faithful, do you see what I see? The image is becoming clear now. . . ."

Eric and Greystone had stayed up late, watching all the old Bogart movies in Eric's library, while Eric planned what to do next. He felt a great deal better about things after his visit to Ria, knowing that Magnus was not only alive, but on Eric's home turf. New York was a rough town to survive, but all of Eric's resources, both magical and mundane, were right here. If Magnus was in trouble, this was the best place on Earth for him to be in trouble in. And the Everforest Gate and Node was less than an hour away by elvensteed—much less, in fact—if they had to get him Underhill in a hurry.

And Ria had been right about the other thing as well. He supposed it was what Oriana would call a "breakthrough." His parents were jerks. They'd always been jerks. They'd proved themselves jerks—twice over. He supposed he should be just as glad they couldn't have a *third* child. . . .

In the morning he'd hit the street and start looking— but *not*, he thought, as Eric Banyon, suave young Bard-about-Town. *That* would be a good way to get himself mugged, and scare off the very people he needed to get close to as well. No, he needed to fit in, and that meant looking homeless and down-at-heel himself.

In the morning he was up early, too keyed up to sleep. A quick cup of tea—skip the shave; he needed the unshaven look for his plans—and he was on his way.

His first stop was a secondhand clothing store down on Canal Street. Not one of the trendy "vintage" places, but an actual secondhand store. There he picked up a pair of frayed khakis, an old Air Force sweater, a trench coat, and a watch cap, all items absent from the current fashionable Eric Banyon wardrobe. Paying for his purchases, he wandered about looking for the other item on his shopping list. There ought to be one in this area. . . .

Aha. There it was.

He walked in through the door of the pawnshop, blinking at the sudden transition from light to darkness.

All around him were the leftovers of other people's lives: everything that somebody might be induced to loan money on, or buy outright. Some of them were pretty strange—cuckoo clocks and mangy animal heads, for example. Others were the usual stock-in-trade of places like this: rings, watches, jewelry. Musical instruments.

"Can I help you?" the proprietor asked.

"I'm looking for a flute," Eric said.

He'd been a homeless street musician before. He figured it made pretty good sense to go back to being one now. But he'd need a flute for that, and it would be way out of character to go around with the $8,000 Miyazawa Boston Classic that he'd bought to replace the flute that Aerune had melted. It didn't raise an eyebrow at Juilliard, where parents routinely took out a second mortgage to give their kids the most expensive instruments money could buy—not that money was a problem for Eric, with Underhill bankrolling him—but out on the street his regular flute would look far too new and expensive to go with his cover story.

"We have several to choose from. Over there." The proprietor pointed casually and returned to his reading.

Eric walked over and regarded the selection. There were six of them, all displayed in open cases, all looking rather battered and certainly well-used. All of about the caliber you'd expect to find being used by a high-school marching band, really. Any of them would be suitable. It hardly mattered which he chose, but Eric still hesitated, gazing at the array of tarnished silver as though sight alone could tell him something of their history and quality.

Was it his imagination, or did one of them look just a little more wistful than the others, just a little more ashamed to be here . . . ? Like the dog in the back of the cage at the pound, knowing that no one would ever take him home, but longing just as fervently for a home as the pup that was performing a complete gymnastic routine at the front of the cage.

"That one," he said, pointing at the flute nestled against the rusty-brown velvet. "I'll take that one."

❖   ❖   ❖

Returning home with his bundles, he dutifully left a message on Oriana's answering machine, letting her know that he needed to talk to her, and went to inspect his new purchase. He'd probably been a fool to buy a pawnshop flute at random, but after all, it was really little more than a prop, and he had a kit here to make minor repairs. Only minor repairs; anything else would need an expert—but he could change broken springs and replace worn-out pads.

Though he was anxious to start looking for his brother, common sense told him it was still too early to begin. Though he and Ria hadn't been able to find Magnus last night by scrying, Eric still thought he stood a good chance of locating his brother—his *brother*!—by magic, if he could only get close enough. The question was, *where* was he? Manhattan was a big place. He'd been shielded last night. Those shields were probably around wherever he slept, and Eric knew from Hosea that street children were mostly creatures of the night. Wherever Magnus was, he was probably still asleep. Eric would have the best chance of finding him once he was up and on the move, and that wouldn't be for a couple of hours yet at the earliest.

That left Eric plenty of time to get ready for his masquerade. He turned his attention to the flute, not expecting very much.

But when he assembled it and blew into it experimentally, the tone was surprisingly good. The silver warmed beneath his hands, as if grateful for the attention, and Eric tried a practice run. That showed him a few stuck keys, and he got out his tool kit.

He'd just gotten everything working properly when the phone rang.

"Eric?"

"Dr. Dunaway." He hadn't expected a call-back this quickly.

"So formal," she said chidingly. "Now." Giving him no more leeway.

"Oriana, I did something really stupid," Eric said, and launched into an explanation of Tuesday. By now, after having explained it already to both Greystone and Ria, he was able to get through it fairly quickly and lucidly.

"I see," she said when he'd finished. "I think you already know that we should talk about this. Unfortunately, my schedule is very full today. Can you possibly come in tomorrow morning, before my regular hours? Or would you rather wait for our regular session?"

Eric sighed. Before regular hours meant eight A.M., and he'd never been a morning person at the best of times. On the other hand, he really thought he needed to talk this out with somebody who knew the whole story. "I'll be there," he said, with resignation.

"Good," Oriana said warmly. "I'll see you then."

Eric hung up the phone, feeling as if he'd attached another lifeline, somehow. He looked down at the flute, and then at the bundle of shabby clothes—his new uniform.

He carefully disassembled the flute again, and took the coil of Magnus' hair out of his wallet. Pulling a single strand free, he coiled it carefully around the mouthpiece of the flute where the join to the body was and fitted the pieces back together. Now the flute was bound to Magnus. As he played, it would search for him, and find him.

And then. . . .

What then?

Worry about that when you get there, he told himself, pulling off his shirt.

With his new flute, his busker's license (no sense being a damned fool about things), and a few dollars in his pocket, unshaven, disheveled, and dressed in somebody else's discards, Eric Banyon reentered the world he'd left (though he hadn't quite realized it at the time) the moment he'd met an elf named Korendil at a RenFaire a few years before.

It was a place where you begged for money while trying not to attract attention. A place where you weren't sure where your next meal was coming from. A place where you weren't sure where you were going to sleep that night—or any night. All right; granted that he had been good enough and personable enough even when he'd been a lush, that he'd usually had an apartment of his own and was able to keep the lights on and food in the fridge—but he acknowledged now what he had resolutely ignored then, that he had been hovering on the edge of that other world, and it would have taken just a little more booze and grass to push him into it. He wandered slowly downtown and eastward, knowing, both from personal experience and from hearing Hosea's tales of his work in the shelters, that he was heading for the part of town where runaways often gathered.

He did not move purposefully, but drifted, stopping every once in a while to play, leaving the flute case open at his feet. The day was bright and cold, and he realized that he'd forgotten gloves—well, he wouldn't tomorrow. And a little warmth was easy enough to summon, even if he did feel a pang of guilt while doing it.

No one stopped to reward his playing with money, but that was hardly the point. He was hunting, not busking.

He found a few hints of his brother's presence, but the magic told him they were old, many days old. And the harder he tried to trace them, to get a sense of Magnus' movements, the fainter they became, though

Eric tried every hunter's trick he knew. It was as if there was a veil over his magic, and the harder he pushed, the thicker the veil got.

And slowly, a new fear was added to all the others.

If he's got this much grasp of magic . . . to be able to cover his trail this well . . . to know *to cover his trail this well . . . who taught him?*

If Magnus had allies, who were they? And more to the point, what did they want with him?

In a small office in a nondescript building in Washington, a man regarded a desk full of reports. They were unsatisfying.

Parker Wheatley was not a happy man.

Everything should have been going his way—this was the perfect time to alert those in power to the existence of a heretofore-unsuspected menace right within their own borders. But at the time he most needed his Otherworld ally, Aerune mac Audelaine wasn't returning his calls.

Served him right for trusting an elf in the first place.

Fortunately Wheatley'd had the great good sense to stockpile a number of Aerune's little toys when Aerune had still been willing to dispense them—the green fabric that rendered humans invisible to Spookies and impervious to their powers; the parasympathetic energy detectors that looked like wristwatches and could detect "magical" energy at a distance; the sheets of transparent material that screened out Spookie illusions. Other items, like the zip guns that threw the slugs of Cold Iron so distasteful to elves, were easy enough to build here.

But he did mourn the loss of the larger items, like the flying car. That had disappeared in Las Vegas, along with a number of fine field operatives, just after they'd lost contact with Aerune. They'd never been able to duplicate it. It was irreplaceable. As were the agents, of course, but the agents hadn't cost several million black-project dollars squirreled away from the Department of Defense to create.

Well, there was no use crying over spilled Spookies, Wheatley told himself with a flash of cynical humor. They could make do with what they had for quite some time, even without Aerune's help. And if they could actually manage the Holy Grail of the Paranormal Defense Initiative, a live capture . . .

Then they could either parlay that into a truly satisfactory budget—for a change—

Or perhaps their new elf would be more cooperative and forthcoming than Aerune had been. He wasn't averse to another interspecies partnership, Parker Wheatley told himself. Only this time he'd be sure to make sure that everyone involved was straight on where the *real* power in the arrangement lay.

He was actually more inclined toward seeking out a new Elven partner at the moment than toward pinning his hopes on displaying a live capture. Despite the early reports last year from Vegas that there seemed to be a whole nest of Spookies running around loose out there, subsequent searches had uncovered nothing, Vegas elves had proved as elusive as Vegas Mafia, and time was running out. The climate on the Hill these days was conservative. Everybody was pulling in his horns, pushing for interagency cooperation and the elimination of deadwood and redundancy . . . and without results, the PDI was headed for the chopping block.

Wheatley was an experienced game player. He could read the writing on the wall as well as anyone. And he knew that Aerune had seduced him into overcommitting himself to the PDI over the last several years. It would be very hard to back out now, to distance himself from the program and try to blend in elsewhere.

No. He needed *results*. And if Aerune wasn't going to answer whatever Spookies used for phones, that meant Parker Wheatley had to find someone who would.

His intercom buzzed.

"Yes, Gail?"

"Mr. Nichol just called. Your appointment is here."

"Good. Let him know I'll be down in just a minute."

"Very good, sir."

Wheatley smiled. Gail was a good girl. A fast hand with a burn bag, and absolutely loyal. He got to his feet, reaching for his suit jacket.

Marley Bell was scared. Not just getting-your-tax-return-audited scared. Nobody who ran a small business was a stranger to audits. But might-be-going-to-die scared.

Everything had been fine this morning. He'd gone down to Bell Books to open up, thinking this was just another ordinary day in his life. Bell Books was an occult book store—not a fluffy New Age shop selling candles, glitter, and unicorns, but a real bookstore, selling new and used occult books, some of them extremely rare. Most of his business was mail order, and many years he was lucky to break even; without the trust fund, he'd have had to pack it in years ago. But he was a member of a fine old Baltimore family, with fine old Baltimore money to match. The bookstore had been in the family for three generations, though it had been Marley who had changed the focus to match his own interests and studies. Scholars flew in from Europe just to *consult* the books on his shelves!

He wondered if he'd ever see any of his beloved books again.

He'd just gotten the shutters up and the front door open—thinking about a nice mug of coffee from the French press he kept in the back of the store—when this big government car had pulled up in front of the shop. The store wouldn't be open till ten, and it was only a little after eight, but he always came in early to check his e-mail and fill orders.

There'd been three of them, all dressed alike. One stayed behind the wheel, while the other two got out of the car: one out of the front seat, one out of the back. They'd been wearing green trench coats, the color so offbeat, bordering on bizarre, that he hadn't taken them seriously for a moment.

That had quickly changed.

"I'm sorry, we're still closed," he'd said, turning in the doorway to face them.

"Yes, you are," one of them said.

They'd walked right up to him, crowding him. One of them had taken the key ring right out of his hand, while the other one had taken his arm and started pulling him toward the car. He'd been too shocked to protest for a moment, until he'd heard the sound of the first one behind him, relocking the door of his shop.

He'd tried to struggle then, but it was too late. He wasn't quite sure what the two of them did— everything got a little hazy—but when he could think clearly again, he had a ferocious headache, and he was sitting in the back seat of the car between the two men in the green coats, and the car was heading in the direction of D.C. Neither of them had spoken to him again.

And now he was alone in here.

"Here" was a small room with a table—bolted to the floor—one chair, and no windows. It looked like the holding cells you saw on television in police shows. He'd been brought in through an underground garage, up an elevator, along a deserted corridor. He'd seen no one.

Why? He'd done nothing wrong, broken no laws. He didn't use drugs, didn't cheat on his taxes . . . he didn't even jaywalk, in the name of all that was holy. He was an only child, never married, his parents were dead, he had no close relatives, he didn't date anyone of any sex. All of his close personal relationships—such as they were—were conducted by mail and over the Internet, and all of them referred exclusively to either the Art or rare books.

Why was he here?

After a while, nervous tension gave way to a kind of numb despair, a growing horrified realization that, no matter how innocent he was, no matter that the men who had kidnapped him seemed to belong to his own government, anything at all might happen to him. And no one would know.

Finally there were sounds of a key in the lock, and the door swung inward. Marley sprang to his feet with a cry, knocking the chair in which he'd been sitting over backward with a crash.

Two men entered.

One was one of the men who'd kidnapped him, wearing a business suit the exact same color of lurid green as his trench coat. The other, Marley was relieved to see, looked normal. He was wearing a plain, charcoal-grey three-piece suit with a burgundy tie, and his thick silver hair was swept straight back from a widow's peak. He looked like an expensively groomed Washington insider and,

paradoxically, that reassured Marley. Career politicos
had plenty to lose. They would not throw it away
on foolish mistakes.

*Mistakes. That's what this is, a mistake. They'll tell
me this is a mistake, and I can go home . . . .*

"Good afternoon. My name is Wheatley. Mr. Nichol
you already know. And you are Marley Tucker Bell.
Bell . . . Bell . . . you wouldn't happen to be a relation
to Miller Stevenson Bell, by any chance?"

Marley felt a disappointment too deep for words
as his last hope of this being a mistake was crushed.
They—whoever they were—had picked him, chosen
him by name. But the dictates of good manners were
strong. "He was my great-uncle, sir."

"Ah." Wheatley smiled. "I thought you had the look
of the family. He was a fine politician, still fondly
remembered, and by all accounts, an excellent preacher.
How sad he'd be to discover that his great-nephew had
grown up to be a black magician."

Shock does *make you light-headed,* Marley decided
with a faint sense of discovery. He reached down,
picked up the chair, righted it, and sat down on
it. His hands trembled, and he knew he looked as
frightened as he felt.

"Perhaps you would be so good as to allow me to
call my lawyer," he said, summoning up the last of
his defiance.

And a psychiatrist for yourself, he thought, but did
not say. He'd long since grown beyond responding to
such petty schoolyard taunts. So Wheatley knew he was
a student of the Art Magical. That was disturbing—hell,
it was terrifying. But studying magic wasn't illegal.
And he was no Black Magician. He harmed no one
and nothing in his practice of the Art.

"Oh, come now, Mr. Bell," Wheatley said. "You've
done nothing wrong. Why would you need a lawyer?

We simply require your help. And you're going to provide it."

Marley stared at him in baffled horror, unable for a moment to think coherently. This was the stuff of nightmares, of bad movies. All it lacked was the Nazi uniforms to make it complete.

"What do you want?" he said at last.

He drew the tiniest of comforts from knowing that his paper files were sanitized, his computer was secure . . . they'd get his mailing list, but very little more than that; and if he didn't log in to his system within 72 hours, it would format itself and that would be lost as well. And his important files and correspondence were triply password-protected *and* encrypted, on a system designed by a Brother of the Art. Bless Ray for that; there was no one better, and even Ray didn't know the passwords and encryption he'd chosen.

The only weak link in the system was him. He had no illusions about his ability to stand up under duress.

Wheatley smiled benignly down at him.

"You're a magician. I don't really care if you're black, white, or purple. You're a good one. The best. I checked. You can conjure up all sorts of things, I'm sure. So conjure me up an elf."

Marley blinked; at first he was certain he must have misheard, then he wondered just what sort of insane thoughts were going on in this man's head. *You've got to be kidding!*

But the man was deadly serious, Marley knew. To laugh would be fatal, though the tension in his soul screamed for release. Irrationally, he felt relief—he had not been brought here to inform on his colleagues. Fleetingly, he wondered who had given Wheatley his name, and dismissed the speculation. It wasn't important now.

He took a deep breath, thinking hard. What the hell was it that this mundane actually wanted? And what were the penalties for guessing wrong?

"Many grimoires concern themselves with the formulae for conjuration and evocation," he began, speaking slowly and watching the madman's face for any clue. "The entities which can be summoned are various, from the embodiments of the Elemental Powers of Earth, Air, Fire and Water, to lesser Elemental Beings—woodland spirits, *genus locii,* aspects of the *anima mundi,* to Greater Powers such as demonic or angelic forces—"

"I'm not interested in any of that," Wheatley snapped, glowering. "You heard me, Bell: I want an elf."

Helpful. But he's not going to like what he hears next.

"—but if what you wish to summon is one of the Princes of Faerie, the Lords of the Hollow Hills, then the matter becomes more difficult." Talking actually made him feel better. This was what he knew best; his life's work. But if they'd just wanted information, why hadn't they come and *asked*? "There's only one book that deals with that sort of conjuration in any detail at all: *De Rebus Nefandis*—'Concerning Forbidden Things.' It was set down around the year 900 by an Icelandic monk who was deploring certain shamanistic practices among his new converts, who had apparently used to have a rather extensive magical system related to the conjuration of *svartálfar* and *ljósálfar,* or what we'd call Dark and Bright elves."

"Well get it, and get to work," Wheatley said irritably.

Marley allowed himself a small smile of triumph. "Unfortunately, there's only one copy, and the Vatican has it. I don't think they'll sell."

Wheatley leaned over the table, bringing his face

very close to Marley's. "I don't think you understand your situation here, Mr. Bell. I want results. I want them *fast*. You can bring one of your fairy princes here, or you can send him a message that I want to see him. I do not care which. But I do know that nobody is going to miss you. And I know that pain makes a man very eager to please."

Marley tried to push his chair back, to get away from Wheatley, but the other man had moved around behind him while Wheatley had been speaking, and was pushing the chair forward, until the edge of the table pressed painfully against Marley's stomach.

And that was the least of what they were going to do to him. He was, alas, entirely familiar with the psyches of the ruthless, ambitious, and mad. There were certain Nazi occultists who had fit that profile—and he had read their diaries. The look he saw in Wheatley's eyes matched the picture he had built up in his mind.

"Please—don't—oh, God—please—"

He couldn't do it. No one could. But he knew he'd try, because if he didn't, they were going to kill him slowly and horribly.

"That's what I like to see," Wheatley said, patting him stingingly on the cheek. "Now, you just let Mr. Nichol here know everything you need. I'll be along to check on you in a day or so."

Wheatley straightened up and left.

"Well, now, Marley, what shall we do first?" Nichol said brightly from behind him. "How about some lunch?"

By the time it was dark—and much colder—Eric was frustrated and fed up. The trail was worse than cold; it was as if every time he got the ghost of a lead, there was a sudden psychic brick wall in his way.

Could Magnus really be doing that all by himself? Or could he have found help already? If he had, Eric hoped it was the right kind of help, and not some modern-day Fagin, protecting kids only in order to exploit them himself. . . .

Not that *that* would be anything new.

But right now he was tired, and hungry, and cold. He'd covered a lot of miles today, and all on foot, and he had to get up early tomorrow to keep his appointment with Oriana. But after that, he'd have the whole day free to search. Reluctantly, he had to admit there was nothing more he could do right now.

He needed to check in with Hosea, tell him about yesterday, and get some ideas about how—and where—to look for Magnus. From his work in the shelters, Hosea was a lot more plugged in to the city's runaway population than Eric was these days. He'd have a better idea of where the kids hung out. Maybe Eric would be able to strike a fresh trail that way. And most of all, if he happened to run into Hosea while he was out wandering around, he didn't want Hosea recognizing him and blowing his "cover."

Besides, he knew that he couldn't spend more than another day, two at most, playing the Lone Ranger. After that, he'd have to call Ria and let her put her specialists on the case, much as his instincts cried out against it. At the very least, he should give her a call later and find out what she'd learned about that Dorland his parents had hired.

As if to underscore the rightness of his decision to go home, when he got out of the subway at his stop, he saw it had started to rain. Only a little rain—more a heavy mist than a real rain, but it made the street slippery and the air even colder. Another few weeks, and this would be snow that stuck; even now, there were a few white flakes mixed with the silvery drizzle, though they melted before they reached the street. Last winter had been unseasonably mild; this one obviously planned to make up for it.

By the time he'd walked the three long blocks to the apartment, Eric was thoroughly damp; whatever waterproofing his trench coat might once have possessed had long departed.

"Nice threads, Banyon."

The familiar voice came just as he reached the stairs. He turned at the sound. He'd been so focused on getting inside, warm, and dry, that he hadn't seen Kayla come up the steps from her basement apartment.

Kayla was just finishing her first year at Columbia, majoring in web design. She was a Healer and an Empath, but neither skill paid the rent, and for someone whose Gift could make close proximity to other people actively painful, it was good to develop money-making skills that would let them spend a lot of time *away* from people. Especially now. She'd spent the months of September and October of 2001 practically in a cocoon.

Kayla walked across the foyer and inspected him critically. "This a new look for you?"

"Um, look, Kayla, I—"

"No," Kayla said flatly. She stood regarding him pugnaciously, hands on hips.

Eric blinked at her in surprise.

"Do *not* come up with some fool dog-and-pony story about leaving your other clothes in a taxi while you were kidnapped by space aliens. Jesus, Eric, this is *me*. You've got two choices here, the way I see it: you can tell me the whole truth straight up or I resort to blackmail, and that takes longer."

Eric smiled in spite of his tiredness. "What kind of blackmail could you possibly use?" he found himself asking, out of a detached professional interest.

Kayla grinned impishly up at him. "Well, either everybody else already knows what you're up to, or they don't. If they do, I bet I could get the truth out of Too-Tall Songmaker in a New York minute . . . or I could just follow you the next time you go out. But why not cut to the chase and level with me? You look like you're trying to pass for street—so why not consult an expert? Which would be me, of course."

Eric had to admit that she looked street—upscale street, but still street. Kayla's look tended to change with the seasons; at the moment it was less Goth than paramilitary, with laced jump boots, the same leather jacket she always wore (all the glitter of its previous incarnation had been sanded off), baggy parachute pants, and a skintight camo-print camisole.

"C'mon," she said, sensing his hesitation. "Let's get you upstairs and out of those wet clothes before *I* catch cold."

Taking over his kitchen Kayla made cocoa—grumbling over the lack of coffee as usual, but Eric had given her his espresso machine as an apartment-warming present, so she had no real cause for complaints—as Eric changed into dry clothes. When he came out, she was waiting implacably.

"Spill it," she said, handing him his mug. Eric was careful not to touch her fingers when he took it from her, or she might have gotten the whole story at once—and not in a terribly pleasant way, either. There were certain rules of etiquette in dealing with Empaths.

He sighed. "There's no way to explain this that doesn't sound really stupid," he said, and launched, once more, into the explanation about how he'd come to find out about Magnus. He was starting to wish he'd gathered everyone together and told all of them the story all at once; he still had Hosea to tell, and it was starting to feel as if he'd told this tale a thousand times already. At least it seemed to hurt a little less each time he told it.

It was new to Kayla, though. She stared out the window for a long moment after he'd finished, her face very still.

"You know, Banyon, even having no parents—or parents that dump you because you get weird, like mine did me—is better than having parents like yours. Some people shouldn't even be let to raise houseplants!" she said at last.

"I know," Eric said gently. Somehow, having someone else upset about it made it easier for him to deal with. "But this isn't about them. Or me. It's about Magnus."

Kayla sighed, and seemed to shake herself all over.

"Right. We've got to get him off the street and under cover before they find him. And that means the next time you go looking, I'm going with you."

"But—" Ria would kill him and hang his scalp in the LlewellCo boardroom, no arguments, if he put Kayla in a dangerous situation. When she'd come East to go to school, Elizabet had made Ria Kayla's unofficial guardian.

Kayla had been supposed to live with Ria, actually. It was Kayla who'd decided that her talents were better utilized at Guardian House, and she'd been proved right a couple of times already. Since the House itself had no objections to her staying—and there was a studio apartment available in the basement—Kayla had moved in, decorating it to suit her own Gothgrrl tastes. And, Eric had to admit, she was a lot more thoroughly watched over by Greystone and the House than she would have been staying with Ria.

"See here, Banyon. Bringing me into this only makes sense. One—" Kayla held up a finger. "I'm a lot closer to Magnus' age than you are. So I can get closer to him. Two—" Another finger. "I've lived on the street a lot more recently than you have—in fact, you *never* lived on the street the way I did. Three— If you go approaching a bunch'a street kids alone and try to get in with them, you'll read as a predator. You may not be as old as you ought to be, but you're too old. Trust me. So we go around together. You find him and point him out. I can get next to him alone and get you in, or he'll accept you 'cause you're with me. And hey, how much trouble can I *possibly* get into with you right there to keep an eye on me?" she added, with a wicked grin.

Plenty, Eric thought, with the wisdom of long experience. But he had to admit that all of Kayla's points were good ones. He looked like he was in his twenties. That was too old to get in with the crowd he was trying to infiltrate, and if Magnus *was* using magic—or was being protected by someone who was—using a *glamourie* to lower his apparent age enough to pass would be like posting a red warning flag above his head.

But Kayla was still in her teens, and looked younger than her age. She'd fit right in. And she was right about being more streetwise than he was.

Besides, trying to keep Kayla out of something once she'd made up her mind to "help" was a losing proposition, as he knew from long experience. . . .

"Okay. Fine. You've got a deal," he said with a sigh.

"Yo! Homes!" Kayla whooped exultantly. "Where do you want to start?"

"I'm going to go see Oriana tomorrow morning—

early—and take my lumps. I should be done about nine. Why don't you meet me there? Then we can head downtown. I'll buy you breakfast, and we can figure out where to go from there."

"Sounds like a plan," Kayla said. "Well, better run. There's a Rutger Hauer retrospective over at the Gaiety, and I promised some friends I'd check it out. See you tomorrow, Morning Man."

"Be good," Eric said, winning himself another smirk.

After Kayla left, Eric made himself an unsatisfactory dinner—he'd been eating out far too much, and getting behind on his grocery shopping, and there really wasn't much in the refrigerator but leftover takeout that was way past its "sell-by" date and the usual assortment of designer water. He finally opened a can of soup, and settled down for some channel-surfing. With expanded cable, he had his pick of almost 500 channels, including several international ones, so he could shop for things he didn't need, watch soap operas or game shows in languages he didn't know, catch up on the latest in sports from sumo matches to Australian football, or learn how to renovate and rewire his nonexistent house.

None of it held his attention for very long.

He realized that he was putting off something he needed to do, and it wouldn't be fair to make this a late night for Hosea. Hosea's days tended to start early—and Eric's day tomorrow was going to start early as well. He stretched out his arm, and snagged the phone.

A few moments later he presented himself at the door to Hosea's apartment. Hosea opened the door. The rich vanilla smell of baking wafted out into the hall.

"You knew I was coming so you baked a cake?" Eric asked, startled.

"Ah'm baking cookies for the shelter," Hosea said, in his slow mountain drawl. "You can have a few, if you're good. C'mon in."

Eric walked down the long hall, following Hosea. The bookshelves were filling up nicely, he saw, and he noticed a few new additions to the art gallery since the last time he'd visited, as well—a large framed poster of *Daybreak* by Maxfield Parrish, and a couple of small drawings of banjo-playing mice that managed to bear an odd resemblance to Hosea—he remembered that Hosea was dating the children's book artist who lived down on Four. What was her name? Kathy? No, Caity.

"Jest set for a spell, I've got to get this last batch out of the oven, and I'll be right out," Hosea said. He disappeared into the kitchen, while Eric wandered around the living room.

Jeanette was there, lying in her open case. Eric gazed at her, wondering, as he often did, just how *present* she was when Hosea wasn't actually playing the instrument she inhabited. He knew that at those times she could see what Hosea saw and hear what he heard, and that she spoke to Hosea through the music, and that only Hosea could hear her. Those were the terms of the original spell that had bound her to "haunt" the banjo until she had expiated the evil she had done in her life. But he did wonder what it was like for her—was she "there" the rest of the time, or just asleep? He'd never asked, though—it seemed sort of intrusive, somehow—and Hosea hadn't said.

Hosea came in a few moments later with a colorful tin tray that bore an old Rockingham teapot and a plate of golden sugar cookies, still warm from the oven. The tray was one of Hosea's many "urban scavenger" finds:

New Yorkers threw out the most amazing things, and many city dwellers had furnished entire apartments from curbside scavenging. Most of the items—from furniture to dishes—only needed minor repairs, or a little elbow grease, to make them perfectly usable. You had to know the right neighborhoods, and get up early, to find the best items, but Hosea was a morning person anyway. Hosea kept some of his finds, and donated the rest, after repairing them, to others who could use them. Somehow, he always seemed to know someone who needed just that thing.

Hosea set the tray down on the coffee table and gestured for Eric to sit. "I was hopin' you'd drop by and tell me how yesterday went for you," he said mildly.

"Well, I made a real dog's breakfast of it—to borrow one of Greystone's favorite phrases—but nobody's dead, and my parents don't even know I was there. But wait. There's more," Eric said. He knew he sounded flip, trying to distance himself from the pain with sarcasm, but what else could he do?

"Have a cookie," Hosea suggested, pouring tea.

Between bites of cookie and sips of peppermint tea flavored with wild honey, Eric told the story: that his parents, having lost one trophy child, had decided to make another one. That this second son—far more rebellious, by all accounts, than Eric had ever been—had run away from home. And was now in New York. Somewhere.

"And I can't find him. Ria can't find him. It's like he's wrapped in some kind of magical cloak of invisibility. I spent all day trying to trace him, and I just kept getting more and more muddled. The harder I looked, the less there was to find. And . . . well, *you* see a lot of runaways," Eric added hopefully.

"That I do," Hosea agreed. "Do you have a picture?"

Eric pulled the bus pass out of his pocket. Hosea studied the picture for a moment, then shook his head. "He hasn't come around when Ah've been there, but most of those kids are wild as jackrabbits, specially if they think somebody might be out to drag them back home. And even the older ones are spooked by *La Llorona*. Some of 'em'll come around for a meal, sometimes, but only if they can be durned sure we won't turn 'em in. If you want to copy this, Ah could show it to Serafina and the others, so they could look out for him."

"Thanks," Eric said. "I'll do that."

"Have you talked to Oriana about this?" Hosea asked, keeping his voice carefully neutral. The last thing Eric needed right now was pity; he'd rarely seen his friend and teacher so brittle, not even just after they'd returned from Chinthliss' domain, when he'd been trying to cope with Jimmie's death, and the battle with Aerune, and—in its own strange way, though she'd died thousands of years before—the death of Aerete the Golden. Not even after the Towers fell, when everyone was in what his Grannie would have called "a State."

He'd found out more tonight about Eric's childhood than he'd ever known before, and none of it good. It was bad enough to have parents who'd bred and raised him with no more love—less, in fact—than a farmer would give to a pig he was fattening for slaughter, but then to find that they'd repeated the sin was a double blow. Because a brother—even a brother he hadn't known about until the day before—wasn't just some stranger. He was *family*, and Eric's responsibility. And then to find that he not only existed, but was lost somewhere in New York. . . .

Well, it was a heavy burden.

"I'm seeing her in the morning," Eric said, with a crooked smile. "And she'll probably read me the riot act, but hell—if I *hadn't* gone when I did . . . Magnus would still be out there, only I wouldn't know to look for him."

"There's truth to that," Hosea agreed. "You stop on by the shelter tomorrow morning. Ah'll have talked to Serafina by then. She knows a lot of the places those kids den up. If you check enough of them, you should find him. But when you do find him, Eric . . . ?"

"I'm not sending him back to Boston." Eric's voice was flat and uncompromising. "Maybe . . . Underhill? I don't know. I haven't thought that far ahead. Ria said the first thing was to find him."

"Well, Miz Llewellyn surely has the right of it. But it's a puzzling thing that yoreshine ain't helping you any."

"Or not much," Eric said with a sigh. "He's in Manhattan, that's as much as I know for sure. If I could just get close enough, I'm sure I could break through whatever protective spells he's got wrapped around him. Ria's suggested hiring specialists— mundane ones—to look for him, and if I don't turn up anything in a day or so, I'll do that. But I'm afraid that if he does realize somebody's after him, he'll run again."

Hosea nodded. "There is that possibility. And he's just the least bit safer when he's not running than when he is, not that being a runaway is any kind of safe at all, bad as the homes some of them run from are. Ah'll do everything Ah can to help. We all will."

"Thanks," Eric said, meaning it. "And maybe I'll get lucky tomorrow. I'll be bringing in a sort of native guide of my own. And Ria would flay me alive if she knew."

"Uh-huh," Hosea said, decoding the sentence without

effort. "Stands to reason that Little Trouble would figure a way to stick her nose in. Well, looks like you're going to have yourself a busy day tomorrow. You'd best get your rest."

After Eric had left, Hosea picked up Jeanette and sat down in his rocking chair, plucking the banjo's strings idly.

"What're we going to do, Jeanette?" he said aloud.

:Let 'em all fry,: the banjo suggested.

"Now you know you don't mean that," Hosea said mildly.

There was a sulky listening silence from the banjo, and finally a defeated sigh. *:Is he turning tricks? Running with a gang? Somebody knows where he is, and trust me, big fella, they'll be happy to give him up for a hundred bucks cash.:*

"Well, now," Hosea said mildly, his fingers continuing to weave glittering patterns of sound in the silent apartment, "Ah don't doubt you, but the question is, who do we offer the money to?"

:Let me think about that,: Jeanette answered. *:I never had any particular connections in New York, and what I did have are years out of date now. You go walking into a Saint clubhouse, and you'll be dead before you can explain yourself.:* Another brooding silence, while Jeanette thought about things. *:Your problem is, you want him alive and in good condition.:*

"That Ah do," Hosea admitted, with a heavy sigh. "Well, we'll both sleep on it. Might could be something will dawn on one or both of us. Good night, sweetheart."

CHAPTER SIX:

BOIL THE BREAKFAST EARLY

Eric settled onto the "non-directive couch" with a large carton of upscale tea in his hand. Oriana usually didn't let patients bring food or drink into the sessions, but she took pity on those who were forced to disrupt their usual routines to come in for an early-morning session. She hadn't remarked on his peculiar outfit—Eric was wearing his "street person" costume—and she heard out the story of his spur-of-the-moment decision to go to Boston in silence, allowing him to tell the story in his own way, without interruption.

"And how did you feel when you saw your parents again?" she asked.

"Shocked, I guess," Eric said, thinking about it carefully. "I'd expected them to still be the same as they'd been when I was eighteen. But they weren't.

And they were, in a way. You'd expect . . . losing a child that way . . . and never knowing what had happened to him . . . to change a person. People. But it obviously hadn't. Or hadn't seemed to. They'd just gone and had another one, like they'd replace a broken microwave."

"Do you feel that Magnus has replaced you in their lives?"

Eric stared at her in surprise. "Well, hasn't he? They obviously haven't told Magnus I ever existed. And they weren't going to tell Dorland—well, me as Dorland—that I'd ever existed. They just had another kid, and tried to duplicate my life, whether that's what he wanted or not." *Or had any talent for. Although obviously he did.*

"And how do you feel about that?"

"Angry," Eric growled. "Very angry."

"At whom?"

Eric looked at her, puzzled, not seeing where this was going.

"Whose fault is it that this has happened? Yours? Magnus? Your parents?" Oriana prompted.

"Not Magnus," Eric said positively. "He didn't ask to be born. My parents, yes. They're the ones who wanted a trophy object instead of a son."

Oriana waited. Eric shook his head.

"And yes . . . me. I guess. A little. I should have . . . no." He shook his head, trying to sort his way through what had seemed simple, and now had revealed more layers than he'd thought existed. "That isn't right, is it? Their actions are *not* my fault."

Oriana still waited.

"But . . . he's my brother. I'm responsible for him. Yeah, I know, I didn't even know he existed before I went out there, and it isn't like I ordered them to brew up another tame prodigy, but he's still my flesh and blood—and that counts for a lot, in magic." That much he was certain of, and he thought he saw a faint expression of approval flit across his counselor's face. "What's more, I think the Bardic Gift bred true in him, too, and that makes another level of kinship. So, this isn't my fault. But it is my responsibility. I have a responsibility to take care of my brother because, hell, nobody else is going to, are they? Not just because he's my brother—although that's enough—but because he's a potential Bard. I have to find him, and keep him from getting into trouble with his magic." *Assuming he hasn't done that already.*

"And your parents?" Oriana asked.

"They just aren't very important," Eric said, with a sense of discovery. It was true. *Magnus* was what was important. As long as Eric could find him, and keep him out of the hands of his parents forever, they weren't really that important, were they?

"You know, they don't matter. They gave over their right to matter to me a long, long time ago." He had a sense, right that moment, of *letting go* of something that had been weighing him down.

"Well," Oriana said, closing her notebook and getting to her feet. "I think we've made progress here, and our time is just about up. I'll look forward to seeing you at our regular time on Monday. And Eric, I think it would be best if you let me know before you decide to get in touch with your parents again, don't you?"

"If ever," Eric said feelingly.

Kayla was waiting for him, appropriately enough, in the waiting room when he came out. Her own appearance had undergone a marked transformation from the day before. Only the leather jacket remained from the previous day's costume. The boots had been replaced

by worn sneakers, the parachute pants by stained and
scruffy jeans, and the camo-top by a faded T-shirt advertising a band Eric had never heard of. She'd washed
all the gel out of her hair, and done something else
to it as well, and it hung lankly down around her face,
looking greasy and dull.

"Wesson Oil," she said cheerfully, seeing his baffled
expression. "The grunge-Goths use it all the time."

"And you had this stuff in your closet?" Eric said
doubtfully.

"What, you think I help Too-Tall refinish furniture
in my best vintage? Get outta town!" Kayla scoffed.
"I figure this is the right look—I just about had to
mug the door guy to get up here."

"Good thing I left your name downstairs, or you'd
probably be sitting on the curb right now," Eric said.
"C'mon. Let's go have breakfast. Then we're going to
go see Hosea."

Kayla made a rude noise.

Eric wasn't unreasonable enough to try to walk
into a restaurant where the way they were dressed
would get them immediately thrown out—or raise a
lot of eyebrows at the very least, which wouldn't be
comfortable for anyone. He took them into a part of
town where their clothes wouldn't attract any particular notice—and the food was just fine. Cholesterol
heaven, in fact.

Kayla ate like a starving teenager—all of her omelet,
home fries, and toast, and most of Eric's breakfast
as well. He didn't really have much of an appetite,
picking at his eggs and toast.

"You're gonna be starving by lunch," she predicted,
piling grape jelly on her toast.

Eric shuddered, pouring more sugar and milk into
his coffee. Had coffee always tasted this bad? Or had

he just lost the taste for it over the years? It really didn't matter. He needed the caffeine to jump-start himself this morning. Tea just wasn't going to cut it. "I'm not really hungry," he said.

"Eat anyway," Kayla commanded, shoving half of his eggs back at him. She cocked her head, gazing at a point a few inches above Eric's head. "You'll do," she said. "But you need to feed the beast. The only reason—other than worry about Magnus—that you aren't hungry is because you aren't used to being up this early."

Reluctantly, Eric shoveled down eggs and cold toast, though the food seemed to have little taste. He did feel better once he'd managed it, though. Kayla was usually right about physical things—not surprising for a Healer.

"I guess I'm just as worried about finding him, as not finding him," he admitted. "I'm not sure what I'm going to do once I do."

"Hell, that's a no-brainer," Kayla said, looking surprised. "You don't think he *wants* to go back to Hell House, do you?"

"Of course not!" Eric said. If there was one thing he was sure of, it was that.

She shrugged, as if the answer was obvious. "Well, then. Ria gets her voodoo lawyers to paper-trip him. He gets a brand-new secret identity, you do a couple of mystic passes, and he gets to be somebody else."

"But . . ." Eric said. He hadn't even *met* Magnus yet! He had no idea of what his brother's situation might be, or what he'd need to do to set things right. Or what Magnus wanted out of life, for that matter.

"Details," Kayla said, waving Eric's protests away. "We can work them all out when the time comes. Trust me. Ria loves to fix things, the more complicated, the better. C'mon. We're outta here."

❖   ❖   ❖

Hosea arrived at Jacob Riis early that morning. He actually spent quite a few more hours there than he was paid for, but he didn't mind. There was always plenty of work to do, and not enough hands to do it, and Hosea liked to feel needed.

Breakfast was served early. The temporary cots put down for the overnighters were taken up at five and stored away, and the tables unfolded in their place. Everyone helped. If you helped, you got fed.

Once everyone in the shelter had eaten, the transients were turned out for the day and the doors were opened to feed the street population. There were already lines outside the door—always.

Sometimes there were eggs for the first through the door. Usually the staff was able to provide at least outdated cold cereal and muffins or bagels and coffee for everyone who came, or coffee at the very least. When donations were especially good, there was hot cereal and juice, but that wasn't often. The street people were philosophical, taking whatever came in enduring silence. The food service closed down by nine, or whenever supplies ran out, and then the kitchen staff got to work preparing lunch, and the rest of the shelter workers turned to their other jobs.

In the little lull, Hosea managed to catch Serafina's eye.

"Ah need a favor," he said.

"You can have anything I have to give—not that that's much," she said. "Come into my office."

Serafina's office had probably once been a linen closet, back when this had been a house. A desk piled high with neglected paperwork, an ailing copier, and two ancient overstuffed file cabinets crowded the small room to the state of the legendary "Fibber

McGee's Closet." There was barely room for her to edge around between the wall and her desk and get into her chair, and just enough room for him to stand in front of the desk.

"Ah need to find a boy," he said. "Came to the city about a month ago. Seventeen, but looks younger."

"Ay!" Serafina threw up her hands. "Only one?"

Hosea smiled ruefully. "It's a favor for a friend."

She sighed explosively. "Picture?"

"I'll have one tomorrow," he promised. "He's white. Upper-class family. Auburn hair, shoulder length when he left home. About five-seven, maybe 130 pounds. Green eyes. Very . . . pretty," he added reluctantly, knowing she'd need to hear it.

She was shaking her head tiredly. "Hosea, you know what happened to him. He didn't get in touch with his family, didn't get picked up by the police . . . he's gone, *querido*."

Hosea sighed. There was no way to explain that they *knew* Magnus was still alive, still here. "Ah know, 'fina. But it's only been a month. Maybe he's still here, somewhere. Or maybe somebody remembers him. You know where the kids go to den up. Give me some hints."

"You're not going to go down where they go," she said, alarmed.

"Ah promise. And Ah'm not going to send his parents there, either—" that was a promise easy enough to make. "Ah don't want the blood of innocents on my conscience. His parents have hired a professional to look for him." And that was the honest truth as well. "Like Ah said, Ah'm just trying to help."

"You promise you won't go looking for him yourself?" she insisted.

"If Ah hear he's at one of the other shelters, Ah might go there—Ah won't lie to you, 'fina. But to follow on any of the hints you'd be so kind as to provide, that Ah won't do. That Ah do promise."

She sighed again. "*Pobrecito.* Well, your friend might start by talking to some of the other boys down under the highway, though I'm sure they'll tell him anything he wants to hear for twenty bucks. He might have gotten lucky—though I'm not sure that's the right word—and gotten taken up by one of the white gangs, like the Dead Rabbits or the Future; I haven't seen Prester in a few weeks, but I'll try to catch him if he comes in. He still seems to know most of the gang gossip. Of course, he's crazy as a fruit bat, which is why they leave him alone, but he might know something useful.

"Another possibility you might want to have your friend check out is abandoned buildings—if he can find one that isn't being used as a gang clubhouse or a crack den. Sometimes the kids move in and take them over for a few weeks or months until the police drive them out—or one of them manages to start a fire and bring in the Fire Department. Most of them are down here, but I've been hearing rumors that there's a big one somewhere Uptown—which would have to be somewhere in Harlem, I guess. I'll try to get you some addresses."

"'Preciate it," Hosea said. "And now Ah guess Ah'd better get out there and make some music."

After the music session—Angelica was gone, and Hosea tried not to think too much what would happen to her—he wandered outside for a breath of air, wondering when Eric would be showing up.

He heard a skirl of flute music from down the street and smiled to himself, following the sound.

He recognized Kayla by her jacket—and the fact that she was wearing the clothes she'd been wearing when she'd helped him paint his apartment—but if Eric hadn't been holding the flute in his hands, Hosea wouldn't have recognized Eric at all, and he could tell that Eric wasn't using a trace of *glamourie* to fool him.

Well, the old story-songs did say that the Bards were masters of disguise, and Hosea was coming to realize more and more every day how much truth there was in the old songs.

It wasn't just the old clothes he'd dug up from Lord knew where; even Eric's closest friends might not have recognized him, walking past him on the street. He looked small and frail, hunched over his flute as though it were his last friend in all the world, playing the mournful notes of his calling-on song.

Hosea walked up to him, digging in his pocket for a handful of change, and tossed it into the open flute case at his feet. If Eric was serious about going undercover, he'd better make this look good.

Kayla looked up. She was sitting at Eric's feet, huddled on a piece of cardboard scavenged from a dumpster. Her face was blank, her eyes wary. She reached out and scooped up the coins as though he might take them back. Eric continued playing, not seeming to notice, and for a moment, Hosea felt a pang of genuine alarm.

"There's hot coffee around the corner at the shelter," he said. "You could come in, get out of the cold for a while."

"C'mon, Boss," Kayla said, tugging at Eric's leg and getting to her feet. "Coffee."

Eric brought the tune to a close and lowered the flute. "Yeah. That'd be nice. I'd forgotten how cold it got out here on the streets," he said softly.

"You scared me there for a minute," Hosea said, as they walked back toward the shelter.

"It just sort of gets to me," Eric admitted. "I start out by acting like a street person and then after a while I kind of become one. I guess it's effective, but . . ." He let the sentence trail off, then laughed shakily. "If that's how much I get sucked into a part, I guess that job on Broadway is right out. Did you get a chance to talk to Serafina?"

Hosea gave a rueful shrug. "She'll ask around. She gave me a bit to go on with. Made me promise Ah wouldn't go pokin' mah nose in mah own self. Says the places the kids go are pretty rough."

Even as he warned Eric, he knew it wouldn't do any good. He could tell Eric that the trail led to the gates of Hell itself, and Eric would still follow it. He glanced at Kayla.

She gave him a glare laden with defiance. "Don't look at me, Too-Tall. Somebody's got to keep him out of trouble, and Banyon doesn't have the sense God gave a goldfish."

Hosea sighed, accepting what he couldn't change. "Come in and warm up. The first thing you'd better do is check the other shelters in the city and see if you pick up his trail near any of them. Ah've got a list of them."

Over coffee, he told Eric what little he'd learned. It wasn't much to go on, but it was all they had. Eric promised to get him a picture of Magnus as soon as possible—but Hosea knew that, rightly or wrongly, Eric would drag his heels there, not wanting to involve any more people in the search for his brother than absolutely needful. If they didn't find him soon, it would have to be done, though. The boy couldn't survive alone on the streets, especially with hard winter coming on.

Predictably, Eric recoiled from the suggestion that

they check with the young rentboys who plied their trade under the West Side Highway.

"They might know him," Hosea said gently.

"Face facts," Kayla said bluntly. "If he isn't doing that, everybody he knows is trying to get him to, believe it. If he's a holdout, he's a legend. He'll be *easy* to find."

"Hard to get them to tell you the truth, though," Hosea said.

"They'll tell me the truth," Eric said grimly.

Show them a face like that, and they'll run like rabbits, Hosea thought, but didn't say so.

"Well, we'd better go," Eric said. "Looks like we've got a lot of ground to cover." He slipped Hosea a folded bill. "Thanks for the help. Go pay for our coffee, would you?"

Hosea smiled. "Find him soon."

After Eric and Kayla left, Hosea stayed. He could have gone busking in the subways—there wasn't much point to aboveground busking at this time of year; your audience wasn't much inclined to linger in the cold—but he didn't have any place he really had to be until this afternoon, when he was scheduled to play at an assisted living facility uptown. He enjoyed that—his audiences remembered and asked for many of the old songs, the ones his grandparents had taught him.

But some instinct encouraged him to linger where he was.

There was a steady stream of people coming through—except when they'd locked up for the night, the Jacob Riis was never really quiet—some seeking help to fill out the endless forms required by the city's Social Services, some seeking information about various programs, some looking for food, a bed for the coming

night, something to steal, news of a friend. The staff
dealt with them all as gently as possible.

"Excuse me."

Hosea turned around. The young woman who had
spoken regarded him warily, glancing over her shoulder to make sure the way to the door was clear. That
gesture alone was enough to tell him she was one of
the street population, and not one of the staff. She was
young, though it was hard to tell her age, bundled up
as she was in layers of clothing against the cold.

"Can I help you?" he said.

He saw her hesitate, on the verge of leaving, and
wished with all his heart that Eric were still here—Eric
could charm the birds down out of the trees with nothing more than a smile, but *he* was only a half-trained
Bard, unable to use his Gift without his instrument
in his hands, and Jeanette was locked in her case in
Serafina's office. He had no Talent to use to convince
her that all he wanted to do was help.

"Nobody's going to trouble you," Hosea said very
gently. "That isn't our way."

She smiled, just a little. Blue eyes, blonde hair—he
could see a wisp of it curling against her cheek,
below the edge of the knit cap pulled low over her
skull, but her face was innocent of makeup, and now
that he could study her, Hosea revised his estimate
downward by several years, into the mid-teens. But
not one of the young prostitutes who frequently came
to the shelter—she didn't have that brittle hardness
to her—though her wariness bespoke a goodly length
of time on the street.

She took a hesitant step toward him.

"I was wondering . . . this is the place where you
can take a shower?" Her voice was soft, with the
faint flavor of the mountains in it, its timbre clear
and unslurred by drugs.

"It's only a few days a month," Hosea said apologetically. "From three to seven, first come, first served. Men and women come on different days. The doors open at three, and usually only the first thirty or forty people get showers. We post the schedule outside, but Serafina has some flyers printed up. Would you like me to get you one?"

The girl hesitated again, wary as a wild thing. "And nobody will bother you? Or . . . steal your things?"

"You'll get a bag for your things, with your name on it. We won't let anybody take them, or bother you."

Trust was an important component of the work they did here. If the homeless population didn't trust them, Serafina had told him when he'd first started working at Jacob Riis, they'd rather die on the street than come in out of the cold. Unless someone's belongings were actively dangerous to the welfare of the other residents, they were left strictly alone and even protected, no matter how much they resembled garbage to the shelter employees.

"Would you like some coffee? It isn't good, but it's hot."

He saw a look of longing cross the girl's face. "I shouldn't. . . ." she said wistfully.

"Why don't you just take a seat—anywhere you like. Ah'll get you that coffee, and a copy of the shower schedule."

He waited until he was sure she was going to sit, and then went back into the kitchen, where he filled a Styrofoam cup with coffee, then grabbed a handful of sugar packets and one of the peanut butter and jelly sandwiches left over from lunch. It was a little stale by now, but he knew she wouldn't mind. He wrapped it in a napkin and came back, setting the items in front of her, then went off to Serafina's cubbyhole.

He picked up the schedule he'd promised, along

with another one listing the addresses of several soup kitchens and free food programs in this part of town—though he was pretty sure she knew about all of them by now—hesitated, and added a handful of pamphlets: the Runaway Help Line, Project Reunion, and a few others. He picked up Jeanette and went back to the table.

Ace kept a wary eye on the door as she tore the tops off half-a-dozen packets of sugar and stirred them into her coffee. And *food,* too. She bit into the sandwich hungrily and wolfed it down in a few bites.

It wasn't that she'd had to go hungry, or not very— not with Jaycie's money to draw on—but meals hadn't been what you could call regular by any stretch of the imagination, and she was getting awfully tired of junk food. It had taken her just about two days to work her courage up to the point of coming in here, but there just wasn't any other way she could think of to keep clean, with the cold weather coming on. One more sponge bath, and she was going to catch pneumonia.

And the man *sounded* nice. She knew you couldn't count on that. Some people were awfully good at lying. And some people could do you a terrible bad turn with the very best intentions. But he sounded nice. She missed that.

He came back and sat down opposite her—carrying a banjo case in his other hand, for a mystery—pushing several sheets of paper across the table. The top one was the shower schedule, and under that was a list of places that gave away food. And under that . . .

Ace started to get to her feet.

"Ah haven't called anybody. And Ah haven't told anybody," the man said quietly. "Ah'd jest like you to think about it."

"Going 'home'?" Ace said bitterly, sitting down again slowly.

"Or jest tellin' somebody about it, if that's all you care to do," the stranger said. "My name's Hosea Songmaker, by the way."

"I'm never going home, Mr. Songmaker. And I'm never telling anyone who I am or where I came from. If I told you—if I told anyone—they'd send me back. Anyone'd send me back. Why not? I come from such a good home. A good *God-fearing* Christian home."

There was a world of anger and bitterness in her voice—and more, an aching need to trust someone, a cry for help that she was too afraid to voice. With Jeanette leaning against his knee he could see it clearly now: she had the *shine* about her, a faint aura that made her seem just a little more *there* than someone who didn't possess it.

"Even the Devil can quote Scripture," Hosea said mildly, "and Ah dare to swear that not every man who says he's a Christian does right by the Book. There are ways to get off the street that don't mean you have to go back to a bad family." Once again he mourned the stroke of bad timing—if only she'd come while Eric was here! Eric would have seen what she was at once, gotten her to trust him . . .

"Not this family," the girl said with weary certainty. "They'd never let me go." She shook her head, looking older than her years, and got to her feet. "Thanks for the coffee."

"Wait," Hosea said. "Won't you . . . at least give me a name to call you by?" he said, willing every ounce of harmless friendliness toward her that he possessed. "So Ah'll know who's askin' after me . . . if you ever come askin' after me."

She took a step backward toward the door, and he

watched her turning the question over in her mind for traps.

"Is that a banjo in that case?" she asked.

"Sure is. Would you like to hear me play it?"

"No," she said quickly. "I hate music. But . . . I guess . . . you can call me Ace."

She turned and walked quickly out the door.

That evening, after his other duties were discharged, Hosea discussed the matter with Jeanette.

"What do you think, sweetheart?"

:DON'T call me that!: the banjo snarled waspishly, between the silvery cascades of notes. There was a brooding silence. *:There seems to be an epidemic of upper-class white kids going slumming these days. Miss Ace-who-hates-music—and I'm sure there's a story there—probably comes from lovely people who were eating her alive. And she probably thinks that the street is better than one more minute of that. And she's wrong. The street is either worse, or exactly as bad, as what she's got at home—whatever it is.:*

"Welladay," Hosea sighed. Jeanette would know if anyone did. Before she'd gone to work for Threshold, she'd cooked meth for a biker gang. She knew the uncertainty of the outlaw life, as well as all the degrees of self-degradation it took for a nice girl from a suburban family to reach it. The rocker creaked beneath him. "At least it's different."

:Oh, yes,: the banjo snarled. Hosea smiled, recognizing all the signs of Jeanette in a temper. *:Strangers can never hurt you quite as much as your own family can, no matter what they do to you. And of course you saw the power coming off her. No wonder she ran away!:*

It was true that young Talents often did not have the happiest of childhoods, particularly if the Gift did not run in their family or—as was often the case—had skipped a generation or more, leaving them the proverbial cygnet in a nest of ducklings.

"I suppose I ought to tell Eric about her," Hosea said reluctantly.

:As if he doesn't have enough to do right now. By all means. Instead of looking for one apprentice wizard in New York—that he has no idea of how to find—he can look for two. Then he'll have a breeding pair, at least. Who knows what might happen then? And—: Jeanette broke off, as if she'd just thought of something she didn't like.

"And?" Hosea prompted.

:If someone—or something—is collecting Talents—and remember, I was—they'll be together.:

"Now there's a happy thought," Hosea said unhappily.

There was a scratching at the window, and Hosea stopped playing, laying Jeanette gently in her case.

Greystone eased open the window and poked his large craggy head inside. "Mrs. Peel, we're needed," he said, giving Hosea a broad conspiratorial wink.

"Wouldn't a phone call have been a mite more sensible?" Hosea said, getting to his feet.

"Ah, laddybuck, have ye no sense o' the fitness o' things?" Greystone said reproachfully.

Less than an hour later, Hosea was in the sort of neighborhood that he had specifically promised Serafina he would *not* visit. He soothed his conscience by telling himself that he wasn't in Manhattan—he was just across the river, in Brooklyn—and he wasn't looking for Magnus.

He was on Guardian business.

The tenement apartment had been a rat-infested firetrap for a century and more. The wood beneath his feet was spongy, like something out of H. P. Lovecraft, and Paul had warned him not to touch the walls, not if he didn't want to bring roaches and worse home with him.

His three counterparts had preceded him, and were gathered in a room that had held a body earlier this evening. Now the body and the police were gone, and the room was empty. The floor was covered with blood and broken glass, as if a hundred mirrors had shattered here at once, though looking around the room, Hosea could see no sign that there had *ever* been a mirror here.

Puzzled, he regarded the others.

"I thought we should all see this," Paul said, gesturing with his sword-cane to encompass the entire room. Paul Kern was a tall elegant black man who carried himself with the grace of a dancer. His voice held a faint trace of a British/Islands accent, and he was wearing his favorite tweed jacket, as if he might at any moment be called away to a country houseparty.

"How many does this make?" Toni asked. She was a Latina with skin the color of buckwheat honey; in daily life the superintendent of Guardian House and single mother of two young sons, an older woman who wore a harried lifestyle and a score of varied responsibilities like an invisible cloak. She was dressed as usual in jeans and a sweatshirt under a down parka, and her blue-black hair was pulled back in a long wavy tail.

"Seven, I think," José Ramirez said. "If our tally is correct." He shrugged, his strong, square, bronzed features settling into a mask of disappointment. "All the same—or close enough."

"Seven?" Hosea said in shock. "But Ah only know of one—and that secondhand, to boot."

The other three turned and looked at him, making

him feel very much like the new kid in school. Paul leaned on his cane.

"Maybe you'd better tell us about it, young Song-maker. The three of us just got around to comparing notes on our own cases a few days ago, only to find this broken-mirror motif—and the murders—running through all of them. There doesn't seem to be any other connection—José's dealing with a gang of demon worshippers, and Toni's involved with a—well, I suppose you'd call it a child-abuse case, although there isn't a child involved. I was chasing ghosts."

"Well . . ." Hosea said dubiously, "Ah'm not sure there's a connection, but the fella Ah know of that got murdered, everybody said *he* was killed by Bloody Mary."

If he'd hoped to stump Paul, he was disappointed; Paul Kern was an expert in the occult in all its guises, from urban folklore to the dustiest grimoire. "Children's folklore. The first cases anyone's collected seem to date from the 1950s, though of course they probably go back farther. Supposedly, if you say her name three times by candlelight while looking into a mirror, she'll come out of the mirror and attack you. Nobody's quite sure where it started."

"It's gotten a little more elaborate than that around here," Hosea said, and gave the other three a condensed version of the Bloody Mary portion of the Secret Stories.

"Ghost? Demon? *Mythago?*" Paul shrugged. "It doesn't seem to fit, somehow. Bloody Mary—both your version and the original—only appears to children. And besides, none of the victims seem to have had any connection with the occult—even José's 'demon worshippers' are strictly amateur night."

"But dangerous none the less," José put in softly. "And I will soon put an end to them."

Paul nodded. "Sometimes the only thing more dangerous than a trained professional is a bungling amateur. But the victims . . . none of them seem to have any connection with each other, so far as Toni's P.D. contacts have been able to determine. All of them were fairly marginal members of society, engaged in rather nefarious—but strictly small-time—activities. All men, all ranging in age from their early twenties to their late thirties. All found lying dead on a bed of shattered mirror glass, covered with cuts on their exposed skin."

"But the cuts weren't what killed them," Toni said grimly. "They all died of heart attacks—in other words, they were scared to death."

Hosea looked around the squalid room. It was hard to believe anyone lived here—or had.

The four of them exchanged wordless glances—Hosea, stubborn, the other three with the dawning realization that maybe they were making a mistake in dismissing Hosea's Secret Stories out of hand. Paul sighed, looking frustrated. "Well, Hosea, perhaps we had better take a closer look at the evidence, and the information *you* have. It looks like your Secret Stories are the first real lead we've got, though it's hard to say how we can follow it up. None of the murder sites were any kind of paranormal locus at all . . . and every spell every one of us has tried here hasn't been able to raise a thing."

"Not even the ghost of the victim," José added, "and that is very odd. This man died this very night, and by violence. His ghost should linger."

"Would you try, Hosea?" Toni said. "I see you've got Jeanette with you. She's a ghost herself. Maybe she'll see something we've missed."

"Worth a try," Hosea said. He unslung the banjo from the soft canvas gig bag in which he'd brought her, and slung the strap over his shoulder. He spent a moment tuning her, then launched into the strains of "Unquiet Grave." It seemed appropriate, somehow.

At times like this—when he was actively working magic through Jeanette—it seemed as if he could see the world through her eyes. It was a world without color, one almost without shape. He could see the other three Guardians, but more as symbols of themselves than in their real forms.

Toni was a quick brightness, sharp and glistening and hard. José was a steady anchor, one that could not be swept away by any tempest. Paul was an infinity of doors, with something behind every one.

He reached beyond them.

There were ghosts here—death was no stranger to these streets—but none, he knew, was the one he sought. Some were faint memories, held by walls and stones, as insensible as a recording. Others—though nothing near—were true spirits that would wander confused for a few days or hours before passing on to the place they belonged. He felt Jeanette yearn toward them, sadly, but she had been bound by her own will and the Guardians' magic into his banjo, and she could not pass on until her work here was complete. Gently, he drew her back, as his fingers wove the song to a close.

"No," he said, opening his eyes. "Nothing more than what you all found."

"Well, it was worth a try," Toni said with a sigh. "Let's go back to my place. We can compare notes, and you can give us the rest of the details about this war in Heaven, Hosea. Though, frankly, if we're going to have to referee something like *that*, I'm not really sure where to begin."

CHAPTER SEVEN:

SLIP JIGS AND REELS

The report on Mr. Dorland was waiting on Ria's desk Thursday afternoon. She had Anita fax it over to Eric's computer, with a note that she'd be out of town over the weekend if he were trying to reach her. She hadn't heard from him since his visit Tuesday night, but she wasn't surprised; Eric would certainly be single-minded in his pursuit of his brother. She made a note in her PDA to call him Monday.

Philip Dorland wasn't the best in his field—which was nice; that meant the best was still available for her to hire—but he was very good, with a sixty percent success rate: astronomically high in the world of missing and runaway children. Of course, Dorland didn't have the advantages of magic to help him hunt, and he was working a month-cold trail. He was probably still checking the Boston area, trying to trace Magnus' movements there.

She'd put an operative on Dorland just as a matter of course; Eric couldn't object to that, and she had no immediate plans to tell him anyway. But it was always best to know what your enemy was doing, and if Eric didn't know that Dorland was the enemy, Ria did.

But for now it was time to turn her attention to other things, and other inquiries.

Early Friday morning, Ria went down to the garage beneath her new apartment, an overnight bag slung over her shoulder, a set of car keys jingling in her hand. She greeted the garage attendant by name, and walked back to her car.

She'd called down earlier, so they'd already taken the cover off the Jag and made sure it was gassed up and ready to go. A 1964 Jaguar E-Type, British Racing Green, and as temperamental as a skittish elvensteed. But the mechanic had given it a complete check-over just last week, and this would be one of the last times she'd be able to drive it this year. Alas, that was the problem with one of these temperamental mechanical beasties; your mechanic saw it more than you did.

She backed out of her slot—the powerful engine purring like a very large kitten—and nosed out into the street. Threading the car expertly into the morning traffic, she headed north.

Once she was on the Saw Mill, Ria was able to open it up a little—nowhere near the Jag's top speed, which was somewhere around 180, but if she decided to come back to the city tonight there might be a stretch of the Taconic where she could give the old lady her head a bit.

Her destination was Amsterdam County, several hours north of Manhattan, along the eastern bank of the Hudson. Taghkanic College and the Margaret Beresford Bidney Memorial Psychic Science Research Laboratory—to give the Bidney Institute its full unwieldy name—were there, and both worth a look, but neither was her destination today.

Once she'd found out about Parker Wheatley, Ria had started doing her homework, but there'd been no sense limiting her inquiries to this side of the Veil. With Aerune out of commission, Wheatley would obviously be trolling for a new Sidhe *padrone*, and Ria didn't move in the right Underhill circles to find out whether he had a chance of finding one.

She could, however, locate and hire someone who could.

Inigo Moonlight billed himself as a Confidential Inquiry Agent and Researcher of the Arcane. Ria suspected he'd been doing pretty much the same thing at least since Queen Victoria had ruled the waves—and why not? The man was—or at least seemed to be—a full-blooded Sidhe (not that she'd ever met him in person). If anyone could tell her whether Parker Wheatley was—still—trafficking with the Unseleighe Sidhe, it was Mr. Moonlight.

So she'd hired him, which presented difficulties of its own.

Inigo Moonlight was . . . eccentric. Brilliant—Ria never wasted her time hiring less than the best—but eccentric. He had a phone but didn't, so far as she'd ever been able to determine, answer it, so there was no use in calling him, and he conducted all his business by letter. And why not? *He* had plenty of time.

Ria did not. If she wanted to know what Mr. Moonlight had unearthed without waiting out an interminable exchange of letters, she'd better go and see him.

Inigo Moonlight lived in an artists' colony named

Carbonek just outside of Glastonbury, New York—another oddity. The colony had been there since the turn of the century—the nineteenth century—and unlike most artists' colonies, it valued anonymity and isolation for its inhabitants above all things.

She supposed there was a certain symmetry to the idea of one of the Sidhe—member of a race with no creativity of its own—living in an enclave devoted entirely to creativity. She wondered how he managed it.

Several hours later she'd reached Amsterdam County Road 4, which wound down into the town of Glastonbury. Glastonbury—most of the towns in this area had fanciful names out of myth and literature; there was a Tamerlane on the other side of the river—was a small Hudson River town, too far off the beaten track to be really touristy—and no passenger trains ran on the west side of the Hudson—but thanks to the nearby college, it had a good selection of shops and services. She drove around a bit until she found a cafe-bakery (named, misleadingly, Bread Alone), and treated herself to an early lunch before driving on.

Taghkanic College had been founded in 1714 on the site of an old cider mill, but everything around it had remained farmland for quite some time thereafter. Even now, the pernicious urban sprawl that was eating the Hudson Valley alive had not reached this far north; once Ria was out of Glastonbury and back on the road again, all she saw was trees, apple orchards, and occasional glimpses of the river. Finally, about ten miles outside of town, there was a small sign off to her left, easy to miss: CARBONEK.

"I suppose it goes along with Glastonbury," Ria muttered to herself, turning onto the narrow, one-lane road.

The road was barely wide enough for one car, and

without shoulders or turnoffs. Though the road was surprisingly good, Ria drove very slowly, mindful of the possibility of other vehicles and of pedestrians—and, for that matter, deer, which were becoming increasingly a problem on the roads. Dense hedges grew right up to the sides of the road, so tall she could see nothing beyond them. If she met anybody coming the other way, one or the other of them had better be prepared to back up for quite a distance.

To her relief, a couple of miles along, the road widened out into a lane and a half, and the high hedges diminished and finally disappeared, to be replaced by a low drystone wall. She could see trees in the field beyond, towering venerable evergreens.

A little farther, and she came to a set of gates.

Two massive fieldstone pillars supported a wrought-metal arch—not iron, Ria noted, but bronze, long weathered to green by time and the elements. The metalwork was in the style of the followers of William Morris, and spelled out one word: "Carbonek."

The Castle of the Grail, which none but the pure in heart and soul might enter. Well, let's give it a shot, shall we?

A brass plaque on one of the pillars announced that this was PRIVATE PROPERTY. The other said that TRESPASSERS were FORBIDDEN. But the gates—massive things of oak, that looked as if they'd just come from Morris's own workrooms—were standing open, so Ria drove through.

Just inside the gates there was a blacktopped parking area—necessary in a region that required plowing and shoveling several times a winter—and the road did not extend any farther. Ria pulled in and parked. There were a number of vehicles already there, from battered vintage VW bugs, to no-nonsense pickup trucks, to a few nondescript vans and sport utilities.

She got out of the car and stretched, looking around. The air was sharply cold, and she could smell the river, though she could not see it. Ria inhaled deeply, relishing the fresh air. City girl she might be, but it was nice to get out into the countryside every once in a while.

There was a large building on her right, as anonymous as a barn, and thoroughly locked. No help there, unless she wanted to break in. She turned to the path leading away from the parking lot. It bisected another drystone wall, and beyond that she could see rows of cottages on either side of the path.

They looked anachronistically English, from their slate roofs and whitewashed exteriors, to the white picket fences outside. She walked toward them. She knew from his mailing address that Inigo Moonlight lived in something called Avalon Cottage, which would be right in line with the Arthurian motif of this place.

The cottages were constructed in blocks of four with cross-streets intersecting. Peering between them as she passed, Ria could see that there were large back gardens, and other cottages beyond. And probably, elsewhere in the colony, there were large communal studios for those whose art required large spaces and specialized equipment. And surely—somewhere— perhaps in the barn she'd passed on her way in, there was a place for the residents to receive their mail, because nowhere did she see a mailbox on any of the cottages, nor did she think a postman would relish tramping all over the quaintly retro Carbonek on foot, especially in the winter.

To her relief, each cottage was clearly labeled on an enameled plaque beside the door, its name easy to read from the gate. All of the cottages seemed to have placenames out of the Arthurian mythos—there

was a Tintagel, a Camelot (of course), a Badon, a
Lyonesse, a Winchester, a Camlann . . .

But no Avalon. Perhaps it came and went, like its
namesake.

All the garden plots were neatly kept, though their
makeup varied wildly, from a full English "cottage
garden" (now bedded down for the winter, of course),
to one empty of growing things entirely, where grass
had been replaced by colored gravel laid in pleasing
patterns, with a boulder or two for decoration.

What they lacked was any rhyme or reason to the
naming. She didn't even know how many cottages
there were. The residents might value their privacy,
but surely this was taking matters to extremes?

"Excuse me, are you looking for someone?"

Busted.

Ria turned at the sound of the voice. A woman
had leaned out of the window of Shalott Cottage.
Her long white hair was pinned up in an untidy bun
on top of her head, and there was a ferret draped
around her neck.

"I'm looking for Avalon Cottage," Ria said, mentally
crossing her fingers. Might as well be hung for a
sheep as a goat.

But the woman did not seem to be inclined to
have Ria flung out as a trespasser. Instead she smiled,
looking pleased.

"Ah, you're looking for Mr. Moonlight." The woman
reached down out of sight and scooped up another
ferret, absently adding it to her living necklace. "Avalon
Cottage is all the way down at the end of the lane,
past Broceliande and Logres. You'll know it by the
roses. He does grow the loveliest roses," she added
with a happy sigh. "Good luck!"

Reaching for yet a third ferret—apparently she
had an infinite supply of them—the woman turned,

her arms full of squirming mustelids, pushing the window closed with an elbow.

Roses? At this time of year? Ria set the question aside for later. She continued down the path, wondering why luck would be called for.

She soon discovered the answer, as the path grew steep, narrow, and twisting. The block of cottages ended, and the trees thinned out as well. The cottages the ferret woman had named were larger than the ones in the cottage-blocks, and each stood alone, surrounded by the ubiquitous white picket fences.

Broceliande's tenant was a sculptor. Ria heard the ring of steel on stone as she approached. He was out in the garden, muffled to the eyes against the cold, hammering away at an enormous block of granite. He did not look up as she walked by. Other sculptures stood about the garden. Ria stopped, and looked, and made a note to find out who he was—and more to the point, who his agent was.

Logres' tenant apparently did not care for plants overmuch. The grass within the yard was neat and very short, and there was nothing else at all within the fence. All the windows were heavily curtained with dark fabric. She had the oddest desire to walk up to the door and demand to know what it was the inhabitant *did*, and strictly controlled herself. *You're far too grown-up to indulge yourself in idle fancies, Ria my girl.*

All the same, the desire to know was very strong. Perhaps he—somehow she didn't doubt it was a "he"—was a reclusive writer, working on some odd literary masterpiece. Or perhaps a jeweler, creating small splendid treasures in secret. This place had a peculiar Brigadoonish aura to it, as if it existed outside of time—partly, she was sure, because the cold raw November weather ensured that she saw so few of the colony's inhabitants. She was sure the place would seem very different in summer.

But even in the cold, she smelled Avalon before she saw it.

She made her way carefully down the last of the path—a path by courtesy, now. The Hudson stretched out before her, and the gentle slope of the eastern bank. Here on the western bank, they were hundreds of feet above the surface of the river, and the cottage was perched on the very edge of a sheer drop to the water below. A racket like roaring surf momentarily assailed her ears, accompanied by the lonely wail of a train whistle; a southbound freight train was running on the tracks far below.

The loveliest roses. Indeed.

The fence, and the cottage itself, were covered in roses—red, white, yellow, pink—and every single one of them was in full bloom.

Roses, Ria told the roses firmly, *bloom in June, not November.*

The roses were unimpressed.

She made her way to the gate. This close, the scent of roses was intoxicating, and Ria could feel the tingle of Elven magic that had coaxed them to bloom out of season. She lifted the latch of the gate and walked inside.

The whole of the garden had been devoted to roses. She was no expert, but it seemed to her that everything here was the older varieties—nothing from later than a century or so ago, at least. These were roses from a time when roses had been prized for their fragrance above all things. The scent was intense enough to drink in like wine.

She walked through the roses and up to the front door. Through the overgrowth of roses, she could

barely make out the enamel plaque beside the door:
AVALON COTTAGE.

Looks like you've come to the right place.

There was an antique bellpull beside the door, and
a brass knocker in the shape of a grinning woodland
imp holding a ring in its jaws. She was hesitating
between the two when the door swung open.

"Come in, Miss Llewellyn," Inigo Moonlight said.
"I have been expecting you."

"I do hope you didn't have any difficulty finding
me?" Mr. Moonlight said, pouring tea.

"None to speak of," Ria said politely, accepting the
delicate porcelain cup. She sniffed the sweet scent
of oranges and cloves appreciatively. It was herb tea,
of course. Inigo Moonlight would as soon drink rat
poison as caffeine—sooner, in fact. The rat poison
probably wouldn't hurt him.

He had not bothered to cast a *glamourie* about
himself, and appeared before her in his true form,
though dressed in mundane, if rather old-fashioned,
clothing. He was quite the oldest Sidhe she had ever
imagined seeing. All the elves were fair-skinned, but
Moonlight's skin was nearly translucent with age. His
hair was white in a way that suggested that all color
had been bleached from it by time. How old could
he be? A thousand? More?

But his eyes were still the intense green of cedars
in twilight, and age, whatever cosmetic changes it had
wrought, had not enfeebled him.

She was resigned to a certain amount of pleasantry
and commonplace, but Moonlight surprised her by
coming quickly to the point, once he had settled her
with tea and cookies in the parlor overlooking the
garden with its splendid view of roses and the river.

"You will be eager to hear my report. And I confess

I was preparing to contact you, as there has been an alarming new development in the past week. I shall, of course, at your pleasure, continue to pursue it as well as the other matters you have asked me to consider, but it had occurred to me that it might possibly be a problem in a sphere in which you yourself might be better equipped to, shall we say, confront the considerations of the world?"

"Something new?" Ria asked, leaning forward. "With Wheatley?"

"Indeed." Inigo leaned back, setting down his own cup of tea untasted and steepling his fingers. "The complete details are in my report, but—to summarize— Parker Wheatley has *not* succeeded either in forging a new Underhill alliance or in successfully making an overture to any member of either Court. Nor have he and his Paranormal Defense Initiative captured any member of any Court, Bright or Dark, High or Low."

"That's good news," Ria said.

"What I am about to tell you is not. I have discovered that Wheatley is making ever-so-discreet inquiries about *De Rebus Nefandis,* a ninth-century grimoire—or, more properly, a book which could be used to construct one. Why this is a matter of particular concern is that *De Rebus Nefandus*—'Concerning Forbidden Things,' as the title might be rendered in English—describes the ancient spells once known to humans, that could compel the Sidhe. Though he did not write them down in his book, the ancient monk who is the author of this tome described them well enough that a superior magician might—would!—be able to either reconstruct them or create something similar, if he could study the only extant text describing them."

"'Only'?" Ria asked. "There's only one copy of the book?"

"The only copy that survives is in the Vatican Library," Moonlight said. "Unfortunately, Mr. Wheatley now knows it is there."

"And," Ria said, "if he gets it . . . ?"

"If he has it, and a Mage to do his bidding, that Mage may call us and force us to appear, bind us, compel us, force us to do his bidding and work no harm against him." Moonlight sighed, shaking his head. "From what you have told me, and what I have since learned from my own young operatives, it would be unfortunate in the extreme were Mr. Wheatley to discover some way to acquire *De Rebus,* or to gain sufficient access to it for his fell purposes."

It would be like Wheatley having Aerune back—on a leash. Ria didn't care for the idea. But something else interested her as well. Normally the Sidhe were impervious to the usual run of sorcery and human magic. The only way to take them out was Elven magic or sheer superior firepower, mundane or magical. Imagine having a set of spells custom-tailored to tie them up in knots . . .

"I'm not suggesting that we let Wheatley get his hands on this book," Ria said slowly, "but I've seen the damage the Dark Court can do to people's lives. Do you really think that humans having a magical defense against the Sidhe is such a bad thing? Maybe everyone needs a few spells like that."

Moonlight picked up his teacup and sipped from it. He did not answer her directly.

"Perhaps you will forgive me for speaking so plainly, but I fear it is the privilege of the old to lecture, and the burden of the young to listen. I have seen much in my life, both good and bad. . . . Magic is for the elves, Dreams for the humans, Miss Llewellyn," he said gently. "Give either race what is the other's birthright, and it does not go well for them, in the end. Oh, the magic of a few does not hurt us—but magic in the hands of the many would be devastating. But without humans, we elves cannot survive, nor would humans long survive without us, I think. You know it to be true of your own knowledge, for did not your young Bard once see a vision of what the world would be like, did the portals no longer connect our two worlds? For each race, a living death, followed by death in truth, so much is the fate of each race intertwined."

Ria thought back to what Eric had told her of his vision of an L.A. in which Perenor had harnessed the Sun-Descending Nexus for his own personal use. A grey, bleak Orwellian place, where no one laughed, no one dreamed . . .

Was that what the elves—who did not dream themselves—gave humans? Dreams?

"So what you're saying is that elves and humans *need* each other?" Ria asked dubiously.

"Danu created us both," Moonlight answered ambiguously. "And humans and elves both are Her children. Each supplies what the other lacks. Though woe betide he, Sidhe or human, who tries to take it for himself."

It wasn't exactly a straight answer, but Ria supposed she was used to that. She already knew that a Sidhe who tried to dream was risking—and often finding—death. And as for humans who practiced magic, well, the burn rate there was just as high, if not higher.

"But Eric is a magician, and he's human," Ria said, puzzled.

"Your young friend Eric is a *Bard*," Moonlight said, correcting her gently. "There have always been Bards among the Earthborn; it is a power they are born with, not something culled from ancient books and pacts with powers best left unroused by humans. A Bard is not a Magus."

Moonlight might see a distinction there, but it was a bit subtle for her. Eric quacked like a duck, after all. He cast spells—didn't that make him a magician?

She shrugged. Arguing with the elves was like riddling with Dragons. Nothing good ever came of it. They returned to the topic of Wheatley.

"We know he doesn't have that book. But he might have a magician. If he does, I need to know," Ria said. "And—obviously—to make arrangements to remove the magician from the PDI before either one can do any harm. Meanwhile, I'll keep working on getting the PDI shut down. If they don't have any real results to show, it shouldn't be too difficult."

"If Parker Wheatley does have a compliant magician, *De Rebus Nefandis* may not be as safe as we hope," Moonlight said solemnly. "The days when the Vatican Library was properly sealed and warded are long past, I fear, and any competent Earthborn Mage may summon one of the Lesser Host to do his bidding. It would be a simple matter to send such a creature to steal the volume—and what I can imagine, Wheatley and his Mage will stumble onto, eventually," Moonlight said unhappily.

"Which means I'd better not waste any time," Ria said briskly. "Looks like I won't be spending the weekend leaf-peeping after all. It's a bit late for it, anyway."

"I shall telephone you if I learn anything of urgency," Moonlight said, surprising her. "Come into the garden. I shall cut some roses for you to take with you."

Heading back toward the city—the cockpit of the Jaguar fragrant with both the scent of roses and the scent of the small parcel of orange-vanilla cookies that Mr. Moonlight had urged upon her at the last moment—Ria's mind roved over all the things Inigo Moonlight had told her, not the least of them the strange interdependency between elves and humans.

He'd spoken as if humans and magic should be completely separate—as if no human should have sorcerous powers, only Gifts and Talents like Eric's or Kayla's. But that only made Ria wonder even more furiously: What about the Guardians?

They had magic.

Where did *they* fit into Inigo Moonlight's cosmology?

It was evening by the time she reached her apartment. Ria took the time to arrange the flowers in a bowl on her coffee table—the huge creamy-pink blossoms made an odd counterpoint to the starkly functional slab of black granite—then phoned Eric.

He wasn't home, and his cell wasn't answering. Neither was Kayla's. She sighed, and called his apartment back to leave a longer message on his home phone, sent one to Kayla as well, then settled down to read Moonlight's report.

It was handwritten, of course, and even though the pages of Spenserian script were as flawlessly clear as any professional calligrapher's, she still found it rather heavy going. But it was all there—plenty of nothing, in exhaustive detail. Wheatley had no Otherworld contacts—and apparently, until very recently, hadn't even had any particular idea of how to go about looking for them properly.

She muttered to herself, setting the report aside. She wondered if Wheatley *had* actually managed to get his hands on a magician—and if he had, if it was one of the rare competent ones who actually knew what he was doing and had the power to do it. Then she dismissed that aspect of the problem from her mind entirely. Let Moonlight follow it up. That was what she was paying him for. She'd attack the problem of Wheatley from another angle entirely.

Pulling out her PDA, Ria opened it to her address book, picked up her phone again, and began making calls.

In the last two days, the two of them had hit up every shelter and flop in Lower Manhattan, and come up dry. And they still had a lot of places to check. On the other hand, Kayla had to admit, Eric was really getting into the role of obsessive weirdo.

He'd probably have still been at it tonight if she hadn't dragged him home with a combination of pleading and threats, pointing out that he wasn't going to do anybody any good—particularly Magnus—if he collapsed himself.

There was no magical trace of Magnus anywhere around the shelters, but they still had the list of addresses that Serafina had given Hosea. If Kayla could get Hosea to sit on Eric long enough, maybe she could convince him to let her check out some of those on her own. It wasn't like it would be all that dangerous, particularly in daylight or early evening when the inhabitants would all be sound asleep—or out.

Or maybe early morning. Yeah, that'd work. Not only would Eric still be asleep, so would everybody at her destination. Runaways, like any other small scavenger, were creatures of twilight and the night, sleeping as far into the day as they could manage. Besides, that way they slept through the heat of the day in summer, and were awake for the worst of the cold in winter. So that was how she'd handle it. And that way she wouldn't have to talk Hosea into going along with her plan.

She finally got Eric herded back into Guardian House, and down to her basement apartment.

"*I* have food," Kayla said firmly. "And you need to eat."

The basement apartment was tiny—one room, with a cubbyhole kitchen and a small bathroom with a stall shower. There was only one tiny window—at ground level, which meant it was high up in the wall.

When she'd moved in, Kayla had painted: the walls were black, stenciled with Celtic borders halfway up their height in a glittery dark purple. The ceiling was the same deep purple as the Celtic border, painted with swirling clouds and a yellow crescent moon by one of the House's more artistic tenants. A bead curtain of iridescent dark purple moons and stars had been set up to screen the studio's kitchen from the rest of the space, and a long mirror wreathed in black silk vines and roses had been hung on the bathroom door. The battered linoleum floor had disappeared under several motheaten but still serviceable Oriental rugs, and the small window was garlanded in a black lace curtain. Fortunately the furniture—a futon, several bookcases, a table, and some chairs, were spatter-painted in lurid shades of pink, green, and purple, or she'd never have been able to find them.

Eric found the effect claustrophobic—the dark colors made the small space smaller—but *he* didn't have to live here, and Kayla seemed to like it.

"I'm thinking of repainting," Kayla said, as she vanished into the kitchen. The bead curtain swished and jingled around her, glittering in the light of several floor lamps.

"Too cheerful for you?" Eric gibed, sitting down on the futon.

"Everybody likes a change," Kayla called back. He

heard the whoosh as the old gas stove lit and the clatter of pots and kettle. She came out with a plate of sliced bread and butter.

"Tea in a minute, chili to follow. I was thinking maybe purple—you know, bring the ceiling color down? And pale toward the floor, almost lilac. And then stencil silver stars all over everything. Doesn't take much talent for that. And Ria called. She wants you to call her back, but it can wait until after you eat. Won't take that long for the three-alarm to heat up."

Eric picked up a slice of bread—thick bakery slices, with a quarter-inch of butter on top—and bit into it, only then realizing how hungry he was.

"You keep your phone in the refrigerator?"

"Wireless e-mail. And *on* the refrigerator, thank you very much. You may have noticed this is not exactly the New York Hilton."

"I *have* seen bigger closets," Eric admitted. Kayla's laptop was crammed into one corner on a triangular desk Hosea had built for her, surrounded by stacks of textbooks and a growing collection of electronic peripherals.

"But it's mine-all-mine," Kayla said with satisfaction. She walked back into the kitchen. "Besides, the rent's good."

After dinner, Eric went up to his own apartment. He thought of going out again—it wasn't that late yet—but he supposed he should at least call Ria back first, and maybe see if Hosea was around. He shouldn't be sluffing off his work with Hosea, and he ought to see how Hosea was coming with that task he'd set him.

But Ria first.

She answered on the first ring.

"Hello, Eric. I was wondering when you'd surface."

Caller ID was a wonderful thing, Eric reflected. It was one of the many shocks, large and small, that had awaited him when he'd first returned to the World Above from his long sojourn in Underhill. Being able to tell who was calling before you picked up the phone had been the stuff of science fiction when he'd been a kid. Now it was the stuff of everyday life.

"I got your e-mail. I thought you were supposed to be away all weekend."

"Plans changed. I don't suppose I need to ask if you've had any luck?" Ria responded.

Eric sighed, a wordless answer. "Kayla and I have had an extensive tour of all the places tourists don't visit, but no luck. A few more places to try . . . Give me until Monday evening, okay? If I can't find him then by magic, we'll try professional help. And how was *your* day?"

Ria chuckled ruefully. "I found a place where roses bloom in December, even in the World Above. I met a woman who juggles ferrets. And I learned a couple of things I didn't want to know. The usual sort of day."

"Sounds fairly typical," Eric agreed blandly—and maybe it was, for people like them. "Roses in December?"

"I admit it's only November, but I'm sure they'll still be in bloom next month," Ria said, sounding faintly puzzled by the notion. "Listen, I— Oh, damn, there's my other line. I have to go."

"Talk to you soon," Eric agreed.

He closed the phone—another item out of a *Star Trek* future—and regarded it unhappily. He knew that calling in help was the right thing to do, but the self-imposed deadline didn't make him any happier. A little more than 48 hours, and some faceless professionals—

albeit ones he'd brought in himself—would be out on the streets looking for Magnus.

And if Eric's brother realized they were looking for him . . .

He'll do what I would have done. Run like hell.

Eric sighed, and got to his feet. He'd go out again after all. He reached for his tattered trench coat, and stopped. For where he was going now, he needed a different look entirely.

She did not know how long she had been seeking the boy, but Rionne ferch Rianten was beginning to despair of finding him.

Bad enough that she had lost him. That was shame enough for a thousand lifetimes.

But not to find him again . . .

The horror of it was nearly enough to drive her mad.

Her hound was dead, and her elvensteed left behind to heal, on the long road that had brought her here, and Rionne missed them desperately, for they would have been aid and companions in her search of this mortal hellpit.

She had followed Jachiel through Gate after Gate, ignoring all treaties sworn by her masters, passing through lands where worse than the Great Death would await her were she discovered therein. And no matter how hard she rode, no matter what spells she summoned to her aid, Jachiel had evaded her.

Until she had followed him here.

Here to where the air stank of deathmetal and of death itself, and her powers failed her in mad prankish ways. But the bond between Protector and Charge endured where nothing else could, and so she knew that Jachiel was here. . . .

Somewhere.

Should one hair upon his head have been harmed
by those who had brought him here, her vengeance
would be terrible, worthy of the songs of a thousand
Bards, but she must find him first. And the task of
finding him, that should have been so simple, had
become unbearably hard, and Rionne feared that she
would die without completing it.

She knew she was dying now—that something
beyond her understanding was happening to her in
this place. Did she not find herself wandering the
streets through the dark hours like one bespelled,
with no notion of how she had come to be where she
was? Sometimes she thought she almost slipped into
Dreaming, thinking she had found him again, but it
was never so. She was always alone, wandering strange
human streets, her very bones aching with the pain
of the lost children that she felt all around her, for a
Protector's heart was bound to the care of children.

It was as much as she could do to survive on these
streets at all, but the closest Gate—the one she had
come through to reach this place—lay firmly in the
control of Gabrevys's enemies, and she dared not
use it to slip back Underhill to rest herself. With
Jachiel to accompany her, she might beg truce and
safe passage through that Gate, for no one—no sane
creature, which these mortals were not—would harm
a child. Without him, she dared not, lest knights of
the Seleighe Court set upon her and slay her for
trespass and truce-breaking, leaving her dead with
her task undone.

It was not death Rionne feared—for she had sworn
an Oath at Jachiel's Naming to give up her life for
his should that be needed—but to fail with Jachiel
unsafe was an unendurable thought. How could the
child, how could any child be safe here?

She could not save them all. That was the bitterest

pain. She roamed the streets at night—for the glare of the sun sapped her strength even further, and she had none to spare—seeking the one to whom she was bound, and heard them, all of them, calling out for someone to help them, to save them from the horrors their mortal kindred inflicted upon them.

She could not save them. She could not save them all, she could not even save the ones she heard. . . .

"Please don't! Please make it stop!"

The cry cut through her like a knife of ice against her bones. Rionne dropped her sword, clutching her head with both gauntleted hands. *No,* she begged desperately. *You are not my Jachiel! I cannot help you!*

But the call, the pain, was too strong for her weakness. Somewhere a child was in danger. A child needed her. They called to her in their dreams, in their waking, with their desperate hearts, willing her to serve their need. . . .

Her form began to shimmer, to change. Elven armor shimmered and flowed like water, becoming long pale draperies. Rionne forgot herself, forgot her name, forgot her purpose. Borne upon a tide of magic, weeping bloody tears of sorrow, she drifted toward the call. . . .

Several hours later Eric was back at Guardian House again. He was considerably lighter in the pocket, as the old saying went, though he'd handed over the money more out of pity than out of any need to use bribes to solicit or compel the truth—a Bard, after all, was a master of Truth in all its guises.

He'd stopped first at Kinko's, where a little work had enabled him to copy and enlarge the photo of Magnus from the bus pass. Some Bardic magic had sharpened and enhanced the image, disguising its origins. Thus armed, he'd gone down to the West

Side Highway, to talk to those who gathered there by night.

Yes, they'd seen him. Some of the ones who said that were even telling the truth. But those who were didn't know how to find him. Someone suggested asking Cleto, but when the name was mentioned, Eric knew that Cleto, whoever he was, was dead. There was no help to be had there.

They were young, terrifyingly so. Youth was their stock in trade, and they bartered it ruthlessly. They didn't know what to make of Eric, and though he ached for them, their hopelessness and their danger, he didn't know how to help them.

It was not that they were beyond help. It was that they needed more help than one man could give. And there were so very many of them.

In the end he left again, sick at heart, casting a *glamourie* over them so that they would forget he'd ever been there asking questions. Even if these children did not know Magnus, their friends might. A careless word, and Magnus would know that the hunt was near. Eric couldn't afford that.

When he got back to Guardian House, he saw that Hosea's lights were still on. He might as well stop in there to see if he could salvage something from the night.

"Ah was hopin' you'd come around," Hosea said a few minutes later, when they were both seated in the Ozark Bard's warm and comfortable living room. "It's lookin' kinda like Ah've got a conflict o' interest, and Ah'm not sure what to do about it."

Hosea explained about having been called out Thursday night to the scene of a murder—which seemed to dovetail with a series of similar murders that the other three Guardians were investigating. And though there had been no trace of occult energy—not even the ghost of the murder victim—at the site, each of the deaths bore a similarity to the one Bloody Mary murder that Hosea *did* know of.

"So," Hosea shrugged, "is this Guardian business—or Bard business?"

Eric frowned, puzzled as well. He had to admit that he'd never encountered a situation quite like this before. He thought hard. "I'd have to say . . . if there's something unnatural out there killing people, that's probably Guardian business. But if it's somehow drawing its power from the shelter kids, then shutting that power off at the source is our business. So maybe it's both." And he felt his stomach twist when he said that, because the *last* time it had been both Bardic and Guardian business, it had ended with the death of one of the Guardians. "And in that case, how are you coming with the tunes, Hosea?"

For the next half hour, Eric listened to the pieces Hosea had composed: short simple songs, easy for a young child to sing and remember. None of them promising more than they could deliver. All offering messages of hope, and encouraging endurance.

Eric offered some advice, suggested a few changes here and there. But overall, the direction in which Hosea was going was good, and he found no fault with it.

Talk then turned to Eric's own quest, and there Eric had little either new or good to report.

"Starting Tuesday, I guess we're going to be doing it Ria's way. And I guess that's for the best," he said reluctantly.

"What's for the best is findin' the little'un," Hosea said firmly, "whatever that takes."

"I just keep feeling like I'm missing something," Eric said. "Something really obvious." He shook his head, unable to follow the vagrant thought to its source. He shrugged, letting it go. "And so to bed."

The Place sort of quieted down after midnight. Everybody was usually out by then, doing whatever they thought they had to do to survive.

Magnus grimaced. They called it "going on dates," but their "dates" had precious little in common with the kind he'd heard about back home. Heard about, but never gone on himself, even though St. Augustine had been co-ed, because Mommy Dearest had been certain that nothing should stand in the way of his glorious future as the next Van Cliburn.

Next David Helfgott, more likely. He'd never bought into all that child prodigy crap his parents had been so obsessed with. There'd been a few authentic ones at Auggie-Dog, and Magnus knew he wasn't anything like that. Real kid geniuses tended to flare up early and crack up early, too, becoming pretty average adults if they stayed in the music field at all. Or else they went totally bonkers.

But after the last few days, he was starting to wonder. Maybe he really had been a musical genius. Because he *was* going crazy.

Magnus sat leaning against the wall, drumming gently on his sleeping bag with his sticks. The sound wasn't enough to wake Jaycie—nothing would wake Jaycie—and Ace was still up, reading by the light of a battery lamp. She was studying for her GEDs, though her chances of taking them, Magnus sometimes thought, were about as good as him getting into a band.

But he had to believe. He had to believe the three of them could get off the street. Somehow. Only he was starting to think it was going to be just the two of them . . . Ace and Jaycie. Because Magnus was starting to think he was losing it.

He'd managed to convince himself that *La Llorona* wasn't coming after him. Maybe the kids had it wrong. Maybe he was too old to bother with. Something. He'd started sticking close to The Place after dark, and had totally given up his late-night roaming, but lately, even during the day, he'd gotten the feeling he was being watched—that something was calling his name, just below the threshold of audibility.

But no matter how hard he tried, he could never see the watcher.

When that happened, he'd stopped going out at all, day or night, and that seemed to help, as if whatever was watching him couldn't see him here. But it hadn't done a thing about his dreams.

In them he was always running. Running from, running to—he was never sure. But running, and there was a voice calling him to come to it, calling urgently, desperately, longingly. And the voice was . . . himself?

He was definitely going over the edge.

"Do you ever stop doing that?" Ace said, without looking up from her book. She didn't sound angry, only curious.

"Nope," Magnus answered, without missing a beat. "You ever stop studying?"

"Try not to," Ace answered, still not looking up. "Never got much chance to, back . . . where I used to be."

"Well," Magnus said, pretending he hadn't heard the almost slip. "I never got much chance to do this, back where I used to be, either."

Ace closed her book with a sigh, marking her place carefully. "Well, that's enough of that for one night. Algebra—geometry—calculus! Lord have mercy!"

"They're not that hard," Magnus said, surprised.

Ace gave him a dour look.

"Well, they aren't," Magnus said defensively. "At least it isn't a bunch of dull novels or poems or something with a bunch of names and dates."

"Like English and history?" Ace said with a crooked smile. "Look here—and I don't mean to pry—but I'm guessing you'll need your certificate same as I will. If you're willing to help me with my hard parts, I can work with you on yours."

"Like I'm going to have to go to college to be a musician," Magnus scoffed.

Ace shrugged, turning away. "Just an idea."

"No—hey—wait—" For some reason, the idea of disappointing her made him feel bad. "It's a good idea. Not that I'm going to need it. But you will. And it'll pass the time."

"Well, I don't want to take you away from beating that sleeping bag to death. There might still be some life in it."

"No, really. When do we start?"

"Tomorrow," Ace said, smiling. "If I have to look at this fool book one more minute tonight I'll tear it up. Well, hello, Jaycie. Decided to join the world?"

Jaycie climbed out of his sleeping bag and wandered over to them, yawning. "I wanted to see what you were doing," he said, sitting down companionably halfway between them.

Without waiting to be asked, Ace passed him a Coke. It wasn't cold by any stretch of the imagination, but it was fairly cool, just from sitting out in here. The Place was warmer than being outside on the street, but that didn't mean it was *warm*.

"Sometimes I do wonder if you're part hummingbird," Ace said teasingly. "Live on sugar syrup and never gain an ounce."

"Perhaps I am," Jaycie said seriously.

He reached out and picked up Ace's book and

paged through it curiously, but Magnus could tell he was only looking *at* it, not reading it. He'd never seen Jaycie actually read anything, and he was pretty sure by now that Jaycie couldn't. Maybe he was—what was that word? Dyslexic? Where you couldn't read or anything? It didn't really seem fair.

So when was it you started expecting life to be fair? Magnus thought sourly.

Jaycie closed the book carefully, and handed it back to Ace with a curiously formal gesture. "This is a work of great knowledge."

"Yeah. I just hope I can get all the 'great knowledge' out of it and into me," Ace said with a sigh.

"It will take time," Jaycie said.

"You got that right," Ace said. She came over and hugged him. "But don't you worry about it. I'll manage. And Magnus is going to help me."

"That's right," Magnus said impulsively, and was rewarded with one of Jaycie's most dazzling smiles.

"Then all is well, with friends to help," Jaycie said. He settled down next to Ace with a sigh of contentment. "Read to me?"

"Okay. Which one do you want?" Ace said. In addition to her textbooks, she had a small library of fantasy novels—scavenged, mostly, out of the dumpsters behind bookstores. Jaycie never tired of hearing the same stories over and over.

That was something Magnus had never been able to figure out. Fantasy. Trying to escape from the real world by reading about a bunch of things that weren't real, that you knew *couldn't* be real . . . he couldn't see the point. It was like trying to lie to yourself. It was more important to know about the way the world *really* worked, so you could do your best to avoid the next horrible surprise it set up for you.

But Ace liked them. And Jaycie liked them. So he kept his mouth shut.

"Read me the one about the elf who gets mugged," Jaycie said placidly. "I like that one."

"Just a couple of chapters, okay? It's long. Let me see if I can find it." Ace rummaged around for a few moments and came up with it—coverless, of course, and rain-spotted, its pages fanned out by many readings.

She sat down on her sleeping bag, next to her light, and patted the space beside her encouragingly. Jaycie came over and sat beside her, and after a moment, Magnus joined him, first tucking his drumsticks carefully away in his bag. The three of them settled down close together—it was warmer that way—and Ace opened the book, holding it so that the light from the lantern fell directly on the page, and started to read.

"*'Chapter One: Never Trust Anyone Over Thirty: It was April 30th and it was raining. . . .'*"

Hell, Marley Bell had decided, was being willing to sell out your principles and not being able to find a buyer.

"Look," he said wearily to the man named Nichol. "If you don't understand what I'm telling you, at least write it down so that someone, sometime, will. Before you kill somebody else. There is a principle in the Art known as shielding. I suppose the mundane equivalent would be a force field. The idea is that nothing goes in, and nothing gets out. The magician controls his own shields. He opens them to admit those entities whom he summons, and to allow his evocations to go forth. There's more, but this is the bottom line, and this is where your problem is."

"And why is that?" Nichol said, as blandly as if they were discussing the weather.

Marley had decided some time before that he hated Nichol. It was the first of the many small defeats that had followed the first and largest, for he had set aside both love and hate years before. But he hated Nichol.

They were back in the interrogation chamber to which Marley had been brought on the first day he'd come here. The only other places he'd seen had been the small windowless cell where he slept and ate, and the workroom that had been set aside for his use. He wasn't sure how long he'd been here. It no longer mattered. He was quite certain he was going to die here.

"Because this place is completely shielded and magic-dead," Marley said in a dull exasperated voice. "It is cut off from the Higher Planes. That means *I* am cut off from the Higher Planes."

At first he'd plotted rebellion—to send a cry for help, or at least a warning—out along the Astral Plane. His kidnappers had found and ransacked his sanctum, and brought everything here—his sword, his knives, all his magical tools and equipment. He'd had—so he thought—the means, even though they'd destroyed half his components with their ignorant meddling and the rest were woefully distempered and out of alignment, nearly useless to him.

At first they had intended to watch him work. He had pointed out that an observer would sabotage his attempt, not daring to object further. They had seemed to accept that, to his trembling relief.

But when he had stepped into the hexagram, even the simplest conjurations had been beyond him. Fire had not come to his summons, nor his familiar to his call, nor would an image form in the speculum-stone. All he had gotten for his efforts had been a crushing headache and a sense of emptiness, but he had continued trying until he was too exhausted to try any longer.

At least he was no longer afraid, at least not the way he had been. He'd despaired too far for that.

"Is all this mumbo-jumbo supposed to mean something to me?" Nichol said pleasantly, jarring Marley back to the unwelcome present.

"Surely you have a specialist to check my work and prove the truth of what I'm telling you," Marley said blankly. It was beyond belief that they didn't. Even a non-Operant . . . but if they didn't, he could be doing anything, committing any fraud—

"We trust you," Nichol said, and hit him.

The beating was dispassionate, delivered in a thoroughly professional manner, but after the first few blows, Marley was in no position to appreciate its finer points, even if he had possessed the particular esoteric skills to assess it. He screamed and cowered, desperately trying to escape that which could not be escaped.

"But maybe you'd better try harder next time," Nichol said, and left him.

When he left Bell's cell, Nichol went up several floors, to the Director's office, and waited to be admitted. He didn't have to wait long.

"How is our project coming?" Wheatley asked genially. He did not invite Nichol to sit down.

"The subject's complaining that the building's shielded," Nichol said laconically. He smiled slightly. "I encouraged him to think outside the box."

Wheatley grimaced. "Well, of course it's shielded! We'd have Spookies all over us otherwise; if we're looking for them, naturally they're looking for us. They're clever, dangerous, and completely without mercy, Mr. Nichol. Always remember that. In the meantime, I trust you didn't damage our little lab rat?"

"He'll be ready to go again in a couple of hours. I didn't even break the skin," Nichol said, with the assurance of long experience.

"Interesting that he should mention it, though," Wheatley said musingly. "There's no way he could have known unless he'd been told. But the Spookies are known to have human agents . . . it's possible this Bell might be one of them. In which case, he might be useful to us in another way, assuming the creatures feel any loyalty at all to their assets. After we've exhausted every other possibility of course. And thoroughly debriefed him."

"I'll make a note in his file, sir," Nichol said.

CHAPTER EIGHT:

CAROLAN'S WELCOME

On Monday, when they weren't even looking, they found him.

Kayla and Eric had spent the morning checking abandoned buildings on the Lower East Side—dangerous in itself, as condemned buildings were condemned for a very good reason, and most of them were falling to pieces. Eric was feeling cross and absent-minded—and trying hard not to share either emotion with Kayla. Not only was getting uptown to keep his appointment with Oriana going to take a big bite out of the afternoon, he'd promised to see Ria this evening to make arrangements to bring in the professionals.

When he came out of Oriana's—the session hadn't gone well, more indication of how foul his luck was running lately—Kayla had suggested cutting across town and seeing what they could turn up at this end of Manhattan.

"Hosea said that Serafina said there was supposed to be a couple of flops up here somewhere around St. John. With all the rebuilding going on, there's a lot of tenements waiting to be torn down," Kayla said encouragingly.

"Sure," Eric had answered. He didn't have any better ideas. Just a lot of dead ends. He'd barely managed to keep from snapping at Kayla when, after they'd crossed Lex, she'd spotted a grocery store and wanted to stop. Didn't she ever stop eating? Where was she putting it all?

"Chips, soda. Feed the beast. It won't take long."

He followed Kayla along the aisles—more from inertia than any interest in making his own purchases—as she dawdled along. He forced himself to remain calm. It wasn't as though there was anywhere he actually needed to be, after all. All they had to look forward to was an afternoon of running down more dead ends. Even a false lead would be more action than they'd gotten so far.

He was watching his feet, rather than his partner, when Kayla suddenly stopped and he almost ran into her. He glared at her with irritation, but she wasn't paying attention to him.

He began to give her a little shove to get her moving again.

"*Eric!*" Kayla hissed, elbowing him savagely in the ribs. Eric looked where she was looking, just as she kicked him painfully in the ankle as a further inducement to silence and attention.

Magnus was walking along at the other end of the aisle, pushing a cart.

Eric quickly looked away, feigning an intense interest in the row of bottles in front of him.

There was a girl with Magnus. The two of them were concentrating on the list the girl held in her hand. Eric moved casually around the end of the row, where he could watch them more easily. He didn't dare use the least hint of Bardic magic, not if Magnus' own magic had awakened. And it did seem to have—he could feel it from here. Talent, raw and untrained.

From behind an end-cap display of potato chips, Eric watched his brother. The teenager looked healthy—not thin, not drug-wasted. Was he in love with the girl beside him? They certainly seemed to be very close. . . .

"When they leave, I'm going to follow them. *Alone*," Kayla said firmly. "Don't argue. There isn't time. One can do it better'n two. I'll fit in, and they can't be going far. Look how much they're buying."

Eric stole another glance. It was true. The shopping cart was filling up with bags and boxes. Nothing that needed a refrigerator or a stove to cook it, he noticed. In fact, most of it was ready to eat.

"All right," he said reluctantly.

"Stay back here," Kayla said, kicking him again to underscore her point. "Learn to love frozen foods."

She drifted away, leaving Eric to watch Magnus and the unknown girl until they, too, passed out of sight. Kayla was right—wherever Magnus had found to live, it must be nearby.

He didn't want to leave following them to her, but he had to admit the young Healer was right. If he couldn't use his magic to disguise his presence, they might notice him far more readily than they'd notice someone close to their own age.

When he was sure the three of them had left, Eric picked up a bag of chips and a bottle of water to account for his presence in the store, and went up to the front.

Paying for his purchases, Eric went outside. The street was empty—at least of the three people who interested him. And he and Kayla hadn't had a chance to set up a rendezvous point afterward.

For a moment, he panicked, then he told himself not to act like an overprotective father. Kayla had more up-to-date street smarts than he did. To a Healer, his magical aura was unmistakable.

Join the twenty-first century, bonehead. Remember your cell? Besides, they both had their phones with them. All she had to do was call if she needed him or couldn't find him.

Eric went to find a reasonable place to set up his pitch.

Before he began to play, he took his flute apart and removed the strand of Magnus' hair from around the mouthpiece. It wouldn't do to call him back now, when Kayla was tracing him to where he slept. Then he reassembled his instrument again and began to play.

The flute's notes soared through the chill November air—songs now of hope and possibility, not longing and loss. Passersby stopped—whether out of curiosity at seeing a street busker so far uptown, or drawn by the joyous optimism of the music—and the flute case slowly filled with coins. Small ones, but amazing that anyone up here felt moved to part with even a penny.

He'd been playing for almost an hour when his phone rang.

He paused, and fumbled it out of his pocket.

"Hiya. I'm over at the diner by the 6 at 103rd," Kayla said. "Wanna meet me?"

"Well?" Eric demanded a few minutes later, sliding into the booth where Kayla sat hunched over a cup of coffee. He was so impatient to hear what she had to say that he was tempted to reach over and shake it out of her.

She gave him a smirk. "Chill, Lone Stranger. We can pick them up any time. It's a big place off 110th. I followed along from about six blocks back, but that's where they went, damn skippy. I figured we could go back and check it out together early tomorrow morning—safest time; they should all be asleep then. But I figure we need a plan, seeing as we've found them."

She made a rude noise at the look of bafflement that crossed Eric's face. "A plan?" she repeated. "Phase One is now complete, Earth Commander. We have tracked the tiger to its lair. Now what?"

Find him and make him safe, Ria had said. Well, they'd found him. But as for making him safe . . . how was he going to do that?

Eric remembered his own days on the street, the early ones before he hooked up with the RenFaire crowd and got himself a seat in a van full of peregrinating buskers, on the run from he wasn't sure what. If someone had walked up to him offering to fix everything, he would have been sure it was some kind of a con. And *he* hadn't been a seventeen-year-old, justifiably paranoid runaway! Magnus would have every reason to be doubly certain that anybody offering him sanctuary was running some kind of a scam on behalf of his parents . . . particularly someone who said he was a brother he had no reason to believe existed. Why should Magnus trust him? Or believe a word he had to say, for that matter?

Of course, no matter how strong Magnus' innate Gift was, Eric had the advantage of training and experience. He could certainly overpower Magnus

and whisk him Underhill before Magnus knew what
was happening.

*Sure. Treat him like an object, the way everyone
else has his entire life. Force him to do what I want,
just because I'm older and stronger than he is, and
I think I know what he* needs *better than he does.
There has to be a better way!*

"If I could just get him to trust me," Eric said slowly.
"Get to know him . . . try to explain . . ."

"Well, getting us in there where you can talk to
him shouldn't be that hard," Kayla said. "They probably aren't the only two denning up there, especially
considering all the stuff they were buying. I just need
to get an invitation from one of the other kids living
there to get us in."

"You think?" Eric asked doubtfully. Those kids—there
wouldn't be one of them that was over eighteen, he
was sure. He had never felt so old before. "I mean,
you know what we used to say, 'never trust anyone
over thirty.' You don't think they'd figure me for
someone trying to hustle them?"

"Well—not if you make like Rainman," Kayla replied,
with a sly grin. "Someone whose ducks aren't all in a
row—harmless, but dippy. Then you use your winning
ways to get next to him, scope out the situation, and
figure out where to go from there," she added, as if
it were the easiest thing in the world.

Eric thought about it. It seemed like an elegant
solution, even if he *would* have to give an impression of a lunatic. If he could get the chance to talk
to Magnus, get an idea of what his situation was—or
what *Magnus* thought it was. The best thing would be
to find some way to break through the spell barrier
Magnus had surrounded himself with, so that Eric's
own magic could work reliably, and so if Magnus ran
again, Eric would have a tag on him.

And at least this way he'd have something to go to Ria with. If he'd already *found* Magnus, there was no reason to go searching for him, and no reason to hire more specialists.

For to see Mad Tom O'Bedlam, ten thousand miles I'd travel. The song rang through his head, unbidden. *Mad Maudlin goes on dirty toes to save her shoes from gravel. . . .*

So here they were, Mad Tom and Mad Maudlin.

"It sounds like the best idea . . . if we can pull it off," Eric said slowly. "But I can't use magic to get us in. He'll sense it."

Kayla made a face. "Every problem in the world doesn't have to be solved by magic, Ultra Bard," she said. "Now come on. There's an alleyway outside the building. Let's find some place where we can watch it . . . and be inconspicuous about it. It's going to be a long cold night, whether we pull this off or not."

"Just give me a minute to call Ria once we get outside," Eric said. "I've got to break a date."

Not that he thought Ria would be unhappy about that. At least, not this time.

She was sure they'd been followed, but Ace hadn't seen anybody. She didn't say anything. It had been hard enough talking Magnus into coming out with her, but he'd been jumpy and cross all day (more than usual), and she'd thought a breath of air—even New York air—would do him some good. Besides, if he came with her on her shopping run, she could buy more stuff, and she wouldn't have to worry as much about being jumped on the street.

She wondered what was bothering him. In particular and lately, of course. Probably somebody was trying to rope him into something—everybody was always trying that. So far he'd had the sense to stay clear, just as she had, but the offers Magnus was probably getting were undoubtedly more tempting than hers. They wouldn't just be asking him to sell his body. No, they'd be asking him to run drugs, or numbers, or do any number of other things that *seemed* cleaner but were just as bad—and far more dangerous over time.

But lecturing him would do neither of them any good—and would probably drive him right into doing them.

When they got back and divvied up what she'd bought, she went to check on Jaycie, as usual. He was right where she'd left him, and Ace breathed a sigh of relief.

He'd given her an almighty fright this morning. She'd been having trouble sleeping because it was so cold. The other kids were still coming in and out, so she hadn't really been doing a good job of getting her head down, and the place was fairly well-lit besides, and one time, when she'd looked over to where Jaycie slept, he hadn't been there.

She'd been terrified. She'd never seen him leave The Place—never!

She'd sat bolt upright, trying to figure out what to do. Wake Magnus? Go out looking for him herself? She'd worked herself up into a fine tizzy and had just been about to shake Magnus awake when Jaycie had come strolling in, innocent as you please.

She'd realized then she was just being foolish. He'd just gone to the bathroom. He couldn't spend *every* minute in bed, after all.

But then he'd seen she was awake, and smiled—that heartbreakingly beautiful smile of his—and taken her hand. And before she'd realized quite what he was about, Jaycie was back in bed and she was holding

a wad of money that would choke a Central Park
carriage horse.

She hadn't told Magnus about that, either.

But now . . .

"He's getting sicker," she said harshly, looking down
at the sleeping boy. He was thinner than before—she'd
seen it clearly this morning when he'd been up and
about. And paler than he had been, almost as if there
were a light shining through him. And he slept even
more than he had when she'd first come here. Now
Jaycie slept almost all the time.

"He isn't," Magnus said stubbornly. "He isn't sick."

"He is," Ace said, not bothering to lower her voice.
"He always wakes up when I come back—but he isn't
waking up now."

Magnus dropped to his knees beside Jaycie and
shook him roughly, which just went to prove that he
was as scared as she was, for all his fine talk.

"Magnus, no—" Ace cried, but it was too late.

You did *not* startle Jaycie, or wake him up suddenly. Both of them knew that. But she'd frightened
Magnus, and he'd forgotten.

She heard a cry—Jaycie's—and then *something*
happened—she didn't know what. And then a yelp
from Magnus as he went flying across the room,
knocking bags and jar candles every whichway. And
Jaycie was on his feet, staring around himself wildly,
about to run.

"Jaycie?" Ace said softly, moving a little so he'd
focus on her. She stepped back, not forward. "It's
me—Ace. We didn't mean to wake you up."

Now *that* was a flat lie, but she didn't think he
was quite awake yet. The important thing was to
wake him up the rest of the way, so he'd know where
he was before he went and did something almighty
foolish. He looked terrified—his face was as white

as scraped bone, and he was panting just as if he'd run a dozen blocks.

"Jaycie?" she said again, very softly. "It's okay. You're safe here."

Finally his eyes focused and he saw her. Some of the wild look left his eyes. "Ace?" he said. "I thought— I saw— I dreamed—"

He reached for her—a rare gesture—and she went to him, holding him tight. She could feel him tremble as she held him, and worse, she could feel how the layers of cloth collapsed inward at her touch. He was nothing but skin and bones underneath all those clothes.

"It's all right," she said again. "I'm sorry we scared you."

He leaned his head on her shoulder, sighing deeply.

"They won't find me here," he said, and there was a faint note of triumph in his voice. "They'll *never* find me here."

And if she could get her hands on the people he was running from, Ace thought grimly, she'd break every promise she'd ever made to herself and sing one more song, a song with every ounce of her Gift in it, a song that would let them feel one-tenth of the pain and fear they'd made Jaycie feel. She knew it was wrong, and she didn't care: wasn't it wrong to do something like this to someone as just plain *good* as Jaycie was? He deserved to be with people who could take care of him, not hiding out here.

"That's right, honey-lamb," she said, giving him one last hug. "Nobody's going to find any of us. Ever. Now—since you're up anyway, why don't you come and see what I've brought back from the store? I got some nice soup—if Magnus hasn't gone and spilled all of it," she added unfairly, "and it should still be hot.

You need to get something into your stomach before you start in on that nasty chocolate of yours."

She stepped away from him and—finally—looked to see if Magnus was okay. He was: Jaycie hadn't *meant* to hurt him. He'd just been startled. And the bag with the cartons of soup and the coffee hadn't been among the ones he'd knocked over, so that was good.

"Must I?" Jaycie said plaintively.

"You must," Ace said firmly. She breathed an inward sigh of relief. At least he felt so guilty about hitting Magnus that she could get him to eat some real food for a change!

"See?" Magnus said smugly, getting to his feet and dusting himself off. "I told you he was fine." He went over to get the soup. "You want chicken noodle or vegetable beef?"

But Ace didn't think so. Magnus didn't want to believe it, but she had eyes in her head, and she knew what she knew. And she didn't think Jaycie was fine at all.

Kayla had been right about "long" and "cold." She and Eric watched from various places along the street as evening faded into night. About half a dozen kids came slinking out of the alleyway at various times—none of them either Magnus or the girl he'd been with—heading toward Broadway. When Kayla followed one of them, Eric followed her.

They passed along the northern boundary of Central Park, heading west, and for the next several hours drifted up and down Broadway, barely keeping each other in sight. Eric was careful to stay in character—not hard, for someone with his years of RenFaire experience, though this was a Faire of a different sort, one in which he didn't think it would be reasonable to try to set up a pitch. This was a rough, edgy crowd, with its mind on everything but music.

The weather was bad, cold and thinking about raining or worse, but never quite able to make up its mind. Despite the weather's nastiness, the streets were full, with people going home, people going out to eat, and people just eddying about.

As the night wore on, the people who had places to go to diminished, but the people whose world was the street remained. A couple of times Eric saw police cruisers make slow passes through the area, but they didn't stop. They were looking for bigger fish than were to be found around here.

He had an academic understanding of what had to be going on around him—drugs and prostitution—but it wasn't all that easy to spot at first. After a while, he was able to pick out the girls, and realize that the ones getting so cheerfully and quickly into the cars that pulled up to the curb didn't actually know the drivers. . . .

He kept an eye on the ones who'd come out of the building that Kayla had targeted, but none of them seemed to get into any of the cars. They hovered around the edges of things, looking nervous and hopeful.

Around midnight, Eric stopped at an open-air juice counter, feeling oddly like an extra in *Bladerunner*. It was on the corner, and the counter went around two sides. You could order greasy gyros, watered-down sugary juice, or toxic coffee, and a purchase bought you a chance to lean at the counter while you consumed it. Eric chose the juice. The awning kept off some of the not-quite rain. Despite the weather and the hour, there were a lot of people around, none of them the kind Eric would have freely chosen as companions.

There was a time, once, when you wouldn't even have noticed them, as long as you had a bottle or a nickel bag in your pocket. He thought back to those days and shuddered.

"Hey, Boss, buy me a coffee?" Kayla whined, in a voice completely unlike her own. "C'mon," she wheedled. "It's cold. I know you got money."

"Buy your own coffee," Eric grumbled, not looking at her.

"Mean," Kayla sulked, pushing in next to him. "Don't be mean to Kayla, Boss, I'll be so nice to you, I'll—"

"If Ria heard you talking like that, she'd boil me in oil first and ask questions later," Eric whispered, fishing a dollar out of his pocket.

"Girl's gotta have a hobby," Kayla retorted in the same low tones.

The counterman brought over a coffee, taking Eric's money. Kayla dumped several packets of sugar into it, sipped, and shuddered.

"We're doing good," Kayla said. "I got to strike up a conversation with Chinaka—she's the black girl we saw in the pink jacket, the one with the silver lipstick? All the pimps around here run strings, and all their strings have territories. You poach on somebody else's territory, you'll get cut up bad. So they're looking for someplace that nobody else is working. That's why they're just hanging around, not going on dates."

"Jesus," Eric said feelingly. Kayla shrugged, but Eric could see she was keeping her face studiously blank.

What am I doing—dragging someone who's a Healer and an Empath out into this?

"My shields are a lot better than the last time I lived on the street," Kayla said quietly. "I'm fine."

"Since when can you read minds?" Eric said, startled.

"Not hard to guess. You'd better do a better job of getting your game face on with them than with me," Kayla said simply. "Or they're going to think you're an undercover cop. Now, we'll just hang around for a couple of hours, and look pathetic and homeless. Maybe they'll take us home to Mama." She grinned wickedly. "That's your job. Remember, they won't expect us to tell them much. I'm Kayla. I don't have a place to stay. I steal things. You're . . . this guy. I feel sorry for you 'cause you're not all there, but you make pretty music, so I look out for you."

"Okay," *this guy* said. "And if it doesn't work?"

"We keep hanging around until it does—or until one of us thinks of something else," Kayla said simply. She finished her coffee and drifted off, the picture of a young grifter looking for wallets to lift. If he hadn't known her, Eric would have distrusted her on sight.

The weather was in their favor. About two o'clock Chinaka and Dakota decided to wait at an all-night coffee shop for their friends to get back from someplace unspecified. Kayla got herself invited along, and Eric attached himself to the group.

They weren't certain about him at first, and Eric realized he was going to have to risk a little magic. Enough to convince these skittish runaways that he and Kayla were friendly and trustworthy enough to invite back to wherever they were staying, or the rest of this wasn't going to work. Magnus shouldn't pick up on that, at least—it wouldn't be directed at him, and as far as Eric could tell, he was nowhere in sight.

So he wove the finest and most subtle spell he could—Master Dharniel would have been proud of him!—around the two young runaways, to convince them that he and Kayla were harmless, friendly, and completely trustworthy.

As it touched them, he saw their faces relax. Chinaka smiled.

"Well, sure he can come with us, girl. But he gonna have to pay, right?" Both of the girls laughed.

Kayla laughed too. "Boss always pays."

"Thanks a lot," Eric muttered under his breath.

The diner wasn't particularly clean, though very noisy. The counterman came out from behind the register when they came in.

"You! Get out of here before I call the police!"

"It wasn't us!" Dakota said quickly, backing up against Eric and looking as if she was about to cry. "It was Shimene and those other girls—we weren't even here—"

"You think I don't recognize that crap jacket of yours?" the man demanded. "Get out."

"Told you you shouldn'ta took it," Chinaka said in a low mutter.

"But it's *mine*," Dakota said, her eyes filling. "She *stole* it! That B. stole my jacket and I wanted it back—"

The counterman was heading back behind the counter, toward the phone on the wall. Kayla slithered out from behind Eric and the other two girls and went over to him. It was too noisy in the diner for Eric to hear what she was saying, but Eric saw money change hands.

"C'mon," Kayla said, coming back. "Let's go sit down."

Both girls stared at her.

"He gonna call the police," Chinaka said suspiciously.

"Somebody stiffed him for the bill," Kayla said, shrugging. "So I paid it. If the cops show up, everybody's going to bail an' he'll be out a lot more'n one check. Who cares? It's too damn cold to go lookin' for another place that's open. Besides, it's not my money." Kayla laughed heartlessly.

Dakota and Chinaka looked at each other for a long moment, then shrugged. They walked on in.

The four of them found a booth in the back. Kayla slid in beside Eric, and Dakota and Chinaka piled in beside each other.

"He paying, right?" Dakota said again.

"I already paid for that other thing," Kayla said, arguing to make it look good. The three teenagers engaged in a long, circular and—to Eric—nonsensical argument about whether Eric should still buy them dinner when Kayla had already paid for Shimene's previous meal, allowing Chinaka and Dakota to come in here at all, even though Dakota hadn't been the one to stiff the diner. Eventually it was agreed that the two of them would pay Kayla back the money she'd spent and Eric would pay for dinner.

It was all pointless. With Underhill backing, Eric had enough money to buy the *diner* if he happened to want to. But he was supposed to be a homeless busker, and Kayla was supposed to be these girls' new best friend.

When the waitress came, the girls didn't bother with menus, but ordered with the ease of long practice—an amount of food that made Eric blink to contemplate it. Kayla ordered a similar amount.

"Coffee. French fries," Eric said, when the waitress looked at him.

"You'd better be planning to pay this time," the waitress said, glaring at all of them.

"Why does everybody *pick* on me?" Dakota wailed.

"Man, that Shimene set you up," Chinaka said admiringly. "She prob'ly wore that nasty-ass jacket all over town, stealin' things."

"It's a nice jacket," Dakota said stubbornly.

It might be, Eric thought, but it was certainly conspicuous. A fashion from a few seasons back, it was quilted denim with studs, rhinestones, fringe, and inserts in several colors of fluorescent lace along the back and sleeves. It was the perfect thing to wear while robbing banks, because if you did, no one would ever remember your face.

"Well, you oughtta trade it, before word get out what Shimene done. Or you tell Ace about her. Maybe she throw her out, 'cause what she done, that almost like stealing."

It wasn't almost like stealing, Eric thought with a sense of unreality. It *was* stealing, though he supposed things might look different to a couple of street kids. Lord knew he'd done more than a few things he wasn't entirely proud of before he'd met Kory.

But nothing like this . . .

Yeah, well, you weren't underage and completely without any way of earning money, were you? You weren't out for more than a couple of days before you were in that van, and you had money in your pocket when you ran out on Juilliard, too. That might have made a difference. . . .

Their food came—the waitress stood right there until Eric paid the bill—and when he had, he realized what this must look like to her: either a pimp out with his string, or worse. He sighed inwardly. He'd never be able to show his face in *this* part of town again!

"Where you staying?" Dakota asked, after she'd finished the first part of her hamburger platter.

"Subway," Kayla said.

Chinaka shook her head in sympathy.

Eric said nothing, not sure how to play this.

"You got any stuff?" Dakota asked.

"Transit cops got it couple days ago," Kayla said matter-of-factly.

"You could—" Dakota began.

"We can't—" Chinaka hissed.

The two of them huddled together in the corner of the booth, arguing in whispers. Eric caught fragments of the conversation—Dakota thought they should bring them along with them when they went back, Chinaka didn't—and a name again: Ace, who seemed to be their leader.

He risked another thread of magic, encouraging them both to trust him and Kayla, to agree that it was a very good idea to bring them back with them.

"Well, okay," Chinaka said, sighing. "He *did* get us out of trouble. So I guess it okay. There a place you could maybe sleep. But you gotta promise not to tell anybody."

"We promise," Kayla said. "Right, Boss?"

"Right," Eric said.

The two other girls were named Graciella—Graz for short—and Alice. They arrived just as the others were finishing dessert. Both of them looked surprised to find their friends in the diner, and it didn't take any leap of logic for Eric to realize that they'd been with Shimene on her last visit here.

Eric quickly wove his spell of trust and friendship around them as well. It wouldn't hurt to have as many allies as they could muster when Chinaka took them back to where they were going. From what little he'd been able to overhear of Chinaka's conversation with Dakota, that place was supposed to be a closely guarded secret, and bringing strangers in was expressly forbidden. He just hoped he'd be able to charm this Ace person—*without* magic—into letting him and Kayla stay.

At least the candles made it a little warmer. She'd lit all of them, so that it was bright enough to read, hoping they'd drive out the dampness, at least. Even Jaycie was awake, watching them study and gnawing on his horrible chocolate.

She had to admit that it was a lot easier with Magnus helping. They'd started out with the math problems, and for the first time it seemed as if she'd be able to get through them eventually. They worked on that for a couple of hours, until Magnus got bored, and Ace was sure that if she closed her eyes, she'd see nothing but numbers.

The Place was noisier than usual. Some of the kids had just stayed inside because of the weather—or gone out and come back early. Shimene was prowling around, trying to look as if she wasn't poking into the other kids' things, looking for something to steal. Ace sighed inwardly. Shimene was a thief and a troublemaker—she'd "borrowed" Dakota's jacket and wouldn't give it back for weeks, but had been suspiciously meek when Dakota had walked out wearing it this evening, having finally gotten it back somehow.

Ace would have been happy to toss Shimene out onto the street weeks ago for the good of the others, harsh as it seemed, but she knew she really didn't have the power to do that. It was as much as she could do to keep the other kids from picking on Jaycie, and she knew she was buying them off with the money Jaycie brought in from . . . somewhere . . . to get that much of a concession.

And when it doesn't work any more? What are you going to do then? Sometimes I feel like a lion tamer

*in a cage. And I'm just hoping they won't notice I
don't really have a whip and a chair.*

She thought about the man she'd met down at
Jacob Riis. Hosea. He'd seemed nice. She wondered
if he'd help the three of them—if he *could* help
them—*her* way, without any names or parents. She
knew this couldn't last much longer, and only a fool
would think it could.

Maybe she'd ask. What he didn't know he couldn't
tell.

"Let's work on your stuff now," she said to
Magnus.

She could see Magnus was reluctant, but Jaycie
turned the tide.

"Stories?" he asked sleepily.

"Stories," Ace agreed. "We could read them aloud.
No elves, though."

"I don't care," Jaycie said, settling down expectantly.

Even Shimene settled down after a while and
stopped prowling around, though Ace couldn't shake
the feeling there was going to be trouble soon.

A couple of hours later—Jaycie had fallen asleep
on her shoulder, and Magnus had gone back to
drumming—some of the others came in.

And to Ace's utter and complete horror, they had
strangers with them.

"No strangers" was the first rule of The Place. The
more kids who lived here, the greater the chance it
would be discovered by the authorities and they'd all
be thrown out—or turned over to Social Services.

And that meant Daddy Fairchild would have her
back, sure as taxes, even if she refused to tell them
who she was. There must be all kinds of wanted
posters of her around, even all this way back East.
And her fingerprints. He'd find her.

Ace shuddered.

The trouble was, none of these kids, wily and feral as they were, had the sense God gave a goose. Anyone they brought in might be just the bully or predator she and Magnus couldn't outface, and then the three of them would have to leave.

She glanced at Magnus, and saw he'd realized the danger as soon as she had.

"Back me up," she whispered, getting to her feet and easing Jaycie gently down onto her sleeping bag. He didn't stir.

She walked over to where the newcomers were standing. They were with Chinaka and Dakota—and Alice and Graz, two of Shimene's posse. Shimene wandered over, moving as if she were underwater. High again, Ace realized, groaning silently. This just kept getting better.

"'Kota," Ace said.

At least the girl had the grace to look guilty, if just for a moment.

"This's Eric and Kayla," Dakota said brightly.

Ace took a good look at them, and her heart sank. Eric was *old*—he must be somewhere in his twenties. No way he wasn't going to try to take over and run everything.

"We can bring people here if we want," Chinaka said aggressively, seeing Ace's expression. "This isn't your place! We were here first!"

"Yeah," Graz said. "What if we're tired of your stupid rules?"

"What if we're tired of your stupid face?" Magnus said, stepping up beside Ace. "So we leave—and take Jaycie with us." He grinned coldly at the girls. "Then you can do whatever you want. How's that?"

The other four looked at each other. They obviously hadn't expected the threat.

"Hey," Kayla began. "We don't—"

"Hey-y-y . . . 'Kota. Nice jacket," Shimene said, her words slurred. She giggled. "You go over to the All-Nite?"

Dakota shrieked and lunged for Shimene.

Ace had known there was going to be some kind of trouble between the two of them, but she hadn't been expecting this. Apparently this guy Eric had. He moved really fast, and got an arm around Dakota before she reached Shimene. Shimene backed up unsteadily and sat down hard on the floor, still giggling. Alice and Graz knelt beside her.

Dakota turned around, sobbing against Eric's shoulder.

"He okay, really," Chinaka said to Ace. "Shim beat the tab over at the All-Nite only the guy thought it was 'Kota on account of her jacket so we couldn't go in there but Kayla made it okay an' Eric bought us waffles an' everything. So it okay they stay, right?"

"No place else to go," Kayla said apologetically, shrugging, looking at Ace. She sidled over to Ace and spoke low. "He's okay, really. I kinda take care of him, y'know. He's got this flute, and he plays music on the street, but he's really hopeless. He's like, twelve or something in his head half the time." She shrugged again wordlessly.

Ace looked at Magnus. He shrugged in turn. She couldn't throw the two newcomers out, and they both knew it. They'd come close to getting thrown out themselves: threatening to take Jaycie—and the money he brought in—away with them was a trump card they couldn't afford to play very often.

"I guess you can stay," she said grudgingly, putting as good a face on things as she could.

"Cops took all their stuff," Dakota volunteered. "But maybe there's a extra blanket around or something."

"I'll make them up a place over by me," Magnus said firmly. "There's room."

Good move, Ace thought. At least that way, if the strangers tried something funny, there was a chance the two of them would spot it.

So here they were, Mad Tom and Mad Maudlin; and they fit right in with the rest of this place and its inhabitants, if Eric was any judge.

The place stank. And it was nearly as cold as outside. And with all those candles, it was a miracle it hadn't already burned down. Eric concentrated on looking vague and harmless. He hadn't expected things to turn so ugly so fast.

He'd barely moved fast enough to grab Dakota when she'd gone after the other girl, and he'd been afraid he'd blown it then, but Magnus and Ace—she was the girl he'd seen Magnus with at the supermarket—had been too worried about other things to pay much attention to him. They were obviously running a delicate balancing act here, trying to boss a bunch of runaways around without any real authority to back it up. But oddly enough, the threat to leave and take someone named Jaycie with them had made the others back down.

And it seemed the two of them were going to be allowed to stay.

With the four girls to vouch for them, they were accepted by everyone else. Everyone was curious about them, and Eric turned down several offers—he supposed they were well-meant—of drugs, cigarettes, and liquor—while meeting most of the rest of the inhabitants of The Place.

There was Tommie, who was from Kansas, and gay. He'd left home when his parents had decided he was possessed by the Devil, and decided to have the Devil beaten out of him by a local faith healer.

Ruthaileen was from Kentucky. She'd left home "after Momma died," and that was as much of her story as she'd tell.

Shimene said that her father was a famous rapper, and she'd run away from home to be with him. And as soon as she could get in touch with him, they'd be together.

Alice intended to become a famous actress as soon as she could get a screen test or an audition.

Johnnie said that here was better than home, and everyone had to be somewhere.

Chinaka said her mama wouldn't miss her anyway, with eight more kids at home, and why bother to go back? Her mama got the check from the Welfare whether Chinaka was there or not, after all.

Graz said it didn't matter, because New York was better than any other place she'd ever been, even if her no-account boyfriend had dumped her when they'd gotten here. Eric wondered how old she was, and where she'd come from; it was hard to tell beneath the heavy mask of makeup she wore.

They were all curious about the flute.

"Can you really play that?" Ruthaileen asked.

Eric nodded.

"Play something, then," Shimene said disbelievingly.

Eric hesitated, but what could it hurt? There wouldn't be any magic in it, other than the magic that was in all music. He got his flute out of his shoulder bag as the kids began to gather around.

He considered what would interest them, then dismissed the thought. A half-crazy street musician wouldn't think of such things. He decided to give them one he'd always liked instead: Vaughn Williams'

Fantasy on a Theme of Thomas Tallis, which itself was a variation on "Star of the County Down." He put the flute to his lips and began to play.

The silvery notes skirled up through the shabby empty space, transforming it, in imagination, to a vast cathedral. It wasn't the best venue, and the acoustics really sucked, but he'd played worse. Eric closed his eyes and gave himself up to the music, and his flute—gallant, played-out old warhorse that she was—did her best for him.

He stopped, and opened his eyes.

"Stupid," Shimene said dismissively, turning away. The other kids mostly looked confused—obviously this was a new experience for them—though a couple of them looked pleased.

"No," a new voice said. "The music is very fine."

Eric turned toward him. It was a dark-haired boy he hadn't met yet. The boy stood unsteadily, clutching a can of Coke in his hand and regarding Eric.

There was a *glamourie* around him. It blurred and shimmered in the air to Eric's trained mage-sight. He didn't need to pierce it to know what it concealed. He stared in horror as the Sidhe boy raised the can of Coke to his lips and drank.

Caffeine in every form was toxic to elves. It worked on them like the worst combination of alcohol and heroin, sending them first into a drunken stupor; then, after long and intense exposure, into the Dreaming—a kind of coma—and in the end, the Dreaming killed them.

With a great effort, Eric restrained himself from knocking the can out of the boy's hand. That wouldn't accomplish anything. He'd just *ken* another one. And if he couldn't *ken* it, he'd get one from one of the other kids.

But what was he *doing* here? Elves avoided New

York for a very good reason. It was full of iron, and iron burned them, as well as making their magic go crazy. The very air here was toxic to them. Even Kory, who was obsessed with all things human, couldn't stay here for more than a day or two, and that only with the help of stronger spells than Eric could see surrounding the boy.

And Eric was very much afraid he *was* a boy. Kory was two centuries old and looked about Eric's age, but Eric had the awful feeling this kid might be about the same age he looked—early teens—in which case he was *way* too young to be out of Underhill alone.

Where was his Protector? Every Sidhe child received one at his or her Naming ceremony. Even little Maeve, who was human, had one, and Lady Montraille was sworn to put Maeve's safety before the defense of her home and her own honor—and certainly before her personal safety. This boy's Protector would never have let him come here—unless he or she were dead or somehow imprisoned . . . or unless he'd been kidnapped and dumped here to die.

Who would do that to a child of the Sidhe? Elven politics were a tangled web, and the Unseleighe Court was as nasty as they came, but Elven children were precious and rare, and even the Dark Court would never intentionally harm an *Elven* child. Even the child of an enemy would be kidnapped and subverted, not hurt nor abandoned in the World Above. And the Bright Court valued *all* children, human and Elven.

Did the boy *know* what caffeine could do to him? Eric couldn't just stand there and say nothing. That would be like standing by and letting someone commit suicide. But an ordinary mortal shouldn't know that elves existed . . . let alone be able to pierce the *glamourie* one had wrapped around himself to walk in the World Above unnoticed.

"That isn't good for you, you know," Eric said softly. Maybe the boy would take his comment as the knee-jerk remark of a health freak. Or maybe he'd see the truth behind it.

The boy glanced up and met Eric's eyes.

"Speak of it, Bard, and I will speak as well," the boy said warningly. His eyes flared wolf-green.

Oh, shit . . . Eric though, his stomach sinking. *He knows exactly what he's doing to himself. He's doing it on purpose.*

"Come on, Jaycie," Ace said, taking Jaycie's arm before Eric could frame a reply. She led the boy away from Eric, back to his own corner of the room.

He knows exactly what he's doing.

Eric sat huddled under a musty quilt with Kayla curled up under his arm, watching Jaycie drink Coke after Coke as Ace read to him out of *Lord of the Rings.* Magnus was sitting with his back to them, drumming out endless patterns on a rolled-up sleeping bag with a pair of drumsticks. It sounded like falling rain.

He was good. Eric could tell. But he certainly wasn't the concert pianist the senior Banyons wanted. Magnus' musical influences were considerably more contemporary than that.

And now Eric's problems were considerably larger than they had been when he'd arrived at The Place, because he could *not* just close his eyes to the problem that Jaycie represented. He not only had to figure out the best way to talk Magnus into coming home with him, he had to figure out what to do about Jaycie.

The only consolation—and it was a small one—was that Jaycie still seemed pretty functional. Eric knew that elves could spend years addicted to caffeine before finally falling into the Dreaming. Terenil had, after all.

But Prince Terenil had been an adult Sidhe, centuries old. Jaycie was still a child. How long could *he* keep this up?

For that matter, what was he doing here? How had he gotten out of Underhill? Elven children were rare, and well-protected. Eric had spent years in Underhill and had never even *seen* a Sidhe who wasn't a full adult.

Why didn't Ace or Magnus *notice?* Not what he looked like—*glamourie* was pretty nearly instinctive for the Sidhe, and Eric didn't expect either of them to be able to see through it—but that a couple of cans of Coke got Jaycie as drunk as half a bottle of bourbon would one of them? Didn't they *care?*

But looking at the three of them together, Eric knew that they *did* care. Watching Magnus and Ace with Jaycie was like seeing himself, Beth, and Kory from the outside, and Eric wasn't entirely sure he cared for the comparison. Sidhe were *enchanting*, in every sense of the word. The other two would never abandon Jaycie—or do anything against his wishes. They'd go with him wherever he ran, and do anything to keep from being separated from him.

And Jaycie had recognized him as a Bard. He'd as good as warned Eric that if Eric made any attempt to send him back Underhill, Jaycie would make trouble. Only Eric didn't know how much Jaycie actually knew—or had guessed—beyond that simple fact. Or how much trouble Jaycie could make.

At least Eric knew who'd been blocking Ria's scrying spells now. And that the Talent he'd sensed in the supermarket wasn't Magnus'.

It was Ace's.

She shone with it. Whatever it was—and that was something he couldn't tell—she was used to using it. Magnus might have a Gift as well—in fact, as

Ria had pointed out, he probably did—but between Jaycie's *glamourie* and Ace's Gift, it was nothing Eric could sense. And he still didn't dare use magic. Jaycie would recognize it instantly. And he had no idea of what Jaycie would consider a threat.

Great. Now I'm at the mercy of a paranoid teenage Sidhe runaway.

But how paranoid were you if everyone really *was* after you?

Maybe Jaycie had fled Underhill for a very good reason.

CHAPTER NINE:

THE IRON MAN

Monday evening, Hosea invited Caity to dinner at his apartment. He hadn't seen anything of her since the previous Tuesday, and that was a little odd. Neither of them had set-in-stone nine-to-five schedules, so they usually took advantage of that to go around to movies and museums during the middle of the week when both were less crowded. Even when Caity was in the middle of a deadline, she usually liked to get away from her work for a few hours.

But Hosea hadn't seen her all week, and Caity hadn't been returning his calls. If this had been an ordinary thing—a dating relationship that one of them was tired of—Hosea would have taken the gentle hint and not kept trying to see her. But he didn't think it was. And so he'd enlisted Greystone's help to find out when she was heading down for the laundry room, and "just happened" to be going down at the same time.

She'd seemed happy to run into him, which had just been puzzling. If she'd wanted to see him, why not answer her phone messages? But he hadn't brought it up, not wanting to come on too much like the jealous boyfriend.

And it turned out she was free for dinner that very evening.

Since free-lancers lived from check to check—often with long dry spells in between—and musicians weren't necessarily all that plump in the pocket, she'd fallen in willingly with the suggestion of dinner at his place.

Promptly at 7:30, she arrived on his doorstep. Hosea had gotten in an hour before—he'd been busking the homeward bound traffic at a nearby subway stop—with just enough time to put on a pot of homemade soup that he'd started a few days before and slide a loaf of bread into the oven. Hosea was a good plain cook, and it was much cheaper to cook for yourself than to eat out.

"Smells good," Caity said, holding out a bottle of wine. "Peace offering? I finally got around to checking my phone messages. I guess you'd called," she said, flushing pinkly. "So did a lot of other people."

"We'd of run into each other eventually, Ah reckon," Hosea said easily. "Ah guess you were all tied up in a piece of work."

"Oh, I put the phone in the closet," Caity said, as if it were the most reasonable thing in the world. "It's less distracting that way."

Hosea supposed it was, and the Lord knew that artists were entitled to a few eccentricities if anyone was, but that sort of behavior hadn't been Caity's way for as long as he'd known her. And if her agent or her clients couldn't reach her . . .

"How about you come and help me set the table?" Hosea suggested, defusing the situation.

It might be underhanded, but Hosea made sure that Caity had the lion's share of the wine she'd brought over the course of dinner. She tucked into her meal with good appetite, admitting that she'd been living mostly on peanut-butter sandwiches and microwave pizza.

"I just can't remember to cook. I've been so distracted," she said, sighing.

That was the second time this evening she'd complained of distractions.

"Is something wrong?" Hosea asked gently.

"Oh, well, I don't know," Caity said hesitantly. "I mean, how could you tell, Hosea? Really?"

"Well, to start with, you might tell your troubles to a friend, and see how they sounded then," Hosea said.

Caity smiled. It wasn't a very convincing smile, unfortunately. "I've met this wonderful man," she began, twisting her napkin between her fingers.

"Not like us, Hosea. Not like that," she added quickly. "But he's good and wise, and so very, very sad. People—the world—have hurt him dreadfully, but he's never complained. Only . . . well . . . you know Tatiana . . . I was talking to her a few months ago—just after I met him—and she said that it's wrong to give people money for training or magic. But what about when you put money in the collection plate at church? That's just the same thing, though, isn't it? Or when you give money to the Salvation Army? And it's not like I'm giving anything I can't afford to give."

She looked at him hopefully, her expression begging for reassurance.

"Caity, honey, you aren't making a lick of sense," Hosea told her gently. "Why don't you start from the beginning? Who did you meet? What's this about money?"

Slowly Hosea pieced the story together, as they moved from the table to the couch and tea and cake. He didn't like what he heard.

Over the winter, at a party thrown by some friends of friends of friends, Caity had met a fascinating and mysterious man. She'd been invited to another party a week or so later, for a smaller group of people, and the man was there again.

"He was just so interesting. He never talked much, and never about himself. And he was so kind. He was so interested in me . . . in all of us. I told him things that, well, I guess I've never told anyone," Caity said.

The parties continued, soon becoming a weekly thing, and Caity realized that they were being held because of this man: Fafnir.

"He never explained anything—it wasn't like we were his disciples, exactly. But somehow we all understood things when we were around him," Caity said. "Everything just became so clear."

"Like what?" Hosea said, careful to keep his voice neutral despite the sinking feeling in the pit of his stomach.

"Oh, about our lives, and our problems. That sort of thing. He has such great power—or he did have, before his trouble happened. And he would give us advice—he could always explain things so clearly. He's so wise—I think he must have lived a very long time. He doesn't look old, of course," she added quickly.

"Because of his power?" Hosea said. Caity nodded.

"And of course we support his . . . his work," she said, a faint note of defensiveness creeping into her voice now. "It's only right, because he does what he does for all of us. That's what the Guardians do, isn't it?"

Hosea had been taking a sip of tea when she spoke. He barely managed to keep from choking. "Guardians?" he said, doing his best to sound puzzled.

Caity heaved a deep sigh. "He never said we couldn't talk about what he does—it's not like the False Guardians don't have other ways of knowing—but I'd appreciate it if you'd keep this to yourself."

"Well, Ah certainly won't go runnin' to Tatiana with it," Hosea said, hoping she'd think that was a promise. He hated to break his word—and he'd certainly think hard about doing it—but he wouldn't hesitate to break a foolish promise if the stakes were high enough.

"Thanks," Caity said with a sigh. "Anyway, Juliana owns a building down on Tenth Avenue, and he's living there now, because one of the units opened up so she gave it to him, and we meet there a couple of times a week. I'm in the Outer Circle, but Neil's in the Inner Circle, and he told me some things . . ."

What followed was muddled and vague, but more than enough to thoroughly alarm Hosea. Apparently someone calling himself Fafnir was claiming to be a Guardian—more than that, *the* True Guardian—and explaining his complete lack of overt magical abilities by the fact that some group called the False Guardians had cast a spell over him to strip him of his powers for some nefarious purposes of their own. He was being supported by Caity and her friends in some amount of style while he worked—so he said—to overthrow the False Guardians and reclaim his rightful position in the world.

It was the oldest con game there was, with some New Age trappings thrown in. But what made it particularly disturbing was that this Fafnir seemed to know at least a little about the genuine Guardians—enough to carry off a bad impersonation, at least.

"And he worries you?" Hosea suggested tentatively.

"Oh, no!" Caity said quickly. "I'm worried *for* him! The False Guardians figured he couldn't be any more trouble when they stripped him of his powers, you know . . . but he's got a plan for getting his powers back and re-founding the Guardians. And if the False Guardians knew that, I don't know *what* they'd do."

Hosea sighed inwardly. *Probably about what I'd like to do to him right now. He's no judge of character, whoever he is, and you're a lot more worried than you let on, Caity-girl. For all you know, you could be talking to one of those* False Guardians *of his right now. And then where would the lot of you be?*

"Well, don't you worry. But Ah'd like to help." That much was the honest day-long truth. "And Ah'd really like to meet this feller of yours. Do you suppose there's any chance o' that?" Hosea asked hopefully.

Caity looked doubtful, and Hosea didn't push things. He had more than enough to go to Toni with as it was. In comparison to Bloody Mary, it was small potatoes—nobody seemed to be getting really hurt, only fleeced—but it was worth talking over. With a *real* Guardian. Because at least part of what made the Guardians effective was the fact that no one—

Almost no one, he amended.

—*almost* no one knew about them.

"So you don't think there's anything wrong with what I'm doing?" Caity said. She stifled a yawn, glancing at her watch. "Goodness, look at the time! I came up here, ate all your food, talked your ear off, you must think I'm a complete fool!"

But she regarded him steadily, waiting for the answer

to her question. And there was only one answer that Hosea could, in good conscience, give.

"Caity-girl, you're a full adult, in charge of your own life. If you're doing what you want to do, if nobody's making you do it, or scaring you into it, or forcing you, or lyin' to you, and it makes you happy to do it, then it's all your own business," Hosea said, trying to conceal the reluctance in his voice. "Ah've always figgered that something that makes you happy and don't hurt you nor anyone else was a pretty reasonable thing to chase. Ain't that in the Declaration of Independence? Pursuit o' happiness?"

Her expression cleared into one of relief and she hugged him quickly. "I knew you'd understand. And I'll talk to Fafnir and see if you can meet him. He's always looking for good people to share the Work."

She left a little while later, promising to meet him for a coffee date in a few days—and to check her phone messages more frequently. But Hosea was far from settled in his mind. Tatiana was right, no matter what Caity thought. Handing over money *was* a warning sign. No responsible teacher of magic asked for payment for their teachings, nor demanded gifts.

Nor *persuaded* people to give them things without coming out and asking for money and presents.

And though she might not be frightened, and it didn't seem that she was being forced, two things were certain.

Caity was being lied to.

And she wasn't as happy as she said she was.

Eric spent the coldest and most uncomfortable night he had in years, curled on several flattened cardboard boxes beneath a couple of thin and none-too-clean blankets, with Kayla curled tight against his side.

He supposed he'd been unrealistic. He'd figured on

being able to come in here and build a relationship with Magnus, figure out some way to talk to him that didn't begin and end with Magnus running off and losing himself again.

Obviously that wasn't going to work. Magnus already had a relationship—two of them, in fact—and that left no place for Eric. The only problem was, one of the people in that relationship was a desperately ill Sidhe boy, and Eric had to get him back Underhill. Somehow.

The easiest, quickest, and most politically correct (in all senses of the word) way would be to call up Jaycie's Protector—if that could be done—and send him home with him or her. Then he could explain—try to explain—to the other two what he'd done, and why he'd had to do it. That would be a start—not the start he'd intended or hoped for, but a start.

But sending Jaycie home might have problems of its own. He didn't even know which Court Jaycie belonged to. That shouldn't matter—not if he was returning a child, presumably to a Protector and parents who must have been looking for him for some time—but he did wonder. Underhill politics was a constantly shifting web of alliances and gossip. The two Courts maintained an uneasy and far-from-friendly peace, but the person of a Bard was sacrosanct, like that of a foreign diplomat here in the World Above, and no matter who came to his call, he should be perfectly safe from attack. Dark Court or Light, he could bring Jaycie's Protector back here, hand Jaycie over, and go on to the next crisis.

And if Jaycie's Protector was dead . . . ?

Then I'll think of something else, Eric promised himself resignedly.

He stood it as long as he could—without windows, there was no light in here except the candles, but by the cheap watch he'd picked up to go with the rest of his outfit it was a little after six—and started to get up.

"Where're you going?" Ace demanded, her voice sharp and awake. Looked like she hadn't been sleeping much either.

"Out," Eric said, keeping his voice soft and vague. "Gotta play."

Kayla yawned and stretched—she hadn't gotten any better rest than he had. "He plays for the commuters in the subway," she told Ace. "I gotta go with him so nobody takes his money."

"Don't come back until after it's dark," Ace said warningly. "And don't let anybody see you."

"We won't," Kayla promised.

So they were being let to stay. That was one thing that had gone right, at least.

"We've got another problem," Eric said, when they were a few blocks away.

"Can we have another problem *later*?" Kayla pleaded. "I am going straight home into the shower, and then I am going to sleep in a real bed."

Eric hesitated. Why burden her with additional problems right now? Besides, it might be solved by this evening. "We can talk about it later," he said. "And meanwhile, we've got the whole day free before I come back here tonight."

"You mean before *we* come back here tonight," Kayla said promptly. "More fun than studying. But I'm going to need some money."

Eric looked at her quizzically.

"I'm supposed to be a pickpocket, remember? Unless you want me to go around boosting wallets this afternoon, I'm going to have to pick up some ill-gotten gains somewhere for show-and-tell tonight. So

I thought I'd hit up a couple of shops this afternoon to pick up some window dressing. And a couple of sleeping bags—I can say I went dumpster diving, or something."

"Good idea," Eric said fervently. Another night on that ratty floor and he'd start feeling his calendar age instead of his real one. "You can burgle my place. I've got a stash in the cookie jar in the kitchen. You already know the combination to my door."

"Works. And you?" Kayla said.

"Going to make an interdimensional phone call," Eric said, brandishing his flute. "See you later."

"Pick you up at your place about seven?" Kayla suggested. Eric nodded, and she waved, moving off.

Central Park was 843 acres in the heart of New York City, stretching north from Columbus Circle all the way to 110th Street—51 city blocks. It was the brainchild of Frederick Law Olmsted and Calvert Vaux who, back in 1858, when city development extended only as far north as 38th Street, decided that New Yorkers needed a "greensward." Despite all attempts to pave it over in the next century and a half, Central Park endured, with its miles of pedestrian paths, lakes, lawns, and woodlands.

There were a number of places in it where a person could be as isolated as they cared to be, particularly during rush hour on a Tuesday morning.

After about half an hour's walk, Eric found himself in an isolated grove of trees. If he shut out the city noises—and ignored the drifts of the faded paper and plastic garbage that accumulated in the months when the Park wasn't policed as often as in the spring, summer, and early fall—the place could do a pretty good imitation of a woodland glade. It was, Eric thought, the perfect place to cast his spell.

There were still more isolated places than the one he'd chosen, but those tended to be visited by serious bird watchers at odd moments—and bird watchers were uncannily good at sneaking up on you unheard. Strange to think of Central Park as a haven for birds other than starlings, sparrows, and pigeons, but it was. He'd run across the birders more than once; they policed the more remote spots for garbage and even had bird feeders set up high in the trees that they kept filled all year long.

Even if Jaycie were a Magus Major, if he was as young as he looked, he was too young to have much mastery of his magic—Elven magical training took decades, if not centuries—and the Cold Iron surrounding him here in New York would make his Sidhe magic work unreliably at best. Eric wasn't worried about being spied upon by Jaycie this far away from The Place, so Jaycie wouldn't know what he did here.

He meant to send out a Call to the nearest Protector in the World Above. Since there shouldn't be *any* Protectors in the World Above—since Protectors stayed very close to their Sidhe charges, and that meant Underhill—the one who came, if any came, should be Jaycie's. Then Eric would explain the situation, and Jaycie would go home before he could do any more damage to himself.

And if no one came . . . ?

Burn that bridge when we come to it, Eric told himself firmly. No matter why Jaycie had fled Underhill, he couldn't stay here.

But suppose you're sending him back to something really bad?

It was difficult to imagine. Protectors were bound with the strongest of oaths to put loyalty to their charges before *anything*—even the good of the Elfhame. A Sidhe Protector would die—literally—before harming their charge, or allowing them to come to harm. If Eric could summon up Jaycie's Protector, he need have no further worries about the boy's safety and well-being. If his own Elfhame was not a good place for him to be, Jaycie's Protector would simply take him somewhere else.

He raised the flute to his lips and began to play.

It was a clear morning—and therefore even colder than usual—and there was still frost on the grass under the shadows of the trees. Eric gazed at it—not really paying attention—as he filled the music with the magic of his intention.

Calling— calling— filling the notes with the image of the boy Jaycie, and the danger he was in from the World Above.

And suddenly spiderwebs of frost raced across from the frozen to the unfrozen grass, turning it all white and glittering in an instant. The trees went white as well, sparkling as if they'd been dipped in sugar.

And the day went dark. Not as if there were clouds, but as if someone had interposed a filter between Earth and the sun, leaching away the light.

Eric Banyon had faced Nightflyers, the Unsleighe Sidhe, the Wild Hunt. He'd riddled with a dragon. He'd traveled through parts of Underhill that were a close approximation of Hell.

None of it had prepared him for this.

He was surrounded by grief—drowning in it. Sheer anguish beat him to his knees. He couldn't tell if it was his own or someone else's. Pain—loss—devastating bereavement bordering on madness.

Shield!

He barely forced his shields into place—*a sloppy discordant wail of clarinets*—when whatever had come to his call changed tactics. Now he was at the center of a physical, not an emotional storm, though he could still sense the grief that lay beneath the attack.

He found himself at the center of a hurricane, but blood, not rain, was born upon the arctic wind. It glittered pinkly, freezing as it dashed itself against his shields, but Eric found time to strengthen them now—*mellow wail of horns*—and they stood firm against the assault as he staggered to his feet again.

What had come against him? What in heaven's name had he summoned? Was *this* what Jaycie was running from?

Grief—anger—terror—pain—

And he dared not risk a moment's distraction to try to communicate with it, whatever it was. Every ounce of his energy was concentrated on defense.

And he still couldn't see what he was fighting.

Then the attack changed again, the blood turning to shards of broken mirror, glittering wickedly in the dim bluish light. He could feel the pressure on his shields, and knew he had to risk an attack of his own, even though he didn't know what direction to launch it in. But anything was better than being battered to death by something he couldn't clearly see.

He ran a line of energy outside his shields—*skirl of piccolos*—and was rewarded with a sound like a string of firecrackers as the next assault struck it. His barbed-energy spell disrupted the mirror-storm, and the shards of glass fell everywhere on the bloody grass. In that instant, Eric got a glimpse of a tall figure standing off among the trees.

She wore long fluttering blue robes, and wept black tears from eyeless sockets. There was something vaguely familiar about her, but Eric didn't have time to stop to think about it. He simply threw everything he had at her.

She'd been preparing another attack as well. The

two spells collided in midair, writhing around each other like mating snakes. The flare was so bright that Eric had to cover his eyes.

When he could see again, she was gone.

Cautiously, he lowered his shields, feeling the last of his energy flow out of him like water into the ground. The battle, brief as it had been, had taken everything he had.

The tree behind where she had stood was burning. The ground around him was covered with blood, as if somebody had dropped a 55-gallon, blood-instead-of-water balloon with Eric as the target. And fragments of broken mirror were sprayed around him in a circular pattern.

But the sun was shining normally again, and his attacker seemed to be gone.

"What just happened?" Eric said aloud. With a shaky gesture, he put out the burning tree, swaying unsteadily on his feet. He felt as if he were going to fall over any moment, but he did *not* want to fall down into broken glass and yuck. Gritting his teeth, he forced himself to take careful steps until he was away from the mess, and then leaned carefully against the trunk of an undamaged tree a few yards away.

What was that? Nothing made any sense. The blood, the lamenting—that pointed to a banshee, but banshees were Low Court elves, tied to a Node Grove. Not only was there no Node Grove for fifty miles, Low Court Sidhe had nothing like the moxie of the thing he'd just faced.

But . . . *blood and mirrors.* There was one creature that description fit perfectly—and if he asked Hosea, he bet the rest of the description would fit, too.

But how had he managed to summon up the shelter kids' Bloody Mary while trying to call Jaycie's Protector?

Eric ran his hand through his hair, wincing at the grimy texture. He'd like to wash it, but he'd better just settle for a hot rinse if he was going to continue the masquerade tonight.

If Bloody Mary had come to his call, he must have tapped into the toxic imago that the shelter kids had created, Eric decided tentatively. *If it's here, and strong enough to be committing murders, and tied to kids in the first place, I guess it qualifies as a kind of Protector. I suppose I just called it up when Jaycie's real Protector didn't respond.*

It wasn't a wholly satisfying explanation, but it was the only one that fit the facts he had.

There was more than one way to skin a cat. The Earthborn had some truly enchanting turns of phrase, really they did. Sometimes Gabriel Horn wondered exactly how many ways there really *were* to skin a cat. . . .

But wondering things like that didn't get him any closer to finding Daddy's Little Angel, did they?

There was, however, one more place he could look.

Humans called it the Astral Plane. The Sidhe called it the Overlight. Neither race understood it very well; the closest the Elven Mages could come to explaining it was that the Overlight was the subtle energy that surrounded All That Was, the way the white of an egg surrounded the yolk. It was bound by fewer rules than even the Chaos Lands, and nothing of flesh could enter it. But magic could open a gateway to it from anywhere.

And there were creatures whose Mage-crafted essence was subtle enough to survive there.

The difficulty with searching the Overlight was that all places in it were everywhere and nowhere at once.

It contained no landmarks, nor could any be forged there. To search it was to search the ocean.

But it was equally true that all magic, both human and Elven, resonated in the Overlight. And that magic could be used as a beacon—did one possess the power and skill, and if the magician were unwary enough—to track its wielder wherever they hid, in Underhill or the World Above.

If one had the proper tools.

Gabriel Horn had the proper tools.

There was, indeed, more than one way to skin a cat.

Night was a time that the wasteful Earthborn used for sleeping. Gabriel used it for other things. He had spent the hours of darkness seated before his Mirror of Air, gazing into the Overlight, looking for the girl.

The flares and flickering beacons of unshielded Elven magics he dismissed at once. At the moment they did not interest him. Likewise, he set aside all investigation of shielded human workings, of humans working in groups. None of these were what he sought tonight, nor were the flares of lesser Talents. He wanted the girl.

At the back of his mind was the minor irritation that when he found her this way, he still wouldn't know where she was, nor would he be able to reach her. But in the end, that didn't matter. She would have disclosed herself, and his hunters would harry her to a place where he could See her directly.

Perhaps it was time to add a few more of them to the hunt.

Withdrawing his attention from the mirror for a moment, Gabriel gestured.

At once the room began to fill with shadows in the way that water might fill a cup. Gabriel smiled. His Shadow Hunt were not bound by the laws that bound creatures of flesh. One by one they came to him, allowing him to stroke their heads with the hand that wore the silver ring and fill them with his purpose, before they leaped through the mirror to run free in the Overlight.

Oh, the Earthborn would have bad dreams tonight.

His Shadow Hounds would search tirelessly, bound by no law. When Heavenly Grace used her Gift—and she would use it eventually, she must—they would mark the beacon and follow it to its source, some of the Hunt returning to tell him that at last his patience and diligence had been rewarded.

And his Shadow Hunt would find her, no matter what blighted, magic-dead hellhole she had fled to.

They were terrifying. She would run. They would harry her from her refuge, back to a place where he could See her directly.

But it would be far more satisfying if he were there for the View. When the last of the Shadow Hunt had slipped through his fingers and run free, Gabriel returned to his contemplation of the Mirror of Air.

He did not have much longer to indulge himself. The sun was rising. In a few hours, he would need to resume his disguise and return to his work. It, too, was rewarding, in its own small way.

But wait—there!

Not Heavenly Grace. Not the quarry he sought. But a beacon of such Power that he was tempted to set aside all thoughts of the girl to claim it.

Perhaps he should go see . . . ?

Quickly he summoned one of the Pack, and sent it to follow the beacon to its source before it vanished. With the Hound as a guideline, Gabriel summoned his elvensteed and followed after.

❖   ❖   ❖

He recognized the place immediately. The Accursed Lands. Almost he left again, but the flare of Power was too rich, too strong to ignore.

Bard.

Human Bard.

Undoubtedly a chattel of his Bright Court cousins, since no Bard bound to the Dark Court would dare to wander so, but what was he doing here? Gabriel ducked reflexively as a bolt of power lit up the sky. Fighting—in that copse of trees over there, just out of sight.

And—what a pity—so far from the protection of his lords and masters . . .

Gabriel waited.

He felt the moment that the Bard's foe vanished, and felt the Bard drop his shields. In that moment, he struck.

A simple spell, a spell of draining, of oblivion. The Bard was already tired. He could feel it. The spell was designed to dissipate the moment it was detected, but if it was not, it would go on, draining first magic, then life, from its victim.

And to make sure of his work, Gabriel cast a second spell, sweeping the area, sending out a Calling spell to those human predators who might well be nearby, calling them to come to the Bard.

And feast.

He would have liked to stay to see the results of his work, but he dared not remain. This place was too dangerous for his kind, and there was the faint possibility that the Bard might see him.

Gabriel set spurs to his elvensteed and vanished, well pleased with the morning's small entertainment.

The walk into the park that had seemed so pleasant on the way in wasn't nearly as much fun on the way out. Eric had a pounding headache, and felt as if he'd gone without sleep for three nights, not one. If he'd had the energy, he would have called Lady Day to come and get him, but the thought of even that simple Call seemed like too much effort. It wouldn't be too hard to find a cab once he reached the edge of the park; he'd go home, pop a couple of aspirin, catch a few hours' sleep, and try to figure out what to do next.

If he couldn't summon Jaycie's Protector, that meant a trip to Elfhame Misthold at the very least. Maybe someone there would be able to summon him or her—or at least, find out why that wasn't possible.

Drained, exhausted, and preoccupied, Eric forgot the first rule of New York: always pay attention.

"Gimme the flute, man. An' anything else you got."

The boy seemed to appear out of nowhere, stepping in front of Eric and grinning nastily.

Eric stopped, confronting his assailant. It was a boy about Kayla's age; a true Urban Primitive: leather jacket, tattered jeans, hair elaborately dyed and gelled. Eric realized with a sinking feeling that he must have wandered into gang territory without noticing—or worse, made himself the target for one of the wilding packs that roamed the park. He could feel and hear others coming up behind him, and saw the boy's smile widen as his friends moved into position. Eric realized he'd missed his one chance to run, but his brain seemed filled with grey fog, and he was so *tired*. . . .

But he dropped the flute instantly, raising his hands and summoning the energy for a spell.

He never got the chance to complete it.

Something hard hit him on the back of the head, knocking him sprawling. He bit his lip, tasting blood, and the world seemed very far away.

He reached out to his magic, only to be hit again before the spell could be fully formed. He felt his magic spin away, out of control, as someone kicked him in the head.

The boys moved in, laughing, continuing to kick and bludgeon him until he stopped moving. And long after.

Around noon, Kayla got up again and riffled Eric's cookie jar, then went off to find the things she needed for her pickpocket masquerade. Unless you were hooked up with a good fence, or were really stupid, the smart thing to do when you boosted a wallet was to toss the credit cards and ID, so she wouldn't come back with any of those. But if she'd grabbed a few purses . . . back when she'd been living on the street in L.A., Connie used to come back with the most amazing junk. Half-used makeup, and all kinds of crap. She could donate some of her own stuff to the cause, and maybe pick up a few donations from Tat and Margot, add a purse from an upscale consignment shop and a backpack from a Goodwill store, and she'd be all set for tonight.

Collecting the items she wanted took most of the afternoon, and then Kayla headed down to Jacob Riis, where Hosea was working. If anybody from The Place saw her, it'd be reasonable for her to be there, and she wanted to check in with Hosea anyway.

She arrived about the time Hosea was finishing up in the kitchen. Kayla drifted in and hung around, but she didn't spot anyone else she knew. Hosea spotted her, though, and his face was what you might call a proper study.

"You look like something the cat wouldn't drag in," he said, coming over to her. Kayla grinned at him.

"Well, I got good news, Too-Tall. We've found him."

"You've found the boy?" Hosea said, keeping his voice low.

"Yup. Alive and well. I'll tell you about it later. But first—Eric and me need something to sleep on for tonight. You got anything like that down here?"

"Think so. Hang on."

Hosea went into the back, and returned a few moments later with a couple of tatterdemalion bundles that might—once—have been sleeping bags.

"We collect 'em—through donations and all—to hand around when we can. You can bring 'em back when you're done. Or replace 'em."

"Thanks," Kayla said gloomily, tucking one of them under her arm and slinging the other over her shoulder. "These look like the real deal."

"As real as it gets, Little Bit," Hosea assured her soberly.

On the way home, Kayla filled Hosea in on finding Magnus and Ace.

"Ace? Little blonde girl, no bigger'n a minute, big blue eyes and plenty of sass?" Hosea asked, startled.

Kayla nodded.

"Ah think she's the same one that came to the shelter a day or two ago. Scared to death and wild as the wind."

"That's her, I guess," Kayla said. "She and Magnus and this other kid Jaycie are real tight. He's kind of a zone puppy, but sweet."

They'd taken the subway uptown. It was still early rush hour, and seats were available, but between Jeanette and the sleeping bags, it was easier just to stand at the back of the car as it rocked its way north.

"She tell you anything about herself?" Hosea asked.

"Hey, Too-Tall, we were doing good not to get

thrown back out on the street again. It wasn't exactly all love and kisses up there. But she said it's okay if we come back tonight. I'm going to meet Eric here at seven and we'll go up there together. He's supposed to have spent the day busking, and I've spent it snatching purses and picking pockets," Kayla said cheerfully.

"Enterprising of you," Hosea commented dryly. "Ah'm sure Miz Llewellyn'll be right proud to hear it."

"Ria's cool," Kayla said comprehensively. "And it's not like I'm whack enough to really do it. But Eric said we've got another problem that he'd tell me about when he got back, and I don't think I want to know. It was bad enough when we just had to explain to this kid that he had a brother who was willing to get him off the streets and protect him from the Evil Clan Banyon, but somehow, I don't think Mags is going to dump his two buddies."

"He shouldn't have to," Hosea said. "But Ah've talked to Ace, remember? She won't go home nohow—and she's got the shine on her, so she might have good reason not to want to go."

"And it's not like people just let you adopt strange teenagers off the street," Kayla said. "Elizabet had to jump through hoops to get her hands on me. So I guess we've got a whole new set of problems. Here we are."

They reached their stop and got out. It was already dark, and they walked the rest of the way to Guardian House in companionable silence, where, by unspoken consent, they went up to Hosea's apartment.

While Hosea lit the stove and put on hot water, Kayla pulled out her phone and left a message for Eric, telling him where she could be found. Then she followed Hosea into the kitchen, poking through his cabinets.

"Tea, tea, and tea. Not even any Lipton's. Don't you ever drink coffee?"

"Ah'm afraid it'll stunt my growth," Hosea said with a straight face. "And you need all the inches you can get, Little Bit."

"Size elitist," Kayla muttered with a grin. She looked into Hosea's refrigerator and shuddered. "Let's order pizza."

Hosea grinned. "Well, okay. If you want to pay for it—the life o' crime bein' so profitable and all."

"There's gotta be something we can do," Kayla said, after three large pies had been ordered. "About those kids, I mean."

"The thing is," Hosea said, pouring tea for himself and instant cocoa for Kayla, "it's hard to keep kids out of the hands of families that want them back, once they know where they are. And most of 'em—like Miz Ace—would rather be on the street than back with their folks." He shook his head. "The halfway houses are full and have waiting lists, the foster-care program is a mess—and it don't apply in most cases—and the social services don't have a lot o' money. So the kids are out on the streets fending for themselves, and Serafina says that the average life expectancy of one of those street kids is about three months, and mostly nobody ever knows what happens to any of them."

"That sucks," Kayla said.

"There's some private programs that will take kids in off the streets, no questions asked, but the thing is, the kids have got to want to come in off the street and stay in the program freely: they're not jails. That means following the rules." He blinked at her, like a curious owl. She read the unspoken question.

"I don't think that would be a problem with Magnus and Ace, but Jaycie—" she shook her head. "Don't know. He's zoned all the time, but I can't tell if it's because he's a stoner or sick." She thought about it. "But you know, he pretty much does what Ace says, and if Ace says 'we go in,' I bet he will, and follow the rules, too."

Hosea nodded. "Thing is, it costs money to get in and stay in, which Ah know ain't a problem because Eric would be more'n ready to write a check, and if he couldn't, Miz Llewellyn would surely do it, as she's a mighty kind lady always willing to help folks in need."

"She'd kill you if she heard you say that, you know," Kayla commented.

"It's the plain truth," Hosea said placidly. "It just don't sound to me like any of these kids are ready to do that. But Ah'll give you the name and address of the place that'll take them in, no questions asked."

"And send the bill to Eric," Kayla said.

"And kick them back out on the street the minute they catch them with drugs, or doing any other bad thing," Hosea said. "Which is why they've always got room."

The pizzas came. Seven o'clock passed, then eight, and Eric didn't show. Finally, at eight-thirty, Kayla got to her feet.

"Damn Robin Hood Banyon anyway. I bet he decided to pull a fast one on me and go back up there alone. Look, I'm going. If he does show up, tell him I went on ahead and to catch up with me there, okay?"

Hosea didn't look happy about the idea. "Ah'm not sure you oughtta be going up there by your lonesome, Little Bit."

"But I'm not going to be alone. I'll be there with all my new friends." *Thieves, prostitutes, drunks, drug addicts, and not one of them within a stone's throw of their eighteenth birthday. . . ."* And I will be incredibly careful. Look, it was hard for us to get in. I can't just throw that away. They'll talk to me. Eric just scares them; we're talking 'The Lost Boys' here; he's too old for any of them to really trust him. If I don't go back now, all that work'll be for nothing. And look. I'll even take my phone with me. I'll call you first thing in the morning. You'll know right where I am. If you don't hear from me, you can call the police, okay? You can call *Ria*. Honest. Besides, Eric's probably already there, so I've *got* to go!"

"Are you sure?" Hosea said, regarding her sternly.

"Hey, this is me, remember? Been to Underhill three times and survived. Not to mention the streets of L.A. I'll be fine." Kayla said, moving toward the door.

Hosea sighed. "Ah surely oughtn't let you do this."

"Look. The least I can do is keep an eye on Brainless Banyon's baby brother for him, right? And Toni's still got her contacts in the PD, right?"

Hosea nodded. "She keeps up with a few of Jimmie's old friends."

"Then if something goes really bad, I'll make sure I get us all arrested and you make sure Toni's friends let you know. And you come down and bail the four of us out. Say you're Ace's brother, or something—you look enough like her for that to pass. And Magnus is her stepbrother. Figure it out."

"Well, Ah'm glad to see you've got a plan," Hosea said dourly.

Kayla blew him a kiss and slipped out the door quickly before he could come up with any more objections.

She'd shown him far more assurance than she felt. If anyone knew how dangerous the city streets could be, it was Kayla. But she had to go back, Eric or not—and what the hell was keeping him, anyway?

She walked over to the A and took it a couple of stops uptown. Even in so short a distance, the neighborhood changed drastically, but New York was a city in which even the same neighborhood took on a different aspect with each hour of the day. She pulled down her cap, and did her best to look as inconspicuous as possible, slouching along as if she belonged here.

Her Gift helped. Even with her shields up, she could tell what people were feeling, just skimming the surface of their emotions. Mostly she could sense if they were paying attention to her or not. Not paying attention was good.

But it was tiring, and she felt very much as if she *had* spent a whole day out on the streets by the time she walked across the park and reached the fetid alleyway that led to The Place. Making sure no one was looking, she slipped in through the back, over to the window.

It was dark.

"This way," a voice from the shadows said.

Kayla suppressed a yelp, recognizing the voice at the last minute. It was Jaycie, Magnus' friend.

"Up here," he said.

Kayla located the window mostly by touch. Why hadn't she thought to bring a flashlight? Although showing a light back here was probably high on the list of Missy Ace's dos and don'ts, come to think of it. She clambered through the window with Jaycie's help.

Once she was inside, and her eyes had adjusted to the dark, she could see the faint glow of light far above. "Come on," he said, taking her hand and beginning to climb the stairs.

❖   ❖   ❖

The Bard was gone, and that was good. When he had left this morning, Jachiel had wished very, very hard that he would go away and not come back. And he hadn't come back. He didn't mind the Bard's friend. She couldn't see him for what he was. She would make no trouble, so Jachiel didn't care whether she stayed or not.

But he really hoped the Bard would never come back.

When she got upstairs, Kayla immediately looked around for Eric. She didn't see him, and her spirits sank. Ace and Magnus were sitting together hunched over a book in front of a battery-powered camping lantern. Jaycie dropped her hand and wandered back to the two of them, leaving Kayla to fend for herself.

She went back to the patch of floor where she'd spent the night, dropping her sleeping bag and backpack. She went and stood over Ace, who looked up.

Showtime, Kayla thought to herself.

"Am I supposed to give you the cut?" Kayla asked.

Ace didn't say anything, just stared at her, hard-faced.

"Every other place we stayed, somebody took a cut. So I want to know, is it you?" Kayla repeated.

Magnus snickered, looking a lot like a Baby Eric. Ace shook her head.

"You don't have to pay anybody to stay here, only I'd appreciate it if you didn't tell anybody else about us," Ace said. "Because if too many people know, the police'll come in, you know?"

"That's fair," Kayla said. "Look, Eric and me, we didn't mean to make any trouble last night."

"Not your fault," Ace said. She looked around. "Do you know if he's coming back?"

"I thought he was already here," Kayla said. "I went off to, you know, do some stuff. And when I came back, he was gone."

She saw Ace looking at the pocketbook slung over her shoulder. You didn't need to be an Empath to catch the wave of distaste that radiated from the younger girl, though Ace kept her face carefully expressionless.

"Another thing," Ace said. "If you want, I can go to the store and buy things for you, if you don't happen to want to go. Just legal things, though. And you've got to give me the money before I go out."

That must have been what Ace had been doing when she and Eric had seen her in the supermarket, Kayla realized. Shopping for the other kids. But it seemed sort of odd that this bunch of kids would voluntarily hand over their money to her that way.

Kayla shrugged, saying nothing, and went to spread out her sleeping bag.

Since none of the other three seemed particularly inclined to chat—Ace and Magnus seemed to be *studying*, of all things, and Jaycie was watching them, drinking a Coke—she made the rounds of the other kids, trading her supposedly ill-gotten gains for useful items like a toothbrush, some hand sanitizer, candles and matches, magazines, and candy. Her barters and outright purchasing done, she went back to her own corner near Magnus and Ace, to read through her new magazines (or pretend to) and wonder where the *hell* Banyon—the other Banyon—was.

It wasn't like Eric to disappear even at ordinary times—and twice as much not now that they'd finally found Magnus.

She'd checked her phone and e-mail before she'd

left, and there hadn't been any messages on either one, other than one from Ria, saying she was going to be down in Washington for a week or so. Nothing from Eric. Nothing that would explain why he wasn't here now. She wished she'd been paying more attention this morning. But all she'd been thinking about was getting home. What the hell had he been saying about where he was going? To make a phone call?

No. To make an *interdimensional* phone call.

That could have a number of interpretations, but considering Eric, the simplest was that he'd had to go Underhill for some reason. Kayla relaxed a little. Time ran funny Underhill. You could stay there for hours, and come back to find out only minutes had passed—or just the reverse. Yeah, she'd found out about that the hard way, going in for a couple of months of tutoring at the deft hands of one of the Elven Healers of Misthold—because she figured she'd better learn how elves were put together in case she ever found one in pieces—and came out to find that it wasn't months she'd spent in there, it was years, and it wasn't a couple, it was lots. Thank God Elizabet had known where she was the whole time, and had definitely approved. Otherwise Elizabet would have been seriously pissed, and a pissed-off Healer had nasty ways of making disapproval felt.

Kayla felt a sudden wave of relief. Eric had probably just gotten turned around coming back to the World Above, or had to stay a little longer than he'd expected to. So she was doing the right thing by being here. Maybe she could even get the other three to like her a little while he was gone.

Man, he must have really tied one on the other night. Eric couldn't remember the details, but he knew it had to have been a great party, because how could he have gotten this thoroughly wasted at a mediocre party?

Well, Faire folk knew how to party. And he was sure the details would come back to him eventually.

It was morning, and the ragged noisy cheer of the SoCal Faire penetrated the sides of the shabby blue tent that had been his constant companion on the Faire circuit for longer than he could remember. You could tell the time by the noise level: the louder the sounds of desperation, the closer it was to nine, when the Faire opened. Judging from what he was hearing, it must be almost that now. Eric rolled over, groping for his flute. His hand encountered a bottle, half full. He shook it, holding it up to the light and squinting at it through bleary eyes.

Bushmill's. Cure everything from a broken leg to a broken heart. Unscrewing the cap, he tilted the bottle back and drank, feeling its warmth lace through him, banishing the cobwebs. *Ah, that's better.* He rolled out of his blankets and crawled out of the tent, dragging on his shirt and groping for his belt.

Pain lanced through his head as he stood, and everything hurt—he must have fallen off Main Stage yesterday, or something—and he crawled back into his tent to find the Bushmill's to speed the healing process. Couldn't take the bottle into the Faire, though, so he took a moment to fill his belt flask, being careful not to spill a single drop. That should see him through the day. That and half a bottle of aspirin.

What *had* he been doing last night?

Whatever it was, I hope it was fun.

The sudden wild howl of bagpipes ripped through his nervous system like a combination of acid and icewater. Eric moaned, and swung around to see Seamus, one of the Wild Northern Celts, tuning up his instrument—if a bagpipe could ever be said to be properly in tune—grinning like a red-headed fiend around the mouthpiece.

"Here, Banyon. You look like you could use this."

Karen Wolfsdottir—one of the German Mercenary Wenches—strolled over and thrust a wooden tankard into his hand. It was warm and steam rose from it. Eric sniffed. Coffee.

"If you finish getting dressed, you can join the parade onto the site. Not that I mind what you're wearing now," Karen said, leering at him appreciatively.

Eric took a swig of the coffee. Hot caffeine joined the Bushmill's in his system, bringing him further awake. He looked down at his bare knees and blushed. He guessed he'd been more ripped than he'd thought. He was just lucky he'd put on his shirt before showing himself to the world—though the Elizabethan smock that was the basis of his Faire costume covered him to mid-thigh, he didn't feel all that covered, particularly with the way Karen was looking at him.

She'd been chasing him all season—Eric remembered now—and while normally he didn't go for the barbarian weightlifter type, he was thinking it might not be altogether bad to let himself get caught. Particularly if morning coffee went with it.

"Sure and it'd be a hard thing t'be explaining to the travelers," Eric said in his best Faire brogue, finishing the coffee in a few burning gulps and passing the wooden tankard back to her. "So if you'll let me go make meself respectable, me fine lady, it'd be happy I'll be to escort such a delicate flower of chivalry as your fine self into the Faire."

Karen shouted with laughter and said something in a language Eric didn't know. In Mundania, she majored in Old English at UCLA, he remembered, and could swear in at least five dead languages. "Hurry back," she said, punching him—gently for Karen—in the shoulder.

Feeling much less like death now, Eric crawled back into his tent and dug through his things until he unearthed his boots and breeches. Quickly dragging a comb through his shoulder-length chestnut hair, he added a "pancake" hat in brown velvet with a long trailing peacock feather and appeared again, buckling his belt with the now-full flask around his waist, and hitching his gig bag over his shoulder: the perfect Elizabethan strolling player.

"Come on," Karen said. "I saved you a place."

Most of the folk were already on site—security and vendors had to be in their places before the doors opened, of course, but a lot of the players liked to go in together and, well, any excuse for a parade. . . .

Seamus and Donal were at the front, and at Seamus' signal, they both began to play, the howl of the pipes sounding like eleven cats in a bad mood, and the little column began to move forward: wenches, jugglers, mercenaries and strolling players of all kinds. Eric recognized a lot of familiar faces—there was Ian with his bodhran, and Linda beside him, dulcimer case slung over her shoulder as she piped away wildly on a pennywhistle; Ranulph the Melancholy Dane; Mistress Althea; a gaggle of Irish step-dancers, laughing as they tried to keep up with the procession and make last-minute adjustments to their ribbons at the same time. . . .

They passed through the Faire gates, going in among the big trees. The morning sun made slanting bars of golden light. All around him Eric saw the booths and signs of the place he'd spent so many happy hours. The last few moments before the travelers entered for the day was an enchanted time—not that Eric saw it all that often, if the truth be told—and if he had to choose a moment when the Faire was at its prettiest, he'd have to say it was now, with everything renewed, reborn . . . *magic*.

And he realized that he was home.

CHAPTER TEN:

O'MAHONEY'S FROLICS

It was a special Wednesday evening meeting of the Inner Circle—Fafnir had the smaller group meeting several times a week now, usually after the Outer Circle met, but tonight, he had told them, was to be special, for them alone.

He had provided them a new revelation last week: an audience with the Master Guardian who lived on the Esoteric Plane, from whom the Guardian Power flowed. It didn't matter that none of them had actually *seen* the image in the crystal or heard the Master Guardian's voice; by now they were all convinced they had.

Eventually, he would hint them around to understanding that the Master Guardian had actively blessed the plan to kill the False Guardians, but that there was no need to worry, that it wasn't murder, since the False Guardians weren't human any more, if they ever had been. In fact, to further soothe their fears, Fafnir would tell them that the False Guardians wouldn't even bleed if you cut them, but simply vanish in a puff of dust like the vampires on *Buffy*, so nobody would have to worry about getting in trouble with the police.

Who knew? It might even be true for all he knew. And once they'd helped him kill Paul Kern, Fafnir didn't really care what happened to any of them anyway.

But he needed to get them to do what he wanted first. Which meant he had to completely convince them not only that the False Guardians were real—and they were fairly convinced of that already—but that the False Guardians were after all of them now, and with deadly intent.

Which required a little assistance.

He glanced over to where Amanda was sitting on her mother's lap. Such a pretty child. Fafnir's interests in her lay in quite another direction than her physical charms. However, Sarah told him that Amanda did modeling work, which was good. It meant she was already used to doing things she didn't like, and following orders.

He'd discovered that the child was a natural psychic quite by accident. The day the Eye of the Inner Planes had first been delivered, Sarah'd had the girl with her. Amanda had stared into the shining ball, fascinated, and Fafnir could actually *feel* the power rising off her skin.

He'd distracted her at once—no telling *what* she

might say if she went all the way into a trance—but he'd started working on Sarah immediately, telling her how fortunate she was to have such a powerful medium in her daughter, and saying how unfortunate it was that most young psychics burned out early because of their inability to properly ground and shield, or lost their powers because no one knew how to train them. It hadn't been long before Sarah was bringing little Amanda to him for lessons.

But the only lesson Fafnir was interested in teaching Amanda was how to go immediately into trance, where her powers would be entirely subject to his control. Once he had that—it hadn't been difficult— he'd started using Amanda as a channel to mold an Artificial Elemental, using her energy, and Sarah's, and his own, to give his own imagination form and life. He'd read about things like that in books, and the directions seemed simple enough to follow. He'd been working privately with Sarah and Amanda for several weeks now.

He'd been very careful. The last thing he wanted to do was hurt Amanda. He just wanted to use her.

And now that he'd laid the groundwork, the Inner Circle could add more energy, feeding his creation, making it grow until it was strong enough for him to take control of directly.

He'd been a little surprised at first to find that this magic stuff actually worked and was so easy, but then, once he'd thought about it, he'd realized there was no reason why it shouldn't be easy. These Guardian guys existed, after all, and some, or maybe even most, of what they did was handwaving and persuasion, just as it had been in Andrew's case. And as far as Fafnir could tell from his reading, magic was just another kind of software. You followed the directions, and if you'd done everything right, and hadn't skipped a step, and the hardware was working right that day, you got results.

The last of the Inner Circle arrived, and Fafnir locked the door behind them. He waited until they had all settled and taken their places, then motioned to Sarah to bring Amanda into the middle of the circle, where the Eye usually rested.

"Last week you heard the words of the Master, of how it will soon be time to bring our battle to the Ancient Enemy. But before we do, it is only right that we protect ourselves against what they may try to do to us. And so, with your aid, I will attempt to summon one of my allies of old: a Protector. But I will need all your help in this."

But they weren't going to summon up an ancient ally. They were going to create something entirely new—their energy, his direction, and little Amanda as the focus and gateway. And then, instead of the protection they thought they'd created, Fafnir would have at his command an elemental assassin answerable only to him. And when his disciples found themselves savagely attacked by paranormal forces—sent, or so he'd tell them, by the False Guardians—well, then he'd have all the cooperation from them he needed, wouldn't he? They'd be convinced that not only what he'd told them was the truth, but that the False Guardians, having discovered that Fafnir had people helping him, were going to ruthlessly and coldly eliminate those people.

And since, without knowing it, they would all have helped create the monster he'd use to stalk them, any little private defenses they might have would be absolutely useless . . . .

"What must we do?" Luke asked.

Fafnir favored them all with his most benign expression, one he'd practiced for hours in front of a mirror.

"All of you know Amanda, Sarah's daughter. She has been sent to us in our hour of gravest need. She is a natural gateway to the Ethereal Realm. When I have sent her into trance, she will be able to carry our call to the Ethereal Plane, and then—I may only hope—the Protector will hear. If it hears, and comes, it will be able to offer us some small protection, for I fear that the False Guardians are very near to learning what we have done and what we plan to do."

He waited, knowing they had to sell themselves on the idea before he went any further. That was the most important part of any con job: never rush the mark. He knew he had them all hooked already, though. Six months ago half of them would have just gotten up and walked out. Now they were all looking expectant, as if he'd offered the lot of them free unlimited high-speed Internet access. After a few moments, each of them hesitantly voiced their agreement.

"You want to help Master Fafnir, don't you, sweetie?" Sarah said to Amanda. "Come on," she said coaxingly.

Amanda hid her face against her mother's shoulder.

"She is shy among so many," Fafnir said, hoping that the kid would for God's sake not make an ugly scene that he'd have to think up some way to explain away. He took his pendulum out of his pocket.

The weight at the end was a faceted sphere of leaded crystal. It sparkled in the candlelight. "Amanda," he said in his most commanding voice. "Look at the dancing light."

Reluctantly, Amanda did.

She didn't want to be here, but she was a good girl, and Mommy said they had to come, and that Master Fafnir was a nice man. But she didn't like him, and

she didn't like looking at the dancing light. She didn't
want to look at the dancing light, but she had to look at
the dancing light, because Mommy said to, and Master
Fafnir said to. Only when she did, everything went
away, and she couldn't make it come back no matter
how hard she tried until they let her, and she hated
that. She couldn't cry, she couldn't move, and Mommy
wouldn't understand why it was so bad.

Please don't! Amanda cried inside, where nobody
could hear her. *Please make it stop!*

But no one listened.

Kayla actually managed to get a few hours' sleep
that night, for a miracle, curled up inside a worn-out
sleeping bag in a Neverland gone horribly wrong. She'd
watched both Magnus and Ace turn down opportunities to go out on "dates," and watched Jaycie eat an
entire bar of baker's chocolate without throwing up,
so she couldn't say she hadn't gotten some entertainment out of the deal. But Eric not showing up had
been a definite bummer.

She watched the three of them, taking mental
notes. Even if she hadn't known that Magnus was
Eric's brother and that Ace was a Talent, she'd have
known there was something not right about the three
of them. Something off, in a different way from the
way the other feral kids weren't normal.

Take the fact that the three of them didn't talk
about themselves, even to each other. The other kids
did, and even if it was mostly all lies, it was still talking. Those three acted like they knew the FBI was
after them, and weren't giving up the tiniest speck
of information, even false information.

Was it the Feds who were after Jaycie and Ace? It
wasn't impossible; she'd been on the receiving end of
one lot of black-project jerks, Eric and Kory and Beth

had been tangled up with two more, and then there was Robert Lintel and Threshold, which had been yet another black-ops thing Ria'd inadvertently financed and abetted, until she found out what was going on. Kayla and Eric knew who was after Magnus, so there was every reason for him to be paranoid, but who was after Ace and Jaycie? More than just parents?

Maybe the three of them would go for that "no questions asked" place of Hosea's after all. The only problem was, someone had to be around to sign the check to get them in, and that meant either Ria or Eric. And right now, Kayla couldn't get ahold of either one.

Around seven A.M.—about the time The Place started to settle down—Kayla slipped out and left. Eric had never showed up. She couldn't shake the feeling that something had gone wrong, very wrong, but she didn't know what.

Lady Day was parked in front of Guardian House when Kayla got there.

"Hey," Kayla said, greeting the elvensteed. "Guess that means Eric's back, huh?"

The 'steed flashed her lights and revved her engine.

"Hey, cut that out," Kayla said, glancing around to see if anyone was on the street. "Somebody's going to notice. And aren't you supposed to be in the back? This is a no parking zone. You want to explain to Eric why you've been towed?"

Although the elvensteed would just Gate out of the impoundment and come right back, Kayla knew. Which would create problems of its own . . .

She started to walk past the bike, but Lady Day moved forward, cutting her off and revving her motor . . . anxiously? Could a bike be anxious? Although

Lady Day wasn't really a motorcycle; she was an elvensteed, a living thing.

"Hey!" Kayla said, jumping back. "Stop that."

She tried walking around the back of the bike. Lady Day backed up, cutting her off again. Kayla swore. "I wish you could talk."

But elvensteeds couldn't talk, not in any of their forms. The most they could do was share emotions through a psychic link with their riders. Which meant with Eric, not Kayla.

"Is there something going on inside you don't want me walking into?" Kayla asked. *Playing Twenty Questions with a Harley clone. I gotta be losing it.*

Lady Day flashed her lights several times and rocked back and forth.

"Is that a yes or a no?" Kayla demanded, frustrated.

"What's going on?" Hosea asked, walking down the front steps of the building with his banjo slung over his shoulder. Then: "What's she doin' out front?"

"I don't suppose Eric came home last night?" Kayla said hopefully.

Hosea shook his head. "And by the look of things, his lady friend here's pretty upset about it."

Lady Day flashed her lights and growled, a deep thrum of engine.

"Just like Lassie," Kayla muttered.

"Do you want us to go somewhere with you, girl?" Hosea asked.

"Took us long enough to figure it out," Kayla shouted into Hosea's ear a few minutes later.

The two of them were sitting on Lady Day's saddle—Hosea holding Jeanette in his arms—as the elvensteed roared across town. Kayla hoped the elvensteed's elvish cloaking device was in full effect, because otherwise they were just begging for half a dozen traffic tickets.

Hosea said something she couldn't hear.

Lady Day reached Central Park, and promptly took off into the park along one of the pedestrian paths, proceeding in a sudden ghostly silence as she stopped making motor noises—which were, for an elvensteed, strictly optional anyway. Kayla guessed that nobody *could* see them, because riding even a bicycle through some of these areas was forbidden, let alone a motorcycle.

Eventually they reached a clearing near the top of the park, and the elvensteed stopped. When they got off, she began racing around in circles again until Hosea sternly told her to stop. She crept off beneath a tree and stood there, looking about as pathetic as a motorcycle—or an elvensteed impersonating a motorcycle—could look.

Kayla and Hosea looked at each other.

"You're the one with the magic banjo," Kayla pointed out. "Do something magical."

Hosea set down his case, opened it, and took Jeanette out, slinging her strap over his shoulder. "Any suggestions?" he asked.

"Well, if Eric was here, he isn't here now. Can you see if he *was* here, maybe?" Kayla asked.

Hosea slung the strap over his shoulder, slipped his picks over his fingers, and carefully began to tune Jeanette.

This looked like a perfectly ordinary—if deserted—stretch of the park, the sort of place he liked to come himself. If not for the fact that Eric hadn't been seen since yesterday morning—and the fact that his 'steed was fretting so about it—Hosea wouldn't give the place a second look. But even a suspicious inspection didn't turn up much of anything. Trees. Grass. Broken bottle glass and discarded trash.

It's up to you and me, sweetheart.

Hosea began to play.

"Mama Tried"—he'd always liked that one. Beneath the music he could feel Jeanette stirring unwillingly, looking around.

:I hate that song,: she grumbled. Then: *:Not dead. And not here,:* she reported brusquely.

"Was he here?" Hosea asked, still playing. He swung into "Banish Misfortune"—that was one of Eric's favorites.

Confusion and irritation from Jeanette as she looked again. Hosea caught blurred symbol images of Kayla and Lady Day from her mind—both of them were easy for her to See because of their innate Power—then a distortion as Jeanette looked in a direction he couldn't follow.

:He was here. He stopped being here. It's all very confused, Hosea. It was a long time ago.: Jeanette's mental voice was a mix of irritated and plaintive.

Hosea brought the song to a close, sighing. The dead weren't bound by time the way the living were, and Jeanette was dead in every way that mattered. But they also tended to get just a little confused by time, and be a good deal better at looking into the past than the future. Either Eric really had been here a long time ago—and Lady Day didn't seem to think so—or something had been here since to muddle the traces Jeanette could pick up.

"He was here, but he isn't now. And we don't know what happened to him," Hosea said grimly.

"He said he was going Underhill," Kayla offered. "When he left yesterday."

"Well, that would make sense," Hosea said after a moment's thought. "Jeanette says he was here a long time ago, and that ain't right. But elves and ghosts don't quite seem to get along any too well, magically." If Eric had opened a Portal to Underhill here, the magic would dirty up the traces of his presence enough to confuse Jeanette's ghostly senses thoroughly.

Lady Day rolled over to them and flashed her lights silently several times. Kayla patted her on the gas tank. "I wonder why he didn't take his ride? That'd be fastest."

"Maybe the trip wasn't all his idea. You got any idea of how to get in touch with the Good Folks?" Hosea asked.

"Well," Kayla said slowly, "I know Eric e-mails Beth and Kory a lot. But I don't know how often they check their mail, and I know he says the Underhill servers run kinda funny sometimes. So if I e-mail them, I don't know how long it'll be before I get an answer."

"And Ah'd hate to worry someone if there wasn't any good reason," Hosea said slowly. "But maybe you'd better get in touch with them. Can't imagine why Lady Day'd be so twitchy if he'd just gone Underhill." He glanced at his watch. "Ah'd better get a move on to get to work. Why don't the two of you go on home and see what you can turn up there?"

Kayla turned back to the bike. "Does that work for you?" she asked.

Lady Day flashed her lights once, rocking back and forth unhappily.

"Look, we know he's in some kind of trouble now," Kayla told the elvensteed, "but until we can find him, there's not much we can do about it, is there? But we'll keep looking for him."

Lady Day sounded her horn in a long mournful *beep.*

❖   ❖   ❖

Back at Eric's apartment, Kayla checked the phone—no new messages from anybody—and then switched on Eric's computer. Instead of sitting down, she wandered around aimlessly, picking things up and setting them down again.

It was funny how different a place looked when you knew its occupant wasn't coming home any time soon.

Dammit, Banyon. You picked a great time to go missing.

The only consolation was that she knew Eric could take care of himself if anyone could. He didn't have the brains God gave a carrot—at least in Kayla's opinion—but he always landed on his feet.

She sat down at the computer and opened Eric's address book, scrolling through it until she found Beth's Underhill address. She clicked on it, opening a new letter.

And stared at it. What could she say that wouldn't have Beth and Kory on Eric's doorstep as fast as their 'steeds could bring them here? Like *that'd* be any help.

But he *had* to be in Underhill. He'd said he was going there . . . hadn't he? Or as good as.

But if he'd gone to Underhill, he'd have taken his elvensteed.

Unless he'd been *kidnapped* to Underhill.

But then Lady Day would have just followed him to Underhill—would have taken her and Hosea along with her without so much as a by-your-leave, probably.

But she hadn't.

She'd taken them up to the Park. Where there hadn't been anything. Where Jeanette had said Eric *had* been, and wasn't now.

And that didn't make any sense either. Because
Eric wouldn't just go wandering off. Not when he
was trying to figure out how to get Magnus to come
home with him.

Reluctantly, Kayla closed the e-mail client, her message unsent. Maybe she'd try a couple of other things
before she scared Kory and Beth half to death.

*I wonder how I find out if somebody's been arrested?
No time like the present, Girl Detective.*

If Toni was home, she'd know.

Hosea had several stops to make that day—no
matter what else was going on in his life, he still had
to cover rent and groceries, and that meant meeting
his obligations.

But there was no reason why he couldn't earn the
rent at the same time. . . .

Now that he knew what to listen for, he was getting more of the Secret Stories, tiny fragment by tiny
fragment. Today, from the girls, it was more about
the Blue Lady; how she not only protected children
from the demons, but from the humans that demons
had gotten to. Physical protection, that meant—which
sure fit in with those murders he and the Guardians
were looking into. But you had to be a Special One to
call her in that way, and you had to be in the worst
fear and pain of your life, because she didn't come
for little things, and when she did come, there had
better be something there for her to protect against,
or she turned back into Bloody Mary.

Kind of like calling on Elbereth Gilthoniel, except
that she'd turn into Shelob if you called her for no
good and urgent reason . . .

From the boys, however, he heard about the angels
and their ongoing guerrilla war against the demons.
They had a base camp in a secret place in the heart of

a tropical swamp, and from there they mounted their ongoing campaign to drive the demons out of Heaven and the strongholds they'd made on Earth. Fighting beside the angels were the good ghosts, who actually could not do much except serve as scouts, spies and messengers to the living, because they had no angelic powers. Oddly enough, the entire campaign, down to the camp in a tropical swamp, had a familiar sound to it; when one of the boys named Julio described the archangel Michael as dressed in fatigues and a beret, bearded and carrying a rifle, Hosea realized why.

He kept an eye out for Ace while he was down at the shelter, but didn't spot her, and that worried him, knowing what he knew now. He wondered who was after her to make her as skittish as she was, and if Eric had managed to get himself tangled up in that, too. He'd been in on the whole Threshold thing; what if there was another black ops project that was using kids instead of adults, and Eric had stumbled into them?

He called Kayla in the middle of the day from the shelter phone, to find out if there was any news.

"I don't think he's Underhill," Kayla said. "I was thinking about it, and if he was, wouldn't Lady Day just have followed him?"

"Maybe," Hosea said cautiously. He had to admit it sounded reasonable, but the amount he knew for sure about elvensteeds could be engraved on the edge of one of his silver banjo picks and still leave room for a couple of Bible verses.

"So I thought maybe we ought to look for him here first before we bothered a bunch of elves," Kayla said tentatively.

"Are you real sure about that?" Hosea asked. "It don't seem to me like it would do any harm to ask the Good Folks if they've seen him."

"And have Beth pitch spinning kittens all over Eric's apartment with Kory along to sing tenor?" Kayla asked crossly. "The weird thing is"—there was a very long pause—"elvensteeds can *track* their riders. Eric told me that once. Over hundreds of miles in the World Above. And across Gates in Underhill. I remembered it when I was thinking about how funny it was that she didn't just take us Underhill after him."

So if she can track him anywhere he goes, why doesn't she know where he is? Hosea thought.

The unspoken question hovered between them.

"Why don't you have Toni help you check the hospitals?" Hosea said, very gently. "Ah'll be home as soon as Ah can."

But it was several more hours before he could fulfill that promise.

On his way into Guardian House, Hosea ran into Caity coming out.

"Oh, there you are!" she said cheerfully. "I was just up knocking on your door." Her smile faded a little as she inspected him. "You don't look like you've been having the best day in the world."

"Ah might have lost track of a friend," Hosea admitted cautiously, not wanting to spoil her mood. "But Ah'm sure he'll turn up."

"I guess this isn't the world's best time to invite you to a party, then," Caity said, drooping a little. "But there's one at Neil's place tonight. *He's* going to be there, and he said I could bring you, so. . . ."

Hosea had never felt less like going to a party in his life, but the only person *he* could possibly be was the mysterious True Guardian Caity had talked about, and getting a closer look at the fellow was important. And Hosea suspected that if he turned down this chance, there wouldn't be another one. So he forced a smile, and said: "It sounds like just what Ah need to take my mind off my troubles. What time?"

Caity beamed. "I'll pick you up about eight." She hesitated. "Wear something nice, okay?"

"Ah'll turn up in my Sunday-go-to-meetin' best," Hosea promised firmly.

Caity stood up on tiptoe to bestow a quick kiss on his cheek, and hurried off. Hosea went on into the building.

He left Jeanette in his apartment and went down to Kayla's. She opened the door at his knock.

"Well, he hasn't been arrested," she said without preamble. "And he hasn't been committed—I called his shrink. She said she'd check the hospitals for me, too, but that I probably wouldn't hear back from her until tomorrow." Her face twisted.

Hosea held out his arms. Kayla flung herself into them, burrowing fiercely, choking on strangled sobs.

"Hush, now," Hosea said. "Wherever he is, Ah'm sure he's just a mite tangled up, is all. You know that boy's got himself a way with trouble. That's all it is. He'll be back in a day or two and apologize for givin' us all such a powerful fright, and everything'll be as right as rain. You'll see."

"You don't believe that," Kayla said, sniffling and pushing herself away.

Hosea fished out his pocket handkerchief and handed it to her.

"Ah do believe that we don't *know*," he said firmly. "And until we do know something for sure and certain, there's no point to borrowing trouble. Now, Eric's got a lot of enemies. But he's got a lot of friends, too, and he's got a powerful shine on him. You're doing the right thing looking for him the way you are, but Ah do wish you'd whistle up the Good Folks to help."

"You don't understand," Kayla said fiercely, scrubbing at her eyes with the handkerchief. "Kory couldn't do much even if he was here. New York is full of iron. Elves can't even survive here very long, let alone use their magic here all that well. So it's really up to us."

"Well," Hosea said, reluctantly going along with her argument, "that does put a different tail on the cat. Why don't you come upstairs and let me feed you? Ah've got to go out tonight, but no sense in either of us goin' hungry, now, is there?"

"Sure," Kayla said dolefully, stuffing the now black-striped handkerchief into her jeans pocket. "Not much anybody can do before tomorrow, anyway."

Hosea was just as glad he'd dressed in his best, but he still felt very much out of place when he and Caity arrived at Neil Grandison's apartment.

It was one of those glass-and-steel towers far uptown, the kind of place that looked as though it were steam-cleaned inside and out once a month, and where the tenants were probably chosen, not only by their financial worth, but by their appearance as well. Hosea wouldn't have been at all surprised to learn there was a building dress code.

As they rode up in the elevator, Caity gave him a number of last-minute instructions—not only to just be himself (as if Hosea would ever consider being anyone else), but to not "bother" Master Fafnir—"or to talk about the Work, because, you know, this is just a social evening, and there will be a lot of people here who don't know anything about it."

"Ayah," Hosea had said laconically. Apparently the Master was looking for a few more sheep, and Hosea set himself to do the best possible impersonation of a lamb ripe for the shearing that he could, setting his other worries—Eric's disappearance; where Kayla was spending her nights; the Bloody Mary murders that the other Guardians—the *real* Guardians, as he still couldn't help but think of them—were pursuing; the Secret Stories—out of his mind for the moment. He could afford no distractions tonight.

The apartment was large, decorated in what Hosea—who had seen more of them than people might expect to look at him—had come to think of as Rich Folks Style: wall-to-wall beige carpet, pale anonymous leather sofas, enormous expensive pieces of pottery, and modern art that didn't seem to go with anything else. Although somehow Miz Llewellyn managed to make her place look a bit more homelike, and Hosea suspected that Miz Llewellyn could buy and sell Mr. Neil Grandison out of pocket change.

There was a banquette set up as a bar in one corner, and the room was filled with people.

"Caity—hi. Is this your friend?"

A very manicured dark-haired man in a grey turtleneck and charcoal slacks came over, a tulip-shaped wineglass in his hand.

"Neil, this is Hosea," Caity said dutifully. "Hosea, this is Neil."

The two men shook hands. "You can put your coats in the back bedroom," Neil said. "*He* isn't here yet," he added, his tone pitched for Caity's ears alone, though Hosea had no trouble hearing him. *Guess Ah'm not supposed to have any idea who he is, although it'd take a pure simpleton not to guess.*

But Caity nodded, looking like a conscientious schoolchild, and bore Hosea off.

They supplied themselves with glasses of wine from the bar, slipped sterling silver wine charms over the stems—a little fairy for Caity and, interestingly enough, there was a banjo that Hosea laid claim to—and then circulated, Caity sticking as close by his side as a hen with only one chick.

Despite Caity's promises that this was to be a purely social evening, there seemed to be only one real topic of conversation, conducted in hints and allusions.

And occasionally outright.

"—well of course I gave him the apartment. It was the least I could do for a man like that. He has such power."

The speaker was a middle-aged woman with long auburn hair—Juliana, it would be, if she was talking about the apartment, Hosea guessed.

"Aren't you looking forward to, well, *it*?" the woman she was talking to asked. She was a few years younger, with shoulder-length, light-brown hair in a complicated style.

"I'll feel better when *it* gets here, if we're going to have to deal with *them,*" Juliana answered cryptically.

Hosea would have liked to hear more—it wouldn't be easy to fill in the blanks, though it ought to be possible—but Caity took his arm and steered him determinedly away. "I want you to meet Gregory," she said firmly.

"So you're Caity's musician?" Gregory said amiably, when they were introduced. "Music can be an important conduit of power."

"Ah wouldn't know a lot about that," Hosea said modestly.

He had a bit of luck then, because someone named Faith came and wanted Caity to go off with her, and Hosea settled himself to listen. People, he'd found a long time ago, tended to talk if you listened, and Gregory—who'd had several glasses of wine—was no exception.

He got to hear a great deal about the ancient brotherhood of Guardians who had been chosen before the beginning of Time to stand against the Darkness, of how their numbers had dwindled over the centuries until there was only one, of how the False Guardians had risen up (from where was an interesting question that apparently nobody was asking) to overthrow the True Guardian, but how one day the True Guardian would reclaim his power and found a new order of Guardians to take up his ancient work.

"—but of course that's all just a legend, isn't it?" Gregory said, belatedly coming to the conclusion he'd been talking too much.

"Ah don't think it is," Hosea said quietly. "An' Ah don't think you think it is, either."

Just then there was a stirring by the front door—*just like when the weasel comes into the henhouse,* Hosea thought uncharitably—and someone who could only be Caity's "Master Fafnir" entered the room.

One of the women hurried forward to take his cloak from his shoulders—and it *was* a cloak, Hosea noted with mild amusement—Master Fafnir wore a cloak, and a broad-brimmed hat, and carried a silver-handled walking stick. *I suppose he must think he's Orson Wells.*

From Caity's description, Hosea had been expecting someone along the lines of Christopher Lee—tall, gaunt, saturnine, and Byronic—but Master Fafnir was none of these things. He was on the short side of average, a few pounds short of pudgy, and had the pale skin of those who spent all their time indoors under artificial light. His short brown hair was combed straight back, making no attempt to conceal a receding hairline, and his face was the sort at which you wouldn't look twice.

But his eyes made up for it all. They had the

intense vividness that his every other feature lacked.
They reached out and *grabbed*—and if it wasn't the
kind of Power that Hosea was used to confronting
in his work as a Guardian, it was a dangerous power
nonetheless.

"And here is our newcomer—our Ozark bard,"
Fafnir said, moving through the crowd to stop before
Hosea. His voice was surprisingly deep for such a
small man, the resonant instrument of a trained
actor—or of someone, like a politician, who knew
just how potent a weapon a good voice could be.
His voice sounded warm and hearty, welcoming,
but Hosea, who could hear the music beneath the
voice, heard another story—of someone who was
calculating, cold, and avaricious, and was already
assessing what use Hosea could be to him. He had
certainly named himself properly—for Fafnir, the
most avaricious of dragons, who amassed treasure
for no other purpose than to possess as much of
it as possible.

Hosea held out his hand, and Fafnir took it in
both his own. He closed his eyes for just a moment,
taking a deep breath. "You could do great things," he
said simply, and moved on.

"Isn't he wonderful? And he *likes* you," Caity said
excitedly, clutching Hosea's arm.

Hosea stood there for a moment, blinking. The man
had a powerful personality. It wasn't hard to see how
Fafnir had gotten all of them to follow him, at least
in the beginning. The fellow was slick as greased ice,
and if he'd been a little less suspicious, Hosea would
have believed that Fafnir had seen right into him and
known him for what he truly was.

But "Ozark bard"—now that was just highfalutin'
poetry. Caity had certainly told Fafnir about him
ahead of time when she'd asked if she could bring

him, and for the rest, who *wouldn't* want to hear that
they could do great things?

He hadn't thought he'd need to worry about shielding himself here, but charisma, and the pull of a large
group all thinking the same way, could exert nearly
the same amount of force as a trained magician's will.
Now that Fafnir had arrived, Hosea could feel the
pull of expectation all around him. Not nearly strong
enough to entrap him, but worth warding against all
the same.

"Listen to your own song," his Gran'daddy had always
told him. *"Ain't nobody can fool with you when you
listen within."* Both Paul and Eric had told him the
same thing, though their words had been different.
Hosea concentrated, until the nagging tug he felt
from the other people in the room receded, and he
felt sure of himself again.

When he looked around, he saw that Fafnir had
seated himself in a large leather chair in a corner—very
much as if by right—and the others had all gravitated
to him, as if, now that he'd arrived, he'd become the
focus of the room. Someone brought him a glass of
wine, and several of the women clustered around him,
sitting on the floor around the chair. Hosea was both
relieved and discouraged to see that Caity was among
them—relieved, because it meant she wouldn't be
dragging him out of any more interesting conversations, and discouraged because it meant she was very
much under "The Master's" spell.

*But if there's one thing Ah know for sure, it's that
you can't save fools from themselves, because fools
have too much ingenuity.*

Though a few people left—apparently not finding
Fafnir as fascinating as their friends did—Hosea stayed,
and since Fafnir had greeted him personally and
seemed to take a personal interest in him, the others

spoke openly in front of him. Fafnir didn't seem to
object to that at all, apparently having decided Hosea
was completely harmless. Hosea hoped that someday
he'd get the opportunity to change the man's mind. *Big
and dumb don't always go together, Mister Weasel.*

He wandered, seemingly aimlessly, among those who
were left, but in fact he was looking for someone in
particular. Caity had said that Neil had told her some
things that perhaps he shouldn't have, and Hosea
was hoping he'd continue the practice if Hosea could
manage to strike up a conversation with him.

At last luck favored him, and he found Neil over by
the bar, playing gracious host among the wine bottles.
Hosea waited until the two of them were alone.

"How are you enjoying our little party?" Neil asked
him.

"Waal, it's real fascinatin' and Ah'm right honored
to meet Master Fafnir," Hosea said, laying on his
country-bumpkin act for all it was worth, "But truth
to tell, Ah'm kinda worried about the Exoteric Plane
consequences of the Work," Hosea said gravely. "Not
on the Inner, you know, but the Outer."

Bless Tatiana for providing him with all the passwords and jargon he needed for this. She'd done a
little skit at the last Basement Party—something about
a bunch of Satanists accidentally calling up a New
Age guru instead of the Devil—that'd been funny, if
peculiar. Paul had laughed until he'd nearly dropped
his drink, though it hadn't made all that much sense
to Hosea. But it *had* included a number of useful
terms for him to trot out now.

Neil seemed to accept that Hosea knew what he
was talking about—and even better, that he had every
right to ask the question. "Oh, you don't need to worry
about that," he said easily. "There won't even be a
body. In fact, as soon as one of them 'dies,' everyone

will forget that they ever even existed. So it's the perfect victimless crime—if you can call it a crime. I'd call it justice, myself. After all, even if they were human once, they aren't anymore." Neil drained his glass, and reached for Hosea's. "Refill?"

"Surely," Hosea said. The potted plants and ornamental vases at the Grandison residence had been drinking well tonight, as Hosea had no intention of taking more than a sip of wine here. No one with any claim to real Power drank much at all, he'd found—of course Eric stayed away from liquor, but none of the Guardians drank much beyond the odd glass of wine, and the Basement Parties were never fueled by anything stronger than wine and hard cider, and not much of that.

If he'd needed any more proof that this was a hoodoo operation, it was the amount of vintage this room full of pretend Guardians were putting away.

Neil turned away and refilled both their glasses, turning back and handing one to Hosea.

"Jealous?" Neil asked, nodding toward Caity.

Hosea looked over to where Caity was sitting, resting her head on Fafnir's knee. The Master stroked her hair as he would pat the head of a dog.

"Ah'd be a pure fool to be jealous of a man like that," Hosea said with complete honesty.

Neil smiled. "You're one of us already. And when we become Guardians—and she's an Acolyte—it's going to be a whole new world."

"Ah can believe that." *A new world somewhere in Upstate New York,* Hosea thought. *And a considerably smaller apartment that has barred windows.*

"You look like you're a million miles away," Neil said. His speech was very slightly slurred now, the pattern of the chronic drinker who was nearing his limit.

"Ah was just thinkin', Ah wouldn't want to have *his*

enemies," Hosea said, nodding toward Fafnir. "You're a brave man to throw your lot in with him like this."

"Oh, Master Fafnir will protect us," Neil said with complete conviction. "He's got *power.*"

Several of them—Caity and Hosea among them—were dismissed soon afterward. In the elevator down, Caity clung to him, giddy with something more than wine. Hosea had watched her closely, and she hadn't drunk that much.

But she was as flushed and coquettish as a woman in love—and not with *him*, Hosea realized glumly. With Fafnir—or worse, with the fantasy that Fafnir'd sold all of them on. And so she'd go on giving "The Master" money in the future—probably more than she could fairly afford—and doing things that made her just a little uneasy, and digging herself in deeper and deeper until she was too ashamed of what she was doing to ask for help to get out.

And right now, she wouldn't take Hosea's help even if he offered it, Hosea knew. She was in love with the whole idea of being part of a grand secret conspiracy for Good.

Would he have been, in her place? If Jimmie Youngblood hadn't had to die to make him a Guardian, if he hadn't already had the music magic? If somebody had walked up to him out of the blue and offered him something like this on a silver platter, promising him the chance to be a hero?

Hosea wasn't sure. But he did know that whatever Fafnir's secret society had started out as, it hadn't been anything like what it had now become, with all its loose talk of tidy convenient executions. Everyone in that room up there had gotten in deeper and deeper by degrees, until now someone like Neil could talk about killing someone as if it were the most natural thing in the world and never turn a hair.

What Fafnir was telling them seemed fairly clear to Hosea now—piecing together the various things he'd heard tonight with what Caity had told him earlier. Some of this group were supposed to become Guardians immediately, and the rest would become Acolytes—Guardians-to-be. And all of that depended on their executing the False Guardians once Fafnir identified them—which wouldn't "count," because the False Guardians would conveniently dissolve away into dust.

But Fafnir himself must know that wasn't true. Even if he did manage to capture and kill a Guardian, all he'd have for his pains would be a dead human being. The man was venal, not insane. He couldn't be intending to set these people up for murder—and even bedazzled as they were, when they were actually holding a knife to somebody's throat, they'd surely balk at using it.

And why should Fafnir give up his soft life just to prove he had ultimate control over the people he'd deluded? He could spin out this nasty game of his for as long as he could deceive his followers, and as long as they never actually tried to execute anyone as a False Guardian, it was simply another sordid and hateful scam, not an actual Guardian problem, wasn't it?

Or was there a plan behind the plan, one that didn't stop at murder?

He saw Caity to her door. She wanted him to come in and stay awhile, but Hosea wasn't even tempted. When he romanced a lady, he preferred her to be in her right mind, and thinking of him, besides. So he made the excuse of an early morning, and waited until he heard her do up the locks on the inside, and went to see Paul.

Paul's business was free-lance computer design, and so he kept owl's hours. Hosea wasn't surprised to see a thin thread of light beneath his door.

"Ah need to talk," he said, when Paul opened the door.

"I was hoping you'd be by," Paul said. "There's been another Bloody Mary murder."

"Another one?" Hosea said, appalled. "I was out—"

"It doesn't matter. I doubt you could have done any more than you did before, and it's not as if we had any warning. Same pattern, same clues that lead . . . nowhere. How do we stop something like that?"

Hosea sighed. "If'n you knew her True Name, maybe. But the little'uns say it's lost."

"Well, the more you can find of the Secret Stories, the better. Maybe there's a clue in there, somewhere. But that won't be what you wanted to chat me up about. Come on in. I've got tea on the boil."

Every inch of the walls of Paul's apartment was covered with books. Software manuals battled for shelf space with esoteric leather-bound tomes, and peculiar curios, both modern and ancient, were tucked into every spare corner of space that remained. What floor space in the living room that was not occupied by a couch, chair, and table was filled with computer equipment, and more computers and books packed every free corner of both bedrooms. The result made Kayla's far smaller apartment look spacious by comparison.

Hosea transferred an armload of books from the couch to the floor and sat down as Paul went into the kitchen, returning with two large white mugs. When Paul said he was boiling tea, he meant it; the brew he brought Hosea was thick and dark, as strong as coffee. Hosea cradled the mug in his hands and wondered where to begin.

"You look like a chap with a problem on his mind," Paul said, settling into the chair. "And I'm supposed to have all the answers."

"Well, it could be a problem for all of us," Hosea said, "since apparently we're the evil False Guardians that this feller name o' Fafnir intends to hunt down and destroy."

"Well, there's an interesting beginning to a story," Paul commented, gazing at the wall above Hosea's head—which contained, of course, more bookshelves.

Slowly, Hosea told him the whole story, as far as he'd pieced it together: that Caity, along with about twenty other people, had fallen under the spell of someone calling himself Master Fafnir, who said he was a Guardian who had been stripped of his power by a coterie of Evil Guardians, and that once the lot of them had hunted down and killed the Evil Guardians and restored Fafnir's Guardian powers, he would be able to make them all Guardians as well. And meanwhile, they were all supporting him, to the extent of free room and board at the very least.

"Fafnir," Paul said musingly. "Interesting choice for a *nom de ombre*. In Norse mythology, Fafnir was the eldest son of the dwarf king Hreidmar, and was turned into a dragon for his wickedness. Guardian of a great horde of gold, which he slew his father—some accounts say his brothers as well—to gain, a horde sometimes known as the Treasures of Light, though by all accounts the treasure was cursed, containing as it did the Rheingold. Slain by the hero Siegfried, eventually, Fafnir was." Paul sipped his tea.

"Knew about the dragon and Siegfried, didn't know about the other," Hosea said, interested in spite of himself.

"As for the rest, I'm sorry that Caity's involved, but I'd have to put the whole mess down to ordinary bloody-mindedness and cupidity on this Fafnir's part. Word does get out about us now and again. Sometimes the people we help talk more than they should, afterward. And a clever con man can put a lot together from very little. But it doesn't sound quite as if he actually knows anything about us and how we operate. After all, you were there tonight and he didn't spot you, did he?"

"Not that I noticed," Hosea admitted reluctantly. But he had to admit that if there'd been anything of True Power in that apartment this evening, he would have felt *something*.

"It's a nasty little game the man's playing," Paul said. "And a lot of people are going to be hurt—emotionally and financially—when it's over. But I wouldn't worry about it too much from our perspective. From what you say, there's no power there, other than the power of overpersuasion and the Big Lie. Those followers of your friend Fafnir's are living in the same fantasy world as all the other Charmed Ones, Chosen Ones, and Mage-Knights that litter the streets of this city, and until they do something actively wicked—or actually illegal—it's nobody's business but theirs, unfortunately. And Caity hasn't asked you for help with her problem. Remember that. We cannot intervene unless we are asked."

If there was one thing that grated on Hosea about the code the Guardians lived by, it was that, but he had no particular choice about accepting it. They could not intervene in a matter until someone asked them for help—or until their own Power demanded they intervene. And so far, neither thing had happened.

"So Ah guess there's nothing we can do?" Hosea said, disappointed.

Paul smiled. "I didn't quite say that. We can certainly

see if the lads down at the Bunco Squad have an interest—it's a long shot, but worth a try. And you can go on being a good friend to young Caity. When she finds out that her guru's promises are nothing more than smoke and moonlight, she'll need one."

"And if they invite me back?" Hosea asked.

Paul considered the matter, gazing off into nothing for several seconds.

"Now *that* might be very amusing," he said at last. "Very amusing indeed."

CHAPTER ELEVEN:

HERE'S A HEALTH TO
THE COMPANY

Ria always found Washington to be an exceptionally unreal city—like Hollywood, it worked very hard at producing the intangible. Each city could point to a finished product, but the work involved in producing that product was labyrinthine and disproportionate—an elephant giving birth to a mouse—and for every finished task, a hundred were begun and abandoned. In both cities, lies and secrets were the order of the day—and the people with the most power were not necessarily those who were the most well-known.

Like every large corporation, LlewellCo did a certain amount of business in the nation's capitol—you didn't survive in the current commercial climate without keeping abreast of the laws and regulations that would affect your company—and so it maintained a permanent residential suite at the Watergate Hotel. It had amused Perenor to make the place his Washington headquarters, and Ria found a certain wry humor in keeping the address. She made good time from the airport, her limousine pulling up at the front of the building only an hour after her plane landed.

There's a certain fitness in my being here, Ria thought to herself. If she was not in Washington to topple a president, she certainly meant to bring down another man who thought himself above the law: Parker Wheatley.

Reaching the LlewellCo suite, Ria tipped the bellman, locked the door behind him, and went over to the desk. It was already piled high with phone messages and mail delivered by the efficient—and very discreet—LlewellCo underling who would be her assistant during her stay. Ria checked her watch and then her PDA. Siobhan Prowse, that was it, and she'd be meeting her here in thirty minutes. Maybe she could get her to unpack as well—or was that considered employee harassment these days?

She opened her briefbag and began pulling out files, the fruit of almost a year's careful intelligence-gathering on their dear Mr. Wheatley. It wasn't much, but she hoped it was enough to alarm the cautious careful men she was going to meet with in the next several days—men who probably would not have been willing to meet with her at all, Ria realized ruefully, if not for what LlewellCo had been in Perenor's time, and for her own very public profile following the Threshold debacle.

She had been able to do one of them a very great favor with the material she'd dug out of Robert Lintel's Threshold files, and she hoped he remembered it now. He was the one she was pinning her real hopes on, but it didn't do to have only one string to your bow, so she'd made several appointments. The first was in three hours.

Ria sighed, resting her chin on her hand and gazing out the window. She had a breathtaking view of the Mall. The city, seen so often in films and television, had a certain surreal quality to it.

Just as her visit here did. How often in the past had Perenor sent her off on assignments that bore too close a resemblance to what she was planning to do here—meet a man, dazzle him, bend him to her (or rather, her father's) will, and bear away the prize?

But this won't be like all those times, Ria told herself, though the promise rang faintly hollow. But it was true in every way that mattered. Though she could certainly cast a spell on any of the men she was to meet with and get him to agree to anything, such a *glamourie* would be only temporary, fading if she did not reinforce it over time. And a failed *glamourie* would be pointless—worse than pointless; it might play right into Wheatley's hands. No, she had to discredit Wheatley with good old-fashioned facts and persuasion.

Not that it should be too hard, if she could only get them to listen to her. Funding a black ops group of ghosthunters and elfchasers was the last thing Washington wanted to be doing—or be seen to be doing—in the current political climate. They should be only too happy to shut down Parker Wheatley and his troop of little green men, if she could play her cards right. These days, there was a great need for scapegoats, particularly expensive scapegoats, to be sacrificed publicly to deflect attention elsewhere.

Four hours later—the man she was to meet had been delayed in another meeting—Ria was sitting across the desk from a senior career intelligence official in an office with a splendid view of the Capitol Building. The nameplate on his desk said JAMES HATCHER.

Not their main offices, of course. Officially, this meeting wasn't happening. Just as well.

"I'm still not sure why you came to us, Ms. Llewellyn," Mr. Hatcher said, smiling agreeably.

"I'm just a concerned citizen," Ria said, her smile equally agreeable—and equally insincere. "And I just think that a program like the Paranormal Defense Initiative is a rather odd way for the government to be spending money at a time like this. Or any time, frankly."

"I did some checking after our phone conversation," Hatcher said, "And I'm afraid I couldn't find any record of such a program."

"Perhaps it's already been closed down," Ria said guilelessly. "Or perhaps I don't have a sufficient security clearance for you to talk about it with me. Why don't I just tell you what *I* know, and we can go on from there?"

She began to speak, reading from the notes in her folder. After about two minutes, Hatcher stood up. "Excuse me," he said.

He walked out a side door of the office. About fifteen minutes later, another man came in.

He was considerably older than James Hatcher had been, and looked as if he ate at least three bureaucrats of Hatcher's caliber for breakfast every morning. He smiled warmly when he saw Ria, and held out his hand.

"Hello, Ms. Llewellyn. My name is David. James tells me you have some interesting information for us."

She shook his hand. "I hope someone finds it interesting. I find it upsetting."

David—apparently he had no last name—seated himself behind the desk. "I'm sorry to ask, but perhaps you wouldn't mind starting from the beginning?"

She repeated what she had told Hatcher, and continued until she got to the end. David listened with an expression of polite attention. Ria tried skimming the surface of his mind, but there was nothing there to hear; the man had a very disciplined mind, one of those who refused to even think about sensitive subjects in unsafe circumstances. She'd encountered one or two like him in her industrial espionage days.

"Well, this is all certainly fascinating," David said, when she'd finished her presentation. "And how did you happen to come across this information?"

"I ran into some people involved with Mr. Wheatley in connection with Threshold," Ria said, sticking fairly close to the truth. "After that I did a bit of digging on my own." She passed the folder across the desk and watched as David paged through it.

"And you say that this Parker Wheatley—a name I've never heard, incidentally—is hunting fairies?"

Now she could pick up a little. Enough to know that this was a lie. David knew Parker Wheatley very well, and didn't like what he knew.

"I believe that Mr. Wheatley thinks he's hunting paraterrestrials—whatever they are," Ria said. "It was the part where he was proposing internment camps for psychics that I found particularly charming, though. Awkward if this should get out."

David looked up sharply.

"Is that a threat, Ms. Llewellyn?"

Ria uncrossed her legs and leaned forward. "David,

LlewellCo is a multibillion dollar multinational company with a finger in a lot of pies. At the moment, one of our partnerships is prospecting for oil in Siberia, and they're using dowsers to locate likely drilling sites. A lot of companies use dowsers to locate everything from water to underground power cables, because they happen to be very effective. And dowsers are psychics.

"I've already been a ninety-day wonder, and frankly, I'm sick of it. Believe me, I have no desire at all to step back into the spotlight for any reason. But the idea that some government agency is going to start a, well . . . witch-hunt . . . it's just going to cost everyone time and money."

"I'm sure your fears are groundless," David said, getting to his feet. "May I keep this?"

"Of course," Ria said, getting to her feet. "I appreciate your time."

One down, Ria thought, standing on the steps of the building a few moments later. The November wind was icy, and she wrapped her cashmere trench coat more tightly around her, turning the collar up to cover her ears.

"David" would know he didn't have the original copies of the information in that folder, and if he was good at his job, he'd probably have someone follow her—purely as a routine check. Let him. She could get rid of a tail if it ever happened to be necessary, and meanwhile, she might as well take the CIA on a tour of the sights of Washington. Tonight she had an appearance to make at a charity gala at the Kennedy Center—LlewellCo had made a large contribution, so Ria might as well show the flag—and there was always the interesting possibility that David's inquiries might bring some of Wheatley's goons sniffing around her as well.

She'd enjoy that. She really would.

✧   ✧   ✧

"You do understand, don't you, Ms. Llewellyn, that *The X-Files* is a television show?"

"I'd appreciate it if you didn't try quite so hard to belittle my intelligence, Agent Babcock. I'm not the one who's set up a secret government department to chase elves, gremlins, and little green men," Ria responded tartly.

Another day, another appointment, this time at the FBI. The J. Edgar Hoover Building.

"So far we only have your word for that," Babcock said.

"I'd be delighted to find out I'm mistaken," Ria said, backing off a little. "It would also be somewhat comforting to know that this was a legitimate government department operating entirely within the terms of its mandate. And since it's operating on American soil with American citizens as its proposed targets, forgive me for assuming you'd either know, or want to know about it."

Babcock looked down at the folder in his hands. "I can't comment on that," he said.

"I appreciate that," Ria said. "And I'm not asking you to tell me anything. Look, anybody with the price of a newspaper knows that the intelligence communities are engaged in one hell of a turf war right now. And one of the ways to hang on to your turf is to make yourself look big and important and indispensable. So what if somewhere there was a little research project that developed delusions of grandeur? That's all it would take, Mr. Babcock."

Nathaniel Babcock had been the special agent involved with sorting out the tangled Threshold mess, so Ria'd had a lot of contact with him over the last several months. She'd decided to take her material to him rather than to someone higher in the organization for just that reason. He already knew her, and—for as much as it was worth—she knew that she'd managed to impress him as being relatively sane and level-headed. And all the information she'd brought him so far had panned out.

She could tell that he'd rather not be hearing about this now. There were already a few rumors floating around Capitol Hill about Wheatley, enough to have filtered down even to Babcock's relatively unexalted level. Wheatley's position apparently wasn't all that secure. But Babcock himself wasn't highly placed enough to take on a crusade of this nature, and hesitated, for a number of reasons that seemed good to him, to push the matter with his superiors.

Even though she was disappointed, Ria could sympathize with his position. There wasn't much hard evidence in what she'd brought him. And whistle-blowers didn't have a long life-span in any field.

He looked down at the folder again and sighed, suddenly becoming more human. "I know we've both seen weirder stuff, Ms. Llewellyn. But this . . . ? Internment camps? It's loony, Ms. Llewellyn. Nobody can just wave their hand and make things like that appear. And besides . . . half the police departments in this country have used psychics on their cold cases at one time or another. For terrorists, maybe, down in Gitmo, but . . . nobody'd go along with this."

"They would if somebody scared them badly enough, Mr. Babcock," Ria said softly. "And I think it would be a very bad idea if they did."

"So do I," Babcock sighed again. "Look, I'll put this in a report and pass it along up the chain. But without something harder to attach to it . . ."

"I know," Ria said. He'd do that much for her, she knew, but he was right: without hard evidence, the report would just vanish into somebody's file cabinet. Without a smoking gun, it would be hard to get anyone excited. And Beth Kentraine—the only human Ria knew of who'd actually encountered any of the PDI's operatives—would make a very poor witness to Wheatley's criminal behavior.

"Well, thanks for seeing me at least."

"A pleasure as always, Ms. Llewellyn," Agent Babcock said, rising to see her out.

Maybe I'm too old for this, Kayla thought to herself, dragging herself into her apartment and collapsing onto her couch with a grateful sigh. She was only a few years older than the kids up in The Place, and it hadn't been so very long since she was living the very same way, but it seemed so much harder now. Maybe because now she wasn't running away from everything, focusing all her energy on looking no further ahead than tomorrow. She *had* a future now, something none of those kids would have if they kept on the way they were. But most of them had already given up and stopped fighting.

Like Jaycie.

Magnus and Ace couldn't see it, and for a while Kayla hadn't been able to spot it either, but the kid was some kind of stoner. She couldn't figure out what his thrill was, though. He didn't smoke, she'd never caught him doing anything harder, and she was positive he wasn't spiking his Cokes. But he was zeeing out most of the time, and it was like neither of them noticed. She'd overheard them talking. Ace thought he was sick. Magnus was sure he was okay.

Yeah, like anybody who sleeps twenty-two hours a day's in the bloom of clean-bodied health.

Maybe she could do something for him. Pull him back from the edge; sweep the junk out of his system.

It wouldn't keep him from poisoning himself again—however he was doing it—but maybe it would scare the three of them enough to listen to her, so they'd go into that program of Hosea's. She didn't know how long Ria was going to be in Washington, but Anita had her number there if Kayla really needed it.

Or maybe Eric would be back by then.

She was putting off checking her messages, because she didn't want to hear any more bad news. But there was no point in delaying the inevitable. And maybe it would be good news. For a big change.

Reluctantly, Kayla heaved herself up off her futon and went into the kitchen to play back her messages.

A couple from friends from school, sounding like strange messages from another world. One from Hosea, wanting her to come see him before she left again this evening. And one from Dr. Dunaway.

"I'm afraid I don't have any good news for you, Kayla. Eric hasn't been admitted at any of the city hospitals. Give me a call or stop by my office between two and three. I'm free then."

Kayla glanced at the clock automatically. Only ten o'clock. Hours before she could call.

And Eric was not in the hospital, not anywhere that Lady Day could find him, not anywhere that Jeanette could find him.

They were starting to run out of options.

Okay. I'm really *scared now. Does that help matters?*

She went back to the living room and huddled on her futon, trying to think.

And trying not to cry.

There was a courier package waiting for Ria when she got back to the Watergate. Someone was certainly following her, but they were far away enough that she could only pick up the faintest wisps of intention, not enough to tell her who they were.

She picked up the package at the desk, glancing at the return address. New York. Something that Anita had sent down, then. She tucked it under her arm and went up to her suite, wondering what could be that important. She'd be going back in three days, and her staff was well-trained; people who felt they had to run to the boss with every little thing didn't last long at LlewellCo.

She went up to the suite and stopped just inside the door. One spell assured her that it was empty now. A second . . .

Oh, this is very interesting . . .

She'd had visitors.

Ria watched as the shadows she'd evoked with her second spell moved about the suite, searching it thoroughly. It was unlikely they'd find what they'd come for, however: not only had she locked her last set of documents in the safe that came with the suite, she'd taken the precaution of rotating it outside of Time with a simple spell before she left. They could search until Doomsday and not find it.

Though apparently Doomsday had come early this year. . . . Ria watched in profound surprise as the colorless shadows quickly located the safe and swung open the hinged cabinet that concealed it. The four shadows clustered around it for several minutes of elapsed real-time before closing the cabinet again and moving on; apparently, while they could locate it, they were unable to break her spell and get inside.

They moved on, performing further actions in ghostly pantomime. What they were doing wasn't that hard to figure out. Their mission complete, the ghosts packed up their equipment and left. Reflexively, Ria stood aside to let them pass, even though they weren't really there, then walked into the middle of the room, knowing that her every move could be heard—and probably seen—by whoever had bugged her suite so thoroughly while she was out.

There were actually very few candidates for that particular honor, considering how easily they'd found the safe—and how long they'd spent trying to get into something they shouldn't have been able to see at all.

How very nice of Mr. Wheatley to take an interest. But since there aren't any residual traces of magic here, I'm very much afraid all of his little toys are about to . . . fail.

It wasn't as easy for her as it was for Eric, or for a pure-blooded Elven Magus. Their magic was innate, born in the blood. All of Ria's sorcery was hard-learned, a matter of years of training, study, and practice.

But it was no less effective for all of that.

She raised her handbag higher on her shoulder and summoned up her shields to full strength, making sure her own electronic equipment was inside them. She'd be wanting it later, and nothing outside her shields was going to be particularly reliable after what she was about to do. Then she called up a particular spell she was very fond of—she'd used it a number of times before—and flung it out to encompass the entire suite.

The room lights flickered for a moment and then steadied. There were a number of hisses and pops from unlikely locations as tiny surveillance devices and their batteries gave up their stored power and memory.

Once her spell had run its course, she walked through the living room, office, and bedroom, making sure.

The phones were all dead. So was the television/ TiVO/DVD/CD player. There was a black smudge on the inside of the lamp over her desk. The lights in the bathroom had exploded in a shower of broken glass.

Ria searched through the debris until she found the camera, a tiny object barely the size of her thumbnail. *Naughty, naughty, gentlemen, putting a camera in here.* She went back through the rest of the suite, searching until she'd collected most of the now-lifeless objects. Several in the lamps. One on the back side of the headboard of her bed.

:Now,: she said, sitting down on the couch and cupping them in the palms of her hands, *:speak to me, creatures of crystal and fire, and tell me what you know. . . . :*

It wasn't difficult to get them to give up their information. The bugging devices had been carried and placed with intent, and each had been individually assembled, so they retained more information than objects that had been mass-produced and expended carelessly. Though they were small, they knew their purpose, where they had come from, and who had brought them here.

A man named Nichol had led the team. Wheatley had found out she was asking questions about him, and wanted to know how much she knew. That answered the "why" of them looking for the safe. As for the "how" of them managing to spot it . . . Kentraine had said that the PDI had some technological method of cutting through the illusions the Sidhe could wrap around themselves, as well as the ability to render themselves magic-resistant and more-or-less invisible—to elves, if not to humans. And it looked like their detecting abilities might extend to sorcery, as well as Elven magery, even if they hadn't been able to break her spell.

Ria set the handful of hardware on the coffee table and regarded it. It was lovely evidence . . . only it didn't point to anyone in particular unless you had psychometric abilities. Anyone with money and connections could dip into this particular bag of tricks these days, and off the top of her head, Ria could name half a dozen people who would have a reasonable motive for wanting to spy on LlewellCo, including both the men she'd paid visits to here in Washington. And while being kidnapped by Wheatley might be an entertaining way to turn over that particular rock, she really had too much on her plate to waste her time playing out that particular end game.

So.

She leaned back, only to be distracted by a crackle of paper. The package from New York.

She fished it out from behind her and tore it open. Inside was a note from Anita that said: "Dear Ria: this came today by special courier marked 'Extremely Urgent,' so I'm overnighting it to you."

The package inside was wrapped in brown paper, tied with twine, and sealed with red sealing wax, superscribed in characteristic Spenserian script. The Post Office would have had no idea of how to handle it; Ria noted it had been delivered "By Hand."

It was a report from Inigo Moonlight.

He said he'd call, Ria thought to herself, vaguely piqued. But when she unwrapped the thick sheaf of documents she realized why he had not.

My Dear Miss Llewellyn—the cover letter began, handwritten, of course; she supposed the man had never even heard of the typewriter—*I believe I have unearthed the identity of the young person who has come to the attention of our Mr. Wheatley, and if I am correct in my deductions, this individual is a wholly innocent pawn in the schemes of that madman.*

A Mr. Marley Tucker Bell has been missing from his home in Baltimore, Maryland, for the last ten days. Following his disappearance, both his home and his place of business, one Bell Books, a shop which deals in new and used books of the sort commonly termed "occult," have been thoroughly searched, and several interesting items have been abstracted from each venue. I attach an annotated list of the items. Mr. Bell has for some years been engaged in the practice of the Art Magickal, with a particular specialization in goetic evocation and historical research, and I believe that it is through his agency that Mr. Wheatley has discovered the existence of De Rebus Nefandis, *and the fact that this volume might well serve his larger purpose. We must not think too harshly of Mr. Bell, however, for few individuals are prepared for the shock of coming face-to-face with True Evil, and I very much fear that our young friend has been exposed to some physical duress to gain whatever cooperation he may have provided. I attach several photos of Mr. Bell, should you chance to come across him in your travels, for it is my conviction that he would under normal circumstances be most unwilling to assist Mr. Wheatley in any operation that this fiend in human form should contemplate. Supporting documentation and my further report is enclosed. As always, I remain your humble and obedient servant, Inigo Moonlight.*

Ria paged through the papers until she got to the photos—several 8x10s that looked like candid shots, obtained Heaven knew how. They were pictures of an enormously average-looking young man—late thirties, she supposed, with the faintly transparent look of Tidewater aristocracy; a face and bone structure that hadn't much changed since it had been exported from England around 1600, and one that would look equally at home beneath a Puritan crop or Cavalier curls. Or, as it was now, in an entirely modern—if a bit Young Republican—haircut. Marley Bell looked like a slightly naive college professor, of the sort that called up most women's mothering instincts. And while Ria had none of those to speak of, she was quite certain that Mr. Bell was in need of help just now . . . assuming he was still alive.

She pulled out the picture of Bell dressed in an argyle sweater-vest and white shirt, behind the cash register of what Ria supposed must be Bell Books, and studied it critically. Wheatley had kidnapped him. And—if she could place any credence in Moonlight's hunches at all—was trying to use him to punch a door through to Elfland, with or without the help of a 9th-century grimoire. Or had been, ten days ago.

She didn't think he'd succeeded. It took a Bard, not a Mage, to pierce the Veil Between the Worlds, and even then it was possible only in certain times and places—and with a Node Grove to anchor the newly-formed Nexus besides. Even the Sidhe Magi Major couldn't do it themselves, with all their power.

This was the break she needed. An actual *crime* to tie Wheatley to—and hang him with.

But it would be ever so much more useful with the testimony of a witness.

If Marley Bell were still alive.

Well, why don't we just go see? Ria said to herself. *There must be a few laws in this town I haven't broken yet. And after all, Mr. Wheatley has invited me so very nicely to come to tea . . .*

She pulled out her PDA and her phone and began making calls.

Michael Myers was not his real name, of course, and Ria had never decided whether his choosing as his *nom de ombre* the name of a fictional Hollywood horror movie villain was an encouraging spark of whimsy or a warning sign of actual psychosis.

In the intelligence community, maybe the two things were identical.

Michael's was the third name on her list. There'd been some items in Threshold's files too sensitive to pass on even to Nathaniel Babcock. Things with international consequences.

It would have been simpler to bury them and forget them, but Ria couldn't bring herself to do that. Eventually the question of how to pass them on safely had led to Michael. The partnership had worked out before, which was why she was trusting him now.

She supposed he must have an office somewhere. She'd never bothered to try to find it. Tonight they were meeting at a place called Xavier's, a trendy District "drinkeateria" located near Capitol Hill. Xavier's was well-supplied with pseudo-Victorian stained glass, blond oak veneer, and even a few ferns. It was the sort of place to which the tragically hip repaired to meet and mate, as anonymous and impersonal as a paper cup. The perfect place to play spy.

Michael reveled in the trappings—or at least pretended he did. Ria was never sure. Michael did everything with utter sincerity, and believed in everything he did.

"You look like a cut-rate Bogie," she said as he sat down.

Raindrops starred the brim of the grey fedora and the shoulders of the tan trench coat of the man who settled into the booth opposite her. Dark hair, dark eyes, middle forties, lightly tinted glasses that he didn't really need. Michael worked very hard at looking just like everyone else. He could be an accountant, a bank manager, possibly even (although that might be stretching things) a dentist.

He wasn't.

"I'm much better looking. And I don't smoke. Which means I'll never die—of lung cancer, at any rate. It's good to see you again, Ria. Or should I say, 'Ilsa'? We really should meet less often."

Usually Michael kept the front of his mind—the interior monologue most people ran without knowing it—crammed with meaningless chatter. Ria had never quite decided whether that was because Michael suspected the existence of telepathy, or because there were a lot of things in Michael's world that he simply preferred not to dwell on. But tonight was different. She'd skimmed his mind out of habit—a bad habit, but hers—and tonight his thoughts were clear and easy to read.

Years of practice enabled her to smile, to carry on as if she'd heard nothing.

"I have something for you. Then I want you to do me a large number of favors. Then we won't see each other again, Michael," Ria said.

No matter what happened this evening, that much was true. And Michael would help her because he didn't care about his future any more, and because it would amuse him to do so, for some reason buried too deep for her to quite catch.

Michael was dying.

It was one of those wildfire cancers that ripped through the system too fast for surgery or drugs. He knew. His bosses did not, but he knew that wouldn't be true for much longer. She could see his plans clearly in his mind: vacation—Greece, Michael had always liked Greece; time the arrival of the documentation of his condition for when it wouldn't matter any more and make sure the body was found so there'd be no loose ends to worry anyone unduly. He wouldn't have to do it this way, except for the fact that he'd lose his passport when he retired; that was just the way it was. And he wanted to see the sun rise over the isles one more time.... *"The isles of Greece, the isles of Greece! Where burning Sappho loved and sung..."*

With a wrench, Ria cut the connection to his thoughts. *More proof that eavesdroppers never hear anything they like.*

"Favors," Michael said, smiling as if he didn't have a care in the world. "Well. I'm from the government, and they say that means I'm here to help you. So what do you have for me?"

Over drinks and dinner, Ria explained about Wheatley and the PDI; giving him the information she'd originally been intending to bring to the meeting.

"You already mentioned this to Babcock over at the Fibbies, and to a dear boy among the Christians In Action who told you his name was David, didn't you?" Michael said.

"I thought I'd share the joy," Ria said dryly.

"But I'm sure you saved the best for me," Michael said encouragingly.

"Today some of Wheatley's goons broke into my suite over at the Watergate and bugged the place thoroughly, though I can't prove it—anybody with a dollar and a dream can buy that kind of equipment these days." She sighed. "There's a certain piquant irony to that which I will probably appreciate in a few years, though I doubt it even dawned on Wheatley. But better yet, I'm fairly sure he's kidnapped a civilian and is holding him hostage somewhere—my best guess would be that it's in his offices here in Washington. So I thought I'd go look," Ria said.

Michael regarded her for a few moments in rapt contemplative silence. "By yourself?" was all he said.

"No. I was going to bring along a couple of experts."

"This would be—ahem!—to assist you in engaging in an illegal search of the premises of one of our intelligence agencies?" Michael seemed to be having some difficulty keeping a straight face, but to his credit, he managed it.

"I'd prefer it if it weren't completely illegal," Ria said demurely. "So if you could arrange for a warrant, and to deputize me and two other people as U.S. Federal Marshals—or whatever you prefer—that would certainly make things easier," Ria said blandly.

"I see. And you would want all of this when?"

Ria checked her watch. "By eleven o'clock tonight."

Michael leaned forward, completely serious now. "Just who is it that's gone missing, Ria?"

"A young man named Marley Bell—the blameless and only surviving scion of a fine old Baltimore family, if that makes any difference. Bell disappeared ten days ago. My sources say that Wheatley is convinced that Bell can help him locate these Spookies he's fixated on." She raised an eyebrow. "Whether or not this is pertinent, I don't know, but I believe that Wheatley is so fixated on his figments of the imagination that he'd ignore an al Qaeda operative driving a tanker full of jet fuel towards the Senate if he thought he saw a goblin across the street."

"And how sure are you that this Bell is squirreled away somewhere in the PDI's offices?" Michael asked.

"According to what I could dig up on them, they don't have a lot of secondary locations and safe houses. If he's anywhere, he's there." Simple logic told her that much. *If he could have been located by magic, Moonlight would have told me exactly where he was—which*

*means he's either behind heavy-duty shielding, or dead.
And the only place with magical shielding that I can
think of is the PDI headquarters.*

"What if he's already dead?" Michael asked pragmatically.

She shrugged; Bell was just a name and a photograph to her. His value was that his abduction proved
Wheatley had gone way over the top. "Then I'm sure
Wheatley's documented it. And I'm sure you don't
care just how you get access to those files."

"And why are you not leaving this to the professionals?" Michael asked.

"Call me a thrill-seeker."

Michael smiled grimly. "I could call you a lot of
things, Ria, but 'thrill-seeker' would be fairly low on
the list. I take it you've done something like this
before?"

She gave him a long look, and a hard one. "More
often than you'd think."

He blinked first. "I'll have to take your word for
that. All right. Let's just say your interests and some
other people's coincide on this one. But there's a
condition. I'm going in with you."

At two o'clock, earlier that same day, Kayla was in
Oriana Dunaway's waiting room.

She could have called, but she hadn't been able to
sit still. She wanted to do something—anything—to
find Eric, but all the things she could think of just
somehow seemed to add to the disaster. Telling Ria,
for example. Tell her *what*? That they'd misplaced
Eric? Ria would lose it big-time.

"You're Kayla Smith, aren't you? I'm Dr. Dunaway."

A slender blonde woman came out into the waiting room. To Kayla's relief, she didn't offer to shake
hands.

Kayla stood up. Dr. Dunaway shook her head, forestalling Kayla's first question. "No, I haven't heard anything new. But maybe if you could tell me a little more about the situation, I could offer a few suggestions. Why don't you come into the kitchen? This is my lunch hour, so I'll have to eat while we talk."

"—so you say that Eric's elvensteed doesn't believe that Eric has gone Underhill, but can't locate him here in our world, nor can his apprentice?"

"Yeah, that's about it," Kayla said, sipping her iced tea.

The kitchen of Dr. Dunaway's apartment was a high-tech marvel in chrome and white that looked more suited to surgery than cooking. Kayla sat at the counter across from Dr. Dunaway. Dr. Dunaway was eating a salad. She'd offered Kayla some, but Kayla was too keyed up to eat.

"And the spirit bound into Hosea's instrument says that Eric isn't dead?"

Kayla nodded, taking a deep breath and willing herself to remain calm. Yelling wouldn't help matters, but Dr. Dunaway's dispassionate calm was almost unbearable. It was as if she didn't *care* what happened to Eric.

Get a grip, Smith. Of course she cares. But it's her business not to get involved. She's a shrink. She couldn't help people if she got all involved in their stuff.

"Well, then. Let us consider what we *do* know. We know that Eric is unavailable to his elvensteed, which would know if he was simply dead, or had been taken into Elfhame. We therefore must assume until we know otherwise that Eric is alive and still in this world, and is for some reason unable to give his name to the admitting physician at any hospital or psychiatric facility in the area, since I've checked with the area hospitals and no patient has been admitted under that name in the last seventy-two hours."

Kayla nodded. "And he isn't in jail. A friend of mine checked that for me. Or . . ."

"Or the city morgue?" Oriana finished for her, very gently. Kayla nodded. Toni had checked that too, even though Lady Day seemed to be certain that Eric wasn't dead.

"Well, it's good to know that all the obvious possibilities have been covered. But let's consider how he could be in the hospital without our knowing. I think the most likely thing is that he *is* in the hospital system somewhere as a John Doe admission. If he disappeared just after he left you, he wouldn't have been carrying any identification, there would be no way for anyone to learn his name from his personal effects, assuming he were admitted to a hospital in a state of unconsciousness. Furthermore, if he *was* unconscious when admitted, there is a one hundred percent chance that anyone who had found him first stripped him of anything valuable, which would include any ID he *was* carrying. So the next thing you'll need to do is search for all the John Doe emergency admissions that match his physical description. Tedious, but not impossible."

Kayla stared at Dr. Dunaway in confusion. "But . . . if somebody just hit him over the head . . . Lady Day would still know where he was."

"My dear child," Dr. Dunaway said chidingly, "an enchanted motorcycle is hardly the most powerful magician at work in the world. If Eric has been placed under a spell of concealment . . . or if, for some reason, he has concealed himself . . . he could be quite difficult to track by magic. But the physical is harder to conceal than the ethereal in most cases. If his body remains in New York, it can be found."

And if it isn't . . . ?

It was time to stop kidding herself and make those phone calls.

Ria had wanted to go in alone—or at the very least, go in with someone like Michael, whom she wouldn't have to take responsibility for. But she needed someone human with her, watching her back, because the PDI's toys wouldn't work on humans. Wheatley's people had the ability to render themselves completely invisible to the Sidhe—and she had no idea how well their equipment would work on someone who was half-Elven. Live-fire conditions were not the time to find out, either.

She'd tried to reach Eric this afternoon when she'd first decided to break in to the PDI, but he wasn't answering either of his phones, which was annoying. When she'd checked in at her office, Anita said that Kayla was trying to reach her, but Ria let that one slide—even if somebody was dead (unlikely), that problem would have to wait until tomorrow. She needed all her attention focused here.

If she couldn't have Eric to watch her back, that left a paid professional. And a very short list.

"I'm so glad you could make it on such short notice," Ria said.

The hotel room was downtown, only a few blocks from tonight's destination. She'd rented it this afternoon without trouble—there were a few perks to carrying a Centurion AmEx—and it was as secure as sorcery could make it. There were two other people in the room.

One of them Ria had met before. His name was Raine Logan. He was only a few inches taller than she was, but he carried himself as if he were six feet tall. His black hair was brushed straight back from a deep widow's peak, and he had the trim, sculpted body of someone who worked out with weights for more than show. Logan had worked for Gotham Security up until about a year ago, when he'd quit to go into business for himself. Gotham Security was the best private security agency in the field, and Logan had been one of their best operatives.

The woman with him was his opposite in every way save her air of utter competence: tall, fashion-model slender, with a frizzy halo of carrot-red hair and a dementedly cheerful grin. She wore yellow-tinted, aviator-shaped glasses that did little to conceal the spray of pale gold freckles across her cheekbones. Both of them wore jeans, sneakers, and dark nylon windbreakers over black T-shirts that concealed the latest generation in Kevlar vests.

"Well, gosh, you're Ria Llewellyn, and all," the redhead said, widening her eyes. "I mean, gee, we saw your picture in *Time* and everything."

Nobody, Ria thought, could possibly be this feather-witted. Still, she gave the kid points for a good act. It probably even fooled some people.

"I want to be very clear on the fact that what I'm asking you both to do is illegal," Ria said carefully.

"So you said," Logan observed. "We're here. Melody stays with the ride."

"That's the plan," Ria said. She didn't bother to ask if Melody was good. She'd specified good. "This time, you're not here to protect me. You're here to protect this man once we find him"—she brought out the best of the photos of Marley Bell and passed it to Logan—"assuming we find him. His name is Marley Bell. If I'm not with you when we leave, get him out, drive him to this address"—a second slip of paper—"and hand him over to whoever's there.

Naturally, I expect to be with you. But if it comes down to a choice, choose Bell."

Logan passed the photo and the paper to Melody, who studied both carefully.

"And after that?" he asked.

"Disappear if you can. If you can't, you'll have LlewellCo's full backing. I've made the arrangements. Your contact will be Jonathan Sterling at LlewellCo West."

Because if I'm not with you, I'll either be dead, in custody, or finding out just what the PDI's position is on human-Elven hybrids.

"We'll be meeting a man there," Ria went on. "His name is Michael. He's getting us in, but other than that, he's running an independent operation. If he gets in trouble, don't wait for him, don't cover him."

"Understood. Time to armor up, then," Logan said. He picked up the case at his feet and opened it onto the table.

He pulled out a light Kevlar vest and passed it to Ria. She slipped it on, pulling the straps until it fit snugly.

"Radios." He set earpieces, throat mikes, and transmitters on the table. Ria picked up one set and put it on, peeling the adhesive off the pickup and placing it against her throat.

"Thermite pencils. Should open most locks. Night goggles. You won't want to turn on any lights. And these are for you." He lifted a layer of padding out of the case, removed two weapons and passed them to Ria. "Your preference, I believe."

A .38 snubnose revolver—a Colt Bulldog—and a Desert Eagle .60 caliber. The one was easy to conceal, with reasonable stopping power against most normal humans. The other could bring down a horse or stop a car.

Holsters, spare magazines, and speedloaders followed.

"Thanks," Ria said, smiling tightly. "I didn't think I was going to need these to lobby my representatives."

She slipped the Desert Eagle into its holster and stood to press the holster against the Velcro patch at the back of the Kevlar vest. It was heavy—the gun weighed almost nine pounds loaded—but it held. Her coat would cover the lump it made. And she shouldn't need to get to it in too much of a hurry. The Bulldog and the spare ammo could go in her pockets.

Logan was already armed—Ria knew he favored the Desert Eagle as well—and while Ria didn't see any weaponry about Melody's person, that didn't mean it wasn't there. She picked up her coat and stowed the last of the equipment in its pockets.

"Let's go."

Their "ride" looked like a showroom stock Lincoln Navigator—black, with tinted windows. Ria didn't ask to see any of the optional extras, but she assumed it had them. Logan was thorough, and she hadn't been coy when she'd told him her needs.

"I'll need a car and a driver. The driver has to be the very best at high speed evasive driving, and know Washington and the surrounding area. The car has to be capable of going off-road, over rough terrain, outrun the local law, stop everything up to an assault weapon—and frankly, I'd prefer up to light antitank, but I won't ask for miracles—blend in, and seat four."

"Do you want a Blaupunkt player with that?" was all Logan had said.

❖   ❖   ❖

Michael was waiting for them at the address Ria had specified. He'd changed his trench coat for a blue nylon bomber jacket and baseball cap and a pair of tinted shooter's glasses. He was wearing fatigues.

"Logan," he said.

"Michael," Logan said.

I guess it makes this easier that they know each other. Or harder, Ria thought.

"Here's your warrants. Try not to need them. They're forged." He handed Ria several blue folders and a badge case. "Welcome to the Justice Department."

Michael turned to the door. Like most of the office buildings in Washington, it had a keycard lock. He produced a card and slipped it into the slot. The light flashed green. The three of them walked inside.

The lobby might have been that of any large corporation—no fancy inlaid seals on the floor here, just a reception desk and security gates similar to the ones in her own building in New York. Two guards seated behind the desk. *One for use and one for show.*

"May I see your identification?" one of the security officers said as they approached.

Both armed. And a panic button within reach that will seal the building and alert on-site security personnel, but no one outside. She's just about to reach for it. . . .

"No," Ria said simply. She made a gesture, and both guards settled back in their seats, staring straight ahead, asleep with their eyes open.

She pointed. Logan and Michael headed toward the elevator, going around the barrier and the screening gate. Ria turned back to the security console.

:Sleep,: she said silently, placing a hand lightly on the security console. Within seconds, all the lights and monitors dimmed to black. She turned away, following the two men.

Michael's keycard opened the elevator as well.

"Where to?" he asked. "I warn you, this is where the fun begins."

"Five," Ria said without hesitation. It had been a number much in Nichol's thoughts, as far as the objects he had handled retained them. And it was as good a place to start as any.

"Here we go."

The doors closed. The car began to move. And everything went completely silent.

Not in a physical fashion—Ria could still hear the mechanical sounds of the elevator, the sounds of breathing and heartbeats, and even—if she Listened—what Michael and Logan were thinking.

But everything else—the hum of Power, the background hum of all the other minds within her reach, the faint sense of other preterhuman intelligences now and again—all that was gone, shut off at the instant the doors had closed.

I guess I've come to the right place, then, Ria thought, fighting down an uncharacteristic wave of anxiety at the odd sense of blindness. This was shielding on an inconceivable scale. It didn't matter how much Power you had. Punching through these shields would be simply impossible. Any form of magic that required Piercing the Veil simply wouldn't work here—human sorcery would be powerless, and Elven magic would burn out quickly, unable to renew itself without its link to Underhill.

But a human/Elven hybrid ought to be able to show them a few tricks, if I'm careful . . .

The doors opened.

"Showtime," Michael said.

He'd tried another conjuration—after what Nichol had done to him he'd been afraid to do anything else.

He'd fasted and prayed, knowing all along it was useless but going through the motions anyway, wondering if he had the courage to cut his own throat.

He should have. But instead he'd kept on, finding safety and comfort in the familiar prayers and invocations, thinking—God forgive him—that at least they'd leave him alone while he was in the workroom.

But they hadn't.

Suddenly—after hours? days?—all the lights had come up. He'd stood there, stunned by the sudden actinic brightness, and two men had come in, walking across his carefully drawn diagrams as though they were meaningless scribbles, dragging him from the room. He was weak by then from fasting, dazed from the sudden interruption. He'd barely had enough sense of self-preservation left to keep from protesting.

He'd been sure, then, that this was the worst thing they could do to him, this disparagement and contempt for his sacred Art.

They'd had so much still to teach him.

They'd brought him to another room. With a last vestige of self-mockery, he realized it was also a workroom. *Their* workroom.

There, time had ceased to have any meaning. Very soon, Marley Bell would gladly have broken the holiest and most sacred oaths he'd ever sworn, only they didn't care about those.

Elves. They wanted to know about elves.

He knew about elves, of course—the medieval inquisitors had been obsessed with them, and no one who studied old grimoires and the history of magic could avoid at least a passing familiarity with the Inquisition.

They hurt him.

He told them everything.

But it wasn't what they wanted to know.

They said he was lying.

And they hurt him again.

He had never understood before that time how the fear of pain and the fear of death could be separated, but in that room they taught him. In that room, they taught him to fear life, for only the living suffered, while the dead were beyond pain. But he was young and strong—they told him that—and his capacity to endure was extraordinarily good.

They said he worked for the elves. He swore he did not—over and over he swore to them; his soul was his own; he hadn't sold it; what did they *want?*

They wanted him to tell them about what he did with the elves.

Nothing—*nothing!*

And they hurt him again.

Perhaps, they said, he worked for the elves without knowing it . . . ?

And dear God, he'd seized upon that possibility, anything to be able to give them answers that would stop the pain, stop the whine of the generator, the lancing of the fire through the electrodes taped to his body.

But still his answers weren't right, though he tried, he tried very hard, he really did, begging them to just tell him what they wanted him to say, he'd confess to it, all of it. . . .

Pain, fire, and the stink of his own burning flesh.

He woke up in his cell, lying on the floor.

He'd been here before, he thought, though by now he knew his memory was not completely trustworthy. Sometimes they stopped and let him rest before taking him back to their workroom again. So he wouldn't die too quickly, Marley supposed.

The first time, he'd thought it was over, that they

believed him. Then they'd come for him and begun all over again, asking the same questions in endless variation. Now he no longer hoped. He'd tried making up the answers they wanted, but when the pain began he couldn't keep his stories straight.

His muscles shuddered uncontrollably, cramping and spasming painfully. His bones felt hollow, and his mouth tasted of bile and blood. His throat was raw from screaming.

Mother always told me the world was going to hell. And she was right. More than that, it's already there.

Was it worth trying to move? Maybe, to get from the floor to the bed. He might be able to manage that. And maybe they'd left him some water.

There was a sudden loud sound. Marley cringed. He couldn't help himself. It came again.

Gunfire.

Suddenly there was a sizzling sound, like frying bacon, from the door of his cell. It began to swing inward. Marley cried out, finding the strength in sudden terror to scrabble backward on hands and knees.

Not now! Not yet!

There hadn't been anything she wanted on Five; a corridor of anonymous doors, deserted at this time of night. Marley *had* been there, briefly, but he wasn't now.

"Come on," she said to Logan. "Michael?"

Michael was regarding the corridor of anonymous doors like a boy with a roomful of Christmas presents, unable to decide which one to open first.

"Oh, I'm fine here. But you'll want this," he said, offering her a second keycard. "Use it wisely. And do try to stay out of trouble."

"Of course," Ria said with grave amusement. She

left Michael there, happily opening doors, and went out into the stairwell.

:Where are you, Marley Bell?:

It was a simple Seeking spell, one she used every day almost without thought, but now she could feel the cost of it, the power that she spent that went unrenewed, draining away like water poured into sand. Ria dearly wished she knew exactly *how* the interior of the PDI was shielded—was it just the whole building, or were some interior rooms separately shielded as well?—because without that information, she might be about to make some lethal mistakes.

But she had an answer—or part of one, anyway.

"Up."

Seven was occupied. The lights were on, and Ria could hear the fleeting hash of thoughts. But there was no one in sight, and that was good.

She knew Bell was somewhere on this floor, but that left a lot of places to look. She hadn't wanted to push for details down in the stairwell—she didn't know how much reserve she had, and once it was gone, it was gone—but now that she was closer, it was worth trying again.

"We need to get out of sight while I look for Bell," she said. Logan asked no questions. They moved off down the corridor, choosing a room at random.

It was dark and empty. Ria looked around. Curious. Doctor's office, some kind of infirmary?

Then she saw the generator in the corner and Ria knew exactly what this room was used for.

"I can't work in here," she said tightly. "Let's find someplace else."

Marley had been in here, and recently. No doubt of that. But he wasn't here now. And her sorcerous psychometry wouldn't be at all reliable against the background noise produced by torture.

Logan nodded, his face impassive, and opened the door.

And a man in a green suit started shooting at them.

Logan kicked the door shut and shot through it all in one swift motion. Ria heard a scream, and wrenched the remains of the door off its hinges.

The man was down, but Logan had shot low. He was still alive. Amazingly, he smiled. "I was right," he whispered. "Right all along."

"*Where is he?*" Ria snarled, grabbing the man's jaw in her hands.

She couldn't hear his mind. His thoughts slid away from her in a peculiar way, as if she couldn't quite reach them.

But he'd been where Marley was now. He'd touched him. And now Ria was touching *him*. And that was all she needed.

"This way," Ria said, getting to her feet and taking off at a run. "Buy me time."

The man on the floor of the cell looked very little like his photographs. Dazed, emaciated, naked, filthy, and covered with contact burns, he scrabbled away from her, whimpering in terror.

She didn't have time to either soothe or reason with him. She crossed the cell in a stride and hauled him to his feet, then slung him over her shoulder in a fireman's carry. She was stronger than she looked, but it was still awkward.

This was it. Her spells were tapped. Blowing the lock on Bell's cell had taken the last of them. All she had left was a little innate ability to read minds, and she didn't require that to see that things were going straight to Hell in the proverbial handbasket.

She hadn't expected the building to be deserted,

though it would have been nice if they could have just walked in, found Marley, and walked out again. She didn't even cavil at a little cold-blooded murder, if it came down to it; anybody who forced her to kill them wasn't likely to be anyone's innocent child.

The only trouble was, the PDI seemed to be even more paranoid than *she* was.

She saw a flicker of movement outside the cell—it wouldn't be Logan; Logan was up ahead, securing the way to the stairwell—and fired at it. It pulled back.

"I'm pinned down," Ria said into her throat mike.

"Coming," Logan said.

Ria smelled smoke.

She fired again, just for fun. An office building was a lousy place for a firefight—all straight lines and no cover. And if the bad guys could get to the cell door and shut it, she'd be bottled up here with Marley, and that would be a fine end to the evening.

She wondered where Michael was.

Suddenly everything went black.

Power's gone out, she realized after a moment's surprise. There was a flicker, then the backup generators went on, bathing the corridor in a faint amber glow. The smoke smell was stronger now.

There was a figure crouching low in the doorway, reaching for the door. Ria shot. In the enclosed space, the Desert Eagle spoke like the Wrath of God. The muzzle flash blinded her for a moment; when she could see again, Ria stepped out into the corridor.

"Three more on this level. I started a fire," Logan said quietly behind her.

"Let's take the stairs," Ria said.

If things had been wrong before, they kept getting worse. When they got to the stairwell, the keycard didn't work—and Ria had no more spells to expend.

"Power failure probably seals every floor as a security

measure," Logan said. "Nice. Melody. Basement retrieval. Find a way."

Logan reached into his jacket for the remaining Thermite pencils and began taping them to the door.

"They'll take about a minute to burn through the lock," he said. "We'll make for the basement level."

He motioned her back around the corner. Ria leaned against the wall, letting it take Marley's weight while she covered Logan and tried to watch in all directions at once. He'd said there were three of them still on the floor. She'd feel much better if she got to shoot all of them.

Logan joined her as the Thermite began to sizzle and flare. Ria closed her eyes against the glare, listening hard.

Something.

Not thoughts, but more of a *disturbance*. The same sort of disturbance she'd felt when she'd tried to read the thoughts of the dying green-suited man.

"Down!" Ria shouted, swinging blindly toward the thought-shadow. Marley slid from her shoulder, hitting the ground as she ducked and fired.

Logan fired just after she did, and when Ria could see again, he was standing over a body.

"One down," he said.

She turned away to check Marley. He was breathing, but unconscious. Just as well. She heaved him onto her shoulder again.

There was a crash as Logan kicked the door open.

The stairwell was dimmer than the floor had been. They took the stairs all the way down, moving as fast as they could. They'd left two hostiles alive behind them, and it would require no great detective ability for the PDI to trace their movements. But there were no interior doors blocking the stairwells, and no one followed them. Bless OSHA and its finicky requirements for government office buildings. Even ones that weren't supposed to exist.

But the door that led out to the basement was steel, and solid, and locked. Very thoroughly locked.

"No good," Logan said, inspecting it. "What I've got left won't get us through."

Ria swore, feelingly. But suddenly she realized something.

She could Hear again.

Whatever shielding Wheatley had put around his little fief didn't extend below the second floor. She was weak, and still far from the top of her game, but she had her external power source back.

She took a deep breath, and reached out and touched the door. *:Open!:*

Magic wasn't effortless for Ria, but it had never been this hard before. She felt herself greying out, needles of strain lancing through her; the forerunner of a really spectacular headache beginning behind her eyes. *:OPEN!:*

After several seconds, a grinding shudder passed through the metal as its locks released. The door shifted in its frame and a crack of light appeared all along the edge. Logan pushed it open. His face showed no surprise. Ria doubted his expression would change if he saw the Four Horsemen of the Apocalypse appear accompanied by the Angels of Mons.

They stepped out carefully into the dark, silent, underground garage, Logan going first. Ria strained her senses to the uttermost, but heard no trace of thoughts that might indicate an ambush. The weight on her shoulders was utterly slack, barely breathing.

"Very nice, Princess, but I'm afraid you're just going to have to put him back."

She knew the Men in Green were shielded against her sorcerous telepathy, and the background hash of other minds had kept her from Hearing the faint trace that did leak through their shields. Ria swung around—awkwardly, with Marley's weight to compensate for—to face the man who stepped out from behind the car.

No wonder they hadn't been followed. The agents had known they were running into a trap.

He was wearing the same green suit they all wore, with Kevlar armor over it, and holding a Mossberg 12-gauge. Ria didn't think it was loaded with rubber bullets. On the opposite side of the garage, two more agents, also in green, also heavily armed and armored, rose up out of concealment.

"Oh, I really don't think she should have to do that," Michael said, strolling into view.

He was holding a grenade in one hand, and a briefcase in the other. The man facing Ria flicked a glance toward him, but his weapon never wavered. Michael stopped a dozen feet away.

"You'll want to know if I've pulled the pin. I assure you I have. You'll doubt me. But it's not being quite *sure* that adds so much zest to our daily lives, don't you think, Mr. Collins?"

There was a squeal of tires and a flare of headlights. The Lincoln Navigator roared down the ramp, headlights flaring.

That got Collins' attention, and in the moment he looked away, Ria put three rounds into his chest just as the other two PDI agents opened up on the Navigator. The impact knocked Collins flying. She could hope it killed him, but she couldn't be sure.

"Ria—*catch!*"

The briefcase came flying toward her. She staggered as she caught it, gripping it against her with her gun arm, clutching at Marley's body with her free hand.

Bullets were flying everywhere, and any one of them could take her down—or kill Marley. She crouched low, using the bulk of the Navigator as a shield. Michael simply stood there, as unconcerned as if there were no men, no bullets, no guns.

The doors of the Navigator popped open and she staggered forward, throwing Marley and the briefcase ahead of her. She clutched at the back of the seat in front of her as the SUV began to accelerate, and barely managed to draw her legs in before the doors slammed shut with a bank vault *chunk*.

In the rearview mirror, she saw Michael drop the grenade into his pocket and placidly raise his hands. The two agents were standing behind the car now, firing directly into it. The vehicle shuddered as it was struck, but the bullets had no other effect.

"Hold on," Melody warned.

They hit the security barrier with a jarring impact as the Navigator accelerated. Ria and Marley were flung back and forth jarringly against the seats as the Navigator bounced over the debris and out into the street, still accelerating.

It had just begun to turn when the explosion shook the night.

"Never lie, Ria. It causes wrinkles," Michael had told her once. The grenade had been live, just as he'd said.

Goodbye, Michael. I'm sorry you didn't get to see Greece again.

"Drive for your life," Ria said harshly.

"Where is he?" Beth Kentraine demanded.

Apparently the e-mail servers to Underhill were working just dandy at the moment. Two hours after

Kayla had sent her e-mail—worded as tactfully as she could, under the circumstances—both Beth and Kory had shown up on her doorstep—or rather, Eric's doorstep.

They walked in—a tall blond man and a shorter, red-headed woman, holding motorcycle helmets beneath their arms. Beth Kentraine's hair had originally been black, Kayla remembered, but the elves had changed it for one of her disguises, and Beth had never changed it back. Both were wearing dark maroon motorcycle leathers, having ridden here from the Everforest Gate on their elvensteeds.

"I don't know," Kayla said miserably, opening the door wider to let Beth and Kory enter Eric's apartment. "Nobody knows. Except maybe his ride, and she ain't talking."

"I will go see what I may discover there," Kory said, turning to leave again. As he left, he rested a hand on Beth's shoulder. Kayla could feel the unspoken communication flow between them.

"You want tea?" Kayla asked.

"I want to know where Eric is," Beth said tightly. "You didn't say much in your e-mail, other than that he'd disappeared suddenly and—"

"Well, so does everybody else," Kayla snapped, interrupting what promised to be a Beth Kentraine special. "Want to know. An' all I know after three days is that he's *probably* not dead and *probably* not in Underhill. And how are you folks?"

"Why did you wait so long to tell us?" Beth half-wailed, sinking down onto the couch. "Eric doesn't just—disappear. We could have helped."

I'm sitting in a building full of magicians with a talking gargoyle on top, and none of them *could do jack,* Kayla thought crossly. But she couldn't be mad at Beth. Of everyone whose life had been disrupted by

Elven magic, Beth's had been the most deeply affected. For the rest of her life, Beth could only be a visitor to the World Above, and not only because every Alphabet Agency there was would be looking for her till the end of time because of her supposed involvement in the Poseidon Project mess.

There was Kory to think of, as well as baby Maeve. Kayla knew that Beth and Kory were bonded together far more closely than any pair of human lovers, but Beth Kentraine was still human, and Korendil . . . wasn't.

Underhill it didn't matter. Here in the Real World, it did. And according to Eric, if Beth spent enough time in Underhill, she'd reach a point where she *couldn't* come out, ever, not even for visits because, unless she was shielded by massive protection spells, she'd automatically attain her true age, the age she would have been if she'd been living outside of Underhill all along. And once enough time had passed, that would mean instant death. So Beth could only make the briefest of visits to the World Above, and pretty soon, not even that.

Beth had the happiness she'd always dreamed of—a loving husband and a child. But—just like in a fairy tale—there was a price to pay.

"That's why I called you guys, Beth," Kayla said. "I do need help. I've been trying to get through to Ria, but Anita says she's tied up with an emergency down in Washington. Hosea's good, but he's still an Apprentice Bard, and he's already looked for Eric and can't find him. Dr. Dunaway thinks Eric might be in a hospital somewhere, shielded so Lady Day can't sense him, and unconscious so he can't give his name. So . . . either Kory's magic can help, or you can hire me a private detective to start checking the local hospitals for John Doe admissions, because they're not going to listen to a college student who's not related to the guy, and hiring help's gotta be faster than doing it ourselves. You know how many hospitals there are in the New York area?"

And what if he isn't in any of them? Let's hope she doesn't bring that up, because I don't have any good answers for that one.

Beth raised an eyebrow in an expression familiar to Kayla from a thousand *Star Trek* re-runs, but Kayla's list seemed to have convinced her that Kayla hadn't just been sitting around.

"So. Tea?" Beth said at last.

The tea was steeping by the time Kory returned. His doleful expression told them he'd had little success.

"She knows he went to the Park, and there he became . . . lost to her," Kory reported, coming into the kitchen.

"Lost?" Beth demanded.

"How lost?" Kayla echoed.

"'Lost' is the only word she has for what she experienced," Kory answered grimly, lifting the lid of the teapot and staring down into it as if the answers he didn't have might be there.

Kayla stared at him, fascinated as always, despite the seriousness of the situation. She knew he didn't really look like what she was seeing. Kory was an elf—pointy ears, cat's eyes, and all—but the *glamourie* he cast showed her a normal—if stunningly beautiful—man. Slender, taller than average, long wavy blond hair flowing over his shoulders, and green eyes to die for, the kind that model bookers would chase down the street waving contracts at, but still human.

"Not dead, not kidnapped Underhill. Only . . . lost," Kory said, sounding puzzled. "And that should not be."

"Where in the Park?" Beth demanded. "What was he doing there?"

"I can take you there," Kayla said. "Or anyway, Lady Day can. Eric said he was going to 'make an interdimensional phone call.' That's what he said *exactly*. So for a while I thought . . ." *You thought he'd gone Underhill to make arrangements for someone to take care of Magnus, and that's why you didn't worry until it was way too late for worrying.*

Should she tell them about Eric's brother? Kayla hesitated. Maybe she'd tell Kory, if she could get him alone, but Beth didn't look like someone who needed additional stress right now. Come down to it, neither did Kayla. She still hadn't made up her mind whether she was going to try to go back up to The Place again tonight. *Not* going felt a lot like running out on Eric when he needed her—there wasn't anybody else to keep an eye on Magnus. But right now Magnus wasn't going anywhere. At least she hoped he wasn't. And Eric might need her help more than Magnus did.

"Earth to Kayla?" Beth said.

Kayla blinked, startled out of her thoughts. What had she been saying a moment before? Running on four hours sleep a night—if that—wasn't doing her brain a lot of good.

"You were saying that you thought Eric had gone Underhill," Kory prompted her, pouring tea.

"Yeah," Kayla said, relieved. "But then, when Lady Day got all upset, it looked like not."

Kory regarded her soberly. Beth might have missed everything she'd left out of that explanation, but it didn't look like her little elf buddy had. Kayla bit her lip, praying he wouldn't ask the next obvious question, because right now she was too tired to come up with a really convincing lie.

"Well," Beth said, "let's finish this and go up to the Park and see what we can see."

❖   ❖   ❖

"See?" Kayla said. "Nothing here."

Beth looked around, wrinkling her nose. "Not a really nice place. I bet a lot of muggings happen up here."

The three of them stood in the same clearing that Lady Day had brought Kayla and Hosea to three days before. Except for the addition of a few more bits of garbage, it was unchanged.

"Probably," Kayla said. "But we should be pretty safe." There were three of them, after all, and the 'steeds could get them out of here at the first sign of trouble. Plus the fact that Kory could probably turn into an Elven Knight at the drop of a hat and pull a sword or something and scare the heck out of anybody who looked at them funny.

"Forgive me for asking," Kory said, "but *how* did you look, when you were here last?"

Kayla thought back. "Hosea had his banjo with him. He used Jeanette to look around."

"And Jeanette is a disembodied human spirit?" Kory asked.

"Yeah," Kayla said. *My homie, the Ozark Bard with the haunted banjo.* "She said he wasn't here and he wasn't dead."

"But perhaps she did not see all there was to see," Kory said. "My power is not great—and in this place it is far less than otherwise—but perhaps it can tell us more."

"Be careful," Beth said.

Kory smiled at her. "With you and Maeve to think of, how could I be less than careful? Yet Eric is our true friend, and I will do no less than all I can for him as well."

Elves. By the time you figure out what they've actually said, they've made off with the keys to the

Mint, Kayla thought in irritable fascination. But she was complaining mostly to distract herself, she knew. If Kory *could* find Eric, or at least find out what had happened to him . . .

Then maybe at least we'll know where to look for you, Banyon.

Kory kissed Beth lightly on the cheek and walked away from the two of them, until he was standing in the middle of the open space. A trampled track of grass, not quite a path, showed where most people crossed through here, and Kory stood just to one side of that. He slipped off his leather gauntlets and set them gently aside on the ground. For several moments, his hands sketched patterns in the air.

At first there was no result, and Kory frowned. He seemed to push against something, and the *glamourie* around him faded away as he funneled all his power into the spell, so that now Kayla could see his long pointed ears, pale skin, and slanted brows clearly.

The patterns in the air seemed to take on more solidity now, becoming faintly glowing shapes, though they sparked and faded away almost at once. Kayla got the impression they weren't supposed to do that, because Kory swore and muttered under his breath, his frown becoming even more thunderous.

But at last they steadied, the pattern burning steadily with a pale blue-green light, hanging in the air before him like disembodied neon.

"I cannot hold it for long," Kory said, sounding a little breathless. "Let us pray that it shows us what we need to see."

And Eric came walking through the Park.

He looked subtly unreal, like bad CGI, but it was Eric, dressed as Kayla had seen him last. He was staggering, exhausted, carrying his flute in his fist. Around him the light was different; though it was late afternoon in the here and now, Eric walked through the light of early morning, adding to the strange sense of disconnection for his watchers.

"*Eric?*" Beth's voice was a symphony of distress. "Oh, Blessed Lady, what's happened to him?"

"This is okay," Kayla said quickly. "He meant to look that way. I'll explain later." She put a hand on Beth's arm. Only the fact that she couldn't sense anything from the Eric image kept her from running over to him. But this wasn't Eric. This was a *movie* of Eric, from three days ago.

But she couldn't stifle a groan of dismay as Eric walked, oblivious, right into the midst of five punks lurking in the underbrush. Didn't he *see* them?

There was no sound, only images, but it wasn't hard to guess what they were saying. "*Give us all your money,*" or something like that.

She watched as he dropped the flute, as one of them hit him from behind with what looked like a length of pipe wrapped in electrical tape, as he fell to the ground and all five of them kept on hitting him. One of them had a baseball bat.

The image vanished.

"I'm sorry," Kory said, staggering back and gasping slightly. "I could not hold the spell any longer. But now we know what happened to him." He shook his head, as if slightly dazed, and Kayla could see—and feel—what the spell had cost him.

"I'll kill them," Beth vowed, in a shaking voice. "I'll find them and I'll kill them all."

Freaks, Kayla thought numbly. *Just an ordinary mugging by ordinary freaks. It could happen to anyone.*

But it shouldn't happen to Eric. Eric was a street-wise New Yorker by now. He knew better than to go wandering through this part of the Park—through any part of the Park—as if he were half-asleep. And what had happened to him just before this? He'd looked like death on toast. Even without his flute, he should have been able to stop them.

But he hadn't.

Kory gathered Beth into his arms and held her close. "We do not know that what this appeared to be was all this was. My spell could show nothing more than the external images of things. But now we know this much. And surely someone must have found him and given him succor," Kory said, as if it were the most reasonable thing in the world.

"Which is the closest hospital?" Beth demanded.

Gotham General Hospital covered several city blocks. It was the largest hospital in the city, and it had one of the best burn trauma units on the East Coast. Jimmie Youngblood had died here.

I never wanted to come back here, Kayla thought, walking up to the information desk. She was just as glad she'd cleaned up and gotten respectable on the off-chance that Beth and Kory might be showing up. Her story wasn't going to make a lot of sense as it was.

"I wondered if you could help me," Kayla said. "I'm looking for my brother."

The woman behind the desk smiled. "Is he a patient here?"

"That's the thing," Kayla said. It wasn't hard to look nervous, frightened, or scared—all those emotions were right below the surface, and she let them well up and spill over. "I don't know. I think he might have been mugged up in Central Park Tuesday morning. Is he here?"

A short time later, the three of them were seated in an office across a desk from one of the hospital's many administrators.

"Why do you think your brother might be here, Ms. Smith?" Mr. Wilson asked.

It wasn't hard to cry, so Kayla did. "It's the closest," she said around a wad of Kleenex. "He didn't come home Tuesday night. I called the hospitals, but there isn't an 'Eric Banyon,' in any of them."

"Perhaps he's just—"

"It isn't going to kill you to check," Beth Kentraine interrupted in a hard voice. "White male, mid-twenties to early thirties, brown hair, brown eyes, no distinguishing marks or scars, admitted unconscious or disoriented and still in that state. Last seen wearing a green raincoat, if that helps. How many of those can you have gotten in here since Tuesday?"

"In New York, quite a large number," Mr. Wilson said, with a faint sigh. "Ms. . . . ?"

"Connor. Beth Connor. I'm Eric's ex-wife. This is my husband Kory. Look, if he's here, we want to find him. And you want to bill his insurance company. Let's help each other out."

Kayla saw Wilson twitch at the mention of the word "insurance"; Beth had struck a nerve there, all right. But he turned to the computer terminal in silence.

After a few moments he turned back to them.

"Are you quite sure your brother was in Central Park Tuesday morning?" Mr. Wilson asked.

Kayla nodded.

"And would you happen to know his blood type?"

"Oh, yes," Beth said calmly. "Eric is O Positive."

Mr. Wilson sighed, sitting back in his chair.

"Ms. Smith, Mr. and Ms. Connor, we have a patient here who may—only may—be Mr. Banyon. The police brought him in Tuesday afternoon, after he'd been spotted by a jogger. He had no identification on him. He'd been . . . severely beaten. He was unconscious upon arrival, and he hasn't regained consciousness. His condition is . . . very serious. He was just transferred out of ICU this morning."

Beth clutched Kory's hand, hard. Kayla hugged herself tightly.

Wilson winced again, though only someone like Kayla would have noticed. "If you'll come with me, I'll take you up to his room so you can make an identification. Please remember, this may not be the man you're looking for."

Who else could it be? Kayla thought desperately.

It took them several minutes of walking to reach the room, and Kayla was lost immediately in a bewildering maze of elevators and corridors. All around her, even through her shields, she could sense the litany of pain and damage from the rooms around her. *A hospital,* she thought wryly, *was no place for a Healer.*

But if Eric was here—if it was Eric—it had to be Eric—she could Heal him, get him out of here—

Mr. Wilson stopped before a closed door.

"I'd really prefer if only one person went in," he said.

Beth started forward, but Kory held her back.

"Kayla will go," Kory said.

It made sense. She was the Empath, the Healer. No matter how messed up Eric was, conscious or not, she'd be able to reach him. Kayla took a deep breath, squaring her shoulders. " 'Kay," she said.

Mr. Wilson opened the door.

The room held six beds. Two were empty. Kayla heard the susurrant sound of ventilators, the faint metronomic beeping of heart monitors, the odd bleachy smell of sick-sweat. It reminded her of the last hospital room she'd been in. Jimmie's.

But no sweet stench of cooking flesh. Not that, at least.

The curtains were drawn around each bed, concealing the occupants. Mr. Wilson stopped at one and parted the curtains at the foot.

"Is this your brother?"

"Gimme a minute." Kayla steeled herself to look, the image of the beating Eric had taken still sharp in her mind.

She was braced for horrors, so she didn't lose it. Not quite.

They'd shaved most of his head, and part of it was covered with an odd lopsided bandage. Both his eyes were swollen shut, the flesh around them black and red. His nose had been spectacularly broken, and it looked as if his jaw had, too; it was held in place by a brace. Both arms were splinted, and one leg was suspended at an angle, held up by a traction brace; multiple fractures, she guessed. Tubes snaked beneath the sheets, some led upward to suspended bags. A machine was breathing for him.

"Eric?" Kayla whispered. *Oh, Jesus, ERIC . . .*

She clutched at the foot of the bed. It would take days, maybe weeks, to repair all that damage. Where did she start?

Start with him waking up. That would be nice.

"Yes," she managed to say, nodding. "That's Eric."

"I'm sorry." He reached out to put a hand on her shoulder, and Kayla moved before he could touch her, going up along the side of the bed to stand at Eric's side. "Could I . . . just stay with him for a few minutes?"

"Of course. Can we get in touch with your parents?"

Kayla stared at him blankly for a moment before realizing that he meant *Eric's* parents. "No. They're dead."

Wilson hesitated, on the verge of saying something

he obviously didn't want to say to her. "I'll be out-side."

Kayla waited impatiently until she heard the door close again.

"Hey there, Sleeping Beauty," she said. "Time to wake up."

She pulled off her gloves and stuffed them into her pocket, then reached out and touched Eric on the forehead. *Come out, come out, wherever you are. . . .*

"—make an appointment for you to talk to Dr. Rodriguez tomorrow afternoon. He'll be able to give you the specifics of Mr. Banyon's condition. And if you can stop by the Admitting Office on your way out, we can get most of the paperwork taken care of," Mr. Wilson was saying to Beth and Kory when Kayla came out.

Beth took one quick glance at Kayla's face and took a step sideways to put herself between Wilson and the young Empath. Whatever had just happened in that room wasn't good, and Kayla looked just about to lose it.

Kory—Lady bless him!—picked up on her cue and shepherded Kayla ahead of him toward the elevator. Beth set her mouth on "babble" and pasted her best insincere smile on her face, the one that had served her well, in a previous life, whenever she'd had to deal with network TV executives.

"Thank you for everything you've done, Mr. Wilson. I'm afraid I don't have Eric's insurance card with me but—do you have a fax number here? I know he's got a fax, I could go home and fax you the informa-tion as soon as we get back to his apartment. Kory and I are staying with him. Eric introduced me to

Kory, actually; we've all known each other for years. I live out on the West Coast now, in fact I was just in town for a few days on a visit; this is such a horrible thing to happen; I told Eric that moving to New York was a horrible idea, but honestly—"

"They'll take care of all that down at the Admitting Office," Mr. Wilson said. "And of course the police will want to get in touch with you."

"Police?" Beth said, her voice skittering up an octave despite herself. "Oh, because he was *mugged!* Well, I don't know what I can tell them. But sure; gosh, I went through that last year out in SF when someone stole my purse. Not that this is anything like that, of course." She laughed, a little jaggedly. *Oh, Blessed Lady, not the police! I don't think I can handle that. . . .*

But she managed to keep right on babbling.

"What's wrong?" Beth demanded, as soon as all three of them were in the open air again.

"Beth," Kayla said, "it's him. *But he isn't in there.*"

CHAPTER TWELVE:

ROCKY ROAD TO DUBLIN

They picked up a tail about two miles away from the PDI, and Ria doubted it was anyone nice, with every LEO in D.C. converging on the explosion.

She'd gotten Marley into her trench coat and managed to get him buckled into the passenger seat beside her. At least, if they *were* stopped, he wouldn't look as immediately suspicious as he would if he were naked.

He was conscious—his eyes were open at least, and he was holding onto a bottle of water—but Ria didn't know how well he was tracking. Still, she had to try. When she showed up at Nathaniel Babcock's doorstep out in Silver Springs, Marley had to have his story straight. She would have liked to have taken him straight to Walter Reed, but that had been going to

be Michael's play. Now she was going to have to fall
back on her second choice. Maybe Nathaniel could
parlay a promotion out of this.

"Marley, can you hear me?" she asked gently.

"Are we going to lose them?" Logan said to Melody.

"We can but try," Melody said cheerily.

Ria shut her mind to the conversation in the front
seat. Either they'd lose their tail or they wouldn't.
There was little she could do about it without more
rest. She felt bruised in places that didn't even have
names, and she had a pounding headache. If she tried
a spell now, and lost control of it, she could do as
much damage to her own side as to the enemy.

"Marley?" she said again.

Slowly, he turned toward her. "I don't know anything," he whispered. He stared at her with an expression of hopeless despair.

"That's right," Ria said. "Parker Wheatley kidnapped
you and tortured you, and you didn't know anything.
I'm going to take you to friends. They'll protect you
from him."

"No," Marley said in that same strangely docile tone,
shaking his head very slightly. "That won't help. He
worked for the government, you know."

"He was a sick, crazy man," Ria said gently. "And if
you tell my friends what he did, they'll see that."

"Elves," Marley said with a sigh. "He wanted to
know about elves."

"But elves don't exist," Ria said firmly. "And anybody
who believes in elves is crazy. So Parker Wheatley is
crazy. When you talk to my friends, they'll understand.
They'll help you."

The Navigator doused its lights and made a sharp
left, bumped up over a curb and down a flight of
steps—across one of the pedestrian malls that were

a feature of downtown—and zoomed on. There was a grinding crunch as it squeezed between a park bench and a piece of sculpture, then a long grating sound as it made its way down an alley just barely wide enough to accommodate it.

"That's done it," Melody said with satisfaction, zipping out into the street and hitting the lights again. "I don't think we're radar-opaque any more, though."

"They won't believe me," Marley said, still in that same flat, dead voice. "They'll believe him."

Ria made herself believe what she said, because Marley was hearing tone more than words right now. "You don't have to worry about Parker Wheatley, Marley. Mr. Wheatley is about to become a footnote to history. Just tell my friends what he did to you."

She patted the briefcase on her lap absently, wondering what was in it that Michael had been so sure was worth dying for.

She'd find out.

It was almost four by the time they reached Babcock's house. Ria got out of the car—the doors stuck a little, but Melody finally got them open—and took a moment to divest herself of all suspicious equipment and weapons. She took the briefcase, and helped Marley out of the car.

"Now disappear," she told the other two. "I'll take care of the rest."

Logan nodded. The Lincoln's doors shut.

She stood there for a moment, holding Marley up, as the Navigator disappeared—more sedately now—into the distance.

It was cold. Her breath fogged the air. She could feel Marley shivering.

"Come on," she said. "Let's go."

He stumbled with her up to the front steps of

the house. All the windows were dark. Ria rang the doorbell. There was a pause, then a sudden wild barking from inside, and the sound of scrabbling at the inside of the door.

Several minutes passed. The dog stopped barking abruptly. Then the outside lights went on, and Nathaniel Babcock's face appeared at the window. He stared at Ria for a long moment before dropping the curtain again.

The door opened on the security chain.

"Ms. Llewellyn?" he said guardedly.

"Yes, Mr. Babcock. It's all right. I'm sorry to bother you at home. I've brought a friend who needs official help. His name is Marley Bell, and up until several hours ago he was being held prisoner by Parker Wheatley and the PDI."

Babcock closed the door and took the chain off, then opened it all the way. He was wearing a plaid wool bathrobe over striped pajamas and looked very rumpled. One pocket of the robe sagged, as if something heavy rested there. In the living room behind him stood his wife, her arms full of a squirming black-and-white cocker spaniel, one hand firmly clamped over its muzzle.

"Bab?" she said.

"Go back to bed, honey. And take Bingo with you, would you? This is business."

The woman sighed and turned away, hefting the dog higher in her arms and letting go of its muzzle. It began to bark again as she carried it off down the hall. The sound continued until it was muffled by the sound of a closing door.

Ria stepped inside, carrying Marley with her. Babcock stared at his bare legs as Ria lowered him gently into the nearest chair. It was pretty obvious that Marley was wearing nothing but her coat.

"What's this all about?" Nathaniel said.

"The short version goes something like this," Ria said, rubbing her forehead wearily. "Mr. Bell owns an occult bookstore in Baltimore. About two weeks ago—I found out yesterday—Parker Wheatley went off the rails and kidnapped him, apparently on the theory that Mr. Bell was an agent of these para-humans he's after. He's had Mr. Bell tortured. A doctor would be nice."

"And where do you come into this?"

"I was left holding the baby," Ria said. She chose her next words with care. If she said anything that indicated she'd committed a crime, Nathaniel would have little choice but to take notice. "A friend of mine entered the PDI tonight with what he told me was a Justice Department warrant. He's dead now. Nathaniel, how much of this do you really want to know?"

"I didn't want to know this much. Are you sure he was tortured?"

In answer, Ria reached down and pulled open the trench coat, exposing one of the burn marks on Marley's chest. Nathaniel's face went very still.

"I'm going to go get dressed and make some calls. Don't go anywhere."

After that, things happened fairly fast. Mrs. Bab-cock, Nathaniel's two boys, and the spaniel Bingo—still protesting, intermittently, these intruders in her domain—were quickly dressed and removed from the house. The expression on Nathaniel's wife's face as she drove off indicated that this wasn't the last Nathaniel was going to hear about this, either. Three unmarked but highly obvious official cars arrived in the Babcock driveway. A doctor made a quick examination of Marley Bell and asked him a few questions before having him taken off to a hospital under full security.

Ria managed a quick look through the briefcase. Michael hadn't had much time inside, but what he'd managed to get should be enough to hang Parker Wheatley from a high gallows indeed. Memos, work documents, position papers—several with Wheatley's own signature—all detailed the PDI's quest to end the "paraterrestrial menace" in plain language that made Wheatley and his band of little green men sound like raving lunatics.

She told a short and highly expurgated version of her story to the senior case agents who arrived at Nathaniel's house along with the doctor, and then, more or less as she'd expected, was driven back into Washington to be interviewed at the J. Edgar Hoover Building several more times by a number of people much higher on the FBI food chain than Nathaniel Babcock. She'd kept her story simple, knowing that they really wouldn't be able to disprove it.

And knowing what she did about Washington politics, they wouldn't want to. If Marley told a different story about his rescue, they'd put it down to the disorientation of his captivity. And they might not ask him about that part at all.

Ria's story was simple and contained a lot of the truth, as the best lies always did. She'd gone to Michael with the information about Marley, and Michael had done the rest. She willingly gave them everything she had about her past dealings with Michael, knowing that at this point there was no one left in Michael's organization to compromise. Michael had taken her with him to the PDI so that she could identify Marley when he brought Marley out. If they thought that was odd, the only person they could complain to about it was dead.

Michael had brought Marley and the briefcase to the car. She gave up the briefcase, admitting freely that she'd looked through it: who wouldn't? Michael had gone back inside. Ria had heard gunfire. There'd been an explosion. Michael hadn't come back. Ria had panicked and driven off.

A nice, neat story. And very nearly true. And if anyone wondered where her car was now, she made sure with a few well-placed spells that they didn't ask. By the time the little spells of Misdirection she'd managed to cast wore off and they *did* ask, she could tell them she'd sent one of her drivers out to pick it up. Just what they could expect from an annoying civilian, when all was said and done.

They'd wanted to hold her for further questioning, of course, but Ria had other plans, and—by now—the magical muscle to back it up. A *glamourie* would wear off eventually, but by the time it did, she would have had a chance to muddle her tracks even more thoroughly and put up a hedge of lawyers around herself. She had every intention of cooperating to bring Wheatley down. But on *her* terms.

One simple spell bought her five uninterrupted minutes' use of her cell phone to call for a LlewellCo car to be waiting for her downstairs. Another—more complicated—series of spells convinced the people she was talking to that she really wasn't very central to their actual investigation after all, and that she might as well be allowed to go back to her hotel until they needed her again. Since that was so counter to their own inclinations, the spell wouldn't hold for long. But then, it didn't have to. Just for long enough.

An agent escorted her out of the building. Her car was waiting. Ria didn't breathe quite freely until its door had closed behind her.

"Back to the Watergate, Ms. Llewellyn?" the driver asked.

She considered it for a brief instant, but no. She doubted Wheatley was the sort to give up easily, and the wheels of justice—or even payback—ground exceeding slow. She'd stung him, she was quite sure he knew by now who his enemy was, and she had ample proof of how little interest he had in playing by the rules.

If he gave her enough trouble, she could certainly make him vanish. But making him vanish wouldn't serve her aims nearly as well as thoroughly discrediting the PDI would.

"No. Just drive around for a while. I'm going to make some calls."

"What do you mean 'he's not there'?" Beth demanded, pacing back and forth.

They'd been about to have this conversation right there on the steps of the hospital, but Kory had made Beth wait until they'd gotten back to Eric's apartment. It didn't make things any easier.

Kayla was huddled in a ball of misery at one corner of the couch, knees drawn up to her chin and arms wrapped around them tightly.

"They really did a number on him," she said, her voice low. "But that shouldn't matter. Hell, Jimmie was *dyin'*, an' she was still there. But I touched him, an'. . . it was like he was *empty.*" She shuddered, remembering. It had been like touching a piece of meat at the supermarket. Warm, and breathing—thanks to the hospital's machines—but . . . empty.

"No," Beth whispered, her face twisting with pain. Kayla winced at the agony she could feel sheeting off Beth. The better you knew someone, the harder it was to shield against them.

"Could he be . . . hiding?" Kory suggested. He stroked Beth's hair, and Kayla felt Beth's pain ease a little.

"Maybe," Kayla said dubiously, trying to forget it was *Eric* in that bed and think. "Elizabet said that happens sometimes. With physical trauma or a bad psychic shock. It's sort of what happened with Ria. It took us almost a year to really put her back together, and it took two of us. I wasn't with Eric long enough to take a good look. And if I am going to take a really deep look, I'm going to need an anchor and some protection. I could use Hosea. Or Ria."

She noticed that Beth didn't make her usual face when Ria's name was mentioned, for a change. That was nice.

"Has anything bad happened to Eric recently?" Beth asked. "Something that could make something like this happen?"

Other than seeing his parents again, and finding out about Magnus, and like that? Kayla thought. "I didn't think so," she said, honestly enough. "He's been seeing that shrink, and everything—I better call her and tell her we found him, and then call Elizabet and ask her what to do. And dig out Eric's insurance card to keep the hospital happy." *And get farther away from you, lady, before I gnaw open a vein just from being around you.*

Kayla swung off the couch and went into the bedroom. Eric would have left his wallet there. There was a second phone there as well.

The first thing she saw, sitting on top of the dresser in plain sight, was Magnus' bus pass. She grabbed it.

Kory reached over her shoulder and plucked it out of her hand. He'd followed her into the bedroom so silently she hadn't heard a thing.

"Gimme that!" Kayla hissed, grabbing for it. She

glanced around him, but Beth had stayed in the living room, for a mercy.

Kory, far taller than she was, held it easily out of her reach.

"A brother," he said quietly, not even needing to look at the card to be able to know—magically—what it signified. "Lost. And Eric was looking for him when he disappeared. Or . . . had found him?"

"He knows where he is," Kayla said, giving up. "He'd run away and come here—to New York. That's why Eric was dressed like that, in the Park. He wanted to gain his confidence a little, so Magnus would trust him when Eric told him he was his long-lost brother and wasn't just going to hand him back over to his folks. Don't tell Beth," she pleaded.

"Because Beth would worry?" Kory said, smiling faintly. "Is he safe?"

Kayla thought hard. Was he? Were the three of them? "For now," she said reluctantly. "He's with two other kids, and Eric said both the other two have Talent." *And he said there was a problem. Was the problem why what happened to him happened?* "If . . ." *If I can't make him wake up, if he stays like that—NO!* "I'll tell Ria where they are and what's going on. Hosea says there's a halfway house they can go to, to get them off the street, if nothing better. I'll make sure nothing happens to any of them. I swear."

Kory regarded her steadily. He looked about Beth and Eric's age, but Eric had told her once that Kory was about two centuries old. Even if the Sidhe lived for about a zillion years, that had to count for something, didn't it?

"A great responsibility for one so young. Yet Eric would not have entrusted it to you were you not capable of it. I only wish . . . had he come to us, the children could all be safe in Misthold even now.

But those days are gone, and we each have our own road to tread. We will keep his confidences between us, then."

He sounded wistful, and sad enough to make Kayla start bawling then and there. But all he did was hand her back the bus pass and leave.

Why does everything have to be so effing complicated?

Kayla stuffed the card into her pocket, and after a moment remembered that she was supposed to be looking for Eric's insurance card and making phone calls. She knew one thing for sure. She wasn't going anywhere tonight. Those kids were just going to have to get along without her for one night. If she was going to help Eric—if Eric *could* be helped—she couldn't do it on four hours sleep on a cold bare floor.

She left a message on Dr. Dunaway's answering machine, and then called Elizabet. It was three hours earlier in California; Elizabet answered after several rings; she'd probably been outside in the garden. November was a milder month in L.A.

"Eric?" Elizabet had caller ID, and would recognize the phone number.

"No, it's Kayla."

"Kayla! Tell me what's wrong."

"If you're so psychic, you tell me," Kayla said, making a feeble joke. She drew a shaky breath. "Elizabet, I need some advice. . . ."

The call took longer than she'd expected, but Kayla felt much better afterward. Elizabet had been able to offer her a number of helpful suggestions, and one strict warning: not to heal Eric's body before she had established a link with his mind. To do so might be to sever the link between the two forever, especially if magic, and not simple trauma, were involved in Eric's injury.

She'd barely hung up the phone when it rang again. Kayla picked it up before the answering machine had time to cycle through.

"Eric?" came the familiar voice at the other end.

"Ria?"

"*Kayla!* Where have you been? I've been calling your phone whenever I could, but nobody's answered, and this line's been busy. I'm sorry I couldn't get back to you sooner. I got your messages. What's wrong?"

"Eric's in the hospital in a coma," Kayla said, too tired to pretty things up.

She could almost feel Ria change gears, even through the phone. "How long?"

"Since Tuesday."

She heard Ria take a deep breath.

"What happened?"

"He got mugged up in the Park. And . . ."

Kayla clung to the phone, unable to go on. *He's in a coma and I can't wake him up, because I can't find him! What if I never can find him! What then?*

"Kayla?" Ria said gently. "I know there's more. Tell me."

"I . . . I tried to wake him up and I couldn't."

There was a longer pause. Kayla knew that Ria understood everything she hadn't—couldn't—say.

"Kayla, I want to come up there, but I can't. I don't know how long until I can. You're at Eric's? I'm sending Anita over there. She'll take care of everything you need. Money, lawyers, everything. Let her handle the hospital. That's what I pay her for."

"Ria? Beth and Kory are here."

Kayla thought she heard a muttered curse—or maybe smothered laughter—but wasn't sure.

"Of course they are. Do they know about Magnus?"

"Kory does. He, uh, found out."

There was another pause. Kayla could almost hear Ria thinking furiously. "Is he going to be reasonable?"

"Depends on your definition. He'll keep his mouth shut for a while, though. But we gotta get them—Magnus and some other kids—off the street, and without Eric around . . . Hosea says there's a halfway house they could go to, but it costs money."

"Have Anita write the place a check. Don't worry about the money, Kayla. Money's for spending. Now listen. Make sure they move Eric to a private room with a special duty nurse. I'll call Anita to give her the details. And get those kids off the street as soon as you can. Dorland's getting close; it's only a matter of time before he finds Magnus. Damn it! That's my other phone! I've got to go. I'll call you again as soon as I can. Take care of yourself."

The line went dead.

Kayla took a deep breath, and ran quickly through a couple of grounding and centering exercises before coming back into the living room. Having Ria in the game made her feel a lot better, even if Ria couldn't be right here right now. There were few mundane problems that LlewellCo-level money couldn't solve.

When she came out, Beth and Kory were sitting on the couch, Beth curled up under Kory's arm. She'd been crying.

"That was Ria," Kayla said. "She's sending her personal assistant over here to help deal with the hospital."

"Why doesn't she come herself?" Beth demanded.

"I don't think she can," Kayla said. Empathic powers didn't work over phone lines, but Ria had sounded really frustrated when she'd said she was stuck in Washington for an indefinite period. And there were very few things that could keep Ria Llewellyn from doing exactly as she pleased.

About forty minutes later, Anita arrived. Anita Sheldrake was Ria Llewellyn's personal assistant, watchdog, and gopher, and if she had any objections to being called out at the end of her workday to run even more errands, they didn't show.

"I'm very sorry to hear about Eric," Anita said, coming in carrying two large plastic bags. "I picked up some Chinese food on the way over. Ria called me in the car and said you probably hadn't thought about cooking." She walked into the kitchen and set the bags down on the table, then came back out, opening her brief bag and pulling out a notepad.

"Now, we can get Eric moved to a private room with round-the-clock private duty nurses tonight. Ms. Llewellyn would appreciate it if you would allow me and Derek Tilford—he's one of our lawyers—to sit in on your meeting with Dr. Rodriguez tomorrow. That's at 2:30?"

"Yes," Beth said suspiciously. "Why?"

"That would be . . . in advance of any problems," Anita said carefully.

"What kind of problems?" Beth asked, starting to sound dangerous.

"Well, Gotham General is obviously going to be concerned that you might take exception to their treatment of what they originally thought was a homeless man, especially now that he turns out to be a rather well-off and well-connected Juilliard student. And Ria said that you'd prefer to be kept out of things as much as possible, Mrs. Connor," Anita said diplomatically.

Kayla felt as much as saw the bolt of blind panic

flash through Beth. Beth Kentraine-or-Connor could hardly afford to have her picture all over the *New York Post*.

"Yes," Beth said wearily, leaning back against Kory again. "Yes, I would."

"So Mr. Tilford will assure them that if they play ball with us, we'll play ball with them—in the nicest possible way, of course. He'll make sure you don't have to talk to the police. Why should you? You weren't even in New York when the incident happened. So if I could just borrow Eric's ID and insurance cards for a moment to jot down some numbers—and I'll leave you my card, and Derek's—we'll meet you at the hospital tomorrow, okay?" Anita said.

Kayla walked Anita out, saying she wanted to see if Hosea was home anyway, which was true. In the lobby, Anita stopped.

"Kayla? Ria wanted me to give you this when I could get you alone." Anita took a plain white envelope out of her brief bag and handed it to Kayla.

"This contains five blank signed checks on one of Ria's slush accounts. You can make them out for a total of up to fifty thousand dollars. If that's not enough, let me know and I'll deposit some more money."

Merry Christmas, Kayla thought numbly. She knew Ria was rich, but it was easy to forget until something like this happened. She folded the envelope several times and stuffed it into her pocket. "Uh . . . this is probably enough. But I'll let you know."

Anita nodded. "I'm really sorry about Eric. Is he going to be okay?"

"We hope so," Kayla said. What else could she say? Anita nodded again, decisively.

"See you tomorrow then."

❖   ❖   ❖

Hosea hated being pulled in several directions this way. He wanted to be out looking for Eric, but his work for the Guardians was just as important. People were dying.

He needed to hear the rest of the Secret Stories. But the children wouldn't tell them except to each other. They believed that bad things would happen to them if any adult knew them.

Maybe that was true. Maybe the real reason that Bloody Mary was loose in the world was because some grown-up, somewhere, knew the Secret Stories and had found a way to use them somehow. But he knew that wouldn't stop him from trying to find out the rest. He was sure that if he knew her Secret Name—the one the littlest children believed turned her from a monster into a protector—it would help. And the clues must be buried somewhere in the Secret Stories.

He hadn't been in the door of Jacob Riis for more than five minutes before Michaela Groom, one of the volunteer day-care teachers, came trotting up to him with relief all over her face. "I'm glad you're here," she said, without preamble, signs of stress in her voice, on her face, in her posture. "We just got a visit from some well-intentioned idiots doing a story for one of the TV stations who got the nickel tour, then proceeded to hand out candy right, left and center before I could stop them. Chocolate—of course—and the kids all stuffed themselves silly. The ones that aren't sick have been vibrating like Buzzy the Hummingbird all morning. They're just starting to come off the sugar high, and those of us that don't have screaming migraines are ready to drop."

Hosea nodded; he knew what she wanted before she asked it, since he had the reputation of being able to calm kids down. "You tryin' to get the little'uns down for a nap?" he asked.

Michaela rubbed her forehead. "And having no damn luck," she confessed. "I picked the wrong week to try and stop smoking."

"Ah'll jest see what Ah can do," Hosea promised, and ambled into the room where the youngest usually took their afternoon naps.

Sure enough, it looked like the aftermath of a tornado. The mats the kids were supposed to nap on were everywhere, and so were the kids. Rather than trying to get their attention, Hosea just settled into a corner with Jeanette, opened her case, tuned her quickly, and started to play, softly, a medley of old lullabies his grandmother had taught him. The banjo notes fell among the screaming, running, fighting children like rain. And, like rain, at first the music just ran off them without any effect. But as he willed calm and peace and sleepiness into the music, gradually fights broke up, kids dropped down onto mats, the noise quieted. Some of them looked up at him in surprise, as if they hadn't realized that he was there; others dragged their mats over to his corner and flung themselves down to listen. Yawns began, and yawning was contagious. Eyelids drooped, heads went down onto arms.

:Whoever the idiot is who decided to hand out candy ought to be shot,: Jeanette said, acerbically. *:No, wait, I have a better idea. We ought to fill these kids full of candy* again *and drop them all off at* his *house.:*

"Not a bad notion," Hosea murmured. His eyes flickered over the little knots of kids who were still awake, but at least now they were sitting and talking instead of fighting and screaming. He strained to hear what they were saying, and thought he caught the words "Bloody Mary."

His concentration lapsed for a moment, and he missed a couple of notes.

:Yo, Music-Man; concentrate on what you're doing, and let me do the listening.:

It wasn't often that Jeanette volunteered to do anything: Hosea snatched the offered help and went back to soothing overstimulated minds and bodies. These were the littlest of the children—none older than six—the ones who had absolutely stonewalled him in any attempt to get the Secret Stories out of them. Either they were too shy, or too afraid to trust him or any adult.

The murmuring went on in the far corner. He played as softly as he could, and hoped that Jeanette was better at hearing what was being said than he was. Finally, as Michaela lowered the lights, the last of the kids dropped off. He let the song he was playing trail naturally off at its end, then picked up the case and tiptoed out through the maze of randomly strewn children.

"How a man your size can move so quietly, I'll never know," Michaela said, shaking her head, when he reached the door and she closed it behind him. He just grinned.

But he was glad that she couldn't see past the surface of his grin, because it didn't go any deeper than the skin. He wanted to have a serious conference with Jeanette, because the little that he had heard of the Secret Stories just sounded worse and worse.

He tucked himself up into an unoccupied corner, and began to play again, softly. "Talk to me, partner," he said, under his breath.

:You already know what the start of the Story is,: Jeanette said, after a moment. *:The demons put Heaven under siege, led by Bloody Mary. They overran Heaven. No one, not even the angels, knows where God is. He*

might be the demons' prisoner, He might be in hiding, He might even be dead. Most of the kids think He ran away when He saw her.:

A bitter start to a sad story, but it explained the hopelessness in the shelter kids' lives. "And the angels regrouped and are fighting back. They have a secret camp deep in some tropical swamp. They're led by the archangel Michael, who happens to look a lot like a feller name of Che," Hosea said.

Jeanette snorted mirthlessly and took up the Story again. *:Heaven's been ruined and is full of demons. There's nowhere for the good dead to go except to the angels' camp. But an angel has to find them and lead them there, because they can't find the way on their own. So the children do their best to help their dead relatives find their way to the angels' camp, by leaving a ticket to the camp on their grave, or where they were killed. Here in New York, it's any pink advertising flyer. At least they can get those.:*

Hosea smiled. He'd wondered why the kids had been so hot about collecting those. Now he knew. "An' the bad dead, well, they go straight to the demons anyway. The demons make all the bad things happen. They made those planes fly into the Twin Towers because they were trying to kill everyone in New York."

:At least it's a reason they can understand,: Jeanette said grimly. She hesitated, almost as if she were gathering her thoughts, as Hosea continued to play. *:The good dead scout for the angels, and where they can, they fight on their side. They come to kids to warn them when they can, and do what they can to keep Bloody Mary away. The kids know that demons can corrupt anyone, even your parents, so no adult is really safe to be around, because the demons can turn them at any point.:*

Hosea winced. The world of the Stories was a

terrible one, where every adult was an enemy, or a potential enemy. But, sadly, it was an accurate reflection of the children's lives. Once again, he took up the tale in turn, adding what he knew.

"Thinkin' about Bloody Mary can bring her to you. She hates kids; whenever one dies, she's happy. Whenever one's turned to the bad, an' is workin' for the demons, she's happy. But she used to be good, the Blue Lady, an' if you're a Special One, you can turn her back to the Blue Lady, an' then she'll protect you. An' that's where Ah don't get it, Jeanette," Hosea said sadly. "Why'd she go to the bad in the first place?"

:Oh, Hosea—: Suddenly Jeanette sounded just as sad as Hosea felt—with none of her usual cynical sarcasm. *:Oh, Hosea. That's what they were talking about just now. She hates children, because hers was murdered. She hates God because He allowed it. The Secret Stories say that once, when people were still good to each other, when there were no wars and no fighting and no drugs, she was able to be good, but when things got awful and her own child was killed, she lost it and became Bloody Mary.:* Jeanette sighed. *:Now the only way to turn her back is either to be a Special One and turn her for a little time, or to learn her Secret Name and remind her of what she was.:*

"Only nobody remembers what it was," Hosea said.

:No,: Jeanette agreed. *:Nobody remembers her Secret Name.:*

It was a long, depressing walk back in the grey dusk, with a faint icy mizzle spitting down out of the sky, and for the first time since he'd come to live at Guardian House, Hosea did not feel his spirits lift when he was inside his own door again. The apartment seemed empty, and conversely, too full of memories of Jimmie.

How, *how* was he to turn so sad a tale around? The misery that had created it had so little hope in it—too little to build on, it seemed. The only "hope" the children seemed to have was for the Special Ones, and even they could only turn Bloody Mary for a few moments. This was too much for him—

Maybe he was more sensitive than usual, but when he heard footsteps in the hall, he knew that it was Kayla, and he knew that whatever she had to say was not going to help the despair that was settling over him. Hosea opened the door at Kayla's knock.

"Come on upstairs," she said. "We've got news, and most of it's bad."

When Kayla got back upstairs with Hosea, Greystone was there, since it had gotten dark enough for the gargoyle to abandon his perch atop Guardian House without being missed. Kayla realized that he and the other two had already met. They were trading small talk that sounded strained. Everyone kept sliding around the subject of Eric, to the point where there was a great, big Eric-shaped hole in the middle of the conversation.

It seemed a relief to have the newcomer among them. For a few moments, anyway.

"Kory, Beth, this is Hosea Songmaker, Eric's apprentice," Kayla said. "C'mon, Too-Tall. Let's get the grub dished up."

None of them really felt like eating—except maybe Greystone, to whom food was an endless novelty—but Kayla chivied the others into it while she filled Hosea in on the events of the day. Even when the mind and heart rebelled, the body still wanted fuel. *Gotta feed the beast,* Kayla reminded herself, filling a bowl with rice and steamed vegetables, and balancing a selection of *dim sum* on top. Anita had brought enough to feed at least six people, which was just as well. There wasn't much in Eric's fridge, and Kayla didn't really feel like shopping. Even with feeding Greystone, there'd be enough leftovers to take care of breakfast.

"You're right lucky you found him when you did, and got him on the insurance," Hosea said, when the three of them had finished bringing him up to date. "'Spect they were fixin' to shut down the machines an' all, an' from what Little Bit here says, that wouldn't be the best thing just now."

Beth stared at him in horror. "You mean, just . . . turn him off?"

"If they couldn't turn up any next of kin, and he didn't look like waking up," Hosea said, "that'd surely be on their minds. Nobody wants to be cruel, but there's only so much money for charity, Ah'm findin' out, and a bed in a big city hospital costs a lot of money, and seems like there aren't ever enough of 'em to go 'round."

"But they can't," Beth protested. "They couldn't."

"Hey, Red," Greystone said reassuringly. "Nobody said it was gonna happen. Right, Hosea?"

"That's right," Hosea said. "Ah just mean to scare you a little, Miz Kentraine, on account of Ah suspect that's what they mean to do tomorrow, if Eric's as bad off as Kayla says. But you just let Miz Llewellyn's folks do all the talkin' there, and don't you pay no mind to what those doctors have to say. Little Bit an' me, we'll find Eric, no matter how long it takes. Ah promise you that. We'll bring him back to you. You can rest your mind easy on that."

Hosea might not be a fully trained Bard as yet, Kayla thought, but nobody could beat his bedside manner.

By the end of the evening, Beth had actually relaxed a little and lost some of her haunted look.

"Ah suspect, too, it might be a good thing for you folks to go on back to Underhill after that meetin' tomorrow as well," Hosea said. "Kory here, he isn't going to be any too comfortable if he spends very long around here, is he?"

"I can stay as long as needful," Kory said firmly, but the guilty look that crossed Beth's face was all the answer to that either Kayla or Hosea needed.

"But neither one o' you wants to be around if people come askin' awkward questions," Hosea pointed out. "Specially if that fancy lawyer can't manage things with the police the way he says he can. You aren't any farther away than e-mail, and if you want to give me your address, Ah can write you myself on Eric's computer. And you can come back every few days. But your baby's going to be missing you."

"He's right," Kory said reluctantly, after a long hesitation.

"I guess . . . I just hate to leave without knowing. But Maeve . . . would you like to see a picture of her?" Beth asked hopefully.

Hosea smiled. "Ah was hopin' you'd offer."

"Me, too," Greystone chimed in.

They all crowded around as Beth dug into her purse and withdrew a small crystal oval. "Not exactly a photograph, but it's what they use Underhill. Here. Look."

She held it up. Captured in the crystal was the image of a golden-haired toddler about a year old, standing in a meadow. She wore a short green gown trimmed in sparkling embroidery, and a little cap trimmed with a rosette of ribbons that fluttered in an unseen breeze.

The picture was moving.

"Hey . . ." Kayla said, fascinated. As she watched, the child's attention was captured by something she couldn't see. Then an enormous butterfly with spectacular purple and turquoise wings floated into view, hovering just above her head. She grabbed for it, then sat down abruptly, off-balance, looking very surprised. The butterfly circled, and came to perch on her cap.

Beth turned the crystal over. The same meadow, but obviously a different day. Maeve again, this time dressed in riding clothes, being led around in a circle on the back of a tiny perfect elvensteed; a full-sized horse in perfect miniature. A tall, red-haired woman in armor was walking close beside her to make sure she didn't fall. Kory held the 'steed's lead.

"There's a couple of dozen in here," Beth warned. "Are you sure you want to see them all?"

"Of course we do," Hosea said, speaking for all of them. "She's beautiful."

"As soon as Eric's back, you gotta bring her around for a visit," Greystone said. "I gotta get my chance to babysit again."

Beth laughed. "You'll have to fight Lady Montraille for that honor. She never lets Maeve out of her sight!"

After all the pictures had been seen, it was time for Kayla and Hosea to go, though Greystone promised to stay and keep Kory company for a while longer, since neither one needed sleep as mortals did.

"Do you really think getting Eric back's going to be as easy as you told Bethie it is?" Kayla asked Hosea. He'd insisted on walking her all the way down to her door.

"Not easy," Hosea said, meeting her gaze unflinchingly.

"But possible, no matter what's happened to him. Eric won't give up, and neither will we. And he's got a lot to come back for."

"Magnus," Kayla said, not needing to say more.

"Ayah. Ah don't say he took the best road there, but he took the road he took. Now you go get yourself a good night's sleep, and get ready to face those doctors in the morning."

"Oh God," Kayla sighed. "Sooner or later they're going to find out I'm not his sister."

Hosea grinned wolfishly. "Well, Little Bit, Ah'd say that by the time they do, Miz Llewellyn's money and lawyers will have made it so they won't care one bit."

Deep night was the best time for sorcery. At night the unawakened hive-mind that was New York was as close to somnolent as possible, and the Etheric Currents could be more easily manipulated.

Or whatever.

The man known to his followers as Fafnir, Master of Treasure, entered his apartment, closing the door behind him. As he did, he sloughed off his mundane persona and its worldly concerns as easily as a snake shed its outgrown skin. The mundane world and its tedious concerns was something he wasn't going to have to worry about much longer.

He went into the bedroom—it had a key lock; it wouldn't do for any of the sheep to wander in there accidentally and see something that would jar their preconceptions of who "Master Fafnir" was—and stowed away his briefcase and work clothes, taking care to cover them carefully in plastic bags as he did. Even this room smelled faintly of the frankincense he burned so profligately.

Changing into one of his Fafnir outfits—it was a

role he lived every moment he could, as befit one that he intended to assume permanently—he went back to the living room again. There was important work to do before dawn and the city's awakening made it impossible.

He lit several of the candles and one of the braziers. Most of what he did was to set the stage for the sheep, but not all. The unconscious mind was a kind of idiot child as well: it required props and staging to be coaxed to perform properly. The trained will could only do so much.

Now they would see what Amanda and the Circle between them had managed to do.

He went into the kitchen to pour himself a snifter of Calvados before beginning—a gift from Neil; very nice. Returning to the living room—the frankincense was smoking nicely—he pulled over a small table and then went to get the crystal.

Setting the box on the table, he opened the lid. The "Eye of the Inner Planes" glowed with the luminescence of fine mineral quartz, and Fafnir smiled. Nothing more occult here than the power of money. Anything would serve—a mirror, a bowl of water, even a ball of ordinary glass—but why not use what his obliging sheep had provided? It was merely a place to rest the outer eyes while the inner eye did its work, after all.

He'd laid the groundwork in all those sessions with little Amanda, not only rendering her malleable and compliant, but preparing the shape and the intent of the Artificial Elemental to which his sheep had lent—and would continue to lend—the power of their credulousness. They hadn't the wit to know the difference between creating something and summoning something already created, and Fafnir had no intention of enlightening them.

It had been done before. It was, in fact, just about the simplest magical operation to perform. There was even a book about it, written back in the seventies, called *Conjuring Up Philip*, by someone named Iris Owen. That was where he'd gotten part of his original idea. Only his creature would be far more powerful than a simple table-knocking, Ouija-board-communicating spirit.

His would be lethal. And answerable only to him.

The others thought it was a Protector, a magical watchdog that would protect them from the False Guardians.

Wrong.

He concentrated on the crystal, letting his mind empty except for the single image. It had come to him when he'd first started working with Amanda, and it was as good as any other. . . .

A gaunt woman, tall, terrifying, her mouth open in a soundless scream of anguish. Pale blue draperies fluttered from her limbs, and she glowed with a spectral light. From eyeless sockets she wept endless black tears. . . .

There was a flicker of blue light in the crystal, and Fafnir drew back with a gasp. The room had suddenly grown cold. He drew a deep breath, rubbing his arms nervously.

Yeah, that should work.

He closed the box, rubbing his eyes. There hadn't been anything there, of course. A trick of the light. But if it worked on *him,* the sheep should be terrified.

Soon he'd call the Inner and Outer Circles together to—or so he'd tell them—make them all known to the Protector for purposes of their protection. That was when he'd call it up to attack them. His creation. Under his control. And he was immune to whatever it would do, of course.

He'd tell them that what happened next was a preemptive strike from the False Guardians. They wouldn't know the difference. He'd chosen them all very carefully: none of them knew enough about magic to challenge him. And they certainly wouldn't doubt anything he told them after his toxic thought-form ripped through the place. It might even kill a few of them, which would make it stronger yet. And then they'd be terrified, willing to do *anything* he said.

Then all he had to do was actually locate one of the Guardians. It shouldn't be all that hard. His sheep had friends in high places, there were very few things secret from a computer, and any reluctance they had to break the law should be gone once his creation had done a little damage. Then he'd find Paul Kern again—the right Paul Kern, the one who'd been a computer consultant at Andrew Reaney's firm about ten years ago.

And then he'd become a Guardian. And have *real* power.

He frowned. Maybe it would be a better idea to hold the meeting at Neil's. He wasn't sure how destructive that thing was going to be, and he had no desire to have *his* apartment trashed.

He took another deep breath, shaking off the last of his unease. Yes. Things were proceeding just as they ought.

At 2:30 the next day, Kayla sat in a hospital conference room with Kory and Beth on one side of her and Anita and Derek Tilford, the LlewellCo lawyer, on the other and listened to Dr. Rodriguez—who'd brought a lawyer along with him as well, it turned out—explain how it was really unlikely that Eric was ever going to wake up again.

The doctor used a lot of words like "massive cranial

trauma" and "intercranial haemorrhagia" and "deep tissue bruising" and "no evidence of EEG activity," but it all boiled down to—bottom line—in the hospital's opinion, Eric was a vegetable, and if he hadn't woken up in the last three days, they didn't think he was going to wake up any time soon. Like ever.

And there were Decisions to be made—the way he said it, you could hear the capital "D" very clearly. And just who was going to make them?

Derek Tilford coughed gently. "Actually," he said, self-deprecatingly, "Ms. Llewellyn holds a power of attorney on Mr. Banyon's behalf to be exercised in just such cases. I have a copy of it here to add to the hospital files. I'm sure you'll find it all in order."

He passed the paper across the table.

Even if the ink ain't quite dry on it yet, Kayla thought. And who knew? It might be the real deal. Ria and Eric were tight, and there wasn't anybody else in the World Above who could stand up for Eric in a case like this.

"Ms. Llewellyn wishes every effort to be made to restore Mr. Banyon to full health," Anita said firmly. "In fact, in the case of the necessity of long-term care, she'd prefer to transfer Mr. Banyon to a private facility of her own choosing. Perhaps you could tell us when that might be possible?"

"Not for at least a week," Dr. Rodrieguez said, on firmer ground now. "Leaving aside the injuries to his head and spine, we've already had to operate once to control internal bleeding. I'd prefer to wait."

"So he could still wake up?" Beth said, her voice tight with hope. She'd kept quiet through most of the discussion of Eric's condition, but could contain herself no longer.

"We can always pray for a miracle, Ms. Connor," Dr. Rodriguez said, getting to his feet. "But I don't want to raise any false hopes. In my opinion, that's what it will take."

Hosea was waiting for them outside of Eric's new room.

"He isn't a pretty sight," he warned Beth as she put her hand on the door. "And he won't know you're there."

"I want to see him," Beth said stubbornly. Hosea stepped back. Beth and Kory went in. Kayla stayed with Hosea. She'd already seen Eric. And she didn't want to be anywhere near Beth when *she* did.

"How'd it go?" Hosea asked, once the two of them were alone.

"'Bout like you said. Hospital was setting us up to pull the plug, but it turned out Ria's got a power of attorney from Eric—fancy that—and LlewellCo wants to keep him plugged in. So now it's up to us." She hugged herself and shivered. "Anita said that Ria wants to move him to a private clinic, but the doctor doesn't want to move him until he's better . . . and I can't even start in on making him better until we can *find* him and put him all back in one piece."

"Which means we do it here," Hosea said. "It'll be a thought awkward figuring out how to work around those private nurses of Miz Llewellyn's, though."

"Damn," Kayla muttered. "Can't your Guardian friends do something about that?"

Hosea smiled faintly, considering the matter. "Ah expect they can at that."

A few minutes later, Beth and Kory left the hospital room. Beth was weeping, and Kory looked stricken.

"You'll help him, right?" Beth said fiercely. "He's going to be all right?"

"Ah promise you, we'll do everything there is to do," Hosea assured her firmly.

"Then fare you well, Bard," Kory said. "And Danu's fortune attend your work."

Late that same night, Hosea, Kayla, and Paul Kern returned to the hospital. No one saw them enter the building, or ascend to the wing that held the private rooms.

The three of them stood in the hallway and watched as Eric's private nurse—a no-nonsense woman in her fifties—left the room and walked down the hall.

"She won't remember leaving," Paul said quietly. "I can keep her out as long as you need me to."

The three of them went into the room.

Paul locked the door as soon as they were inside; with Greystone's help, his spell would keep nearly everyone from seeing or hearing anything that went on in here, but there was a tiny percentage of the population that was completely impervious to magic, and there was no point in taking chances.

Hosea set down his banjo case and opened it.

"You're not going to play that thing, are you?" Kayla asked, alarmed.

"Won't know till we come to it," Hosea answered mildly. He slung the strap over his shoulder and began to tighten the strings.

Kayla went over to the bed. Eric lay unmoving beneath the sheet and blanket, just as she had seen him before. It might be her imagination, but the sense of *absence* was nearly palpable.

"I'm just going to do a quick check," Kayla said. "Elizabet said not to Heal him before we got his mind to come back, but I want to make sure there ain't something goin' wrong in there that the doctors maybe missed."

"You need an anchor for that?" Hosea asked.

"Nah," Kayla said, taking a deep breath. "It's just physical stuff. Easy-peasy." *Yeah, right.*

She stuffed her winter gloves into her pocket and reached out and laid her fingers, very gently, against the side of Eric's face.

The hospital room fell away.

She raced through his body. Torn muscles; flesh cut by the surgeon's knife; the hard alien presence of surgical sutures; bruises and broken bones . . . she felt the power well up within her, wanting to reach out, to begin the work of Healing, and held it back with an effort. Not now. Not yet.

Even through the drugs coursing through his bloodstream, she felt the pain. With an effort, she blocked it out, searching further, memorizing the damage so that she could ignore it later. All this, terrible as it was, would heal on its own in some way or another, given time. There was nothing here that was immediately life-threatening. The surgeons had done good work.

With an effort, she lifted her hand away, leaving her work undone.

"Fascinating," Paul said, watching her.

Yeah, I'm just a dream walking.

"There's nothing here that can't wait," Kayla said aloud, taking a deep breath.

"Then let's go," Hosea said, reaching out his hand.

Kayla took it, and reached out to Eric once more.

This time she forced herself to close her Healer's senses to the song of pain and damage that his body sang, isolating it and shunting it aside. She was seeking something else. She was seeking Eric himself.

As before, when she had sought Jimmie's consciousness in the Guardian's charred and ruined body, she found herself in a house.

It wasn't real. It was a construct, a symbol, a kind of fantasy that allowed her to do her work, the way she sometimes saw the bodies she worked on as machines, or video games, or even songs. She didn't waste her time trying to see the truth behind the symbol. That was pointless. It was okay for her to see a house. All she had to do was hunt through the place until she found Eric.

Simple. Not.

The place she found herself in wasn't Eric's apartment—or rather, only part of it was. This place had a lot more rooms, all of them dark. She summoned up a flashlight and used it to light her way.

"Eric?" she called. "Eric? It's Kayla."

No answer. And worse, no sense that there was anyone here listening.

She passed from a room that looked more or less like Eric's living room at Guardian House, down a long corridor lined with doors, all shut. Conscientiously, she opened every one and looked inside, stopping at intervals to call Eric's name and identify herself, and always receiving the same sense of *absence* in response.

Some of the rooms looked as if they were long-deserted, cluttered with ancient junk. Some looked as if they'd been used, at least until recently. Some of the rooms had more doors leading off them, and there might be closets as well. She hesitated, considering searching them. *Try the main rooms first,* Kayla told herself. *You can come back here later if they don't pan out.*

It took her quite some time to finish checking the main rooms of Eric's mind, though she knew her subjective sense of time was no indication of how long had passed in the outside world. No matter how many rooms she passed through, and how fantastic their contents, all of them were dark and empty. Deserted.

At last she found herself standing before a gate—all lacy wrought silver, with touches of gold. It wasn't locked. She pushed it open and went inside.

The room beyond was huge, giving the faint impression of a cathedral, though, looking around, Kayla couldn't quite say what it was that gave her that notion. The chamber was round, the arching ceiling a fantasy of interlocking vaults. When she shone her flashlight up there, the roof sparkled.

She shone the light on the floor beneath her feet, and discovered it was a mosaic, each tile no larger than her smallest fingernail. The pattern was something elaborate and geometric in blues and greens, as detailed as the finest Persian rug. All around the edges of the room was a young forest of miniature flowering trees, every one in bloom, each in an elaborately painted pot that echoed the colors of the floor.

In the center of the room was a fountain.

This isn't like anything I've ever seen, Kayla thought, puzzled. But the images she saw when she Healed could come solely from her subject's mind as well. She wondered if there was something in Underhill that looked like this.

She also wondered what the room was *for.* Every "room" in a subject's mind was keyed to a talent or memory. She looked at the fountain again. Wasn't water supposed to have something to do with creativity, at least according to some symbol systems?

She walked over to it.

The fountain towered twenty feet in the air, and covered a good portion of the floor. From what she could tell, it was one of those things that ought to be spitting out jets of water in all directions, and possibly even play tunes—water harps, they were called.

But the water in the basin lay still and unmoving, and the fountain was silent.

If this is the symbol of Eric's creativity, we are seriously screwed.

She hesitated for a moment, then passed on to the small doorway on the far side. It was barely wide enough for her to get through, but no gate blocked it. It led down a steep flight of stone steps.

Going down. Sub-basement, collective unconscious, repressed memories, childhood traumas, right this way . . .

The stairs were steep and slippery; not a place Eric visited in his own mind very often, if she had to guess. But—if she was right about what the fountain room symbolized—a place intimately connected to his creativity.

Have I mentioned lately how much I really hate pop psych?

At last she reached the bottom. Wherever she was, whatever this place was to Eric, it looked to Kayla like the basement of a very old building. It was walled off in places by hastily built brick walls, now dusty and crumbling with age. Some of them had been torn down. Others had holes knocked in them. Some still stood firm. She felt a faint flicker of hope. He could be down here, behind one of those walls, and that might be why she'd been unable to sense him.

Oh, please, let that be it.

"Eric?" Kayla said aloud. "Eric, it's Kayla. Are you here?"

Nothing.

"Eric, it's Kayla," she said again. "We need you to come back to us. You've been hurt, and I know you're confused, but you can't stay here. You need to come back."

She didn't know if he heard her. Hell, she didn't even know if he was here. *She* didn't want to be here: it felt too much like trespassing, with all of the guilt and none of the thrill. She'd never been this deep in someone's mind before, not even Ria's. She shone the light around the walls, searching for something, anything, that would tell her where he was—or failing that, which way he'd gone.

A door.

There was a door in the back wall.

She knew it wasn't there, not really—neither the door nor the wall—but she saw them. She ran over to it, the light from her flashlight swooping crazily over the walls of the dark basement.

It was wood, old thick shabby splintery dusty wood, of the same vintage as the rest of the basement that wasn't really there. There was no handle, no way to open it. The only thing that was new was the padlock and hasp on it, gleaming brightly in the light of her flash, mocking her.

Kayla grabbed the lock and yanked. If she could tear it free, she could probably pry the door open.

No go. It was like trying to yank open the wall itself. The lock held firm.

As she stepped back, she stepped on something soft. She squawked and jumped, then turned her flashlight on it. Something dark blue and dusty . . . and familiar. She bent down and picked it up.

Eric's cap. The watch cap he'd been wearing that day up at The Place.

It was here. *He'd* been here, by this door. This was a clue, a sign that this was the right way. Only how was she supposed to get through the door?

Kayla blinked, straining to see the lock clearly, and suddenly she realized there was a reason she couldn't.

The light from her flashlight was dimming.
She concentrated, willing it to burn brighter.
And it didn't.

CHAPTER THIRTEEN:

OVER THE WATERFALL

There was a jarring moment of discontinuity, then she was back in the hospital room again, staggering back against Hosea.

"Whuh . . . what?" Kayla gasped. She coughed, and took a deep breath, realizing she hadn't been breathing for a little too long. Nausea made her shudder.

"Come over here and sit down," Hosea said firmly. He led Kayla over to a chair and pushed her into it, then reached into his backpack and took out a bottle of apple juice. "And drink this."

Kayla gulped down the apple juice thirstily. Being jarred out of a Healer's trance was no fun, but she suspected the alternative would have been worse. "What happened?" she asked hoarsely, handing the empty bottle back to Hosea.

"Not much from where Ah stood, until you stopped breathing," he said soberly. "Right then Ah figured it was time for you to come on home. Ah called to you, an' you didn't answer me, so Ah yanked you loose. Ah'm sorry if Ah hurt you some, but you weren't lookin' any too good."

"I'm glad you did," Kayla said honestly. "I think I went a little too far. But it still wasn't far enough."

She explained where she'd been, and what she'd found.

"So I think that Eric's somewhere on the other side of that door. But I don't know what the door means, or where it goes. And from what you say, trying to find out nearly killed me."

"Hmn." Hosea made a noncommittal sound. His fingers moved over the strings of the banjo, raising faint echoes of melody. He cocked his head, as if listening. After a moment, he raised his head.

"Jeanette says you should let her try," Hosea reported. "She says she's dead already, so going down there won't hurt her none."

"Let her try? How?" Kayla demanded.

"Let her go through you into Eric," Hosea answered. Absently, his fingers began picking out a soft counterpoint on the banjo's silver strings.

"Can she do that?" Kayla asked dubiously.

"There are records of ghosts temporarily possessing the living. I suppose this situation would be analogous," Paul said, speaking up from his position by the door for the first time.

Kayla grimaced. She didn't like the idea of just letting a ghost walk into her, much less the semi-reformed ghost of Jeanette Campbell.

But what choice did they have? She could try getting through that door again herself—and fail, get hurt, or possibly do serious damage to Eric. If Jeanette failed, they probably wouldn't be any worse off than they were now.

"I guess it's worth a try," she said reluctantly.

Hosea smiled just a little. "Jeanette ain't any more eager to do this than you are, if it makes you feel any better," he said.

"Not a lot," Kayla admitted. "What do I have to do?"

"Let down your shields and give her a link to Eric," Hosea said. "Show her where you went. But . . ." Hosea hesitated, "you'll need to keep the link tight, whatever happens. If it breaks while Jeanette's all stretched out like that, Ah don't know what'll happen to her. Or to Eric, for that matter. Nothin' good, seems to me."

Kayla thought about it. It was a risk. But it was a risk either way. They couldn't just *leave* Eric like that.

Sure, there were other things they could try. They could wait for Ria to get back, maybe have her cast a spell to yank Eric back from wherever he was. Or Paul might be able to do it.

But either of them would be working blind. And Kayla wasn't sure it would be a really good idea just to yank Eric out of wherever he was, without seeing just where that was. They might do even more damage that way.

Sending Jeanette in might be the best thing. At least Kayla could see what she was doing. And she wanted to make up for her past, so it wasn't as if she couldn't be trusted to do her best.

"I can handle it, Too-Tall. You just concentrate on your ghost-wrangling. Well, here goes . . . something," Kayla muttered, taking a deep breath and getting to her feet again. "But if this doesn't work, I'm taking up tatting."

She resumed her position at the head of the bed,

taking Hosea's hand again. His free hand, she noticed, he kept firmly pressed over the banjo's strings.

She touched Eric's forehead again. There was a spark of contact, but she waited, not letting it pull her down inside this time.

And then *cold*. Colder than anything she'd imagined. She felt cold flow through Hosea and into her; through her, and into Eric.

Don't break the link. If you do, they're both toast.

But all her instincts screamed at her to let go, not to follow them down into death; Elizabet had warned her. . . .

And then she was there.

"Well, come on, where do I go?" an irritable voice said from behind her.

Kayla turned around. She was back in the darkened apartment again, inside what was currently passing for Eric's consciousness.

And there was Jeanette.

The only time Kayla had seen Jeanette Campbell alive, her body had been completely reshaped by Aerune mac Audelaine's sorcery into that of a half-Elven sprite; his hellhound. She'd Seen Jeanette once after she'd died, but that had been in Aerune's dreamworld, and the connection hadn't been really good. There Jeanette had been mostly a blur, her image flipping back and forth between her hellhound form and what she'd really looked like in life.

This, Kayla guessed, was Jeanette as she really had been: a moon-faced woman in boots, jeans, and a biker jacket, her long light-brown hair pulled back in a ponytail.

"Get with the program, would you?" Jeanette said impatiently.

"Come on," Kayla answered, hefting her flashlight.

❖   ❖   ❖

"Down those steps. There's a door at the back. It's locked. I think he's somewhere on the other side, if you can get through."

"Nothing to worry about there, kid. I brought the key along." Jeanette patted her pocket.

Kayla didn't ask what she had in there. She had a feeling she'd rather not know. "Do you, uh, want to take the flashlight?"

Jeanette looked surprised that she'd asked. "Don't need it. Every place looks the same to me now."

She went through the smaller door and disappeared.

Kayla stared at the doorway, although she was pretty sure it wasn't going to do anything interesting. *What do I do now?*

And how long do I wait?

This was the best year the Faire had ever had. The weather had cooperated—not too hot, not too cold—and the travelers had been generous; he'd made enough to buy a new shirt and a pair of those fancy custom boots he'd had his eye on for as long as he could remember. There were good parties every night, and he never, ever, had a hangover.

Eric was having a great time.

Sometimes he wondered if there was something he was forgetting. In the moments before he was quite awake some mornings, he was *sure* there was. But he could never quite remember what it was—and now that he'd moved into Karen's big tent, there weren't a lot of mornings that he got to spend time in quiet reflection. Karen was definitely a morning person. Eric was not.

On the other hand, there were advantages. Coffee. Breakfast. Not missing Morning Parade. And those were just the G-rated ones. . . .

But . . .

Had the Faire always used to go on all week? He couldn't remember going back to the mundane world once since he'd gotten here.

It was hard to think about something so irrelevant during the day, and the evening parties had their own logic, but Eric had finally remembered to ask Karen about it one evening, when they were gathered around the fire with some of the Wild Northern Celts and the rest of the German Mercenary Wenches.

"Hey, Ian!" she'd shouted. "Eric wants to go back to Mundania!"

"What would he want to do that for? We come here to get away from there!" Ian had shouted back merrily.

"Faire isn't good enough for you, Banyon?" someone else had called amiably out of the darkness.

Someone played a mocking trill on a pennywhistle. There was a ruffle of a bodhran; whoever had it actually managed something that sounded perilously close to a rim shot. There were cheers and scattered applause.

The wench on Eric's other side—a brawny lady named Hulda—had elbowed him robustly in the ribs, nearly making him spill his tankard of mead. "If you're bored, Banyon, we can think up a few more distractions for you. . . ."

He'd never really gotten an answer. But he guessed it didn't matter. The Faire was the Faire, and how it ran was Admin's business, not his.

It wasn't like there was any other place else he was supposed to be, after all.

And the weather was good.

The perfect Faire.

The perfect summer.

✧   ✧   ✧

So this is what's behind the door.

Jeanette pulled it open—it wasn't locked, no matter what Kayla had said—and stared.

On the other side was . . . summer.

Summer, and . . . a parking lot? An open field, actually, though the cars were parked in neat rows, hundreds of cars. Jeanette noted, even though some of them were obviously new, none of them were recent models.

I can see—and feel!

Everything was *real* again, as real as it had been when she was alive. Jeanette stepped through the doorway, taking a deep breath. She could smell summer and dust, and hear wind, birdsongs, and distant traffic. When she looked down, she could see herself—and feel her leather jacket beneath her hands.

It was like being reborn.

The world was in color again, a thing of shape and depth, experienced through her own senses, not in stolen glimpses through Hosea's eyes and thoughts.

If she had this much reality here, no wonder the kid had nearly died. Any place that was good for ghosts couldn't be good for the living.

She took a moment just to *feel* the sensation of sun on her face—why didn't people appreciate things like this before it was too late? To be able to feel her lungs fill when she took a breath, to be able to feel the wind pass over her face, to be able to feel the warmth of the sun; the living could experience those things every day of their lives, and they didn't care. . . .

But she had work to do. And no matter how real this felt, it wasn't. It was somewhere between a dream and an illusion; either way, it was bad news for somebody.

It would have been easy to get sucked in, if she hadn't been what she was and—even more—*who* she was. If she hadn't gotten every dream she'd ever had twisted and used against her by a mad Sidhe Prince. After Aerune, no pretty little paradise was ever going to suck her in, because her experience told her that no matter what she saw, there was *always* going to be something nasty lurking under the surface.

Maybe that was why the Secret Stories hit her right in the gut she didn't have anymore. No matter how rotten her life had gotten—a lot of which was her own fault, she could see now—at least she'd been able to keep some of her secret dreams intact almost to the end. Those kids Hosea worked with had gotten *theirs* shattered before they got two digits in their ages.

Jeanette walked on, into the open field, looking around curiously. There were people driving up and getting out of cars, and walking toward a destination in the distance. She could hear faint scraps of music on the air, something sort of medieval. All the signs for the parking were done in antique script as well. There were bigger signs in the distance, welcoming visitors to the Southern California Renaissance Faire.

Very bizarre.

A gleam of sunlight on chrome off to one side caught her attention. There was a big cream and maroon Harley touring bike parked under one of the few trees here in the field. It looked oddly familiar. She walked over to admire it.

The word "Mystery" was written on the gas tank in flowing gold script.

That's my bike!

"What the hell are you doing here?" Jeanette said aloud. The Harley had been her pet, her one self-indulgence when she'd gone to work for Threshold

and there'd been good legal money coming in for
the first time. She'd lost it somewhere in Flyover,
West Virginia, when Elkanah had kidnapped her,
and never known what had happened to it. Stolen
by someone, undoubtedly.

So what was Mystery doing here? This wasn't *her*
fantasy world.

She automatically groped in her jacket pocket, not
surprised to find that she had the keys.

If she just took her bike and rode away, where
would she get to?

Was it any place she wanted to be?

She looked toward the gates of the Faire, then
back at her bike. But she was supposed to be looking
for Eric Banyon, and if Eric was anywhere, he was
probably in there.

And it might seem like paradise—someone's paradise, anyway—but there was probably a nasty surprise
waiting somewhere around here the moment she let
her guard down.

She sighed, and turned away from Mystery. Maybe
she'd see her best girl again in Heaven, in the
unlikely event she ever qualified for that particular
destination.

Hunching her shoulders, she strode toward the
gate.

A Renaissance Faire, Jeanette quickly discovered,
was a bizarre place full of annoying losers dressed
in weird costumes who simply *lived* to make fun of
people by talking like Shakespeare.

Full of people—where had they all come from?
Most of them were tourists, and she didn't think
Eric would be one of them. But there were a lot
of people dressed in costumes. Some of them were
wandering around playing instruments, or juggling, or

giving impromptu puppet shows. Others were selling things in booths.

Unfortunately, she suspected that shooting them with the gun she discovered that she'd brought with her wouldn't help things along.

She hadn't thought she'd have to *talk* to people to find Eric. Jeanette hadn't had very good social skills while she was alive, and death really hadn't improved them. And finding herself in someplace that looked so . . . *real* . . .

Was this some kind of spell? An actual *place*, like Underhill? A disused part of Eric's mind? Did it, in fact, actually matter, so long as she found him and got him back out and up those stairs again before Kayla got bored standing around?

Probably not.

What would happen if the link with Kayla *did* get interrupted for any reason was something Jeanette preferred not to think about. Would she just vanish? Or would she be permanently stuck here in La La Land's version of Shakespeare in the Park?

No, that was too much to hope for. What happened would probably be whatever was most horrible. Not that she didn't deserve it, she supposed, after what she'd done in life, but that didn't mean she was going to go racing toward her karma with open arms.

She wandered through the crowds, hoping to spot Eric. He had to be here somewhere, didn't he? Or why was she here?

Finally she spotted a booth that looked promising. It had a large sign over it that said INFORMATION—LOST AND FOUND.

Well, Eric was lost. And she was trying to find him.

"I'm looking for a guy," she said, coming up to the booth.

"What's his name?" the woman behind the counter said. Despite the fact she was dressed like something you'd see on PBS, she seemed to be efficient enough.

"His name's Eric Banyon. I was supposed to meet him here," Jeanette said, stretching the truth only a little.

"Is he a traveler or a player?" the woman asked.

Jeanette stared at her. *Riddles? Next she'll be asking me, "What has it got in its pocketses?"*

The woman smiled. "Does he work at the Faire, or is he just visiting?"

"Oh." *I hate people. Even people who don't exist.* "He's a player. He's got a flute."

"Oh, sure an' ye'll be meanin' O'Banyon the Irish Rogue! Friend of his?" For some reason the woman suddenly had a thick Irish accent, but to Jeanette's relief, she quickly dropped it.

"Kayla said he'd show me around the Faire," Jeanette said, unable to think of anything else to say but a version of the truth. Apparently this made sense to the bimbo in crushed velvet, because she pulled a sheet of paper out from somewhere Jeanette couldn't see, and made some marks on it, talking all the time.

"He's on the Main Stage right now, but the show's about over. You should be able to catch him when he comes off. Here's a map. I've marked the Main Stage. Good luck!" the woman said, smiling cheerfully.

She handed Jeanette a sheet of paper with a map of the Fairesite on it, with the Main Stage circled in yellow Magic Marker. Jeanette took it and walked off.

She found the Main Stage without much difficulty. The woman said there was a show, so Jeanette followed the map until she heard music, then followed the music.

The Main Stage was a raised platform with a curtained backdrop, facing enough benches to seat maybe seventy very friendly people. Up on the stage, what looked like a cross between the cast of *Robin Hood* and the cast of *Riverdance* with a few walk-ons from *Braveheart* thrown in were making an almighty Celtic racket. It was a lovely sound. Jeanette stopped, so enchanted by the music that she forgot for a moment to look for Eric.

I miss the music most. Why couldn't Hosea play a guitar or something sensible instead of that damned banjo?

Then the sound of a flute soared up through the opening notes of "Banish Misfortune," and Eric Banyon stepped to the front of the stage.

Yes, that was him. He'd looked different the last time she'd actually been able to see him—and she'd been in too much pain, then, to really care—but that was definitely him. Younger, she thought. Longer hair. But him.

She stood and watched for a few minutes. She'd heard Eric play often, of course, whenever he played with Hosea, but this was different. Better. Sure, the costumes were dorky, but the music. . . .

Couldn't we just stay? Jeanette thought wistfully. *What's out there that's so important, compared to the music?*

But she knew they couldn't. It would be wrong. Eric was needed back in the Real World. She was here to bring him back. That was all.

Besides—

It occurred to her that if this was Banyon's dream, there was absolutely nothing keeping it from becoming his nightmare. And she'd be trapped here with him.

She blinked, as the thought settled into place with a sense of solid *rightness*. Yes. *That* was the nasty surprise just waiting to spring up out of the ground and bite her in the ass. And she did not want to see what Eric Banyon's worst nightmare could be like. She already knew he'd faced down a Dark elf-Prince as well as assorted unpleasant things and people associated with the Threshold Lab, and those were by no means the only horrors he'd dealt with, according to Hosea. So if his worst nightmare incorporated any of that—

No. She very definitely did not want to be trapped here when the pretty dream turned into a nightmare.

Going wasn't only right, it was necessary. And the journey had brought enough rewards.

I got to see my bike again, and hear this. More than I deserve, I guess.

I know I haven't come anywhere near to paying what I owe. Not nearly. Hosea'd better plan on having kids to pass me on to. But when I do . . . will I know?

There was no point in wondering about something that might never happen. What Hosea did wasn't all that safe. It was far more likely she—or more precisely, the banjo that held her—would be destroyed before she could complete her atonement.

Or maybe we'll all get careless, the Healer kid'll blink, and it'll be over tonight. She shrugged the thought aside irritably. Worrying about things you couldn't affect was a quick ticket to the boneyard, whatever that meant for someone like her.

When it seemed like the show was winding up, Jeanette started moving around the edge of the crowd, toward the back of the stage, where the performers would come out when the set was finished.

❖   ❖   ❖

It had been a good show—one of the best. The audience had been right with them, and everything had gone off without a hitch. Eric was feeling really good about everything, right up to the moment that the strange traveler walked up and called him by name.

"Eric."

He turned toward her. She was nobody he'd ever seen before, but it wasn't like he was exactly anonymous. He gave her his best bow and a charming smile.

"O'Banyon the Irish Rogue at your service, milady. And what is it that I can do for you this foigne Faire day?"

She stared at him as if she'd never heard anyone speak Faire cant before.

"I'm Jeanette Campbell. You don't recognize me. Kayla sent me."

Now it was Eric's turn to stare.

She frowned, clearly annoyed. He couldn't imagine why. "Don't give me that doe-eyed gaze! You've got to remember them! Kayla, and Hosea, and all those other people you left hanging back in New York—"

That was all Eric needed to hear. "New York" meant only one thing to him. Juilliard. His parents. The people who wanted to drag him back to a life he'd sworn he was never going to have anything to do with ever again.

He pushed through the crowd of players around him and took off running.

After a stunned instant Jeanette followed. *What the hell—?* He'd gone pale as chalk the moment she'd mentioned New York. Damn, damn, damn. And she absolutely guaranteed he knew this dreamworld better than she did.

She was keeping him in sight—just barely—as he
fled up the hill and toward what her map told her
was the edge of the Faire. In a tiny part of her mind,
she wondered if she could corner him, or if they'd
both run forever.

"Where do you think *you're* going?"

A woman dressed in furs and armor stepped out of
a would-be tavern right into Jeanette's path. Jeanette
tried to dodge around her, but the woman grabbed
her by the arm, dragging her to a stop.

Jeanette kicked out expertly—not that engineer boots
could do much against iron shin protectors—but the
damage had been done. Eric had gotten away, and
two more Babes in Armor had shown up. All three
of them looked like they ate weights for breakfast,
not just lifted them.

"I need to talk to Eric," she said sullenly.

The first woman grinned nastily, not letting go.
"Well, if it was Eric I just saw lightfooting by, I'd say
Eric doesn't want to talk to *you*, Traveler."

"And you make all his decisions for him, do you,
Big Chunk?" Jeanette snarled. "He's needed back in
New York. I was sent to tell him so."

"And who could *possibly* need Eric in New York?"
the woman sneered. "You?"

"I want to talk to Eric," Jeanette repeated, with what
passed, in her, for patience. "It's important. Eric will
agree that it's important. I came a long way to talk to
him, and if I don't get to talk to him, people are going
to die who shouldn't have to die, okay? People who
are sitting in a hospital in New York right now."

"Oh, wow," said one of the other Babes, "you mean
you want to talk to him about, like, donating a kidney
or something? My cousin donated a kidney last year.
But he might not be a good match."

"I need to talk to him," Jeanette repeated, wondering

if this might be Hell already, instead of Heaven. "I've come a long way to talk to him. Now we can do this the easy way, or I can go and find whoever's running this insane asylum and rope them in. Your call."

"Come inside then," the woman who'd originally grabbed her said, letting go reluctantly. "Someone will go look for him. And no funny stuff."

Funnier than sending a dead drug dealer to go looking for the soul of a Bard in a coma? Hard to beat that.

But Jeanette allowed herself to be led into the back of the tavern, and sat down at one of the benches. Jeanette waited nervously. How long could she spend here? What if she couldn't manage to convince Eric to be reasonable?

Finally, an idea occurred to her, straight out of one of those old *Twilight Zone* reruns she'd used to watch. But it was the only thing that occurred to her. She had to break through, get him out of this reality and into the—ah—"real" reality. He didn't want to go, and she guessed she could see why—but maybe if she could lead him back to the door she'd come through—if it was still there, and visible—it would jolt him enough to make his memories come back.

Eventually Eric arrived, flanked by two guys in kilts. He looked as wary as someone arriving at his own execution. He scanned the room until he saw the Babe, and came over and hugged her.

"Thanks, Karen," he said. He looked at Jeanette, his expression hostile.

"She says she just wants to talk to you," Babe Karen said.

"Privately?" Jeanette said.

"I guess," Eric said reluctantly. "Don't go too far, okay?"

"We could just throw her out," Karen said hopefully. "Accosting one of the players?"

Eric sighed, shaking his head. "They'd just send somebody else. Might as well get it over with."

He stood across the table from Jeanette, not bothering to sit down. "Well, go ahead."

Jeanette hesitated, but she'd played to tougher audiences while she was alive. "Nothing about this seems at all odd to you? And you don't remember Kayla, or Hosea, or Ria? Being a Bard? Your brother, Magnus?"

"I don't have a brother," Eric said. But he sounded doubtful, and he'd started, just a little, when she'd said Magnus's name.

"Okay, here's one: tell me your home address."

A stricken look crossed Eric's face, quickly masked. "Look, are we done here?"

She shook her head, and decided to give her crazy idea its best shot. "No. I could give you the whole explanation, but if none of those names mean anything to you, the explanation won't help either. But I know one thing: you really want me to go away and never have to see me again."

"You got that right," Eric said feelingly.

"Okay, here's the deal. You walk out of the Faire with me, across the parking lot. There will be a doorway. If it's there, you walk through it with me. You can bring anyone with you that you like as far as the doorway, but only you and I go through. Deal?" Jeanette said.

Eric had a strange expression on his face. "Um . . . Jeanette, right? There isn't a doorway out in the parking lot. And we're not supposed to leave the Faire during working hours."

She hardened her expression. "This is the deal, Eric. You want me to leave. Do this with me and I will.

Look, down inside you know you aren't supposed to be here. You know there's something wrong. It won't hurt to go look. I can't wait until the Faire shuts down for the night. We don't have that long. And don't give me the official party line. You know they won't miss a couple of you for a half hour or so."

"Why should I trust you?" Eric demanded.

What are you, deaf as well as paranoid? "I'm not asking you to trust me," Jeanette pointed out in exasperation. "I'm asking you to walk across the parking lot with me and trust the evidence of your own eyes."

"And if the door isn't there?" Eric said cannily.

Then I'm in big trouble.

"Then I leave. You go back to the Faire. You'll never see me again." *Because if the door isn't still there, I'm going to take Mystery and ride as far as I can before whatever's going to happen catches up with me.*

"And this . . . Kayla? How do I know she won't just show up next?" Eric asked.

Jeanette was losing the small amount of patience she'd started out with. Her voice was curt as she answered. "She sent me because she couldn't come. Stop wasting time. Do we take a walk?" *Or do I have to see if I have a hope in hell of getting you out of here at gunpoint?* It was something she didn't want to try. It would definitely put a hole in his reality—but it might be the kind of hole that would turn dream into nightmare.

"What the hell," Eric said, shrugging. He turned away and went over to talk to Karen for a moment. She looked puzzled as he spoke, and kept glancing over at Jeanette, shaking her head vigorously.

Jeanette got to her feet. "Come on, Eric. You think I've got a van with the A-Team in it waiting for you outside the gate? Get real. If you see anything like that, run. We're just going for a walk. And I guarantee: whoever you think sent me, didn't."

"You do anything to hurt Eric, and I will break every bone in your body," Karen hissed, walking over to Jeanette and leaning in close.

"Fine," Jeanette said. *Just try it, and we see how well guns work in the Faire.* "Can we go now?"

Karen and her two girlfriends went with Eric and Jeanette. All three of them were armed with knives, swords, and axes: Jeanette had no idea of how well they knew how to use any of those things, but she did know that all three women were bigger and stronger than she was, and their furs and armor would get in the way of some of her better bar-fight moves, and maybe even stop a bullet.

She really hoped it wouldn't come to that.

They didn't go out through the Main Gate. Eric said that would attract too much attention, and Jeanette supposed he cared about that, still thinking this place was real. He took them around through the Faire and then out through a side gate that led through what looked like a campground. There were tents in all shapes and sizes.

"This is where we stay when the Faire shuts down for the day," Eric said.

"You don't have to talk to her, Eric," Karen said edgily.

Jeanette looked around, wondering if all this ever had been real, some where-and-when. It actually looked like it might have been fun, she thought grudgingly.

They passed through the camping area and worked their way through the players' parking and out into the main parking lot.

"Where's this 'door' of yours?" Karen demanded. "I don't see it."

Fine talk from a figment of somebody's imagination.

"It's on the other side of the parking lot," Jeanette said, not slowing down. *I hope.*

She spared a longing glance for Mystery as they passed the bike again. *Maybe someday, girl.*

The door was right where she'd left it, an impossible hole in reality.

Eric stopped as soon as he saw it.

"Come on, Eric," Karen said nervously. "It's time to go back."

"There's the door, Eric," Jeanette said harshly. "Right where I said it would be. The door back to the real world. Where you have people who love you, and a brother who needs you. This is a fantasy. It isn't real."

Eric took a hesitant step forward.

"Eric!" Karen wailed.

"Is this a dream, Karen?" Eric asked, turning to face her. "Is that why everything here is so perfect? Why the Faire never ends? Why the sun is never too hot, why it never rains, why the travelers never get drunk and ugly, and there's always a good take in the hat? Is this Neverland without Captain Hook? Am I a Lost Boy?"

"You're happy here," Karen said pleadingly, not answering him directly.

"It isn't real," Jeanette said. "You know it, down deep inside. Face the truth."

"I *am* happy here," Eric said slowly. "But—" his face twisted, and if it hadn't been so sad, it would have been funny. "But it *isn't* real. So I guess . . . I have to see what's on the other side of that door."

"No," Karen said, a pleading note in her voice.

Suddenly the air seemed charged, as if a storm was brewing, though the sun shone down pure and changeless.

"Don't make *me* get real, bitch," Jeanette said, stepping between Karen and Eric. She slipped her hand into her pocket, closing her fingers over the pistol. "Get going, Eric."

But suddenly Karen's face crumpled into tears, and she turned away. Her two friends put their arms around her, soothing and patting as they led her back toward the Faire.

When she was sure Karen was going to keep going, Jeanette turned back. Eric had walked away. He'd almost reached the door, and Jeanette didn't know what would happen if he went through it without her. She ran until she caught up with him.

"Tell me . . . what happened?" he asked, hesitating on the threshold of the open doorway. "What made me come here, I mean?"

His brown eyes were wide and troubled, searching her face for some hint of hope or reassurance.

Jeanette felt something twist inside her. He looked so vulnerable, so young and lost. No wonder Karen had wanted to keep him! She had to tell herself that this Eric wasn't real, any more than the Faire that she'd dragged him out of was real. He was a shadow of his true self, a shadow inhabiting a shadow world.

"You got mugged. You're in a coma. But you'll be okay. Through the door, up the stairs, and you're home," she said gruffly. *And you'll never be as happy again as you were here, I bet.*

And if they'd met in real life, someone like Eric would never have looked twice at someone like her.

"You're sure about this?" Eric said dubiously. "Because I don't—"

Losing the last of her patience—with herself and him—Jeanette shoved with all her strength, pushing him through the door, and followed him through.

❖   ❖   ❖

Kayla's fingers were icy cold in his. Her face was white and drawn. Beads of sweat trickled down her face, and shudders of chill wracked her body, but she never moved. A faint halo of blue light, difficult to see in the fluorescent illumination of the hospital room, played over her fingers and Eric's face. Her breathing was deep and raspy, but at least she was still breathing, thank the Good Lord.

Hosea kept glancing from her face to the banks of machines monitoring Eric. One green line for heartbeat—a steady jagged pulse—another for brain activity, flat and ominous. The steady thump of the ventilator, breathing when Eric could not.

Suddenly Kayla began to cough and twitch, like a hound chasing rabbits in his sleep. Her fingers jerked and twitched in his grasp. At the same moment, Hosea felt a wave of freezing chill wash into him.

Jeanette was coming home.

The EEG monitor *eeped* and began to mutter to itself, its display showing spiky patterns. At the same time, the blue glow in Kayla's hands expanded and brightened, covering Eric's entire body. Hosea felt the last of the cold pass from her fingers, through him, settling safely back into the banjo again.

"Kayla!" Hosea said sharply.

Kayla's eyes fluttered open. "Not . . . done," she said, in thick ragged tones. Her voice sounded slurred, and he wasn't entirely sure she knew where she was.

"Stop now," Hosea commanded firmly. *"Now."*

"But—" Kayla sounded plaintive.

"Stop," Hosea repeated, putting all the authority he could muster into that one word.

Kayla lifted her hand from Eric. The azure glow around his body faded and died away. Her eyes rolled back in her head and her knees buckled. Hosea barely caught her in time.

He picked her up and deposited her in the chair, though—if truth were told—his own knees weren't as steady as he'd like. Gently he felt her wrist, scanning her face apprehensively. She was breathing normally and her pulse was strong. She'd just overextended herself, or so he hoped.

Once Kayla was settled in the chair, he ran his fingers over the strings of the banjo. "You okay, Sweetheart?"

:Leave me alone!: Jeanette snarled furiously.

Hosea smiled faintly and began detuning the banjo. By the time he had the instrument locked away safely in its case again, he felt better, and Kayla was sitting up.

"Don't you move, now," Hosea warned her. "You keeled over, and Ah don't want you doing it again."

"Hah," Kayla said a bit groggily. "Eric?"

"According to the medical equipment, Mr. Banyon is doing much better," Paul said, coming over to inspect the readouts. "Brain function is well within normal parameters."

"Then how come he ain't awake?" Kayla demanded, trying to get up.

Hosea pushed her back down into the chair without effort. He pointed over his shoulder at some of the bags dangling beside the bed. "Ah'd say that the mess o' painkillers they've stuck him with might have a little bit to do with that. Now you just rest here for a few minutes and have some more to drink. Then we're goin' home."

Kayla opened her mouth to argue. Hosea held up a finger.

"You're in no shape to finish Healin' him up tonight, and that's the plain and simple truth. And even if you did, it'd be sure to cause more'n a bit o' talk. They can explain away him comin' out of a coma to their satisfaction, but not broken bones that heal overnight."

"I guess," Kayla muttered sullenly.

"Now drink up," Hosea said, handing her another bottle of juice. "You're just tetchy from doing all that work."

A few minutes later, Kayla felt strong enough to stand up, though she was pretty sure she wasn't going to feel really *warm* any time soon. *I bet I've got ghost prints on my liver.* She stood up carefully, leaning on Hosea for support.

"Ready to go then? All right," Paul said briskly, unlocking the door and pulling it open.

Kayla cast a last longing glance back at Eric.

"Later," Hosea said firmly. "Now walk—or be carried."

"Bully," Kayla muttered, heading slowly toward the door.

Eric's night nurse was just coming back up the corridor as they walked out into the hall.

She walked into the room. A moment passed as the other three watched and listened, invisible, in the hall.

The call light went on over the door.

An aide came over to the door and stepped inside.

"Get the doctor on call *now*. Mr. Banyon's come out of his coma."

Hosea got Kayla home and made sure she ate something before letting her go to bed. He saw that she was tucked up warmly before letting himself out of her apartment and taking the stairs up to Eric's.

Just as well Miz Llewellyn wasn't around. She'd

have his hide for a rug if she knew what he'd got up to with Little Bit tonight.

But there hadn't been any way to test Jeanette's idea. Only to try it.

And it seemed to have worked. Eric was back in one piece—or back in one place, anyway. And Little Bit could take care of the rest, over time.

Now Beth and Kory would be wanting to know the good news, and Hosea owed it to them to let them know as soon as possible. It was already late. A few more minutes before he got to bed wouldn't make any difference.

He let himself into Eric's apartment and switched on the computer. Hosea's own finances didn't quite stretch to one yet, but he borrowed Eric's from time to time, or used one of the many public Internet connections available in the city.

He dug around in his backpack until he found the scrap of paper on which he'd written Beth's e-mail address, and logged in to his Hotmail account. Typing her address into the "To" field, he began composing his message.

"I want to go back to New York," Ria said, pacing back and forth restlessly in the living room of her suite. Her two bodyguards watched her incuriously. There was another one on the outside door. Ria ignored them. They were a fact of life under the current circumstances.

"It isn't that easy, Ria," Zachary Standish said patiently.

He was a well-groomed and formidably efficient legal shark; she'd wooed him away from private practice to walk point for LlewellCo in the wake of the Threshold debacle, and had been able to keep him busy ever since. Her competitors had been astonished—Standish had made his name by suing corporations, not working for them—but Ria had dangled an irresistible bait.

"Fair dealing, Mr. Standish. No compromises. Ethics and responsibility. I can always use another still small voice of conscience on my staff. And with what I'm going to pay you, you'll have the resources to go after a lot more pro bono work, I'd imagine."

"Even if it touches on a LlewellCo company, Ms. Llewellyn?" he'd asked.

"Threshold was a LlewellCo company, Mr. Standish," she'd answered implacably. *"I'm cleaning house. Want to help?"*

Neither of them had yet regretted the partnership.

Zachary had flown down from New York yesterday with his entire staff. They were occupying most of the rest of the floor, and a considerable amount of the resources of Gotham Security as well. Ria had no intention of seeing any of her people take a bullet for her.

"Zack, if it were easy, I wouldn't be paying you the enormous amount I do. I need to get back there. A friend of mine's in the hospital. I want to sit by his bedside and wring my hands. *Do something.*"

Though her words were light, they did little to conceal Ria's frustration. It had been almost a full day since she'd heard about Eric's condition, and everything she'd been able to do since then—for him and for herself—had done little to take the edge off her anxiety.

She'd changed hotels, and surrounded herself with round-the-clock security. She'd thrown up a thornbush of law around herself, including Zachary Standish.

She'd put Anita on the case back in New York to take the heat off Kayla, and arranged for Eric's transfer (as soon as circumstances would permit) to a small private hospital that she used frequently. The staff there was very discreet. She was also having a room in her apartment outfitted as a fully functional sickroom, in case it would be possible to have him transferred directly there. The report on his condition that she'd gotten from Anita wasn't good, but it didn't particularly worry Ria; she'd seen Kayla work miracles before. None of Eric's physical injuries were a real problem—hell, all of them could be fixed mundanely with enough time and money.

Except for one . . .

"Get me out of this city, Zack," she repeated, stopping and staring down at him imperiously. "You're my legal counsel. Do something legal."

"I am. I'm advising you to stay put. You're in a very tenuous position here. Breaking and entering—"

"You've seen my statement. I was in the car the whole time."

"Kidnapping—"

"I assisted in the rescue of a kidnap victim."

"Assault with a deadly weapon—"

"Exactly who am I supposed to have assaulted—and with what? All my entirely legal handguns are still locked up in my safe in New York. Where are you coming up with this nonsense?"

"From a counter-brief Parker Wheatley filed with the Justice Department this morning, accusing you personally of murder, pillage, arson, impersonating a Federal Marshal, and a few things I actually had to look up. My specialty is corporate law. You need a criminal lawyer, Ria."

"He's blowing smoke," Ria snapped. Whether Wheatley's accusations were true or not didn't actually matter as much as whether he could drum up political support for them. Did he still have friends in high places—or not?

"Maybe. But it's going to take time for the smoke to clear away," Zack said.

"Oh, I don't think so. Either the smoke goes away, and I go home . . . or I go public. I'm sure the Great American Public would really like to hear that the U.S. Government is spending tax dollars kidnapping and torturing harmless bookstore owners and planning to put tea-leaf readers into concentration camps because it's taking the UFO menace so seriously." She smiled coldly.

Zack winced. "I really don't think you should do that, Ria. If . . . there's a possibility you might find yourself detained as a material witness," he said carefully.

"Sent to jail for shooting my mouth off, you mean?" Ria began to pace again. "I don't have to be available to break this story, and I'd be a fool to make a threat they could neutralize by just locking me up. I came to them, Zack. If I hadn't, Wheatley would still be going his merry way. I don't expect either gratitude or a long memory for past favors, not in this town. I just expect special treatment now. Tomorrow can take care of itself."

She sat down on the couch, suddenly tired.

"I need to get back to New York—which was still, last I heard, a part of the U.S. I'm not going any farther than that. They'll have my full cooperation—including my silence, if that's what they want. Or my testimony. Their choice. I'm not a flight risk, because I'm not a criminal. Just a concerned citizen and campaign contributor. *But I have to get home.* Now for God's sake, Zack, go find someone to explain that to before I have to renew acquaintance with my friends over at the *Washington Post.*"

Zack got to his feet, closing his briefcase. "If you're sure that's the way you want to play it?"

"Yes, Zack, that's the way I want to play it," Ria answered, her voice flat.

The ringing of the telephone jarred Kayla awake sometime—not long enough—after she'd gotten to bed. She opened her eyes. Daylight. Must be morning, then.

The phone continued its annoyingly cheery chirping, until Kayla finally located it—she'd gone to sleep clutching it, for some reason. She fumbled at it until she hit the "On" button.

"Hello? Kayla?"

"Ria? What's wrong?" she croaked.

"Things are going right for a change, not that I need to tell you. Anita called a few hours ago, but I thought I'd let you get some sleep before I touched base; it sounds like you had a busy night. The official story at the hospital is that Eric has made a miraculous recovery from his coma and is doing much better. They should be willing to transfer him to my private clinic day after tomorrow instead of the end of the week, and then you can really get to work on him," Ria said.

"Yeah. We did all right." Kayla sat up and ran a hand through her hair, still groggy. And ravenous. She wondered what there was in the fridge that didn't need cooking. Maybe she'd go out. "I wasn't there for most of it."

"Weren't there? Where were you?" Ria sounded confused.

"I was sort of there. But he was stuck off someplace I couldn't get at, so we had to send Jeanette in after him."

"You sent *Jeanette Campbell* in to find Eric?" Ria was almost sputtering suddenly, and Kayla would have thought it was funny if she still hadn't been so tired.

"Yeah. Trust me. It was the only way. I still don't have all the details. It was kinda late when we finished up." *And linking up with a ghost really takes it out of you.* "Ria . . . where are you?"

"Still in Washington. I've got a few more things to straighten out here—unfortunately—but I'll be home as soon as possible. If I'd known this was going to take this long—and what was going to happen up there while I was gone—I might not have come, but it turns out it was a good thing I did."

"Yeah, go all cryptic on me," Kayla said, and Ria laughed harshly.

"How's the other matter coming?" Ria asked.

Magnus, she means.

"I'm going to go up and see Eric," Kayla said, "then I guess I better go check out that place Hosea mentioned and give them some money. Then tonight I'm going to go back up to The Place and see if I can't get the three of them to go over there." She was just as sure as Eric had been that Magnus wouldn't move without Ace, and neither one would stir a step without Jaycie. So it looked like all or nothing.

"It sounds like a good idea," Ria said. "Don't overwork yourself."

"Like I could, with all the yentas I've got looking over my shoulder here," Kayla said, only half joking. *And sometime before the end of my so-called vacation, I've got to make some time to hit the books. I've got a couple of papers due.* "Don't worry, Ria. I'll be fine."

"I'm counting on it," Ria said. "Take care."

"You too," Kayla said.

Looking at her watch after she closed the phone again, Kayla discovered it was already 2:00 P.M. Better get moving, then. Respectable for her to visit to the hospital and Somerset House, then back here to grubby up to go back to The Place. Kayla wasn't really looking forward to another night spent on unheated bare floors, but the way she felt now, she could sleep on a bed of nails, and she really couldn't afford to spend another night away. She'd manage.

She still had her visitor's pass from her previous day's visit to Gotham General. You were supposed to turn them in when you left each day, but she'd kept hers. It was a lot faster that way than having to wait in line at the Admissions Desk.

But when she got up to Eric's room, it was empty.

Not empty as in "he was temporarily somewhere else and would be right back." The bed had been made up, the life support machines were gone, the room was obviously waiting for a new occupant.

Kayla headed for the Nurses' Station at a dead run.

"Hey! You!"

The nurse behind the desk looked up from her paperwork with a frown. "Can I help you?"

"The patient in 2418. Eric Banyon. Where is he?"

"2418?" The woman consulted her charts. "I'm sorry, there's no one in that room."

I know that! "Was he moved?"

"What was the name again?"

"Eric Banyon."

The woman consulted her charts with maddening slowness, then checked the computer. "I'm sorry. There isn't an Eric Banyon in this wing."

But he was here yesterday! And last night!

Seeing Kayla's stricken expression, the nurse smiled gently. "This is a big hospital, and a lot of the floors do look alike. And patients do get moved, and sometimes it takes a little while for the system to catch up with them. Why don't you check with the front desk? I'm sure they'll be able to find him for you."

I don't think so.

But because she couldn't think of anything else to try—other than checking every room on the floor, and she knew she wouldn't get very far with that—Kayla went back down to the front desk.

"I'm here to see a patient," she said.

"His name?" the woman behind the desk said.

"Eric Banyon. Room 2418," Kayla repeated.

She waited, hoping against hope that the woman would say that Eric had been moved, would say it had all been a mistake, a computer error. But instead, after frowning at the computer for several minutes, what she said was: "I'm sorry. We have no patient by that name here. Are you sure you're in the right hospital?"

This is bad. She wasn't quite sure how bad, or in what direction, but she knew it was bad. Kayla found herself out on the sidewalk, walking aimlessly away from the hospital. She didn't know where she was going. It hardly mattered now.

She wanted to cry. She wanted to hit something. She settled for finding a diner and calling Ria.

"Hello?" Thank all the Gods, real and unreal, that Ria answered her phone. If she hadn't, it would have been the very last straw.

"Ria? This is Kayla. What time did the hospital call you to say that Eric was better?"

"What's wrong?" Ria demanded, instantly suspicious.

"I'll tell you in a minute."

"Let's see. Anita called them this morning about nine-fifteen and talked to Dr. Rodriguez. She talked to him for about ten minutes and called me just after that."

So Eric had been at Gotham General—had *existed*—at nine-fifteen this morning. At least Ria still remembered he'd been there. Kayla felt a faint sense of relief at that. At least she wasn't the only one in the world who remembered that Eric was supposed to be in the hospital.

"Well, I was up there around three. He wasn't there. Furthermore, they said he never had been there. No such patient."

"I'll take care of it." There was a tone in Ria's voice Kayla had never heard before.

"Ria?" She'd been scared a moment ago. Now she was *really* scared.

"Listen to me, Kayla. It doesn't take magic to produce effects like that. Computer records can be changed. People can be bribed. I'm involved with . . . some rather annoying people just now. Anybody backchecking me might turn up Eric and decide to get to me through him. Call Anita. Tell her to look into it. And . . . it might be a good idea for you to drop out of sight until I get home. That, or go on up to my apartment and let me call in a security team for you."

"Just what are you *doing* down there?" Kayla demanded.

"Opening a nastier can of worms than I expected to, apparently," Ria answered, her voice distant and cold. "But if they've harmed Eric, I guarantee that when I'm through with them, they'll think Lord Aerune was one of the Backstreet Boys."

"Now you're scaring me," Kayla said nervously.

"Good. Then you'll be careful. Now call Anita. Warn Hosea, just in case. Will you go to my apartment?"

Kayla thought about it. But that would mean staying out of sight until Ria showed up again, and she'd

already been out of touch with Magnus and his friends
for too long. A day was a lifetime when you were on
the street. Anything could happen. Anything might
already have happened.

"No. There's things I gotta do that can't wait."

Ria sighed, acknowledging defeat. "Then play least-
in-sight for another twenty-four hours or so."

"Are you sure about this?" Kayla demanded.

"Better safe," Ria said cryptically, and hung up.

My life has just become a John Grisham novel, Kayla
thought, staring at the silent phone. Who were these
people that Ria thought were after Eric and might
be after her? What can of worms?

What the hell was going on?

It was a safe bet that nobody here on Sixth Avenue
was going to have any answers for her. She stirred
more sugar into her coffee.

Dutifully, Kayla called Anita, telling her that Eric
had disappeared from the hospital and, as far as anyone at Gotham General was willing to say, had never
been there in the first place. Anita promised to check
into it. Kayla told her to call Ria if she found out
anything—much as she wanted to hear the answers
herself, it wouldn't do her street cred any good to
have her phone ring while she was playing Homeless Street Kid.

After that she called Hosea, who didn't carry (or
for that matter, *own*) a cell phone. She thought it
over, and left a message on his answering machine,
stressing the fact that she was safe, that Ria thought
Eric's disappearance from the hospital might be related
to her problems in Washington and not really to do
with Eric at all, and that because of that, Ria wanted
everyone connected with her to keep a low profile
until she could get back.

Kayla was pretty sure she'd covered everything

in the phone message. But it would be just as well to see Hosea and give him the message in person. She knew his schedule varied, but he might be down at the homeless center. It was worth a shot, anyway.

But she was closer to Somerset House than she was to Jacob Riis, and if she was going to try to talk Magnus and the others into going there, she'd better go and drop off one of Ria's checks. She dug through her backpack, looking for the notebook in which she'd written the address.

Somerset House was on the Upper West Side. It looked like a perfectly ordinary apartment building, except for the fact that there was a desk in the lobby with a book for signing in and out, and a woman with a name tag sitting behind the desk.

"Can I help you?" the woman asked, as Kayla approached.

People keep askin' that lately, and the answer always seems to be "No."

"Um . . . a friend of mine down at Jacob Riis referred me here. He said you might have vacancies?"

The woman pressed a button under her desk. In a moment, another woman entered the lobby. "If you'd come this way . . . ?"

Kayla followed her into a bright and cheerful office that had once, obviously, been a ground-floor apartment.

"I'm Miranda Sherwood. I'm in charge of Admissions here. What do you know about our program?"

"That it's private, that it costs money, that you don't send kids back to their parents or tell their parents that they're here, that they have to be clean and sober and follow the rules. It's not for me. I'm here to pay for three other kids to come in."

Miranda raised her eyebrows. "I thought I'd heard everything. Where are they?"

Kayla hesitated.

"Please don't lie, Ms. . . ."

"Smith." Abruptly, Kayla realized how that must sound. "No, really. Kayla Smith. It's my real name. I can show you ID."

"Maybe that would be a good idea," Miranda Sherwood said consideringly.

Kayla hesitated, but everything she could sense from this woman told her that Miranda Sherwood could be trusted. And she was going to have to trust somebody, sooner or later, even if only a little. She dug around and pulled out her Columbia student ID. Miranda studied it for a moment and handed it back.

"So, Kayla Smith, what's your interest in these 'three other kids'?"

"I want to get them off the street before they die," Kayla said bluntly. "There's no possibility they'll go home. I think I can get them to come here." She hesitated. "Not if they know I had anything to do with paying for it."

"Ms. Smith, it costs us over a thousand dollars a month per child to keep this place going. You don't think the kids come in with that kind of money, do you? As soon as they have jobs, they contribute to their upkeep, but—"

"Actually, LlewellCo's paying for it," Kayla said.

"Ria Llewellyn?" Miranda said, sounding surprised and dubious. Kayla nodded. She wasn't surprised that Miranda Sherwood wasn't buying it. She didn't exactly look like the kind of person who hung with Ria Llewellyn.

"Is this some kind of a joke?" Miranda said, starting to become angry. "Because if it is—"

"Fifty thousand dollars," Kayla said quickly.

"I beg your pardon?" Miranda said.

"You've got openings right now, don't you?"

"Yes, but—"

"I'll give you a check from Ria Llewellyn for fifty thousand dollars," Kayla said. "You take the kids. Call her bank. Better yet, call her personal assistant. I've got her number right here. Her name's Anita Sheldrake."

"Could you wait outside for a moment? There are chairs in the lobby."

"Yeah, right."

Kayla went outside and sat down. Miranda was probably calling the police right now. They'd come and arrest Kayla on suspicion of making an eccentric charitable contribution.

She rested her head on her knees, wishing she were still asleep in her bed. She wished Eric was here. She wished Ria was here. Either one of them could have finessed this operation a whole lot better than Kayla just had.

But if either one of them'd been around, she wouldn't've been in this situation in the first place.

Eventually she sighed and sat up. Feeling sorry for herself wouldn't get her anywhere. She couldn't do anything for Eric right now, but Magnus, Ace, and Jaycie still needed her help. If Miranda Sherwood would just cooperate, maybe there was something she could do for them.

While she waited, she saw a number of kids coming in and out, singly and in groups. All of them stopped at the desk to sign in or out, showing their IDs as they did.

Kayla bit her lip. Could she talk the kids into coming to this place? Would they think the street was better and safer? Kayla knew it wasn't, but she had the benefit of a couple of years and a lot of experience.

And you had to get clean and stay clean to be here. She knew Ace and Magnus qualified. But Jaycie?

Kayla could clean out his system; sweep out whatever junk was in there. But she couldn't repair the emotional damage that had led him to choose that form of escape.

"Ms. Smith?"

Miranda was back. She was smiling, and her aura read puzzled.

Kayla followed her back into the office.

"I just spoke to Ms. Sheldrake. She described you in detail. We had a . . . very interesting conversation."

I just bet.

"Apparently Ms. Llewellyn's offer is on the level," Miranda said. "And Ms. Sheldrake indicated that LlewellCo would not be averse to providing additional funding to our program beyond your initial contribution."

"Yeah. That's the kind of thing Ria does a lot of. So you'll take them?" Kayla said with relief.

"We'll be happy to. But they won't receive any special treatment. We don't force anyone to stay here, and if they break the rules, they have to leave. So: no drugs, no drinking, no tobacco, nothing illegal—and that includes sex."

"Sex is illegal?" Kayla asked, surprised. Not that casual sex was a big item in the future of a Empath. But she always liked to know when she was breaking the law.

Miranda smiled. "If you're under eighteen it is, and almost all of our residents are, except for a few special cases. Here, let me give you a couple of brochures. They've got our address on them, in case your friends want to come in on their own."

"And you'll keep my name out of things?" Kayla said quickly.

"We have a policy of not lying to our clients, because it's very important to us to build a trust relationship with them, but as far as I'm concerned, Ria Llewellyn has made a generous donation to our facility that has made it possible for us to accept your friends. I can't say I won't ever tell them, but I certainly won't volunteer the information, and I don't really think it will come up immediately. Now, I believe you have a check for us?"

A few minutes later Kayla was back out on the street, having signed over the contents of what Anita had called Ria's "slush account" to Somerset House.

She hoped she'd done the right thing. But now, this way, at least Magnus and the others would have a safe place to go, and could stay as long as they wanted or needed to. And if they didn't come here, Miranda Sherwood could certainly put the money to good use helping a lot of other kids.

She was exhausted, thinking longingly of her apartment and her bed. She stopped on the street to phone Hosea's apartment, but he still didn't answer. She supposed she'd better head on down to the shelter. At least they'd give her coffee.

She walked over to the A train and caught it all the way downtown. It was getting into rush hour now, so the trains were running more frequently, and she made good time. The trek across town woke her up a bit; it was already dark when she got back up onto street level, and getting colder. And she was hungry again. Well, she'd taken a lot out of herself in the last twenty-four; had to pay it back one way or another, calories or sleep. She bought some dried apricots from a street vendor and ate them as she walked across town, toward the shelter.

Gotta feed the beast.

She was a block away from the shelter when she saw the last person she would have expected to see.

It had been risky—she'd been scared to death the entire time—but it'd been worth it, even with having to get down here at noon to be sure of having a place in line, the long wait, and then being afraid her things would be stolen. But if she'd left the important stuff back at The Place, she could be almost sure it wouldn't be there when she got back, the way things were there these days. So with much hesitation, Ace had brought the money along. There was quite a bit of it, even with Jaycie not bringing in as much as before, and the other kids holding out because they knew she'd pay for food and things.

But being able to take a shower . . . ! To be clean, really clean, all over, and *warm*, even if it was only for a little while, and wash her hair. Even though she'd had to get right back into the same dirty clothes she'd come in, she still felt better. And she was sure she smelled better, too.

And Hosea Songmaker hadn't lied. Nobody had given her any trouble. And everything had been right where she'd left it.

She'd better hurry now. She'd had to wait a long time in line to get in. It was already dark, and she didn't like being on the streets after dark. She didn't like leaving Jaycie alone for very long these days, either. Magnus was there, but sometimes he didn't see things quite the way she did. He still thought Jaycie was doing okay, when Ace knew he wasn't. And whether Magnus was willing to see it or not, things were getting worse all around up at The Place.

The three of them had to get out of there. That fight with Chinaka and Shimene and the others last week had been bad—and when Eric had just disappeared, and then Kayla, they'd accused Ace of going behind their backs and getting the two of them to leave. Now Chinaka wanted the two of *them* to leave—they'd want to keep Jaycie of course, but they had another think coming there. But where were the three of them going to *go*?

She was walking back toward the subway when she saw a familiar figure walking toward her.

"Kayla!"

Kayla stopped. It was Ace.

Busted.

She glanced down at herself. Same jacket she'd been wearing the last time Ace had seen her, and she supposed the rest of her outfit would pass muster if someone weren't too suspicious.

Only she knew "suspicious" was Ace's middle name. And last, probably.

"Hi," Kayla said resignedly.

"You're too late to get a shower. All the slots're filled," Ace said.

Kayla shrugged. Shower? "Next time, I guess."

"So," Ace said, a little too casually, "are you and Eric coming back?"

She wants *us back*, Kayla realized with surprise.

"Can't find him," Kayla said honestly. "Been looking all over for him. Guess he took off without me."

"Too bad," Ace said sympathetically. She seemed sincerely disappointed, which puzzled Kayla. "Guess it's just you, then. We kept your stuff."

"Sure," Kayla said, falling in beside her and turning away from the shelter. *What does she want?*

She hated the thought of missing the chance of

talking to Hosea, but he might not even be there anyway. The message on his answering machine would have to do. And hooking up with Ace was more important.

Hosea returned home around seven, having played for the subway crowds. He could shower and change, go up and see Eric during evening visiting hours, then maybe head back down to the shelter and see if he could do a little eavesdropping on the children to try to pick up the last missing pieces of the Secret Stories.

Bloody Mary's True Name was the key—he was sure of it. But what could it be? What sort of demon could a four-year-old child imagine that was terrible enough to frighten God Himself?

The answering machine message light was flashing spastically when he got in. He hurried over to it to play back his messages, thinking that perhaps Caity had called.

But no. It was Kayla. She'd had to call several times to leave her full message, because the machine kept cutting her off.

Eric had vanished from Gotham General sometime this morning, and no one there remembered he'd even been there. Miz Llewellyn thought it was connected to her problems in Washington. Kayla intended to disappear until Ria got back. Hosea might be in danger himself.

"What . . . a . . . mess," Hosea said, at a loss for words. "Greystone?"

After a few moments there was a scrabbling on the fire escape, and Hosea's bedroom window opened. Greystone came clumping into the living room, his carven simian face grave.

"Trouble, boyo?" he asked.

"In every size and shape you care to name," Hosea said grimly. "Listen to this." He played back Kayla's messages.

"Well," Greystone said, "the lass sounds half-demented, and who's going to blame her, with Eric gone missing again." The gargoyle sighed. "And things were going so well, too."

"What am Ah goin' to do?" Hosea said. "Ah don't have much to worry about—it's not likely anybody'd be comin' after me, and Ah can take care o' myself, what with bein' a Guardian and all. But Little Bit's got more confidence than common sense, sometimes. An' Ah don't know where she's gotten herself to. But you do," he said, fixing Greystone with a level blue-eyed stare.

"Ah, now, laddie, sure an' you wouldn't be askin' me to trespass on the sacred bound of confidentiality," Greystone said, taking a step backward.

"If somethin' bad happens to Kayla because Ah don't know where she is, Miz Llewellyn is going to turn you into driveway gravel—and Ah might be persuaded to help her," Hosea said meaningfully. "Right now Little Bit's the only one who knows where Eric's brother is. That don't do anybody any good."

"You're right." Greystone sighed. His wings drooped. After a long pause, the gargoyle spoke. "The kids are holed up in a condemned tenement up near Harlem—hold still and I'll show you where it is."

Greystone concentrated, his features contorting in a grimace of concentration. A picture formed in Hosea's mind, and suddenly he *knew* where The Place was, and exactly how to find it.

"You aren't planning on making any bull moves, are you, laddybuck?" Greystone asked anxiously.

"Ah guess not," Hosea said slowly. He felt better knowing where Kayla was. Not the best neighborhood in Manhattan, but her empathic abilities should give her the ability to avoid trouble if she could. And *somebody* had to keep an eye on Magnus. "Ah just wish Ah knew where the devil Eric was."

"Aye, don't we all?" Greystone agreed somberly.

CHAPTER FOURTEEN:

GRAVELWALK

In a typical New York example of bad luck, Ace and Kayla's subway train went out of service at 34th Street, dumping several hundred irritated commuters out onto the platform. The train then closed its doors and sat there sullenly, blocking the tracks, with no relief in sight.

"C'mon," Kayla said. "Let's walk up a couple of stops. Maybe they'll route around it or something. And at least we won't be stuck down here."

Though she didn't have a lot of choice about taking the subway to get around the city, Kayla didn't like it much, especially at rush hour. With all those bodies packed in like sardines, you couldn't help touching people, and that meant she got to know a lot of people a lot better than she really wanted to sometimes. In an hour or so, not only would the blockage on the line clear up, the trains would clear out, too.

So they walked uptown for a while.

When they reached Times Square, they found that a street preacher had set up shop on the traffic island in the center of the square. He had an amplifier with him on a wheeled cart, and was shouting into a cordless microphone. His grossly amplified words echoed through the space around him.

"Yea! And the Sabeans fell upon them and took them away! Yea! They have slain the servants with the edge of the sword, and only I am escaped alone to tell thee!"

"Job 1:15," Ace muttered in disgust. "And he hasn't even got it right." She put a hand on Kayla's arm, trying to pull her past the crowd that had gathered around the man.

Kayla looked at her in surprise. Ace hadn't struck her as particularly religious, let alone someone who could quote the Bible, chapter and verse, on the fly. But suddenly her attention was riveted by the god-shouter's next words.

"Brothers and sisters, on that terrible day, *I* was there upon the Field of Blood, and God Himself reached out His Mighty Hand to shield me from the terrible destruction from the Towers. Daily I praise Jesus for giving me this miracle, and preserving me to bear witness to all of you that His Glory endureth, yea! Though the Sabeans fell upon them and took them away! Though they have slain the servants of God with their fiery sword, *I* am proof of Christ's miraculous love—"

Kayla pulled away from Ace and started elbowing her way through the crowd, pushing to the front. The preacher was a white-haired old man in a long black coat and clerical collar that she bet he wasn't entitled to. There was a folding table beside him, with a jar for contributions, and taped to it were photographs of the Towers in flames, with a sorrowing Jesus crudely Photoshopped over them.

It had not been an easy year for an Empath in New York. She *knew*, better than anyone other than the sufferers themselves, just what thoughts occurred in the panic of the moment, in the dark of the night, in the lonely times, in the times when even family said, "It's time for closure, get on with your life."

Sure, as many people as had died that day died in car accidents every month . . . but *not all at once*. Not sacrificed to hatred, dying in terror, some of them knowing their fate for hours or minutes beforehand . . . and with the tragedy leaving a gaping unhealed wound in the very flesh of the city, visible for all to see.

And not in a way that left survivors feeling guilty, so guilty, for being one of the ones that got out—or who hadn't been there at all. Wondering, "Why did I live?" or "Why didn't they?" Leaving the survivors—*all* the survivors—wondering if it *was* punishment, somehow . . . and wondering just who was being punished. Feeling angry, so angry, that a loved one hadn't survived that day. Bearing scars, visible and invisible. Wanting revenge, wanting to punish the people responsible, and knowing that would never, ever happen.

What had happened that day was and would be inescapable: like other tragedies, needing only its name to invoke its memory in all the years to come. Dallas. Challenger. Oklahoma City. September 11th. It had been horrible. It was still horrible, though the shock and the rawness of the grief, if not the magnitude of the tragedy, diminished with time.

And then—this.

"You!" Kayla shouted, interrupting him. "Just who do you think you are?"

The preacher stopped dead, and stared at her.

"Hey!" Ace hissed, tugging at her elbow. Kayla ignored her.

"Even if you *aren't* lying through your teeth, which I *doubt*," Kayla continued savagely. "Just what makes you think *you're* so especially holy and deserving of a miracle? Are you trying to say that those people in the Towers and the planes and at the Pentagon *weren't*? That they *deserved* to die, and you and you alone *deserved* a miracle?"

The preacher's mouth worked, but no sound came out. Ace stared at Kayla in horrified fascination, but Kayla had just gotten started.

"What about all the babies that died?" she snarled into the bubble of silence that had formed around them. "Do you think you're so much more pure than a baby that you deserved a miracle more than they did? Do you go around saying to everybody who lost someone that day that their loved ones were so horrible that they *deserved* to die and you're so wonderful that you *deserved* to live? Is this the way you show people that God *loves* them?"

The preacher's eyes were blank and expressionless. She shouted at him in frustration. "Am I even getting through to you? Are you thinking at all? If God could have made that kind of a miracle, don't you think He would have kept the whole thing from happening at all? Does it even occur to you how much you're hurting people every time you open your mouth to claim that *you're* a better person than someone who was just in the worst place at the wrong time? Or are you just thinking of how much money you can get out of it? Dammit, how does doing something like this make you any better

than the people who flew those planes into the
Towers in the first place?"

She turned to the crowd. "We're better than this!
We have to be! Or else— Or else—" Her eyes filled
with tears, and she couldn't continue.

The crowd began to applaud, shouting derisively at
the preacher as he tried to resume his harangue.

Ace was beside her, putting an arm around Kayla's
shoulders.

"Or else it was all for nothing," she said quietly.
"All those deaths, and all the good everybody's tried
to do since."

They went down into the subway again to wait
for a train. Kayla could tell that Ace wanted to say
something. For herself, she was still shaking all over
with anger. People like that "Reverend"—people who
took other people's pain and turned it into a cash cow
for themselves—they were the lowest of the low.

"What you did back there," Ace said, "that was
good. I wish I'd had the nerve to do that. A long
time ago."

"I hate people like that," Kayla said feelingly.

"So do I," Ace said. "C'mon. Let's go home."

"If you—" Kayla began. *If you had someplace else
to go—someplace better—would you go there?*

But just then a train pulled into the station, and
the opportunity for that conversation was lost.

When they got back up to The Place, the tension
in the atmosphere hit Kayla like a slap. Chinaka hurried over as soon as she saw them.

"Kayla! Thought we wouldn't see *you* again!" she
said, giving Ace a poisonous look. "Doin' all right,"
she said, giving Kayla's clothes an appreciative glance.
"Where's Eric?"

"Been lookin' all over for him," Kayla said. "Guess he's moved on."

"Wouldn't be surprised—with how welcome *some* people made him feel," Chinaka said. "You wanna hang with us? We got smoke."

Kayla slid her eyes sideways. Ace had drifted off, unwilling to provoke a further confrontation.

This must be why Ace had been so relieved to see Kayla again. Feuds as well as friendships developed quickly on the street, and Kayla and Eric coming in had been enough to tip the balance. And those spells Eric had cast to make Chinaka and the other girls like him probably hadn't helped matters any . . .

"Catch you later," Kayla said. "I got some stuff to do."

She went over and sat down next to Ace, who was sitting with Magnus over in their corner. Something had happened here, too, though Kayla wasn't quite sure what it was. Magnus seemed tense, and Ace was unhappy.

Looking at the room, even though everyone was spread out all over it, Kayla could almost see the invisible dividing line: Ace and Magnus and Jaycie, and everyone else.

"You sure you want to be here?" Ace said, a little bitterly, though she made room for Kayla to sit down.

"I couldn't stop them," Magnus said, resuming the conversation he'd been having with Ace before Kayla'd come over. "I was afraid they'd go for Jaycie if I did. They didn't take much."

Looking around, Kayla could see that Ace's makeshift bookshelf was gone, and the tidy orderly piles of things were all scrambled.

"Just my books. And most of our food," Ace said wearily. She turned to Kayla. "You hang with us, you aren't going to be real popular."

"I choose my own friends," Kayla said. "And you look like you could use some."

Ace let that pass without comment. "But Jaycie's okay?" she asked.

"Sure," Magnus said, shrugging. "He didn't even wake up."

Kayla winced, feeling the sudden flare of fear and anger. But Ace had a good tight rein on her temper—outwardly at least. She just got very quickly up off the sleeping bag and hurried over to the corner where Jaycie was sleeping.

"Hey," Magnus said. "You better not wake him up. Ace! Remember what happened the last time—"

But Ace wasn't listening. She knelt down beside Jaycie.

"Jaycie, honey, wake up. It's Ace. It's time to wake up now."

Jaycie didn't move.

Ace reached out and shook him, ignoring Magnus' protests. Still no response.

Kayla came over, Magnus following her a little warily.

"You'd better not get too close," he told Kayla. "He can get really upset when you wake him up suddenly."

"Can't you see he isn't going to wake up?" Ace burst out angrily. "I told you he was sick, but you wouldn't listen!"

"He sick?"

Shimene had wandered over to what Kayla thought of as "their" side of the room. Two of the other girls stood behind her—Graz and another girl whose name Kayla couldn't remember. Shimene gazed down at the four of them, her expression simultaneously smug and frightened. "He gonna die?"

"Go away," Ace said, not looking up.

"You don't tell me what to do, white girl," Shimene said angrily. Behind her, her two girlfriends muttered encouragement.

"If he's got something horribly contagious, I'd sure hate for you to catch it—and die," Kayla said sweetly. "You haven't touched him or anything, have you?"

"Yeah, you aren't looking so good, Rent-a-Butt," Magnus chimed in. "Better back off."

Shimene took a step backward. "He sick, you better get him outta here," she said, retreating hastily to the other side of the room.

"He won't wake up," Ace groaned, sounding truly terrified.

"Look," Kayla said, "I don't think he's sick, exactly. And I think I can help. But I don't want to do it with all those other kids here. The way things look like they're going right now, there might be a riot. And the three of us can't take all of them on."

"You're right," Ace said. She stroked Jaycie's forehead. The boy didn't stir at all. Except for his slow steady breathing, he might have been dead. "He feels all right. There isn't any fever . . . and Shimene's *always* been trouble. Some of the others, well, they won't start trouble, but they won't stop it, either. Oh, Jaycie . . ."

All at once she seemed to come to a decision. She turned away from the sleeping boy and faced the other two, smiling a dangerous smile.

"You want them gone so you can help Jaycie? I'll get rid of them. Here," Ace said, holding out her hands to the other two. "You hold my hands, both of you. It gentles it some. And whatever you do, don't let go."

Kayla took Ace's hand reluctantly. She was wearing gloves, and so was Ace, which provided some insulation, but it was still an intimate thing. She tightened her shields as much as she could, but as soon as she took Ace's hand she still felt the younger girl's anger and despair flood into her, swamping her own emotions until she could no longer tell which were her own feelings and which were Ace's. And with the emotions, a stray scrap of thought.

I swore I'd never do this again—but it's for Jaycie—

Ace took a deep breath and began to sing.

At first she sang very softly, almost in a whisper, but slowly the volume of her song grew, drowning out the rap music from the various CD players in the room.

"Ladybug, Ladybug, fly away home . . . your house is on fire; your children will burn—"

A nursery rhyme or a folk-song; Kayla couldn't remember which. Ace had a strong trained voice; it filled the room with ease. And Kayla felt the uprush of Power from the other young Talent—and more. She felt absolute terror, a primal need to get *out* of this place, to be somewhere, *anywhere* else.

She watched in amazement as the effects of the song struck the other teenagers in The Place. If, as Ace said, holding her hands "gentled it some," they had no such defense. Suddenly every one of them—even those who had been asleep when Ace began to sing—was consumed with the single desire to be *gone.*

Kayla looked on as they hastily grabbed anything that they could, just as if The Place really were on fire.

Ladybug, ladybug—

And rising up from somewhere, *Bardic* power. Young, unawakened, unaware. But there, waiting to be roused. Suddenly it flooded into her as well.

And with that, Kayla's shields crumbled. She felt like a penny in a fusebox, barely able to retain her identity beneath the uprush of a power she'd never been meant to carry. She resonated to the terror Ace was projecting like a tuning fork, her own Empathic power turning itself somehow inside-out, projecting itself as Ace's did, projecting raw fear; broadcasting emotion instead of receiving it.

That which can heal can also harm.

Ladybug, ladybug—

It had started out as a rotten day and was now going on to be a weird one. A few hours after Ace had left, some of the others had come over and started rooting through her things, saying they just wanted to "borrow" some stuff.

Yeah, right.

Just as Magnus had told Ace, he'd tried to stop them, but then a couple of them had gone for Jaycie, starting to pull him out of his sleeping bag. Jaycie hadn't even stirred, and that had scared Magnus even more. It had been pretty clear to Magnus that he could either protect Jaycie, or his and Ace's things. Not both.

He knew they'd been laughing at him for not fighting back. But he'd had no particular desire to get knifed or razored. Or shot, for that matter.

Then when Ace finally showed up with Kayla, she went ballistic—not (as Magnus had expected) over her stuff getting trashed, but because Jaycie slept through it all. Shouldn't that be a good thing?

Next, this Kayla person went all over psychic healer on them, saying she could help Jaycie—weird thing number two—and—weird thing number three— Ace went for it. And when Kayla said she needed privacy, Ace offered to clear The Place out.

By . . . singing?

By now the weird things were piling up too fast to

count. Ace never sang, and didn't much like music, as far as Magnus had been able to tell. He guessed he was willing to hold hands with her, because she'd had a rough day.

But after that . . .

He wondered if he'd gotten hit on the head by one of the other kids and just managed to forget about it, because when Ace started singing, he started hallucinating.

Heat flowed from her hand into his, just as if she'd plunged his arm into a tub of hot water. He tried to pull his hand away, but her grip was too strong. And even though she was just singing some stupid nursery rhyme, over and over, he could hear *music* behind it: a full orchestra.

And he was afraid.

Of course he was afraid. He was losing his mind. He was so hot all over now that he was sweating, just as if it was summer, not winter.

And the other kids . . .

They were scrambling to get out of The Place, grabbing everything they could in a hurry, throwing on coats and shoes and grabbing for backpacks and stashes.

If it's my hallucination, I wonder if I can affect it?

He tried thinking the orchestra louder. *Wagner* louder.

It cooperated.

He could feel the floorboards tremble under him, just as if the music were real, but Magnus didn't care. This was just a hallucination. Somebody'd probably slipped him some drugs. So he'd deafen them in return. Fair was fair. Magnus cranked an imaginary amplifier up a few more notches.

He could feel the whole building vibrating now—with

the invisible orchestra that loud, he shouldn't have still been able to hear Ace singing, but somehow he could. That contributed to the comforting feeling that none of this was actually happening, and made him a little less afraid.

Jachiel ap Gabrevys had finally lost himself in the shadowlands. This time, at last, he knew he would not waken. He did not know if this was what human-kind called sleep, this condition he could only reach through the foods of mortal lands; he only knew that this dark oblivion was a sweet thing that he courted desperately.

He would be very sorry to leave his human friends. If he only had their mortality, there would be no need to slip into Dreaming. Were he only mortal, there would be no need for any of this.

But he was what he was. Every day of his life he had dreaded the thought that the day would come when he must begin to learn the arts and disciplines of magic, the day when he would begin to be of some *use* to the Prince, his Father. He could not bear the thought. He dreaded it, all of it: the magic he felt ripening in his very bones, the uses he would be forced to put it to, the politics and necessities of the Court.

And so he had run away, to a place he had only heard of in Bards' legends. The World Above. A place without magic, without elves. A place where the Dreaming was possible.

And now—at last—he had what he sought.

But something was pulling him back. Something that wasn't supposed to be here at all.

Magic.

Hot silver threads of magic. Not as strong as in Underhill, but far stronger than they ought to be here in the World Above. They cleansed his blood, roused him toward life once more.

The Hound lunged through the Mirror of Air, dancing and capering to gain its master's attention, but Gabriel Horn didn't need that additional warning. The silver ring on his finger burned hot and true.

The wench had used her Gift.

Quickly he reached out his hand and touched it to the mirror.

Nothing happened.

It was as he had thought. She had gone to ground in one of the blighted places. But that would not save her now.

"Go to her," he told the Hound. "Seek her out. Hunt her tirelessly, and harry her back to me. . . ."

The Hound leapt through the mirror again, and vanished.

With a gesture, Gabriel banished the Mirror of Air.

Now the game began. True, he could follow the Hunt himself directly, but he had gone into the Accursed Lands once, after the Bard, and knew they were dangerous to his kind.

Besides, his plan was to break the girl's spirit, render her subservient to his will. What better way than to harry her a hundred leagues with creatures of nightmare following always at her heels, driving her inexorably homeward? In a day or two at most he would be able to See her directly, and able to decide whether to drive her to her own doorstep under her own power, or to let her be found by his agents.

But there was one thing he knew for certain.

Soon he would have the lost lamb back in the fold once more, and after what he would do to her then, it would be a very long time before she even *thought* of straying again. . . .

"—*fly away home*," Ace finished, and stopped. Tears of self-reproach glistened in her eyes. She pulled her hands free of Kayla's and Magnus'.

The Place was completely empty.

"What . . . was that?" Kayla asked raggedly, drawing a deep breath.

"What I do," Ace said harshly. "Why I left. Only . . . it never worked quite like that before," she said, sounding puzzled. "Guess maybe because I haven't done it for a while."

Or maybe because you never did it while linked up to a Healer and a Baby Bard, Kayla thought, still shaken. She wondered if any of those kids was *ever* going to come back.

"Hey," Magnus said, sounding pleased. "You can do things like that? That's cool."

Ace rounded on him furiously. "No, it isn't! It's wicked and dishonest! It's like stealing from people— only it's stealing their right to make up their own minds what they want to feel! And they don't even get a chance to defend themselves against it, because there's no way a normal person can defend themself from a freak like me—no, I just sneak up on them with a song, and before they know it, they—" Ace shut her mouth abruptly, refusing to finish her sentence.

"You're not a freak," Kayla said gently. "You're just different. Some people are born different, that's all. I'm different too. I can Heal people."

Ace stared at her, eyes glittering dangerously. For some reason, that had been the wrong thing to say.

"Not like faith healing," Kayla said, feeling her way carefully. "You don't have to believe anything. I mean if you had a bullet in you—or you had a broken leg—and I touched you—I could Heal it. That's my Talent, like singing that way is yours."

"Boy, your folks must have loved that," Ace said, relaxing her wariness just a little.

"My mother loved it so much she abandoned me when she found out," Kayla said bluntly. Let Ace think it had happened a little more recently than it had. It wasn't quite a lie.

Ace winced. "Sorry. I just . . . but does that mean you can Heal Jaycie?"

"I think so." Kayla didn't say that she thought Jaycie was the one making himself sick. Once she'd Healed him, she'd know for sure, and she could say something then. "And I know a place the three of you can go. A place that's better than this, that won't send you back to your parents, or tell them where you are, either."

"Huh." Ace was noncommittal, refusing to believe it. "Jaycie first."

"Hey," Magnus said, sounding pleased, though still a little rattled both by what had just happened and Ace's furious outburst. "He's awake."

"Jaycie!"

Ace jumped to her feet and hurried back to him, dropping to her knees again at his side. His eyes were open, but he seemed disoriented, and when he spoke it wasn't in any language the three of them knew.

"Sounds like Gaelic," Magnus said dubiously. "A little."

"Jaycie, honey, wake up," Ace pleaded. "Kayla's here. She's going to make you better."

"Nay . . . no." Jaycie's eyes opened wide. He was awake enough to speak English now. He stared at Kayla in horror.

"She won't hurt you," Ace said. "She wants to help."

Jaycie struggled up onto his elbows, and now even Magnus could see how terribly weak he was. "But she lied to you, Ace," he said. Though the words obviously cost him great effort, he smiled triumphantly as he spoke. "She and the Bard both. Lied to make you trust them." He took a deep breath, summoning the strength to say more. "I don't need help. All I need is sleep."

He fell back against the sleeping bag, exhausted.

Oh, shit, Kayla thought. *He knows Eric's a Bard. But how the hell . . . ?*

"Looks the picture of health, don't he?" she said aloud.

"What Bard?" Ace said. Her voice shook with fear. Kayla could feel how desperately Ace wanted to trust her, and how terrified she was of doing so.

"I guess he means Eric," Kayla said, fudging desperately. "Look. I haven't told you any lies. And I'm willing to swear on anything you want that whatever happens, it isn't going to end up with either of you being taken back to your parents. Not because of me or anybody I know, anyway."

"Funny you should mention that," Magnus said.

"You want to tell me you're living here for your health?" Kayla shot back angrily. "I don't know about you, dude, but I'd guess a few people know what Ace can do. And I'm betting they want her back so she'll keep doing it. So they're looking for her. Now, you guys can't stay here—"

"I bet you got a place all picked out for us, right?" Magnus sneered.

Kayla dug in her pocket for the flyers from Somerset House. She pulled them out and threw them at him. They fluttered to the floor. "Read 'em an' weep, moron. It's legit, it's been around for a while, and it's got nothing to do with me. It takes runaways in off the street and protects them. It'll take the three of you. But Jaycie'd better be able to walk to get there."

Hesitantly, Magnus stooped down and picked up the flyers. Ace, still looking confused, came over and took one of them from him.

"It's a real place," Ace said slowly. "But there's a waiting list. And I don't believe they wouldn't tell your folks if . . . if they knew who you really were."

Now that Kayla knew what Ace could do, her paranoia made a lot more sense. A Talent like that—to make her hearers experience any emotion she chose—would be worth millions to whoever controlled her. No wonder she'd run away. But why hadn't Kayla ever heard of her? With an ability like that, Ace's face—if not the name Kayla knew her by—ought to be on billboards all over the country.

"It's got vacancies now. I checked today," Kayla said. "Just go and talk to them. If you don't like it, you can leave. They won't stop you. Now, let me work on Jaycie, okay?"

"Don't let her," Magnus urged.

"Yes!" Ace said. "I believe her. I don't think she's told us the whole truth, but I believe her when she says she hasn't told us any flat lies. And he's *sick*, Magnus. I don't know what's wrong with him, but he's awful sick—and whoever his folks are, they've got to be worse than yours and mine put together, the way he cries at night. We've got to help him. *You've* got to help him, Kayla," she said urgently.

"I'll do what I can," Kayla said. "Now, when I touch him, there's going to be a kind of light. Don't touch me or him while I'm working, okay? That could mess things up."

Magnus grinned without humor. "Just be careful. He could start struggling—he does that sometimes if you startle him—and he's a *lot* stronger than he looks. Knocked me all the way across the floor once."

Oh, this just keeps getting better and better, Kayla thought. She nodded, and went back to where Jaycie was sleeping. Though they'd been talking—and arguing—in normal voices, the boy was sleeping soundly again.

Kayla crouched on her heels, preparing to spring out of the way at the first sign of movement from Jaycie. She unzipped the sleeping bag and peeled it back, revealing Jaycie in a parka and gloves. That was no good. She needed to touch exposed skin for the best results, and all she could see was a bit of his cheekbone at the moment. She sighed and pulled off his watch cap.

Long silky black hair tumbled free.

Huh. I wonder how he keeps it so clean?

He didn't move, and she relaxed a little.

Very cautiously now, she brushed it away from his face, but he still didn't stir. His eyes were closed, long black lashes stark against his milky skin. *I'd have to use two tubes of Max Factor to get the same effect. It isn't fair.*

Showtime.

She glanced up. Ace and Magnus were standing several feet away. Apparently they hadn't been kidding about how violently Jaycie reacted to being awakened, though she doubted he could be as strong as Magnus said, not now. Well, at least her health insurance was paid up.

Kayla pulled off one of her gloves, flexed her fingers—it was cold in here—and reached for his cheek.

A spark of blue fire leapt from her fingers to his skin. She touched him, and the glow raced over his body.

He isn't human.

He was—

He was *Sidhe*.

But elves don't sleep—

Suddenly Kayla thought of every time she'd seen Jaycie with a can of Coke in his hand, of all the pound bars of Baker's chocolate she'd seen him wolf down.

It's the caffeine.

She'd known Jaycie was an addict just from watching him, and hadn't been able to figure out what he was using. Now she knew. Coca-Cola. Chocolate. Caffeine was deadly to the Sidhe. And he'd come here to poison himself with it.

Focus!

He was Sidhe, so caffeine was a poison—a drug—like any other. She concentrated on sweeping it out of his system, repairing the damage. She knew the way that the Sidhe "were" now, familiarly, intimately. Once you knew that, every system was alike to a Healer: it wanted to be well and whole.

But Jaycie didn't.

The stronger she made his body, the stronger she made *him*. He began to fight her.

Where's the off *switch on this thing?*

Normally she could simply send an unruly patient to sleep. But a healthy Sidhe didn't sleep. And he was getting healthier by the minute. He began to struggle, trying to push her away.

She reached up his spine and cut off the nerve impulses to his muscles—tricky, that, and she couldn't leave the block in place for long. Dimly, she sensed his body going limp again.

But that left his mind—awake, aware, and fighting.

Will you chill out? I'm trying to save your life!

A wordless response: fury, grief, despair . . . and

terror, as if life was something to be fled from at all costs. Kayla soothed him as much as possible, but Healing the mind was a delicate thing, and she couldn't afford to split off too much of her attention from Healing his body.

At last she'd taken care of the worst of the damage—as much as she could in the time she had before she had to remove that spinal block, anyway. She pulled the block, releasing control of his body—

A blow from Jaycie sent her sprawling, breaking the link.

"How *dare* you?" he shouted, standing over her and glaring down at her, fists clenched. His eyes flared green in the dim light of The Place. "How dare you meddle in my life, you foolish mortal wench?"

Kayla stared up at him, mouth quirked in a half smile. He'd knocked her sprawling, she was dizzy from the abrupt breaking of the link, and her stomach hurt where he'd punched her, but whether because of the Healing or because she'd gotten him well and truly wound up, he'd dropped his *glamourie*. She could see his pointed ears plainly. And if she could, so could Magnus and Ace.

"You've got an audience, elf-boy," she said breathlessly.

"*Oh.*" Jaycie looked truly appalled. He turned around.

"Magnus— Ace— I did not mean—"

"What did you do to him?" Ace cried.

Gee, thanks a bunch. "I didn't do anything to him," Kayla said, taking a deep breath and getting to her feet with a wince. "This is what he actually looks like. Your friend Jaycie is an elf—a Sidhe. And he's a junkie. Elves can't handle caffeine in any form. It poisons them. Coffee—chocolate—Coke—they've all got caffeine in them. And he's hooked on it."

Jaycie took a step toward them. Ace hesitated.

"Elf?" she said blankly, stunned. "Like in my books?"

"There's no such things as elves," Magnus said flatly.

"Yeah?" Kayla said. "Tell that to him."

"Magnus? Ace?" Jaycie repeated uncertainly. "I didn't want to lie, but—"

"Oh, you damned fool!" Ace cried, and threw herself into his arms. "You can be an elf if you want—I don't care—but how could you do something like that to yourself?"

"It isn't true," Jaycie said quickly, putting his arms around Ace. "She's lying."

He reached out a hand to Magnus. Hesitantly, Magnus took it, grinning in relief.

"I'm not lying," Kayla said. "And I'll tell you something else that's true. Elves do just fine a lot of places in our world, but not in New York City. There's too much iron in the air here, or all around them, or something like that. If Jaycie stays here very much longer, even without caffeine, he'll get even sicker. And die, maybe. I dunno for sure; no Sidhe I know of ever stayed around long enough to find out."

"Die?" Magnus said, looking past Jaycie to Kayla, his grin fading. "But you did that thing. We saw you."

"I fixed most of the damage that's already been done. Not the damage that hasn't been done yet," Kayla said patiently, walking over to the three of them. "Every time he takes a breath, he's hurting himself again. He needs to go home."

"Home!" Ace said cynically, stepping back from Jaycie and looking at Kayla. "None of us needs to go home."

"Jaycie does," Kayla said. "Because if he stays here

in this world he's going to die. He doesn't need to go back to his own folks. Just to . . . Underhill."

"No," Jaycie said quickly. All of a sudden he looked human again, though just as stunningly beautiful as Kory had looked. Apparently the elves didn't know how to cast a *glamourie* to make themselves look ordinary. "I won't go back. And if this is the only place in the World Above that the Sidhe don't go, then this is the only place I can be."

"You *did* lie to us," Magnus said accusingly to Kayla. "Maybe you weren't looking for me or Ace—but you were looking for *him*, weren't you? How else would you know so much about elves? How else would you know they even existed?"

She could feel the three of them drawing together, drawing away from her. Jaycie didn't want them to trust her, and he had a lot more influence over them than she did. All Kayla could do was tell the truth, and hope that Ace and Magnus cared enough about Jaycie to try to keep him alive.

"I've met elves before," Kayla said. "Lots of times. There's more of them around than you'd think. Just not here. Look—" she said desperately. "It doesn't matter what trouble you're in, any of you. Here or in Underhill. Just let me and my friends help."

"No one can help—" Jaycie began. And stopped.

It was getting darker.

Kayla stared around The Place. All the candles and lamps were still lit and burning just as brightly as they had been a moment before, but somehow it didn't seem to matter. The Place was filling with shadows. And it was getting colder. Lots colder.

"*No!*" Jaycie cried, sounding suddenly terrified. "Run! Run now!"

He grabbed the hands of the other two and began dragging them toward the stairs. Kayla followed.

The stairwell was absolutely black. Maybe Jaycie could see in the dark, but the other three couldn't. Ace and Magnus stumbled and cried out as he dragged them all the way to the bottom, slipping and skidding across the trash and garbage.

"Hey! Wait—" Magnus said as they passed the half-open window.

"There is no time!" Jaycie shouted out of the darkness. "If the shadows touch you they will take your will, and you will be nothing but mindless prey!"

They ran down the last flight in the dark. There was a wrenching, ripping sound, and Jaycie tore the chained and locked street door open. Light from the street shone in across the filthy lobby.

The four of them ran.

Eric drifted in an aimless, healing sleep. Something exceptionally bad had just happened—or almost happened. He was aware of that, dimly. And also that he'd been in pain, terrible pain, and had fled from it with all the power at his command.

But now that was over.

It was okay to wake up.

So he did.

Eric opened his eyes. He felt good. In fact, he felt much, much better than good.

He was lying in a bed in a room he'd never seen before. It was . . . he was somewhere Underhill.

What was he doing Underhill?

He tried to think back. His memories were jumbled and discordant. He remembered going to see his parents—Magnus—The Place—

And after that . . .

He'd been back at the SoCal Faire. But he *couldn't* have been! The Fairesite had been bulldozed years ago.

He remembered seeing Karen.

But . . . hadn't he heard that Karen had died in a bombing overseas? And Beth had said that Ian had died in a car crash a few years back.

Had everyone he'd seen there been *dead*?

But *he'd* been there. Only . . . not as he was now. He'd been Eric Banyon at 20: feckless, irresponsible, with no particular thought for the future, living from party to party.

And there'd been a lot of parties.

He grimaced, sitting up. He supposed it had been . . . nice, in a way. But the clearer those memories became, the less he liked them, and the less he liked that Eric, the one who ran like hell from anything that looked even remotely like a commitment. He knew where he'd been, now.

TirNaOg. The Land of Eternal Youth.

A fine place—if you were an Irish warrior whose idea of Heaven was somewhere that held all of your other friends, and where you were all young and strong and in the prime of life forever. A lovely place, if your choice was never having to grow up. He hadn't been that far off the mark when he'd asked Karen if he was one of the Lost Boys.

But I've done a lot of growing up since then. It's all been hard, and some of it's been painful, but I wouldn't trade the life I have now for the life I had then—even an idealized version of it. I like being a grown-up.

"Ah, Bard Eric, you have awakened."

An ancient Sidhe entered the room, obviously one of those who had repaired the damage done in a catastrophe the details of which he still couldn't quite remember. Its face was androgynously beautiful; between the long flowing robes, and the Sidhe's great age, it was difficult to tell the Healer's gender—and some Sidhe just liked to keep you guessing, anyway. Eric could feel the nimbus of Power around—him? her?—without any effort.

"Yes. I, ah . . ."

"I am Healer Avalnate of Elfhame Misthold. When young Korendil told Master Dharniel of your plight, he begged of me and my sisters that we travel to the World Above to succor you in your distress. We sought and found you there, yet it was thought unwise to attempt any work of Healing in such a polluted place. So we returned with you here." Avalnate smiled coolly. "Perhaps you would have died there."

"Perhaps," Eric said, just as formally. "And so I thank you for your great care of me, and for your work on my Master's behalf."

If there was one thing Master Dharniel had managed to beat into Eric's head along with his Bardic training, it was a basic understanding of Elven protocol. If Dharniel had actually unbent so far as to ask a favor on his behalf—and it looked like it had been a very big favor—it would absolutely not do to be anything less than very formally polite.

"You will wish to dress and to see your friends. They have been as impatient as mortalkin, both young Korendil and the *lennan sidhe*."

Lennan sidhe, Eric knew, was the old term the elves used for a mortal who left human lands to live Underhill with one of the Sidhe. At the moment it didn't seem to be particularly complimentary, at least not as Healer Avalnate used it.

But he kept his face smooth, simply bowing again as well as he could from a sitting position. Avalnate turned and left.

Eric threw back the covers, only to grab them again as Beth came rushing into the room, closely followed by Kory. It almost seemed silly—she'd seen him a great deal more than naked, plenty of times—but before he could sort out the impulse, she'd flung herself on him, toppling him back into the bed, weeping and covering his face with kisses.

"Eric—oh, Eric—I thought you were going to die—oh, God—when Kayla sent that e-mail—when I saw you in that hospital bed—if I *ever* get my hands on those punks from the park—"

"Hey— wait a minute— slow down—" Eric gasped, arms suddenly full of the both of them. "What hospital? What punks?"

Beth drew back and stared at him in disbelief. "Don't you remember?"

Eric thought hard. "I remember going up to Central Park . . . Tuesday? Yeah. Tuesday morning." But why had he been going there? *That* he couldn't remember.

"Don't worry about it," Beth said, hugging him so fiercely Eric gasped for air. "You're alive and whole, and that's all that matters!"

"Yeah—but what *happened*?" Eric demanded plaintively.

"You were set upon by ruffians," Kory said somberly. "And did not defend yourself. They beat you until you were driven from yourself."

"Some trick," Eric said, puzzled. But a head injury would account for the scrambled memories, he guessed. He hoped he hadn't forgotten anything important.

"Kayla went looking for you—you'd lost your link to Lady Day, and she went ballistic," Beth said. "She's here, by the way; she followed you Underhill and showed up a little while after you arrived; she's down in the stables now. Anyway, Kayla *finally* got around to letting us know, and Kory was able to cast a spell that let us see what happened to you. So then we checked the hospitals until we found your body—"

"I was dead?" Eric interrupted, alarmed.

"No, just in an irreversible coma," Beth said, finally

able to make jokes now that it was all over. "And in traction. You looked like Frankenstein's Mummy. So. They were just about to shut down your respirator—"

"*What?*"

"Do not tease the Bard, my heart," Kory said. "You were grievously injured, Eric, that much is true. But the worst hurt was to your mind; when Kayla attempted to touch your consciousness, she found it absent, and the Healer Elizabet counseled her not to attempt to restore your body until your mind was within it once more. So she sent us from the World Above, all being in good hands, since Ria Llewellyn was able to stand as your worldly kinsman once she was aware of your plight—"

"Ria!" Eric said. "Where's Ria now?"

"Tied up with some business thing," Beth said, shrugging. "She didn't come to the hospital, anyway. But boy, did everyone start jumping once her personal assistant started name-dropping. You should have been there," Beth said with malicious satisfaction.

I was. Sort of.

"Kayla and Hosea assured us that they would do all they might to bring you back to yourself, and when the message arrived of their success though saying how much more work yet remained, I thought we might spare them that necessity. So I petitioned Prince Arvin to send Healers—though of course it was Master Dharniel who asked, since the Sisters bow not to the command of any, and Dharniel is your Master," Kory said, taking up the tale again.

And would be until the end of Time—at least technically, and for the terms of Elven protocol—Eric knew. Well, at least now he knew what sex Avalnate was.

"And the Sisters brought me down here and magicked me up good as new," Eric said, piecing it all together. "Did they tell anybody?"

Both Kory and Beth looked blank.

"Hosea, Kayla, Ria? The hospital?"

"I think they used a spell of Forgetting on the hospital," Kory said hesitantly. "So no one would see them, or remark on their presence, or that of their elvensteeds. It would have been a very strong spell," he added reassuringly.

Maybe strong enough to wipe all memory of me out of the minds of everybody in the hospital. Or not. Magic works in freaky ways in New York.

"How long have I been here?" Eric said, climbing out of bed and looking for his clothes. *And how long has it been since Tuesday?*

"It's just been a day, really," Beth said. "I can go e-mail Hosea and Kayla right now, Eric. Surely you can stay for just a little while? At least see Maeve before you go."

"No," Kory said, surprisingly. "Eric must go, and as quickly as may be. He has responsibilities in the World Above that will not wait. He will return as soon as he can, I know. And we will visit him, and soon."

Because this can be TirNaOg too. Sorry, Bethie. I've got to get Magnus safe . . . and there might be something else going on I can't quite remember.

He looked at Kory; Kory nodded, as if he had heard all those thoughts. Then Kory kissed Beth upon the forehead, got to his feet, and helped Eric find his clothes.

By the time they reached Broadway, Jaycie felt safe enough to slow down a little. Kayla looked back. No shadows in sight, other than the normal ones.

"What was that?" Kayla demanded.

"Magic," Jaycie said bitterly. "Elven magic. Hunters that make their prey run in terror before them so that the huntsman may slay it." He turned away, hunching his shoulders against the cold, his long hair streaming in the wind.

"You said elves couldn't come here!" Ace said to Kayla accusingly.

"I said it wasn't safe for long," Kayla said. "*He's* here," she pointed out inarguably. And Kory came to visit Eric, too, though he was careful not to stay more than a few days.

Where could they go that was safe? The barriers at Guardian House would keep the shadow things out, she was pretty sure, but Ria'd said that might not be a safe place for her to go. And if there was going to be trouble—men-with-guns kind of trouble—Kayla didn't want to drag a bunch of innocent bystanders into it.

But Ria's apartment was shielded and warded too—well enough to keep a bunch of nasty elvish nightmares out. She hoped. And Ria had suggested she go there in the first place. So that meant it must be a place trouble wouldn't be looking for her.

"How long are they going to follow us?" Magnus asked edgily.

Jaycie didn't say anything, but his expression said everything it needed to. *Forever.*

"I know a place where we can go," Kayla said cautiously.

"Where?" Ace said.

"Don't trust her," Magnus urged.

"It's a trap," Jaycie chimed in helpfully.

Kayla could cheerfully have strangled both of them on the spot. She was pretty sure Ace would trust her, if the boys would just *shut up*.

"Okay," she said. "*Don't* trust me. So where are *you* going to go to get away from those things?"

Both of the others looked at Jaycie.

He looked scared—and fresh out of ideas. "There

is nowhere. Once they have the scent of their prey, they are tireless. Not quick, but sure. And *you* must sleep." He said the last word longingly.

"We could take a train—or a bus," Ace said desperately. "Outrun them."

"Where?" Kayla said brutally. "And what's to say that you won't run into someone *else* looking for one of you?"

Magnus looked guilty and worried. Ace looked just plain scared. Neither of them said anything.

"Look. A friend of mine has a place uptown. I know this is a lot to take in right now, but it's got magical wards around it—defenses—and I don't think those shadow-things will be able to see through them. She isn't there right now, but it's okay if we use it."

For a long moment nobody said anything. Kayla could feel their suspicion, their resistance.

"Please don't trick us," Ace said softly.

"I won't," Kayla said. "I promise. It'll be a shock, but I promise. No tricks."

Hosea wrestled with his conscience for almost two hours before giving in and getting his jacket.

He was going to find Kayla and Magnus.

With Eric gone, Ria incommunicado—he'd tried both her numbers and gotten no answer at either one—and Kayla in danger, there was only one thing for him to do. Little Bit was doing the best she knew how, but she'd never stopped to think that if the people Ria was worried about *were* after her, they might already be following her.

And she might have led them right back to Magnus and a bunch of scared, helpless, defenseless street kids.

There wasn't much he could do for the lot of them—but he *could* get his hands on Kayla and

Magnus and bring them back here, if he had to drag them back to Guardian House kicking and screaming. And he'd keep Magnus here if he had to tie the boy to a chair to do it.

He owed it to Eric.

He looked regretfully toward Jeanette, but he couldn't take her with him this time. Still, there were a few tricks he could manage to pull off without her. Enough to make Magnus come along quietly, he imagined.

But when he reached the abandoned tenement, trouble had already come calling.

The front door was hanging open, half ripped off its hinges. Ignoring the crowd of people gathered out front, Hosea summoned up his shine and walked past them and into the building. No one had gone in yet, which meant that whatever it was, it hadn't happened that long ago.

None of them noticed him. It wasn't invisibility. More like *unnoticeability*. People could see him if they looked at him. They just preferred to look elsewhere.

He went up the stairs, treading carefully in the dimness. When he'd gone up a couple of flights, he could see a glow coming from above, and the sound of hip-hop music playing.

But when he reached the place where it was, there was nobody there.

There were sleeping bags and piles of blankets scattered all over the floor, and dozens of candles left burning all around the room. Someone—a lot of someones—had been living here very recently. But there was nobody here now. And in a few hours, when people came up and looked around, none of this stuff would be here, either.

He walked to the middle of the room, looking around. Clothes—food—CDs and music players. Nobody—especially the homeless—left that kind of stuff unattended, especially with the downstairs door hanging open like that.

Something bad had happened here.

As he stood there, not moving, something familiar caught his eye.

Kayla's backpack. She'd been here.

He hurried over to it and picked it up, tearing it open and rummaging through it. Her phone and PDA were both there. So was her wallet. She'd never leave that behind.

Not if she had a choice.

He slung it over his shoulder.

The mage-sight that Eric was trying to teach him didn't come easily yet, but after a struggle he managed to call it up and use it now, checking for clues. His vision seemed to blur and shift, and suddenly the world appeared in colors it wasn't meant to.

And he could See . . . something.

Traces of magic burned red on the walls, like spatters of blood. There were pools of dull silver near where he'd found the backpack—a different kind of magic, a better magic—but there were only a few of those, in a small area, and the red magic was everywhere, as if it had flooded the place and then seeped away. The stains seemed to pulse with a malignant life.

He turned around. The bad magic had flowed down the stairs behind him, trickling out onto the city street.

Follow the magic? He wasn't sure he could. Once it reached the street, its faint traces would be lost amid the pedestrians, the lights, and the traffic. Concentrate too hard on following the trail, and he could end up in the hospital just the way Eric had, and for much the same reason.

Suddenly Hosea froze, blinking away the mage-sight.

Someone was coming up the stairs.

Eric pulled into the parking lot at Guardian House and swung his leg over Lady Day's seat. The elvensteed purred smugly, having enjoyed the run back from the Everforest Gate, especially because it had been taken at top speed under a cloak of invisibility.

Eric hurried inside, his thoughts fixed on finding out—first—*what day it was,* and then getting back up to The Place to resume his masquerade. Or . . . forget that. He was going to level with Magnus tonight and get him somewhere safe—hell, all three of them—Ace, Magnus, Jaycie. He didn't care what they were running from. He'd protect them from it. That's what grown-ups did. They protected kids. Kids were the future.

A faint confused feeling momentarily distracted him. There was something he'd forgotten. Something important. He knew it.

But whatever it was, it would have to wait. Even with the best Elven Healing in the world, he'd taken a major knock to the head. Scattered memories took time to resurface.

He went inside.

Hosea wasn't home, and neither was Kayla. Eric went up to his own apartment.

Greystone was waiting for him there.

"You're back," the gargoyle said, sounding guilty and unhappy. "Oh, laddybuck, I wish I'd known you'd be coming a few hours ago."

"What? Why? What's wrong?" Eric demanded sharply.

"Well," Greystone said, "maybe I'd better start at the beginning."

"Talk while I change," Eric said. He was still wearing High Court finery, and needed to get into something a little more Earthly before putting in an appearance Uptown. He walked into the bedroom, pulling off his cloak and tunic as he went.

"Well, Kayla was that upset when you vanished from the hospital this morning, and everyone there was sayin' you'd never been there in the first place," Greystone began slowly.

"This morning?" Eric said, not paying a lot of attention. That's good. "What day is it?"

"Wednesday," Greystone told him.

"I've been gone a week?" Eric yelped, suddenly focusing on Greystone's words.

"Been a helluva week, boyo," Greystone said. "You were missing for most of it, and that scooter of yours was raising the roof."

Eric grinned faintly in spite of himself. Kory and Beth had told him that part. "So what happened then?" He pulled on a pair of jeans and a sweater, the closest analogues in his wardrobe for his missing "street person" garb.

"So Miss Ria thought you goin' missing might have something to do with her problems down in Washington with the hardboys, and told Kayla to hide out with the kids. So she does, and then Hosea comes around and—I couldn't help it, Boss—none of us knew where you were, or what had happened, and when—or if—you was comin' back!"

Eric turned around to face him, a black leather duster in one hand, a pair of boots in the other.

"What did you do?" he said slowly.

The gargoyle hung its head.

"I told him where The Place was. And now he's gone up there to bring Kayla and Magnus back."

Eric sighed, and shook his head. No wonder Greystone was upset. He'd told Hosea something he could only have known from reading Eric's thoughts. Eric guessed that for Greystone to do something like that was almost like a priest violating the sanctity of the confessional.

But what if he hadn't come back? What if he *had* been kidnapped by enemies, and not taken Underhill by friends—or allies at least? What if he hadn't gotten back from Underhill as quickly as he had? Hosea was his friend and his student, and Eric trusted him to do the best he could.

"Don't worry about it," Eric said gently, setting down the boots and putting a hand on Greystone's shoulder. "I would have done the same thing in your place. It'll work out." *It's going to have to.*

He stomped into his boots hastily and swung his duster around his shoulders. He'd been planning to cast an illusion over them to make them look like the clothes he'd worn before, but there was no point to it now. "How long ago did he leave?"

"About an hour ago," Greystone said with a sigh.

Eric patted the gargoyle on the shoulder. Well, whatever was going to happen had already happened by now. "Look—would you tell everybody I'm back, and fine? Everybody who knew I was gone? Kory just called in a couple of favors, and some friends of his took me Underhill to finish healing me up. Only they weren't too careful about letting anyone know I was gone." *Or covering their tracks. Or maybe the word there is* too *careful, if nobody at the hospital remembers I was there in the first place. Never mind.*

"I'll do that," Greystone promised. "And you bring the kids back safe."

"The kids, Hosea, anybody who doesn't run away too fast," Eric said, forcing cheer into his voice. "You'd better put a new wing on this place, my friend."

CHAPTER FIFTEEN:

BEARDANCE

Eric ascended the stairs of The Place slowly, having left Lady Day well down the block—and invisible—when he saw the people gathered in front of the building. The sight of the open door disturbed him, and he could sense the residue of baneful magic in the air, but that was no reason to go rushing blindly into a trap.

He got to the top of the stairs. The room inside looked empty, but he could *sense* someone waiting just inside the doorway.

Someone familiar . . .

"Hosea?" he called. "It's me. Eric."

"Eric!" The big man appeared in the doorway and enveloped him in a crushing bear hug, lifting him off his feet. "Boy, am Ah glad to see you! Where've you *been*?"

"Underhill," Eric said briefly. "It wasn't exactly my idea."

Hosea set him down and studied him critically. "Well, you're looking a sight better'n you did the last time Ah saw you. Got your hair back, too."

Eric put his hand up to his head, feeling his hair. It was all shoulder-length again; he'd wondered about that, but he hadn't gotten around to asking anybody about it before he'd left Elfhame Misthold.

Oh. Brain injury. They must have shaved my head at the hospital.

"We've got trouble here," Hosea said gravely. "Kayla was here. An' she left in too much of a hurry to take her backpack. The place was like this when Ah got here."

Eric looked around at the deserted flop. It was *never* empty this early in the evening, as he remembered— and Jaycie, Magnus, and Ace didn't go out at night at all.

"And something was chasing her—or them—or someone that was here," Eric said, piecing things together. There it was again, the sense that he was forgetting something vitally important. "I wonder what it was?"

Now that he looked—really looked—at the traces of magic on the walls, he could almost make out the thing that had left them. He whistled a few bars of "The Rising of the Moon," calling up his Power, and suddenly the traces burned bright and clear again.

Elven magic.

Unseleighe magic.

Shadow Hounds. They were a magical creature specifically adapted for use in the World Above. Not much use Underhill, where the least breath of magic could sweep them away, but here, in the human world, they were deadly.

And Jaycie—

"*That's* what I was doing in the Park that day!" Eric burst out in alarm, remembering at last. "Jaycie's a Sidhe—I was trying to summon his Protector to take him home, but I called up Bloody Mary instead! I was so worn out from my battle with her that I walked right into that wolfpack of kids without noticing them until it was too late! *That's* what happened!"

"What—whoa—slow down—" Hosea said. "What does Bloody Mary have to do with these kids?"

"I don't know," Eric said. "I thought at the time I just dialed the wrong number, so to speak, but now I'm not so sure. What if Bloody Mary's Jaycie's Protector?"

Hosea shook his head, obviously thinking that Eric hadn't quite gotten over his knock to the head. "Then why ain't she Protecting him?" he asked, reasonably enough.

"I don't know. Maybe she's lost. *He's* sure lost. And slugging back Coke like there's no tomorrow—that's going to kill him—or send him into Dreaming at least, and I don't know what that would do to a Sidhe this far from a Node Grove. And now the Dark Court's looking for him, too—that's got to be it. We've got to find them—all of them!" Eric said urgently.

It was all coming together at last, and the picture it made wasn't a pretty one.

"If Kayla's with Magnus, and Magnus's with Jaycie, and Ace is with the lot of them, then find one, you'll find 'em all," Hosea said pragmatically. "Only how're you going to do that?"

"Now that I've been around them—and if Kayla's with them—maybe a Finding spell," Eric said hopefully.

Eric summoned up his magic again, but no matter how hard he tried—and even with Hosea lending his own Power to the Finding spell—he could gain no clear idea of their location.

After a few minutes, he gave up.

"No go. My guess is Jaycie's shielding them somehow, which means the four of them are together at least, but I have no idea where." He hesitated for a moment. "Look, Kayla probably has at least some idea of what that thing was that came after them. Where do you think she'd try to take them?"

"Maybe back to Guardian House," Hosea said, after a moment. "Nothing unchancy's going to be able to get inside. She'd know that."

"Or maybe Ria's apartment," Eric said. "That's got shields too, and Kayla's got the entry codes to get in even if Ria isn't there. We'll have to split up. You take Guardian House. See if they've made it back there. If they have, *sit on them*. And whatever you do, don't let Jaycie out of your sight. I don't know how much magic he's got, but what I do know is, if the Dark Court is hunting a Sidhe child, there's going to be *big* trouble."

"I'll take Ria's place. It's right on the Park, so I'm going to try calling up his Protector again. He or she has *got* to be here somewhere—or dead. Whatever shows up, I'll at least try to talk to it and explain about Jaycie."

"Risky," Hosea said consideringly.

"We've got to get him back Underhill before anything worse happens to him," Eric said. "And preferably without starting a war. If I can't find his Protector, I'll have to take him back through the Everforest Gate and dump a huge political hot potato right in Prince Arvin's lap, and that could be really awkward." *In fact awkward doesn't even begin to describe it. . . .*

"Let's get a move on, then," Hosea said.

✧   ✧   ✧

"Here?" Magnus said in disbelief.

The four of them stood outside the lobby of Ria's building on Central Park South. Kayla sighed. Now came the tough part—not that getting them here had been easy.

"Your friend lives here," Ace said tonelessly. "And you were sleeping up at The Place."

"I said it would be a shock," Kayla said, keeping her tone deliberately neutral. "But those things can't get into her apartment. They shouldn't even be able to track you once you're inside. It's safe."

"Just tell us which one of us you were after, and we'll go in," Magnus said, smirking at her nastily.

Kayla felt a sinking feeling in her stomach. It was the question she'd have asked in his place. The three of them were terrified, and finding out about Jaycie and then being chased out of The Place by demonic shadows had been a real shock, but none of them was stupid.

"Is that a promise?" Kayla said coldly.

"You said there's nobody there?" Ace asked, hedging.

"I'll ask before we go up, okay?" Kayla said.

"That's fair," Ace agreed, nervously.

"So," Magnus said.

"Do you promise?" Kayla repeated.

"Yes," Ace said, looking as if she was going to be sick.

"All three of you?" Kayla insisted.

"Let's go away," Jaycie said.

"Where?" Ace demanded. "With those *things* after you? Where can we go? We left all our stuff back at The Place, and I'm sure not going back for mine."

Finally—with Ace glaring at them—the other two grudgingly promised to go inside.

"I was looking for Magnus—but *not* because of

his parents. For someone who's about as fond of his parents as he is. Someone who wants to keep him away from them at all costs. So Eric was trying to find you before that hotshot PI they hired did," Kayla said, speaking half to Ace and half to Magnus.

"*Eric?*" Magnus said blankly.

"Yeah," Kayla said. *Might as well tell him the whole thing.* "You've got an older brother, moron. He ran away from home before you were born—your 'rents tried to make a musical prodigy out of him, too, and he didn't like it either. So he finally goes back to see them, and finds out about you, and that you've bailed too, only you aren't eighteen like he was, and they're going to drag you back."

"So what— How come— Why—" Magnus stammered, flustered.

"Because he found out they hadn't told you about him, and he didn't think you'd believe him if *he* told you, and he was afraid you'd just run off again and get your ass in a sling. And now he's disappeared, and nobody knows where he is. And now these things are after us, and we're standing in the street where they can get at us. So will you come *on?*" Kayla snarled.

They went inside.

"Good evening, Ms. Smith," the security man said.

"Hi, Ramon," Kayla said, sighing inwardly. "Is Ria back yet?"

"No," Ramon said cheerfully. "But you can go right on up."

"Thanks," Kayla said. "They're with me," she added, waving in the direction of the other three. *I hope.*

She ushered the other three over to the penthouse elevator at the far end of the lobby and punched in Ria's code. The doors opened.

The kids hesitated, unwilling to get in.

"Come on, guys," Kayla pleaded, "I've been straight with you."

But she could tell that seeing the elevator—the *penthouse* elevator—and hearing Ramon greet her by name had been too much. She was losing them, losing even the fragile trust she'd been able to build.

Jaycie reached out—

A flash of light exploded in her face, and Kayla fell back, stunned.

Hosea got back to Guardian House in record time. The place was quiet. Kayla's apartment was empty—he still had her spare set of keys, so he checked it, just to be sure.

Eric's place was similarly deserted—he knew Kayla had the code to Eric's apartment—the upstairs apartments all had key-code pads instead of key locks—so she might have gone there.

Last of all he checked his own apartment. Maybe she'd called from a street phone.

She hadn't. But someone else had.

"Hosea? It's me. Caity. Oh, I wish you were there! Listen. Julie just called. There's something tonight—in a hour—up at Neil's place. Something big. And . . . I don't think I like it much. Hosea . . . Sarah's daughter Amanda's going to be there. She's only four. I just thought . . . I think . . . That can't be *right*, can it? Anyway, I just thought . . . But there isn't anything you can do. I wish—"

The answering machine cut off, and Hosea never did find out just what it was that Caity wished.

He knew, though. Clear and plain, in the silences and unfinished sentences of the answering machine message was one simple plea: *Hosea—help me!*

At last he had the freedom to interfere with Master Fafnir's group.

And it had come at the worst possible time.

He grabbed Jeanette and slung the strap of her carrying case over his shoulder, and ran downstairs to Toni's apartment.

Fortunately Toni was there. She opened the door at Hosea's frantic pounding, took one look at his face, and ushered him into the bedroom where they could be private. He could hear the television going in her living room, and knew that Raoul and Paquito, Toni's two young sons, were probably firmly ensconced in front of it at this hour.

"What's wrong?" she asked.

"Caity's called for help," Hosea said shortly. "Apparently this cult she's gotten tangled up in is throwing a big party tonight, and she says that they're bringing the four-year-old daughter of one of the members to it."

"That's bad," Toni said, making a face. "You know where?"

Hosea nodded. "And nothin' Ah can't handle. But Eric an' me are tangled up in another matter right up to our eyes too, an' Ah'd appreciate a little help there." Quickly, he laid out the details of what he and Eric had discovered earlier that evening up at The Place, plus what Eric had told him about what had happened up at Central Park a week before.

"Wait a minute," Toni said. "Eric thinks that Bloody Mary and this Elven Protector are the *same thing*? And he can *call it up*?"

"Ah don't credit it myself," Hosea said. "The first part, anyhow. But that he can call it up somehow, or that it's drawn to him somewise—that Ah believe."

"Well, then, at least we have a place to start. Finally," Toni said. "When the rest of this is over, we'll have to ask him for a demonstration, and get rid of her once and for all. Meanwhile—go. If Kayla and the other kids show up here, we'll grab them. I'll have Greystone keep a special eye out. And if any shadow-things show up, we'll be prepared."

Eric, riding Lady Day this time, returned to the place he'd originally cast his first spell. Lady Day's magical senses were a lot keener than his own, and the elvensteed would protect him from casual muggers—by Gating him to Underhill, if nothing else would serve. And if he actually was dealing with either a crazed Protector or something Unseleighe, he'd prefer not to risk any innocent bystanders being hurt when it showed up.

If it showed up.

This time, having some idea of what his Calling might summon, he took time to build defenses— serious defenses—around himself and Lady Day before he started. When he was done, the spell walls were almost visible to the unMagely eye, hanging in shimmering purple and green curtains around the two of them.

Eric summoned up his Flute of Air and began to play "God Bless The Child," wrapping his Calling spell around the melody—now *there* was an appropriate tune. He thought of Jaycie as he'd last seen him. Scared, and lost, and angry—and drugged on caffeine—surely somebody cared that he was missing? Surely somebody wanted him back?

Suddenly—just as before—the temperature dropped sharply and the dark night went darker. Just as before, Eric was surrounded by a howling storm of grief bordering on madness, but this time he'd come prepared, and his shields deflected the worst of it.

"I've seen him!" he shouted, hoping he was talking to the right person. "I've seen your charge! He's alive and well!" Not well exactly, not mainlining caffeine

the way he was, but this was no time to equivocate
or go into details.

Had he guessed right? Did the violence of the storm
battering his shields seem to draw back, to lessen?

"He's somewhere in Manhattan!" Eric shouted.
"The Dark Court has sent a Shadow Pack after him!
You've got to find him before it's too late! I'll help
you search, if you'll let me!"

And suddenly the storm was gone, without answering.

Cautiously Eric lowered his defenses, wary of further
attack. But Jaycie's Protector—if it *had* been Jaycie's
Protector—was truly gone.

Had he really accomplished anything, other than
proving he could, indeed, summon the same being
twice? Maybe. He wasn't quite sure—maybe he'd
given hope where there'd been none before.

Or warned Jaycie's enemies that there was someone
on their trail.

Though now that he came to think of it, a Shadow
Pack was an odd weapon to send against one of the
Sidhe. Even a very young Sidhe . . .

"Are you all right, Ms. Smith?"

Ramon was standing over her.

She was lying on the floor. Her head hurt where
she'd banged it against the wall.

Jaycie had done . . . something.

*When I get my hands on that elf-boy, I'm gonna
tie his pretty pointy ears in knots*, Kayla vowed furiously.

"Yeah. Yeah, I'm fine. Slipped." Kayla struggled to
her feet.

She looked around. The three of them were gone.
Of course.

"Did you see . . . ?" she asked hopefully.

Raoul shrugged apologetically. "Just ran out of here like their tails were on fire. You sure you're all right?"

"Yeah. Kickin'." Kayla walked stiffly to the door of the lobby and looked out.

Nothing.

She rubbed the back of her head. She leaned back against the doorway, closing her eyes for a moment. This day had gone on *way* too long. Last night she'd been up at Gotham General, trying to put Eric back together. This afternoon she'd found out somebody'd stolen him. Then Ria told her that somebody might be after her. Tonight she found out Jaycie was an elf and somebody was after *him.* It'd been a busy day.

"Maybe you oughtta come over and sit down awhile," Ramon said, sounding anxious.

"I'm fine," Kayla said. "Really. Thanks." *And I've got a killer headache. And I just realized I left my wallet up at The Place. Good-bye Visa card, cash, ID . . . My life is now officially perfect.*

She still had her keys and her subway card, though. She could get back to Guardian House. Or she could go upstairs. Ria kept some cash there. She'd be a lot more mobile with that. She could call Hosea. Maybe her backpack was still up at The Place. Maybe—against all odds—they'd gone back there. He could check for her. And then she could take off after the kids.

She turned around and walked back into the building and called the elevator again.

Forget The Place. The shadow-things had scared them out of there and, like Ace had said, they wouldn't go back there. So where were they *really* likely to go? They'd be too paranoid to try to get into any of the shelters, it was too cold to try to sleep in the open— they'd be risking arrest anyway—and they knew they had those shadows chasing them—what had Jaycie said about that? Slow but sure? So they wouldn't want to stop and hole up anywhere for fear the things would catch up with them, just for starters.

The elevator doors opened and Kayla walked out into Ria's penthouse.

She'd spent a certain amount of time here when Ria had been moving in—funny how Ria hadn't wanted to take any of her decorating hints—so she knew where everything was. Her first stop was the guest bathroom, where she grabbed a bottle of Excedrin and made for the kitchen. She opened the fridge and pulled out a bottle of orange juice, and slugged down six Excedrin along with half a quart of OJ straight from the bottle.

Excedrin. Sixty mg. of caffeine per tablet. Another elf designer drug du jour.

She rummaged around Ria's refrigerator further—fully stocked with the latest weekly delivery from Balducci's, all untouched because Ria hadn't been here—until she located a carton of something that looked good. She grabbed a spoon and wolfed it down cold, barely stopping to chew. She grudged the wasted time, but Healing Jaycie had taken a lot out of her, and she knew she needed to recharge. She finished the orange juice and then went in search of the play money.

It was in a drawer in a desk in Ria's study—what Ria called "pizza money"; only a couple of hundred dollars. Kayla took it all, stuffing it into her jeans pocket.

Then she called Hosea. No answer. She slammed the phone down in disgust, not bothering to leave a message.

Looks like I'm on my own.

But where was she going to go? Where would *they* go?

*They can't stop, not for more than a few minutes.
So they have to keep moving. Subways won't work,
because the trains always come back to the same
place and the shadows might be smart enough to
figure that out.*

*And they know—at least Ace and Magnus know—
that New York isn't good for Jaycie. So they'll want
to get him out of here.*

*So that leaves train or bus, to get out of the city.
And bus is cheaper, and stops in more out of the
way places.*

"Next stop, Port Authority Bus Terminal," Kayla
said. *And hope I'm right.*

"What did you do to her?" Ace demanded, when
they finally stopped running.

"Nothing," Jaycie said. "Just . . . nothing. A little
shove. But we had to get away. I don't trust her. She
was lying."

"She *had* to be lying," Magnus said, sounding desperate. "I can't have a brother! And for it to be . . . Eric?
It doesn't add up. He'd have to be, like, *old,* and that
guy wasn't. Not *that* old, anyway."

"Well, we can't go back there now," Ace said pragmatically. "So where are we going to go? I've still got
Jaycie's money." *At least we have that much.*

"And I can get more," Jaycie said positively.

Ace pulled them into the shelter of a doorway
and dug out her wallet. It was thick with cash. She
counted it quickly, and blinked at the total she arrived
at. Almost a thousand dollars.

Where could they go? Big cities were best—nobody
looked twice at you in a big city. But maybe all big
cities would make Jaycie sick. And people were looking
for all three of them, she knew that now. Whatever
else Kayla had lied about, she didn't think she'd been

lying when she'd said Magnus' parents were looking for him. And Magnus seemed to think they were, too.

Move now. Think later.

"Come on," Ace said wearily.

Eric had gone to try to reach Jaycie's Protector first for two reasons—one, if it had worked, it would have simplified everything and given him a powerful ally. And two, it would have been much more difficult—and possibly dangerous—to cast the spell with the kids in tow, assuming he'd actually caught up with them at Ria's.

But now Eric wondered if he should have skipped that step. Even with Lady Day to get him around the city quickly, he'd lost valuable time. And the windows of Ria's penthouse were dark.

Still, checking to see if someone was there—or had been there—would only take a minute or two.

He parked Lady Day in the yellow "no stopping, standing or breathing" zone in front of the building and walked in.

"Hi, Ramon. Anybody home?"

"Hi, Eric. Good to see you again, sir." It had taken Eric weeks to get the staff of Ria's building to use his first name, because he *loathed* being called "Mr. Banyon." He still couldn't get rid of the "sirs," though. He supposed that was part of what most of the tenants in a place like this paid for.

"Ms. Llewellyn's still away, and you just missed Ms. Smith. She was here for a few minutes with some friends of hers. They didn't stay. And she left about half an hour ago," Raoul said helpfully.

There was something odd about the way he put it. *They didn't stay . . . she left . . .*

"Were they together when she left?" Eric asked, on a hunch.

"Oh, no, sir," Ramon said. "They left, and Ms. Smith went on up to the penthouse alone."

That didn't make any sense. Ramon had to mean that Kayla had been here with Magnus, Ace, and Jaycie. But if they'd split up, he ought at least to be able to locate Kayla now.

"Thanks, Ramon. Have a good evening."

He went back out to Lady Day and mounted, letting the elvensteed find her way out into traffic again.

"Let's find Kayla!" he shouted over the noise of her engine, and felt the elvensteed's eager assent.

They caught up to the taxi at a light.

Kayla was sitting inside—alone—hunched forward on the seat, looking cross. Eric leaned over and knocked on the passenger window.

She glanced up—angry, startled, not recognizing him at all, even though he'd taken the obvious precaution of removing his helmet so she could see his face. Then her expression cleared into one of utter relief and delight, and she made a grab for the door.

At that moment, the light changed and the taxi pulled away.

Eric followed, watching the silent pantomime of Kayla arguing with the driver, but it was another several blocks before the man managed to find a hole in traffic and pull over. He pulled up just behind the cab and dismounted from Lady Day once more. She balanced, rather smugly, on her two wheels, but he didn't worry about anyone noticing, not right now. If anybody saw, they'd probably just think it was some new kind of motorcycle. New Yorkers were notoriously unflappable. They took pride in it. Unsinkable, unflappable New Yorkers.

Kayla flung herself at him and hugged him hard.

"Oh, Jesus, Banyon, where've you *been*?" She pulled

back and punched him in the arm. Hard. "We were worried half to *death*. I thought Ria was going to lose it big time. You better call her if you want to live. And . . . nice hair." She grinned, reaching out to flip his hair back over his shoulder.

"First things first," Eric said. "There's an Unseleighe Shadow Pack after Jaycie. He's—"

"An elf. Yeah, I got that part. I Healed him up earlier this evening an' he dropped the moonlight and roses long enough for Ace and Magnus to see what he really looked like. And then this dark stuff started boiling out of the walls and we ran like hell. That's the short version. I tried to get them to Ria's, on account of its being shielded there, but they wouldn't go for it. Almost did. But at the last minute, the elf-boy knocked me on my ass with a light show and they bolted."

Eric winced. "Any idea where they're headed?"

"I'm guessing Port Authority. They know they gotta keep moving because of the Shadows, an' I told them the city's making Jaycie sick, and I think Ace believes me."

"Come on then," Eric said.

Port Authority Bus Terminal, at Ninth Avenue and Forty-Second Street, on the western end of Times Square, was open 24 hours a day. It had been built in 1950, and gotten a multimillion dollar overhaul that had finished at the end of 2001. The terminal itself covered five stories, plus a three-floor car park on the top level, and on a typical day, 200,000 people used it. It was big, sprawling, and complicated, and over thirty bus lines called it home. Not an easy place to search, even at this time of night, with most of the place shut down.

Eric left Lady Day outside the main entrance, not

bothering to park—the elvensteed could fend for herself, and move if she needed to.

They went inside.

"We'll check the ticket windows first," Eric decided, looking around. "They might still be buying their tickets. Then the gates."

"Sounds like a plan," Kayla said doubtfully.

"Best we've got," Eric said grimly. "I just hope they're here—or it's back to square one, and we're running out of time and choices."

"Which one?" Magnus said, as they walked into the bus terminal. He'd been here once before—on his way down from Boston, but he hadn't been paying a lot of attention then.

"Greyhound," Ace said decisively. "It goes the most places, and we can get off at any of the stops if we see someplace we like. Come on."

She led the other two over to the ticket window and studied the list of destinations critically. Miami. That was good. Three one-way tickets would only be a little over three hundred dollars. Miami was a long way from New York. And at least it would be someplace warm.

She told the clerk her destination, hoping nothing would go wrong. It seemed to take a long time to print out the tickets. The clerk told her the gate number, and added: "You'd better hurry. It's a long way to the gate, and the last bus for tonight leaves in half an hour. Next one won't be until tomorrow morning."

"Thank you, ma'am," Ace said politely. She turned around to hand the tickets to the boys.

And stared.

Magnus was right there, looking bored and irritated.

But Jaycie was gone.

She grabbed Magnus by the arm and hustled him out of earshot of the ticket agent. By now Magnus had realized that Jaycie wasn't with them, and was looking around wildly.

"Where is he?" Ace hissed.

"I just—"

"Well, *find him!*" As an afterthought, she thrust Magnus' ticket at him, precious little good it was going to do him now, since certainly neither of them was going to leave without Jaycie. She looked up and down the concourse. It looked like the world's largest shopping mall, even with half the places closed up for the night. Jaycie was nowhere in sight.

"You check down that way—I'll go this. We'll meet at the gate in half an hour. That's when the bus is supposed to leave. If we've got him, we can go. If not, we can keep looking for him together."

"What if he just . . ." Magnus said, and stopped. Neither of them wanted to be the first to say it. *What if he's just run out on us?*

"He wouldn't do that," Ace said, but there was no certainty in her voice. "He needs us." *We need him. Jaycie . . .*

She turned away, starting to run.

His head hurt. He was sick. And everything was going wrong. He wanted chocolate. He wanted Coca-Cola. And most of all, he wanted it to be *yesterday*, before that Healer girl had come back and spoiled everything with her tales.

Jaycie wandered through the terminal, looking into the barred windows of the closed shops. What he wanted was in there, but he couldn't get in. Simple locks were no problem, and he could charm nearly anyone he met into giving him anything, but these

doors were sealed with bars of steel, and there was
no one about to charm.

All he wanted was a few cans of Coca-Cola. And
some chocolate. He didn't feel at all well without
it. And it would be hard to talk Ace and Magnus
into letting him have them now. They might actually
believe the Healer girl had been telling the truth. And
he wasn't completely sure of his ability to convince
them otherwise.

He'd go back to the others once he had what
he needed. And maybe he could talk them out of
leaving the city. The Healer girl—who knew far too
much about Jaycie's kind—had said this was a safe
place, a place the Sidhe didn't come. They should
stay here.

But the Shadow Hunt was here. So that meant
this place wasn't safe either. But who would send a
Shadow Hunt after *him*? It made no sense.

Then he saw bright lights up ahead, and a familiar logo, and forgot all about the Shadow Hunt. He
couldn't read the languages of the World Above, but
he knew its symbols very well.

Coca-Cola.

"There he is." Kayla's voice was a low whisper. She
nudged Eric and pointed.

She'd had the advantage—at least she'd known what
the kids were wearing when they'd started running.
That made Magnus easy for her to spot.

She and Eric slid over to him.

Knowing what he now knew—that it had been
Jaycie's magic he and Ria had sensed in the beginning, not Magnus', Eric was free to cloak himself
and Kayla in an invisibility spell, so they were able
to approach Magnus unseen. He might not have
noticed them anyway; he was alone, walking quickly

through the Terminal, obviously searching desperately for something or someone.

"Miss me?" Kayla said, stopping in front of him just as Eric dropped the spell.

To Magnus, it must have seemed as if she'd appeared out of nowhere. He staggered backward, and bumped into Eric.

The boy had fast reflexes. He gathered himself to bolt just as Eric grabbed his arm, and between Jaycie's true appearance and the Shadow Hunt, he'd seen enough strange things tonight not to waste time boggling at inessentials. He struggled for a moment, but Eric was stronger than he was—and had the advantage of having been trained in swordplay Underhill besides. That put muscle on you.

When Magnus realized he couldn't break Eric's grip, he stopped fighting.

"I'll scream," Magnus threatened.

"Call the cops," Eric pointed out reasonably, "and you go straight back to Boston."

Magnus shut up as if he'd been gagged.

"Where are Ace and Jaycie?" Kayla demanded.

Magnus remained stubbornly silent.

"Look," Eric said. "I don't *want* to send you back to Boston. I want to help you."

"Yeah, she already told me you're my brother. I don't believe it," Magnus said flatly.

Stalemate.

Where would he go? Ace wondered desperately, running through the half-empty terminal. Suddenly Kayla's words earlier came back to her—about Jaycie being a junkie, kind of, hooked on Coca-cola. She remembered how he'd drunk it practically every moment he was awake, back at The Place, going through two or three six-packs a day.

He hadn't had any all night.

She looked around for the nearest security guard and ran over to him, taking a deep breath and trying to look calm.

"'Scuse me, sir, could you tell me what's open to get something this time of night? Just candy bars or Cokes?"

He thought about it for what seemed a maddeningly long time.

"Well, not much this time of night. There's Hudson News—there's one up on Third Floor North, but I think that's closed this time of night. The one on Second should be open, though. There's a map right over there."

"Thank you!" Ace said. She hurried over to the map. There it was, smack in the middle of a bunch of other shops, as many as a mall. She got her bearings, and headed for it at a dead run.

Jaycie stood in front of the cooler at the back of the newsstand, happily chugging down Coca-Colas. He drank three immediately, and felt much better. He tucked another six into the pockets of his parka for later, set the empty cans back into the cooler, and turned to walk out of the kiosk.

"Hey—you gonna pay for those?"

Jaycie smiled—it had always worked before—and *wished* very hard that the man would just let him walk away. But he was a little dizzy from the sudden rush of caffeine—his system wasn't as used to it after the Healing as it had been before—and the man only frowned.

"You gotta pay for those, you know," the man repeated. Not angry, but not letting Jaycie walk away, either.

Jaycie took an uncertain step backward. He didn't

have any money. He'd given all of it to Ace. Should he run?

Slowly the lights began to dim.

There was a sudden blast of light down the concourse.

Eric's first thought—everyone's first thought these days—was: *bomb!*

Eric flung Kayla and Magnus to the ground, throwing up as much of a shield over all of them as he could in that instant. But the seconds passed, and there was no shock wave, no fireball, no rain of debris. He looked up, abruptly sensing the currents of Sidhe magic.

There was an Elven Warrior in the Main Concourse of the Port Authority Bus Terminal.

She was tall, wearing full battle armor that gleamed bright silver, a long blue cloak hanging from her shoulders. With a gleaming two-handed broadsword she was swinging at shadow-things that boiled and snapped around her, half smoke, half dog. She'd already pretty much demolished the newsstand. Alarms were going off—Eric could hear them—and in moments police and security would arrive.

He hauled himself up off Magnus and Kayla and went running toward her.

The Shadow Hunt had found them. Jaycie turned to run. There was no time to argue, to even try to cast a *glamourie*, or to try to sweep the Shadows back into the Overworld. He had to find the others and run before it was too late.

Then the world exploded in a flash of light, and *she* was there. She'd found him and she'd take him back, to all the terrible things he'd fled from.

He ducked away from her and fled in the only

direction left. The man behind the counter leaped out and began to pursue him, only to be knocked sprawling with one blow from his Protector's armored fist.

Suddenly the air was filled with bells. Mortal bells. Warning bells.

"Jaycie!"

Ace grabbed him. He struggled, but she clung to his jacket, and he could not throw her off without hurting her.

"She comes for me!" he cried in terror.

Ace turned to run, and found herself staring directly into the barrel of a security guard's gun.

They all started gathering together at Neil's about ten o'clock. Fafnir had picked tonight because it was his night off, and he wasn't sure how long this would take, especially if something really dramatic happened. It would be nice to have a good solid payoff after putting up with all their crap for a whole year and more. Sure, September 11th had helped—after that, everybody had wanted to believe that there were Secret Good Guys out there working behind the scenes to make everything better. But it was over a year since then. He needed to hammer them a little. Make sure he got some really nice Christmas presents.

With both the Inner and Outer Circles gathered, and no outsiders tonight—tonight he wasn't looking for new blood—there were almost two dozen people there. That number jammed Fafnir's own living room to the walls, but Neil's living room wasn't even really crowded. Fafnir felt the dull angry heat of resentment. Why should Neil live in a place like this just because he had that nice soft brokerage job, and Fafnir be crammed into that grubby downtown apartment, even if it was free? It wasn't fair. He deserved more. He was *better* than Neil, better than all of them. He was smarter. He had more imagination. He'd *made all of this up*. All the stuff about the False Guardians, and the True Guardian and the Secret Master, and the Inner Planes—he'd gotten some ideas from the comic books, and a little from what Andrew had told him, but most of it was his own idea. *He* was the one who deserved to be living like this, not a Wall Street drone like Neil!

Well, they'd see. After tonight, they would definitely see.

He saw Sarah come in with Amanda, and crossed the room to her, smiling warmly. Without little Amanda, he was pretty sure none of this would work. And it *had* to work.

"Sarah. Tonight will be a very special night—for all of us." He concentrated on turning up the charm. He needed Sarah to keep Amanda in line, if nothing else.

"Oh yes," Sarah said. She was carrying Amanda, and the girl's head lolled sleepily on her shoulder. Fafnir frowned.

"She was so fussy earlier," Sarah said apologetically. "I had to give her one of the pills her doctor prescribed. I didn't know what else to do. I would have gotten a sitter, but you said I really ought to bring her."

"It is necessary," Fafnir said austerely. Why couldn't the idiot bitch control her own daughter? Amanda wouldn't be any use to him at all if she was asleep! And he could hardly give her a couple of lines of blow to wake her up, even though he bet Neil had some stashed away around here somewhere.

"She'll wake up soon," Sarah said anxiously. "They're really mild."

"Of course," Fafnir said kindly. "Sarah, you know I do not like to interfere in the sacred bond between mother and child, but those of us with the Etheric Gifts are not quite as ordinary men and women, and drugs which are perfectly safe and even wholesome for others to take can have unfortunate consequences for us, shutting down—or even forcing open—senses that we try hard to discipline through constant effort. Forgive me for speaking, but Amanda and I have worked so long and hard together. . . ."

Sarah's blue eyes filled with tears. "Oh, Master, I'm so sorry! Forgive me—I didn't think—"

"It is Amanda whose forgiveness you should ask, Sarah, dear, not mine," he said gently, and moved on.

There. That should book that brainless meatbag on a nice guilt trip.

The last two to arrive were Caity and Juliana. Caity'd tried to say she couldn't come this evening, so Fafnir had sent Juliana down to pick her up. Caity was the fat little artist who'd come to the Open Party with that enormous hillbilly, and Fafnir had no intention of letting her get away. She was generous and—up until now—had been a fervent follower.

Why hadn't she wanted to come tonight? That was unusual, and he didn't like the sheep doing unusual things. It might mean they were trying to think for themselves. And he couldn't allow that, especially now.

Fafnir went over to the two of them, smiling beguilingly. Juliana—as usual—melted like a schoolgirl with her first crush. Usually Caity did too. But not tonight.

"Caity, dear girl. You look troubled." He took her hand and brought it to his lips. He would have kissed it, but she hadn't taken off her mittens yet. He settled for gazing commandingly into her eyes.

"I've been worried, Master Fafnir," she said softly.

"Child, you may always bring your deepest troubles to me. I will always hear them," he said. Finally he felt the last of her resistance dissolve, and suddenly he thought he could guess the reason behind her hesitation. "And after tonight, we will all be safe. That is why I wanted Amanda with us. If her mother is to be a target for the wrath of the False Guardians, how could I in good conscience leave her innocent daughter unprotected?"

Relief flooded Caity's face. "Is *that* why?" she said. "I thought—"

"You thought I would use the child as a mere tool. Oh, Caity—that is the action of our enemies, not my work," he said chidingly.

Caity blushed a deep scarlet, and Fafnir knew he had guessed exactly right. Stupid cow.

"Now come. Remove your outer garments, and prepare to take your places, so that the Great Work can begin."

In preparation for this evening, Neil had bought several cases of jar candles, and now he began setting them out around the edge of the room. Three large braziers—also bought new, to save the trouble of bringing the three up from Fafnir's apartment—were prepared and lit, and soon fragrant frankincense smoke began spiraling up toward the ceiling.

"It isn't going to stain anything, is it?" Neil asked anxiously.

"Shut up, Neil," Juliana said poisonously.

"Please," Fafnir said, raising his hand. "No anger now. We face enough anger from those who wish us harm."

His acolytes subsided, focusing all their attention on him, as was only right.

They were gathered in three concentric rings around

him and Amanda. The two of them were in the center.
Fafnir was seated in his favorite chair, his back to the
window. The drapes were drawn. Amanda, still a little
groggy, was seated on his lap.

On a small table before them stood the Eye of the
Inner Planes, the only ritual item Fafnir *had* brought
from his apartment. Around them were his acolytes,
closely packed together, the knees of those behind
against the backs of those in front of them.

"Now, Evan, turn out the lights, and we shall begin,"
he said.

One of the Outer Court acolytes in the outermost
ring got to his feet and turned out the living room
lights. Now the room was lit solely by the light of
the ring of flickering candles. The crystal ball in the
center of the circle seemed to draw that light to itself,
glowing a lunar blue.

Fafnir sat there in silence for almost a minute, letting the months of conditioned response take effect.
The darkness, the candles, the incense, the sight of
the crystal ball, all had their effect. The room was
absolutely silent, the closely packed group of people
swaying slightly as they slipped into an entranced
state.

"Concentrate, my young Guardians-to-be," Fafnir
said. "Reach down into yourselves. Summon up the
power that is within you. Call forth the Protector!"

"The Protector—the Protector—" they began to
chant softly.

Amanda was drowsy enough that he hardly needed
his pendulum to put her under this time.

"Look into the crystal ball, Amanda," Fafnir whispered in her ear, under cover of the soft chanting.
"See the lady in the crystal ball? Remember the lady
in the crystal ball? Call her. Bring her here."

And Amanda did.

CHAPTER SIXTEEN:

BATTLE OF AUGHRIM

"Stay here!"

Eric ran toward the Protector—hoping it *was* Jaycie's Protector, and not some new menace from Underhill. He needed to put a lid on this situation *now*.

He stopped a few feet away.

"Look. He's right there."

Eric pointed. Jaycie and Ace were standing staring at a very nervous security guard, who obviously couldn't make up his mind whether they were part of the problem or innocent victims.

Quickly Eric reached out with his magic, spreading a ring of Sleep around the immediate area. A little sloppy—Master Dharniel would criticize his performance—but it would keep anybody from getting shot. The guard—and all the rest of the emergency personnel arriving in answer to the alarms—quickly crumpled to the ground, deeply asleep.

"Jaycie!"

He heard Magnus shout from behind him, and heard Kayla yell in protest. Magnus ran past him, oblivious to the danger the Elven Knight presented, heading directly for Jaycie.

She lashed out at him with her sword, striking him with the flat of the blade and knocking him skidding across the floor, and advanced on Jaycie.

"Magnus!" Eric shouted, turning toward him, terrified. *If this is what parenthood feels like, I don't like it.*

"He's okay—he's okay!" Kayla said, kneeling over him, and yanking off her gloves. "Busted rib—that's all. I'm on it!"

Eric turned back to the Protector. "Now, look—" he said.

Suddenly she recoiled, dropping her sword and beginning to wail.

It was a horrible sound, a sound of death, and loss, and bereavement bordering on madness. He'd heard it before—in the Park, when he'd tried to call her. But Eric could sense no form of attack. Either it was a spell only she could sense . . . or prolonged exposure to New York had driven her mad.

As she howled she began to *change,* her armor shimmering and flowing like water, turning into long flowing robes. She clawed at her face—whatever was happening to her, the Elven Protector was obviously fighting it—and losing the fight.

"No, no, *no!*" Magnus screamed. *"Don't let her get me!"*

Kayla had finished her Healing, but the boy was obviously terrified half out of his wits, staring over her shoulder at Jaycie's Protector and trying to scrabble away.

:Lady Day, come and get us out of here,: Eric thought to his 'steed. *:Quietly.:*

Abruptly the Protector vanished.

The wailing stopped.

It was suddenly very quiet. Jaycie started to back away.

"*Stop.*" Eric put all the force of a Command into that one word. Jaycie stopped where he was. Ace clung to his arm, staring at Eric.

They had to get out of here. Fast. Before more police showed up. And more to the point, they had to cover up the damage they'd done here tonight, starting with the kiosk.

A simple spell—like Elven *kenning*, but one that a Bard could perform—repaired the damage to the newsstand, as he asked the kiosk to "remember" its previous condition. Next, a spell of Forgetting on everyone here to cover kids, Shadows, and Elven Knights. It wouldn't take care of everything, but they'd come up with explanations of their own. Maybe they'd put it down to a malfunction in the alarm system. Eric knew he was going to pay for this later, but that was then, and this was now.

Lady Day rolled in down the Main Concourse.

"Come on," Eric said.

He gathered them all together, standing close around the elvensteed. Jaycie was still docile—thanks to Eric's Command—but the spell wouldn't hold past the Gate.

"Take us home," Eric said.

"Very funny," he said a moment later. "Now go in the bedroom. I'll figure out how to get you downstairs and out of the apartment tomorrow."

Lady Day, very meekly, wheeled herself down the hall, nudged open the door of Eric's bedroom, and slipped inside.

Eric looked at the four of them.

Magnus still looked terrified; so terrified, he barely noticed he'd been teleported into Eric's apartment. Kayla was holding onto him, just as she had been when she'd dragged him over to the 'steed back in the Port Authority.

"She— That's— If you see her, you'll die," Magnus said, almost stammering.

"Nobody's going to die," Eric said firmly. He went over and stood directly in front of Magnus, forcing the boy to look at him. "We're going to talk," Eric said firmly. "Which we should have done in the first place, except I guess I still had a little growing up to do. Magnus, I really am your brother Eric. I don't look as old as I should because I've spent quite a bit of time Underhill with the elves. Learning magic."

"There isn't any such thing as magic," Magnus said desperately, blinking hard to hold back tears.

Kayla moved away from Magnus over to Ace and Jaycie, putting her arm around the younger girl and speaking to her soothingly. Eric caught the words "Ria Llewellyn" and "lawyers." He wondered what Kayla was saying. He turned his attention back to Magnus.

"Yes, there is. I've got the talent for it. Since you're my brother, you probably do, too. If that's the case, you'll have to learn how to use it properly. Or keep from using it, if that's what you want. Either way, you're not going back to Boston. Our parents don't deserve to have custody of a houseplant, let alone a child."

"You can't stop them," Magnus said sullenly. "I'm only seventeen."

"Oh, yeah?" Eric said. "I'm of legal age, and I'm

your brother. I'll sue for custody. And you aren't going to spend another minute beneath their roof. I promise you that."

"I hate classical music!" Magnus burst out desperately. "I want to be a drummer like Neil Peart! I never want to play the piano again!"

"Fine," Eric said. "Just let me help."

"And Jaycie? And Ace? Them too?" Magnus asked.

"Yes," Eric promised. He already knew he had to help Jaycie somehow—whether by reuniting him with his Protector, or by taking him Underhill—and as for Ace, if Ria and all her lawyers couldn't do something there, Ace could simply disappear Underhill as well. There were certain advantages to having the Sidhe for friends.

At that moment, the window opened and Greystone poked his head in, looking around. "Och, laddie, ye fair deafened me with that last blast. Is this the wee bairn, then? Faith, bucko, you've given us all a good bit o' trouble! Greystone, at your service." He bowed.

"It's a talking mon—stat—mut—*thing*," Magnus said faintly.

"No such thing as magic, huh?" Ace said scornfully. She was holding up pretty well, all things considered— but then, from what Kayla had told him on the way to the bus terminal, from using her Talent, Ace already had a certain amount of experience with what she considered "magic." She looked at Eric.

"Greystone is a gargoyle," Eric said. "And he's my friend."

Suddenly there was a hammering on the door.

"Ah, that'll be Ms. Hernandez," Greystone said.

"I'm on it." Kayla went over to open the door.

Toni burst in breathlessly, stopping to stare at the room full of people.

"Eric—you're back," she said. "Good to see you. First you set off a depth charge at Port Authority—at least Greystone said it was you—and then you rattle the windows here. Gotta say, you know how to make an entrance."

"Good to be seen. This is my brother Magnus—" how odd it felt to be saying that simple sentence! "—and this is Ace, and Jaycie—"

"Jaycie?" Toni asked, puzzled, looking around.

"Jaycie!" Ace yelped, staring around the room wildly.

The Sidhe boy was gone.

Eric swore. He'd only taken his eyes off him for a second, and Kayla or one of the others would have been watching.

But all the Sidhe possessed the *glamouries* of illusion, of trickery, of misdirection; hard to catch, harder to hold. As Jaycie had just proven.

"Should have tied him up when I had the chance," Eric muttered.

"Where did he go?" Ace demanded frantically.

"Can't you find him with this magic stuff?" Magnus pleaded.

"It's not that easy. But it might be possible. I bespelled him once," Eric said, thinking fast. "That might give me enough of a link to follow. Toni, you'd better get Paul and the others and follow me. I think there's something wrong with Jaycie's Protector, and if she finds him again, I might need backup."

Quickly he sketched out for Toni's benefit what had happened at the Port Authority, when Jaycie's Protector had appeared.

"I don't understand it," Eric finished. "She *ought* to have just taken him and gone home, but something stopped her. I don't know what. *Nothing* is supposed to come between a Protector and the welfare of their charge. They'll defy everything Underhill and in the World Above for them—and they're within their rights. It's the most sacred bond the elves know. Nothing is allowed to come before it for a Protector—not their honor, not even their life. But something's hurting her."

"Something's hurting a lot of people," Toni said dryly. "She's killed almost a dozen people looking for this kid—if it was her."

"And that doesn't even answer the question of why she's turning into a fairy tale," Eric said. While it was true that the Sidhe took a positive delight in shaping themselves in the forms dictated by human myths and legends—and cartoons and comic books, for that matter—generally the transformations were entirely voluntary.

"Killed?" Ace said in a small voice.

Abruptly Toni realized who else was in the room.

"I'm afraid so—Ace, is it? So we'd kind of like her to stop," Toni said gently.

"But Jaycie *can't* go home!" Ace said. "His folks hate him!"

"If that's really true . . ." and Eric doubted that it was; *all* elves valued children, any children, and Elven children were especially precious and rare, " . . . then his Protector will guard him even from his own parents. He knows that's true—or he should. And if she can't, I will."

Magnus looked at him doubtfully.

"He can do that," Kayla said firmly. "And I'm coming with you. If there's trouble, you'll need a medic."

"We're coming too," Ace added. "We can talk sense into him."

"There isn't time to argue—not if your runaway elf-boy is on a collision course with Bloody Mary," Toni said briskly. "Get going, Eric. Take your phone. Call me and give me your position."

"Right." He went into the bedroom.

"Come on, girl."

He wheeled the elvensteed out into the living room again and glanced at the others before heading toward the door. It was a hell of an introduction for Magnus to the Eric Banyon life-style, but Magnus would manage. His brother was a good kid.

Hosea had no trouble getting into Neil's apartment building. Doorman building or not, they wouldn't stop what they didn't see, and Hosea very much didn't want them to see him. And fortunately he remembered the address from last time.

The other Guardians had swords for occasions like this. Jimmie's sword was his now, he guessed—it still hung, in its scabbard, on his bedroom wall. Paul said that swords were strong and important weapons, both exoterically—that meant in the real world—and magically, but somehow Hosea had never felt comfortable with a sword in his hand, even though both Paul and Toni had told him it was first and foremost a symbol of his Will, his intent, and need never be used to draw blood.

"What are you going to use, Hosea? A banjo? Bard or not, I've never met the demon yet you could exorcise with a banjo—even a haunted one," Toni had said to him once.

Even so, Hosea just didn't feel comfortable facing down the Dark Folk with a sword instead of music. Maybe that might change after he'd been a Guardian a while longer. But for now, he simply preferred Jeanette. Besides, he'd look mighty silly hauling a sword—no matter how well disguised—all over New York. Not to mention how much it would upset people.

He made his way to the proper floor, and hesitated. What now? He didn't have any sense of anything being *wrong*, though he could smell the faint scent of frankincense creeping out from under the door, so he knew Fafnir was in there and up to his nonsense.

But nothing was actually happening.

Just in case.

Hosea set down the banjo case and got out Jeanette, slinging her strap over his shoulder and beginning, very quietly, to tighten her pegs.

Suddenly he heard—faintly, through the door—a young child's high scream of terror. Hard upon its heels, drowning it out, came the sound of breaking glass.

He needed to find Rionne. Everything was all wrong here in the World Above, and somehow he'd hurt Rionne. He'd never meant to do that. She was the only person who cared about *him*—not his father's rank, not the politics of the Court of Elfhame Bete Noir. When he'd seen her again in Port Authority, he'd been afraid at first, thinking she might be angry with him, but that was wrong. Rionne was never angry with him, no matter what he did.

Why had he run from her? He'd been afraid. He'd thought she wouldn't understand. But when he'd heard her scream, seen her fighting the Shadow Pack—he'd realized that the Prince his father's wrath must have fallen upon her.

He had to find her. He had to fix things. He had to make things right. For *her*.

He'd gone back to the Port Authority. The trail there was easy to follow, thick and foul with the evil alien magic that had claimed her will and forced her from his side—more proof, not that he'd needed it, that magic was a terrible and frightening thing, to be avoided at all costs.

He hid in the shadows—the place was filled with police, all talking about the mysterious malfunctioning of the security system less than half an hour before. He didn't linger. Now that he'd found Rionne's trail, Jachiel didn't need to. He knew where he was going.

Rionne had saved him many times.

Now he had to save her.

He pulled a can of Coke from his pocket and drank it quickly as he hurried from the bus terminal. It was warm by now, but he didn't care. It made him feel better.

He would go, he would find Rionne, and he would tell her that neither of them ever had to go back Underhill.

Once Eric was away from the apartment, he tried summoning Jaycie's Protector back again. It was risky, here on the Upper West Side, but with Lady Day's help, he thought he had a good chance of stopping her before she did more harm.

But this time she wouldn't—or couldn't—come when he called.

Next he sent a Seeking spell after Jaycie. It homed in on the residue of his previous Command spell and found the boy easily. He was heading Uptown, moving fast enough that he had to be in a cab or a bus. Elves hated the subway system—all that iron—and he doubted Jaycie was an exception to that rule.

He sent Lady Day in pursuit—linked to his mind, she could follow the spell trace as easily as he could—and pulled out his phone.

For a moment he hesitated about making the call. Kayla had looked exhausted when he'd caught up to her, and he hated the thought of dragging Ace and Magnus into more danger.

But he needed Toni and the other Guardians for backup. And Ace was right; Jaycie *might* listen to her and Magnus.

He made the call.

"Toni? I've picked up the trail. Jaycie's heading north. He might be going into Central Park—I found his Protector twice there before. I'm heading over to Sixth—I think he's in a cab. If I can spot it, maybe I can catch him before he gets where he's going."

"Right, Eric. Stay on the line. Give us landmarks," Toni said.

"Gotcha." Fortunately, he didn't need to hold on to the handlebars—or really drive Lady Day in any sense of the word. The elvensteed did all the work. All Eric needed to do was follow Jaycie's trail.

But though he followed the trace as fast as he could without overrunning it, the few minutes' head start Jaycie had gotten was enough to keep him ahead of Eric.

Suddenly a thunderclap of magic—Elven magic—rocked the night. Eric clutched at Lady Day's handlebars, nearly dropping the phone. Something *big* had just happened.

"I've got to go," he said tersely.

"Never mind," Toni said, sounding shaken. "We can follow *that.*"

Eric shoved the phone into his pocket. Without any urging, Lady Day stretched herself to the utmost.

He didn't know who—or what—had just caused that enormous magical disruption he'd felt, but there was no way he could ignore it.

A few moments later he was outside one of the luxury high-rise apartment buildings that dotted the

Upper West Side. Magic radiated from one of the upper floors, as though a meteor had struck it. Eric flung himself off the elvensteed and ran inside.

A quick encouragement to Sleep took care of the doorman and the security guard.

Which floor was the disturbance coming from? He could tell approximately, but to search several floors would take too long.

No sign of Jaycie in the foyer—but to Eric's dismay, he realized that the Sidhe boy had in fact come this way, and only minutes before. Whatever disaster lay ahead, Jaycie must be in the thick of it.

Mage-sight told Eric which elevator he'd used. Once inside the car, Eric was able to tell which button Jaycie had pressed. That gave him the floor he needed.

The ascent of the elevator to 20 seemed to take forever.

When the doors opened, even his ordinary senses could tell Eric there was trouble. The whole hallway smelled faintly of incense, and he could hear screams.

Eric ran.

Though she fought it desperately, the foul sorcery of this place had its way with her yet again. In the moment that should have been her triumph, when Rionne ferch Rianten gazed upon her Jachiel's face once more, saw him sick and terrified—but alive, *alive!*—she felt the demon call reach out to her, enfolding her with the evil magic she was powerless to resist.

Somewhere, there was a child in danger.

But not my child! Not Jachiel!

In vain she fought against it. She was too weak. Her battles against the Seleighe Court Bard and the Shadow Hunt had both drained her, and she had no energy left with which to resist this call. The magic to which her kind was particularly vulnerable—that of imagination, of will—enfolded her, drawing her away, reshaping her in the image of its own desire.

And she came as she had been called.

Fafnir hadn't been expecting much. Maybe for the room to go cold, or the candles to blow out. Maybe for some glowing lights to appear and some of his more suggestible sheep to throw some nice hysterical fits. Maybe.

Not this.

Amanda began to scream and cry. It was embarrassing, but Fafnir didn't have long to be embarrassed. Seconds later, Neil's big picture window exploded inward in a shower of glass. It was safety glass, so all of it that wasn't caught in the curtain starred the floor like diamonds. The curtain had come down with it as well, lying on the floor in a puddle of dark fabric. Immediately, the icy winter wind began whipping into the room, blowing out most of the candles.

There was a woman there as well. A monster. The woman he'd seen—he'd thought he'd seen—just for a moment—in the crystal. She wasn't shadowy or insubstantial at all. She was as real as anyone else in the room.

She was tall—at least six feet—and wearing some kind of long flowing blue draperies that fluttered in the icy wind. And her *face . . .*

Where her eyes should have been, there were nothing but dark gaping holes. Bloody tears streamed down her face.

"We're under attack!" If he hadn't memorized the line, and been thinking about it all along, he never would have managed to say it. What he was thinking was: *Jesus, this is REAL.*

Even without eyes, she somehow seemed to be

able to see. Her face turned toward him. She took a step toward him.

Reflexively, he clutched Amanda even tighter. The kid was screaming like a siren now, but so were a lot of other people. He got to his feet, still holding the screaming, struggling child by the arm.

Should he command the woman to stop? Would it do any good? Why was she just *standing* there? He wished everyone else wasn't making so much noise. It made it really hard to think.

:Freddie. Freddie Warwick.:

Oh, god. She'd said his name. His *real* name. Had everyone heard her? He didn't dare look around to see. Everyone else had scrambled back out of the way, huddling in the corner of the room—except Sarah, who was cowering at his feet, too scared to either grab Amanda or retreat.

:Come to me, despoiler of children.:

"Wait. No. You've got it wrong." He didn't care any more what he sounded like to the others. He didn't even care that he was talking in his Freddie voice, not his Fafnir voice. He didn't care about anything but keeping that *thing* away from him. He'd never been so scared in his life.

He held out his hands, trying to show her that he was harmless, to push her away. To do that he had to let go of Amanda. As if the blue woman had been waiting only for that, she took a step forward, smiling.

Her smile was the most terrible thing Freddie had ever seen. His heart hammered painfully in his chest. He would have given anything to be able to run away, but somehow he could do nothing but gaze into her ruined face, unable to think, unable to *breathe*, as the pain became numbing agony, radiating down his arm and up into his brain.

He tried to scream, and could not.

He dropped to his knees.

Bloody Mary gazed at the room full of cowering acolytes.

:All of you. Despoilers and endangerers of children.:

Hosea burst into the room just in time to see Master Fafnir fall to the floor at the feet of an apparition that matched the shelter children's description of Bloody Mary exactly. The floor was covered with glittering glass and shards of mirror, and the picture window had been completely shattered. A few feet away a woman knelt clutching a screaming child. Bloody Mary turned toward her.

She's going to kill everyone here unless you can stop her.

You've got one chance. If you've guessed right.

If he had, he knew her Secret Name, the one that would turn her from Bloody Mary into the Blue Lady, protector and defender of all children instead of their murderous avenger.

If he'd guessed wrong, they were all going to die.

He swept his hand down over the banjo's silver strings and began to sing, putting everything he knew of magic into the words.

"When Joseph was an old man—An old man was he— He married Virgin Mary—The Queen of Galilee . . . He married Virgin Mary, The Queen of Galilee—"

He felt the power of the good holy words of the old song sweep outward, clashing with the power that held the creature in thrall through the terror of the people gathered here in the room and the spell Fafnir had cast. Poor demon—as much a victim as anyone here, if the Secret Stories were anything to go by.

The Virgin Mary—who else could it be? She who had lost Her child—a loss which God had not prevented, and who was Queen of Heaven—who else?

As the first notes of music sounded, the woman stopped, as if spellbound by the music. That was right. The old story-songs spoke of how you could enthrall—even trap—one of the Good Folk with a song if you played well enough. And some old tales said that fallen angels and the Good Folk were one and the same.

But Hosea wasn't here to trap anyone tonight. He was here to set someone free.

Bloody Mary stopped in the act of reaching for the mother and child huddled together on the floor and straightened up, staring straight at Hosea as if listening intently. He swept into the second verse:

"As Joseph and Mary walked through an orchard green, There were berries and cherries as thick as may be seen— There were berries and cherries, as thick as may be seen—"

Now she took a step backward, raising her hands to her face. Her hair paled from red to blonde, the terrible wounds on her face healed. She became a beautiful young woman surrounded by a pale blue glow. Her fluttering draperies stilled, became less tattered, became a simple blue robe only blown as much by the wind as the clothes of anyone else in the room, not whipped by an eldritch gale.

"Amanda!"

The little girl tore herself free from her mother's arms and ran to the glowing stranger, who knelt to take her in her arms.

"Rionne!"

A boy came tearing into the room, through the

door Hosea had left open. The boy ran through the huddled mob of terrified acolytes, straight to the robed woman, too fast for Hosea to stop him.

And the woman began to change again.

Where an image of the Virgin Mary had stood a moment before now stood a fully armed and armored Elven Knight—as dangerous in her own way as Bloody Mary had been. She thrust both the children behind her and raised her sword.

Hosea stared for a moment in shock. This was no part of the Secret Stories. He'd been expecting one transformation—not two.

But this was no time to sight-see. The Elven Knight raised her sword, and Hosea lunged forward. He reached Sarah—from Caity's descriptions, it must be her—just in time to drag her to safety as the sword flashed down where she'd been. From the look of her, the Elven Knight was as willing as Bloody Mary had been to slaughter all of them. It was a good thing Hosea *didn't* have a sword. That would mark him as an immediate enemy.

"Oh, *shit* . . ." Eric said very softly, at his shoulder. "Jaycie, tell her to let the little girl go."

"Oh, my baby," Sarah whimpered, clinging to Hosea's arm. "Oh, please, don't hurt her!"

"She would harm the child," the Protector said grimly, speaking aloud at last.

"No," Eric said desperately. "She's been very foolish, but she won't do anything like this ever again. She didn't mean to do anything that would hurt Amanda. Truly. I tell you this—" Hosea heard Eric's voice strengthen, and the Elven Knight blinked and straightened from her fighting crouch, "—I *swear* you this, by my name as Bard. She was led astray by sweet words, but never thought harm would come to her child from them."

"Let her go," the boy—who must be Jaycie—said, tugging at the Elven Knight's cloak. "Rionne, please. It was you they wanted to hurt, not some Earthborn babe. All because of me! I never meant to hurt you!"

Eric walked cautiously forward toward the Protector, putting himself between her and everyone else in the room. The whole room was a soup of conflicting currents of magic—both the spell Hosea had cast and the one Fafnir's circle had accidentally cast, and all around him the people that Fafnir had gathered were starting to react to it—badly. He could hear moans and sounds of retching, and forced himself to ignore them. He could not afford to be distracted now.

Somehow Jaycie's Protector had provided the power for whatever spell Fafnir had been trying to cast, becoming the focus for the toxic imago the shelter children had created and becoming tangled in it, and then being bound to Fafnir's circle in turn. Ill as Jaycie was, he was probably the picture of health next to his Protector—Eric wasn't sure how much she understood about where she was or what was going on, but he did know that she'd do anything to protect Jaycie—and the little girl—from anything she saw as a threat. Things could turn deadly in a heartbeat.

Jaycie was clinging to her, weeping, talking to her in a voice too low for Eric to hear. And finally, after what seemed like forever but what was actually only a minute or two, she released the little girl. The child ran past Eric to her mother. Hosea quickly swept them both out of harm's way.

Eric looked directly at Jaycie, knowing that he, at least, would understand what Eric was saying. "I am Eric Banyon, Bard of Overhill and Elfhame Misthold, and I offer you both the protection of Elfhame Misthold in Prince Arvin's name."

"The Bright Court!" Jaycie drew back in horror.

Eric stared at him in shock. Jaycie was an *Unseleighe Sidhe*? Then his own people had been hunting him . . .

This was worse than he'd thought.

"Even so," Eric said gently, bowing slightly. "I give you my word as a Bard. The sanctuary of Elfhame Misthold. For *both* of you."

"Why did you run from me, my heart?" Rionne said sadly, sheathing her sword and putting her arms around Jaycie. She ignored Eric completely.

Jaycie simply shook his head, clinging to her.

Toni had wanted the kids to stay in the car, but nothing short of handcuffs was going to keep them there. At least Eric had a head start on them.

And to her relief, by the time they got there, the shooting part of things seemed to be over.

"You want to stay out here, *querida*?" she asked Kayla. The young Empath's face had gone white as they reached the half-open apartment door, and she swayed on her feet.

"I'm just peachy," Kayla said, gritting her teeth.

"Then stay behind me, at least," Toni said, easing the door open and walking in carefully, sword in hand.

She was no Empath, and her psychic senses were the result of Guardian Powers rather than inborn Gift, but even she could feel the sludge of unexpended magics that filled the living room and foyer of the apartment. The room was dark, lit only by the light of a few flickering candles in jars, and the city light coming in through the hole in the far wall that had once been a nice picture window.

The room was icy cold.

Silhouetted against the shattered window was a tall armored figure with her arms around a boy in street clothes. Eric was standing in front of them, his hands spread. Between Eric and the knight was a body—no doubt of that—and the rest of the room was filled with almost two dozen people in various stages of backlash shock. Besides Eric, the knight, and the boy, Hosea was the only one on his feet. She realized Hosea was playing softly, spreading the equivalent of a psychic Band-Aid over the scene. It wouldn't hold for long, but it did explain why there wasn't a full-scale riot going on now.

"Shut the door," Toni said in a low voice. *Contain the scene.* That was what Jimmie had always said; the first rule of crime scenes, magical and otherwise. They had to keep all these people from going anywhere until they could get this sorted out. At least things were quiet right now, and Paul and José would be here soon to provide as much backup as she needed.

Behind her, she heard Kayla close the door.

"Jaycie," Ace whispered.

As if he'd heard her, the boy looked up. His eyes glowed green in the dim light of the room. If that was Jaycie, then he was the Sidhe-child Eric had spoken of, and the armored knight must be both his Protector, and the specter the Guardians had been tracking.

At that moment, Eric beckoned the others forward.

Hesitantly, Toni walked into the darkened living room, bringing the children with her. She kept her sword down, doing her best to make it look like a tool, not a threat. She put her free arm around Magnus—of the two kids, he was the more skittish, and she could tell that the whole scene had him pretty spooked.

They reached Eric's side.

"This is Rionne ferch Rianten, Jaycie's Protector," Eric said quietly. "She comes from Underhill." He thought it was just as well to leave out the Unseleighe part of things. It didn't matter at Jaycie's age, and Rionne's loyalties were to Jaycie, not to either Court.

"Is she going to take him back?" Ace said harshly.

"I have to go," Jaycie said, still clinging to Rionne. He wore no *glamourie* now, and appeared fully Elven. He gazed past Eric, at Ace and Magnus, willing them to understand.

"I never should have come here. I never should have . . . loved you both. But I was afraid of my magic, of what I would learn to do with it—of what my father would want me to do with it. So I ran away. But that just made things worse."

Rionne held him tightly. "Nothing you could ever do would be wrong in my eyes, my heart," she said to him fondly.

Jaycie closed his eyes for a moment. "I know. I should have thought of that. But I was scared. And now . . ."

"And now we will go, on the Bard's promise, to the Bright Court and Elfhame Misthold, where we shall cry 'Sanctuary' and you may be healed of the ills the mortal world has dealt you. And when we have had time to consider matters further, the Bard will speak to the Prince, your father," Rionne said firmly.

I will? But Eric guessed he'd volunteered for the job, in a way. And serving as envoys between Courts was one of the traditional jobs of Bards.

But . . . an elf who didn't want to learn magic?

"So you're just going to *leave*? And we're never going to see you again?" Ace asked.

She sounded utterly lost. Romances were common between the Sidhe and humankind; the elves found humans just as fascinating as humans found elves enchanting. But such romances were commonly brief. And usually, when they were over, the Elven partner clouded the human's memories to spare them the pain of bereavement.

Not this time.

Eric could see the moment when Jaycie realized just how badly he'd hurt his mortal friends. By the time he was mature enough by Sidhe standards to leave Underhill again, many years would have passed in the World Above. Ace and Magnus would be very old, if not dead.

"Perhaps you will be allowed to come and visit me Underhill," he said softly, taking a step away from Rionne. "I am sorry, my friends. I never meant to hurt you."

"Eric," Magnus said urgently. "Can't you stop her? Can't you keep him here?"

Eric turned to his brother. Magnus' face was white and strained, with the panicky expression of someone very much afraid he's about to cry.

"They have to go, Magnus," Eric said, very gently. "If they don't go, they'll both die. There are places that elves can live in the World Above, but New York isn't one of them. And Jaycie needs help that he can't get here."

"He'll be safe? And happy?" Magnus said desperately.

"Yes. That much I can promise. Maybe—" He thought quickly. "Look, I have friends Underhill with e-mail. It'll take some time, but I'll fix it so you can e-mail each other. More than that, I can't promise." He turned back to Rionne. "I'll loan you my elven-steed, Lady Day—you'll find her below." He spared a bit of magic to take his promise to the elvensteed, who was taken a bit aback for a moment, but then agreed. "She awaits you; she can take the two of you through the Everforest Gate to Elfhame Misthold. You'll find Sanctuary there."

Lady Rionne bowed her head in acknowledgement. "That makes good hearing, Bard. And perhaps—when the child is grown—I shall return to your world. From what I have seen here, your children need a Protector also."

For just a moment, the Elven Knight vanished, and the form of the radiant Blue Lady appeared in her place, then Rionne stood before them once again.

"Child, it is time to go."

"One moment, Rionne, please," Jaycie said.

He walked over to Ace, and stared down at her for a long moment. "I lied to you before, because I was afraid. The Healer and the Bard both told you the truth. About everything. You should trust them. They'll protect you."

"I know," Ace said, her voice thick with tears.

"I wish I could stay," Jaycie said. "But it isn't right for me to." He put his arms around her and held her very tightly. "You humans have so very many wonderful things, and you never appreciate half of them!"

Then he let her go and turned to Magnus.

"I'm sorry I hit you—more than once, I guess. You were a good friend to me, one I didn't deserve. Let your brother help you, or, or—or I shall send Rionne to make you heed him!"

"Yeah, right," Magnus said raggedly, as Jaycie hugged him very hard.

"Now," Jaycie whispered, stepping away from Magnus, toward his Protector.

Rionne stepped forward—

—and suddenly the humans were alone in the room.

"Elves know how to make an exit, gotta give 'em that," Kayla said into the silence.

"That's all very well," Hosea said, "but just now we've got more than a little housekeeping to do here."

He nodded his head at the room full of bespelled people.

"Right," Eric said, thinking hard. "I think the best thing is for everybody to forget that tonight ever happened. The whole thing will just fall apart without Fafnir, anyway."

Hosea nodded. "A little healin', a power o' forgettin', and let their own minds do the rest. Sounds good."

Having set the terms of the spell, Eric summoned up his Flute of Air, and let the Bardic magic spill out in a skirl of notes.

First music to cleanse and heal, sweeping away the last of Fafnir's toxic and baneful influences from the area. In a way, it was like jazz improvisation, the flute and the banjo winding around each other, each taking its turn to lead the melody. Eric could see Kayla's face relax as the last of the psychic and magical mess was swept away, and even Eric felt better once it was done.

But all that was like cleaning up a kitchen before you were going to cook in it. Now they were going to cook. And once they were done, all of Fafnir's former disciples would go home, forgetting all about tonight—and particularly about Fafnir's death. Over the next several days, they'd forget all about Fafnir and the whole True and False Guardians scenario, retaining only as much information about their Fafnir-related activities as they needed to make sense of their day-to-day lives. But none of the things relating to Fafnir would seem very important, or very real, and in a year or so they'd forget about him, and what they'd done in the "Guardian" cult entirely.

His intent lodged firmly in his mind, Eric began to play.

He chose an old Gospel song—it seemed fitting,

somehow: "On The Wings of a Dove." He knew
Hosea would know it.

But to his surprise, on the second repeat of the
melody, Ace joined in as well, singing the words.

Her voice was high and true and pure, filled not
with Bardic magic, but with the power of her Talent.
The song's words spoke of love, of endless forgiveness
and healing, and as Ace sang, everyone in the room
felt those things, blending into the magic, soothing the
frightened panicky people, making it easier for the spell
to do its work. She drew all of them together: Healer
and Guardian, Bards and Bard-to-be, drawing their
Powers and Talents gently together into a whole.

And as the spell worked its way over them, Fafnir's
people slowly got to their feet. They looked confused
and distracted, but no longer frightened. Moving as if
they did not see anything out of place—Eric, Hosea,
Toni, the kids; Fafnir's body; the broken candles or
shattered glass—they moved through the apartment
like sleepwalkers, retrieving coats and hats and purses.
In a few minutes all of them—including, presumably,
the apartment's rightful tenant—were gone, and the
others were alone.

Eric brought the song to an end and released the
spell, knowing the magic would follow them out into
the world to finish its work.

The living room went silent, and suddenly Eric
could really feel the cold for the first time. It was a
lot colder twenty stories up than it was at street level,
but when he'd walked in and seen Rionne standing
there, he'd been too focused to pay much attention to
it, and things had been moving too fast since then.

Ace shook herself as if she were rousing from a
dream, and glared at Eric and Hosea with confused
suspicion.

"Who *are* you people?" she demanded, taking

Magnus' hand protectively. "You—I saw you down at the shelter," she said to Hosea.

Hosea nodded.

"Ah guess we might ask you the same thing," Hosea said with a smile. "You surely gave us a goodly bit of help there. Made the helpin' we did for those poor folks go down a mite easier."

Ace made a wry face. "It's what I do," she said bitterly. "I can make anybody believe any kind of lie."

"But you weren't lyin'," Hosea said. "You were helpin' them see the truth. Girl, ain't it true that there's love, an' love forgives? Ain't it true that God—whatever name you want to call Him by—don't want nothin' for us but what's right and good for us? It's a powerful Gift, if you use it rightly. Have you ever thought that if you were given a goodly gift, you could choose to do goodly things with it?"

Ace stared at him for a moment and began to cry. It wasn't the kind of crying of someone who was hopeless. It was the kind of weeping that came from someone who had just been offered hope, unforeseen, unexpected.

"Oh. Oh, *jeez,*" Magnus said, sounding horrified, angry, and disgusted all at once.

"Have we come at a bad time?" Paul Kern asked, walking into the living room, closely followed by José. "My, what a mess."

"You don't know the half of it," Kayla said fervently.

She walked over and tried the light switch—there wasn't any reason to leave the lights off now, and she wanted to see if they still worked. They did. The sudden tasteful brightness further reduced the scene to ordinariness.

"I'll go see what's in the kitchen," Toni said briskly. "I think our host owes us a few refreshments."

Hosea had led Ace over to the couch—far away from the body—and gotten her to sit down, sitting down beside her and offering her a large white handkerchief. José came out of a back room with a bedspread and draped it over Fafnir's body. Even though everybody knew what was under the lump, it was better not having to look at it.

"I turned the heat up to 'high'," Kayla said, coming and perching on the couch next to Ace and Hosea. "Not that it'll make much difference with that honking big hole in the wall."

Paul followed Toni into the kitchen, presumably to get her version of the night's events.

Magnus looked at Eric.

"Things always this much fun around here?" the boy suggested, in tones that indicated it had been anything but.

"No," Eric said. "Usually it's quiet for, oh, months at a time."

"You meant it about not sending me back to Boston, right?" Magnus said aggressively. Eric nodded.

"I'm not a musical prodigy," the boy continued.

"I know you're not," Eric said.

The boy looked startled and a little annoyed. Well, having been told from the time he could walk that he was a musical genius, it was probably a little offputting to have his talent so casually dismissed.

"You're undoubtedly a very good musician. That much certainly runs in the family. You might be a Bard—or Talented in some other way. I'm not in any hurry to find out," Eric said, with a gesture of indifference. "All I want is to get you some space to find out for yourself what you want and what you're good at." Eric said.

Magnus shrugged. "Fine with me. What's a Bard?"

Just then Toni and Paul returned, carrying bottles of juice and a bag of paper cups. "Our host has an amazing collection of liquor, and quite a wine cellar, but I managed to find some juice," Toni said.

She passed around cups, making particularly sure that the young Talents—Ace and Kayla—had some. Ace had gotten herself back under control now, but still looked rather strained. As would anyone whose greatest secret had been dragged out into the open for everyone to see.

"It doesn't matter *who* your folks are," Eric heard Kayla tell her. "Ria Llewellyn'll eat 'em for breakfast."

"Oh, I do believe she could," Ace said. "If she wanted to."

"She'll want to," Eric said.

"But right now we have another problem," Toni said. She pointed toward the corpse on the floor.

"Looked like he died of a heart attack," Eric said.

"He did," Hosea said quietly.

Eric smiled. "Well, I don't see why this guy shouldn't have a heart attack in his own apartment and be found there, for one thing. Greystone?"

A moment later, the gargoyle—who had landed on the roof about the same time Paul and José had come in the door—flew in through the open window and waddled over to the body on the floor. He peeled back the cover and regarded it critically.

"Nasty piece o' work this," he said. "Troublin' poor Miss Caity and all those others the way he did. Some people do improve life by the leavin' of it. Just leave this to me, folks; there isn't an apartment in the five boroughs I can't get into when I'm of a mind to. I'll even make the 911 call from his apartment so they find him before too long. How's that?"

"Perfect," Eric said.

Greystone slung the body over his shoulder and climbed to the windowsill again. He sprang out into the night, falling like a, well, rock. Ace gave a small squeak of alarm, but a few moments later they saw a dark speck silhouetted against the moon: the gargoyle with its burden.

"That takes care o' everything but Mr. Neil Grandison's window," Hosea observed a moment later.

"I'd just as soon leave it, rather than repair it by magic," Eric said, after a moment's thought. "He'll need some reason why he went out tonight. And big birds do fly into them and shatter them from time to time."

"Ayah," Hosea said approvingly. "Probably that's jest what happened here."

"It's been a long night," Toni said, looking around. "Let's go home."

"That means you guys, too," Eric said to Ace and Magnus. "You're with me."

For a moment the two runaways looked at each other.

"Hey, Ace," Magnus said. "I bet Eric's got a television with all the channels—"

What? The non sequitur made no sense to Eric. But tired as she was, Ace's face lit up with secret mischief.

"Internet access—?"

"A refrigerator and a stove," Magnus said.

"Coffee—" Ace said next, with the air of one playing out an old game.

"*A bathroom and a door that locks,*" the two of them finished in chorus, before dissolving into helpless, and slightly hysterical laughter.

CHAPTER SEVENTEEN:

BOYS OF THE LOUGH

This Thanksgiving Eric had even more than usual to be thankful for.

He'd found Magnus alive and well.

Having a "baby" brother was still a whole new world for Eric, and one that was going to take a lot of getting used to, for both of them. For one thing, he was going to need a larger apartment. Toni had promised to give him the first two-bedroom that she could manage to free up, but that would take a while. For now, Magnus was sleeping on the couch in the living room, and Eric had spent the past week shopping for clothes for him, and trying to decide what to do about school and other such mundane necessities.

The two of them arrived at Ria's apartment around two, having spent the morning down at Macy's, watching the parade with the rest of the New York crowds. They'd had beautiful—if ice-cold—weather for it, and a good view of all the performances. Christmas decorations were already up on most of the buildings, which Eric thought was hardly fair—Christmas was weeks away, wasn't it? And it looked like it was going to be a white one.

Ria had argued, logically enough, that as she had the largest apartment and the biggest dining room table, Thanksgiving should be held at her place, and Eric could see no reason to disagree with this plan. She had the biggest kitchen, too, even if (he suspected) everything was going to be shipped in from an upscale caterer.

But when the private elevator opened into the foyer, Eric's nostrils were assailed by the smells of . . . cooking?

"Hey," Magnus said appreciatively. "Smells like *food.*"

"You can't be hungry," Eric protested. Magnus had eaten three hot dogs during the parade, assuring Eric they wouldn't spoil his appetite for dinner at all.

"Can," Magnus said simply, heading off in the direction of the food smells without bothering to take off his jacket.

Ace waved as they appeared in the doorway.

"Boy, when I said I wanted a kitchen, I wasn't expecting something like this," she said, grinning.

"Hey . . . wow," Magnus said, and for once Eric knew he wasn't thinking about food.

A week—and a shopping spree—had worked radical changes on the young teenager. Her pale blonde hair had been cut so that it haloed her face in a trendy mop of curls. Small gold hoops glittered in her ears. Expert makeup made her blue eyes seem enormous, and mascara darkened her lashes. And tight blue jeans and a form-fitting sweater didn't hurt matters either.

She looked, in fact, like a normal, healthy, teenage girl. Pretty, too.

Accent on the teenage, *Banyon. Mind your manners.* "You look great," Eric said, as his brother had apparently just been struck dumb. "But what's all this?"

"It's dinner," Ace said. "When Ria said she was going to get a bunch of store-bought stuff, I said I'd cook. She's done so much for me—and I like to cook."

"You can cook?" Magnus said, drifting toward a platter of devilled eggs.

"Out!" Ace turned, quick as a flash, to intercept him. "You haven't even taken off your coats yet. You go take off your coat, Magnus Banyon, and wash your hands, and then—maybe—you can come back into my kitchen and I'll give you something to keep body and soul together until dinner. Which won't be for a couple of hours, because Ria called and she's running late, and—as you can plainly see—Hosea and Kayla aren't here yet. And the turkey isn't ready anyway. So scat."

"Come on," Eric said to Magnus, taking his brother's arm and leading him out of the kitchen. Once Ace was sure her devilled eggs weren't in immediate danger, she turned back to the stove, picking up a wooden spoon and giving one of the pots a stir.

It looked like Ace was settling in with Ria just fine, Eric thought with a grin, as he led Magnus back to the foyer and a closet where they could hang up their coats. Fortunately, Ria had finally been able to get out of Washington a day or two after the final blowup, so Ace had been able to move in with her. Otherwise things at *chez* Banyon would have been even more crowded than they were right now.

When Ace had finally unbent enough to tell the others her entire story, Eric and Hosea had no difficulty understanding just why it was she'd been hiding so desperately.

They'd already had ample evidence of her Gift—to influence people's thoughts and emotions through her singing, and more, to draw on the Power of those around her to intensify her Gift. When she'd told them about her past, the others had learned that she'd been born to a revivalist preacher, and that Billy Fairchild had not been in the least shy about exploiting his daughter's ability.

But even with Ace's help, Billy Fairchild had been strictly small-time, until a man named Gabriel Horn had come on the scene about two years ago. He'd frightened Ace—whose real name was Heavenly Grace, and Eric could see why she didn't want to go by it—so much that she'd run away from home, and she'd been hiding ever since. It hadn't been hard to track down information about Billy Fairchild Ministries on the 'net, and verify every bit of it. Including the ongoing deception that "little" Heavenly Grace was supposed to be attending a strict Bible college at this very moment.

"Well, that's over and done with," Ria had said firmly, once Ace had finished her explanation. "You don't have to go back there, and you certainly won't be using your abilities that way ever again."

Ace had looked at her skeptically. Ria had only laughed. "My dear girl! There are half-a-dozen ways to keep him from coming after you! Blackmail is the easiest; I imagine Mr. Fairchild has any number of secrets besides your abilities that he'd prefer not to have made public knowledge—or the subject of an IRS audit?"

"I suppose," Ace had said uncertainly.

"Besides," Ria had said briskly, "We'll just file a petition for emancipated minor status for you. Your family won't contest it if they know what's good for them. And that's that."

"'Emancipated minor'?" Ace had said, confused.

"Giving you the privileges of adulthood a few years early, assuming the court grants your petition. And they will," Ria'd said, with no doubt in her voice.

"But what will I *do*?" Ace had said, sounding flustered and doubtful. "I don't know how to do anything but sing."

"Stay here in New York with me," Ria had answered. "Go to school, at least for the next few years. And help me with a certain project I have in mind."

Though Eric had asked Ria about her project, she'd just smiled and looked mysterious. Maybe he could get more details out of her today.

And if Ace did nothing else with her future, she could certainly get a job as Ria's full-time majordomo, Eric thought, as he followed Magnus back to the kitchen.

Ria arrived, amazingly, only forty minutes later.

"Half day for you?" Eric gibed, when she joined the others in the kitchen.

"Hah," Ace said, lifting a tray of cornbread out of the baking oven to cool. "She lit out of here at six this morning. You get away from that!"

"I wasn't doing anything," Magnus protested—reasonably enough, as he was still seated on the far side of the kitchen.

"You were thinking," Ace said.

"I was not thinking," Magnus said virtuously.

Ria raised an eyebrow at Eric, and Eric grinned. She indicated the living room with an inclination of her head, and he followed her out. Behind them, they could hear an elaborate and amiable argument continuing about whether or not Magnus thought—or, in fact, *could* think.

"How are you doing?" Ria asked. "I'm glad you got your hair cut again, by the way. Those toy-boy tresses gave me quite a start."

"Courtesy of the Underhill M°A°S°H Unit," Eric said, with a grin. "But kind of hard to explain when I went back to school. We're doing okay."

We.

It was odd to think of things in those terms, but for the next several years—and maybe longer—that was how things were going to be. Magnus was his responsibility now, someone even more dependent on him than an apprentice was. "A little cramped, though. Toni says she might be able to work something out in a few months, though."

"Something with soundproofing, I hope, if your brother is set on being a rock 'n' roll superstar. And what about the magic?" Ria walked over to the couch and sat down with a sigh.

"Too soon to tell. And I'm not going to push it. He's been pushed around since before he was born. I'm going to let him find his own level."

"Nice idea—if the world will cooperate. Meanwhile, you'll be pleased to know that Philip Dorland—remember him?—is off looking for Magnus in Miami, having given up on finding him in New York. That should buy the two of you some time, at least, while you decide how to play things."

"Good thought. I figure on waiting until spring before sticking him back into school. Who knows? Maybe he'd like Juilliard after all?" Eric sat down beside her on the couch.

Ria snorted eloquently.

"And what about you? What's this special project you want to get Ace involved with?" Eric asked.

Ria turned to face him, a wicked gleam of mischief in her eyes. "Well, you know how you've always said I'm not doing enough *constructive* with my money, just becoming filthy rich. So . . . I've decided to do something you'll like: the Ria Llewellyn Foundation."

"For homeless elves?" Eric joked.

"For homeless Talents," Ria said, her expression turning serious. "Ace's story made me think. What if she hadn't run into you? For that matter, what if I hadn't been around? There *has* to be something to do with kids with capital-T Talent besides squirreling them off to elf Hill to be raised by another species. I'm going to do it."

Eric stared into her eyes for a long moment.

"What? You're going to found Professor Xavier's School for Gifted Youngsters?" he finally said.

"Something like that," Ria said. "Without the funny uniforms and supervillains, I hope. Ace is going to be my pilot project. She already has a handle on her Talent. Maybe she'll be willing to help me find and take care of kids who don't. Maybe Hosea will be willing to help as well. And then kids like her—and Kayla—will have someplace to go besides institutions and the street. A place where people will understand them and teach them to understand themselves. It will take time and money. But I have both. And I think it's something worth doing."

"Well . . . yes," Eric said. "But it's not going to be easy. Just keeping Ace out of her family's hands is going to involve a heck of a fight. I've been surfing the 'net—when I can get the computer away from Magnus—and I might never have heard of Billy Fairchild before Ace mentioned him, but he's not exactly nobody. In fact, he's building a Casino of

Prayer over in Atlantic City right now. I'd imagine he can afford some pretty good lawyers to get his daughter back."

Ria smiled wolfishly, and patted his knee. "Why, Eric," she cooed dulcetly, "so can I. And I'll just adore reducing that insufferable little maggot to a grease spot, him and whoever this Gabriel Horn is. You've just got to stop thinking of Underhill as the answer to all the World Above's problems . . . even if the two are . . . linked," she finished musingly.

"Linked?" Eric asked, puzzled at the change of subject.

"Did you ever wonder why the Guardians exist? When they started? What they're for?"

What has that got to do with Gifted youngsters or elves? Eric wondered.

Ria frowned impatiently.

"Oh, come now, Eric: when we met, you weren't one of the world's deep thinkers, but you've grown up since then. Everything in Nature has a purpose. Look at humans and the Sidhe."

"All right," Eric said agreeably. "And maybe you'll tell me what this has to do with your plan to found Hogwarts in New York."

"Maybe nothing directly. But a specialist I consulted during the recent unpleasantness was adamant about the study of magic being bad for humans, though he had no problem with inborn Talents, like Ace's, or Kayla's—or yours, and frankly I can't see a lot of difference between your magic and a Guardian's, right? Magic is magic. But he was adamant about magic being for the elves and creativity for the humans, and if that's the case, how did the two ever get tangled up together? Remember Aerune's dream?

"So I've been doing a lot of thinking and research, back to the bad old days, and Perenor's project, and wondering how and why the two realms connect. Remember that vision you told me you once had, of the world as it would have been if Perenor had gained control of the Sun-Descending Nexus and sucked up all the magic for his own use? All grey and dismal, with no light and laughter anywhere? There are places in the world already like that, as we both know, more of them all the time. Everybody always believes that the world used to be better, but nobody can quite imagine just when that used to be. The closest thing to a golden age was that fantasy world in Aerune's mind, of the way things were in Aerete's time—when humans had *no* magic—but I don't think being some Sidhe's pet is the right answer either. But that only begs the question. If humans have imagination and elves have magic, where do the Guardians—humans with magic—come into things? Where do they *fit*? What are they *for*? Aerune seemed to recognize Toni when we all fought him together; that implies that elves know something about the Guardians, doesn't it?"

Eric remembered something Master Dharniel had said, about the elves remembering the Guardians even if the Guardians had forgotten them. He said so.

Ria nodded. "Another thing to ask my specialist about; I'm sure he knows. And the fact remains, however the relationship started out, elves and humans have been together now for an awfully long time: elves need humans because humans can dream, imagine, create—all things that elves can't do. And humans need elves—hard as that is for me to admit—to add magic and wonder to their lives by just existing. So it seems to be a symbiotic relationship: Faerie and the World, interlinked. Whether they started out together or not, by now they've grown so closely intertwined that I don't think you can separate them any more.

Destroy one and you destroy the other. That's why I put so much effort into getting rid of Wheatley's little task force, and I'm pretty sure that after his last adventure, the PDI is history—I'll tell you the whole story of that another time."

"I'll hold you to that," Eric vowed. "But about the Guardians . . . you know they act only for good. Why do you want to, well, meddle?"

Ria kissed him gently on the forehead. "Because I don't like mysteries, Eric. Never have. And if elves are so convinced that no human can have innate magic, I want to know more about people who *do*."

And Eric wondered if there was anything he could possibly do to stop her.

Kayla was the next to arrive. She'd restored herself and her jacket to full Goth glamour, and was wearing enough leather to upholster a small chair: skirt, bustier, her leather jacket, boots, and cap. Her eyeshadow and lipstick were both bright orange, and she was wearing a tiny Pilgrim dangling from each ear. Kayla liked to dress for the seasons.

"Where's Hosea?" Eric asked, greeting her at the door. "I thought he was coming and bringing Caity." Paul and José were spending Thanksgiving with Toni's family in Queens, but the three of them had said they might stop by on the way home, for dessert. From the number of pies Eric had seen on cooling racks in the kitchen, Eric thought there'd be plenty left. It looked as if Ace had been cooking for as many hours as Ria had been working. He hadn't known there were that many pots and pans in Ria's kitchen. Probably Ria hadn't known either.

A faintly guilty look crossed Kayla's face. "I guess you'd better let him get into that."

She shrugged out of her biker jacket and opened

the closet. Beneath it, she was wearing an orange Chinese silk jacket that just covered her shoulders.

"Oh good," Magnus said, coming into the foyer and seeing Kayla, "Ace says you can help me set the table."

Kayla thrust her jacket and cap at Eric and followed Magnus, effectively ending the conversation.

Fortunately Hosea arrived just as the turkey was coming out of the oven, and before Ace began to worry about holding dinner for him. But he arrived alone.

"Ah was jest helpin' Caity with her packing," Hosea said, explaining. "An Ah ran a little late."

Packing? There had to be more to the story than that, to judge from the glum expression on the big man's face, but Eric didn't want to push for an explanation in front of everybody. And Hosea seemed more than willing to let the subject drop, helping the others carry food to the table and complimenting Ace on her cooking.

"I'm not a very religious person," Ria said, when they'd all taken their places around the table, "but I think it's a good idea every once in a while to stop and take stock of what you have to be thankful for. Your health, if you have it. Your life, if it's been endangered—and even if it hasn't. Your freedom, always. And your friends. Without them, the other three aren't worth much. So here's to us, and to another year lived."

"Good words," Hosea said, bowing his head.

Ria raised her glass, and they all drank.

"And I'd like to say," Ace said, blushing furiously, "that we should be thankful for love. And—hope. Because even if you don't have any of those other things—or think you don't—if you can love, and hope, you can at least get to where you do. Someday."

"Amen to that," Eric said.

❖   ❖   ❖

After the meal was done, Eric and Hosea volunteered to scrape plates and load the dishwasher—emptying it of the now-clean pots and pans that Ace had filled it with before they'd sat down to eat—while the kids went off to channel-surf and Ria returned a few phone calls.

Besides, it gave him a chance to talk to Hosea alone.

"Anything you want to tell me?" Eric asked.

"Ah supposed we'd get around to that," Hosea admitted glumly. "No reason not to tell you. Caity's moving out of the city. She's decided she can do her drawing just as well back home in West Virginia. So that's where she's going. Ah was helping her with her packing."

Eric digested the news in silence. "I'm sorry," he said, after a moment. "I know the two of you were friends."

Hosea sighed. "Well, Ah don't think she'd take any too kindly to findin' out about me bein' a Bard—or any o' the rest of it, 'specially after what happened with 'Master Fafnir.' She's taken it into her head that he was just some kind o' con man, feedin' her and the others a line o' country to get money out of the lot of 'em. Which ain't any too far from the truth, when you come down to it, really. And she's so mad about it all, and at herself with bein' roped in by it, that she's decided to put a good deal o' distance between herself and the big city. Ah'll miss her." Hosea sighed.

"So there's going to be a vacancy at Guardian House," Eric said, hoping to turn the conversation to a topic less painful for his friend. *Unfortunately, not a two-bedroom.* "I wonder who's going to move in?"

"Whoever it is, Ah hope they're a restful sort," Hosea said. "But there's one other thing you should know about Caity. While Ah was helpin' her pack, she did tell me one interesting thing. Ah'm not sure whether knowin' it sooner would've made any difference, or not, though. Seems Fafnir had already picked out the feller he was going to have his little group execute, once he'd got them scared enough to take leave o' their common sense."

"Anybody we know?" Eric asked lightly.

Hosea regarded him steadily. "Paul Kern."

Eric blinked, and took a deep breath. "Well, he had the right guy. Paul's a Guardian, all right. But how did he know—or *did* he know?"

Hosea shrugged. "Ah suppose we won't ever know the answer to that, any more'n we'll ever know just what attracted Jaycie's Protector to her particular victims. Toni checked with the PD, though, and there were children—young ones—at all the places at the time o' the murders."

"So Rionne was protecting them—or trying to—or at least thought she was. The same way she was trying to protect Amanda," Eric said slowly. "Only she'd spent so much time in New York looking for Jaycie that she'd lost her ability to resist human imagination and human belief. . . ."

"Ayah. She must have started out looking in the shelters. The little'uns made her a part of their Secret Stories, and then 'Master Fafnir' made Bloody Mary a part of his spell," Hosea said consideringly. "Ah never thought of the Good Folk as being quite so vulnerable."

"Just as vulnerable to human creativity—belief—as humans are to Elven magic, I guess," Eric said. "But it takes a lot more belief over a longer period to affect one of the Sidhe than it does for a spell to affect a human. She was just in the wrong place at the wrong time for too long."

"There's a lot of that goin' around," Hosea said. "But sometimes good does manage to come out of it, along with all the pain."

For a while the two Bards scraped, stacked, and loaded dishes in companionable silence. When everything was finished, and the dishwasher had begun to run, Hosea spoke again.

"Do you think she'll come back, the way she said?"

"Maybe," Eric said. "You can put that in one of your songs, too."

"Ah reckon Ah will," Hosea said, smiling.

EPILOGUE:

THE WIND THAT SHAKES
THE BARLEY

In early December, Parker Wheatley attended a meeting he'd very much wished to avoid.

Things had been going badly for several weeks. His calls hadn't been returned. People who'd been happy to know him this time last year were distant and evasive. Even his own people were less than responsive—and as for interagency cooperation, that had vanished as of the night Ria Llewellyn had broken into his offices and kidnapped a traitor to the human race.

She'd had high-level help, of course. No one would believe him. That was one in a long list of things about which Parker Wheatley could suddenly find no one to believe him. His credibility—the true coin in which Washington bargains were made and sealed—had suddenly vanished as if it were faery gold.

Faery gold. As they did so often, his thoughts turned to Aerune mac Audelaine, who had so inexplicably abandoned him after seducing him with false promises. Without Aerune's meddling, his career wouldn't be in ruins now.

And it was. Only a fool would think otherwise. The meeting today would only put the official imprimatur on what everybody knew.

But still the forms must be observed, so he presented himself at the appropriate offices at the appointed hour, wondering what his punishment was to be. He was fairly certain that the PDI itself was to be dismantled, but it was his own future that he was concerned with now. What would they do with him? A demotion in grade with associated pay cuts? Revocation of some of his security clearances? A minor desk in some out-of-the-way bureau?

An attaché met him at the elevator, and walked him silently back to an anonymous conference room. There were seven people seated around the conference table, and Wheatley was dismayed to realize that he didn't recognize three of them. One of the others, Caleb Buchan, was the head of the newly formed Joint Oversight Committee on Intelligence. He had a thick folder in front of him.

No introductions were offered.

"Sit down, Mr. Wheatley," Buchan said.

Wheatley sat.

"I've been going over the mission statement for the . . . Paranormal Defense Initiative, is it? Very interesting reading. And of course, I've been brought up to date about your recent activities."

There didn't seem to be anything to say, so Wheatley said nothing. This was going to be worse than he thought, if the FBI and CIA were sitting in on it.

"We don't believe that there's any further need for your project, Mr. Wheatley," Buchan said. "Your resources will be reallocated. Your assets will be debriefed and assigned elsewhere as appropriate."

There was a pause. Buchan leafed through the file in front of him—an unnecessary gesture, as he'd certainly had plenty of time to familiarize himself with it before the meeting.

So far, things had gone about as Wheatley had expected them to. The PDI was history. He'd expected that. But what had been built once could be built again, given time.

"And now, I imagine you're wondering what we're going to do with you," Buchan continued, looking up. "Considering that your actions border on criminal lunacy, that's only reasonable."

Wheatley shifted in his chair, keeping his face expressionless with an effort. He certainly hadn't expected this sort of language from a Washington insider.

"Fortunately, Mr. Bell and Ms. Llewellyn are both willing to cooperate with us to keep this low-key. They're trusting us to take care of it quietly, for the good of the people. *Pro bono publico*, a phrase heard all too rarely these days. I see from your personnel records that you haven't taken a vacation in twelve years, Mr. Wheatley. Is that correct?"

It took Wheatley a moment to realize he'd been asked a direct question. "I . . . yes. Sir."

Buchan smiled. It wasn't a nice smile. "Well, then. You'll have a great deal of leave time accumulated. I suggest you take it. And you can apply for early retirement while you're at it. I'm absolutely certain the request will be granted. I understand there are wonderful opportunities in the private sector these days."

He got to his feet, indicating that the meeting was over.

"In fact, why don't you start now? I'll have my assistant call yours. She can pack up your office and have your personal things sent to your home. That way, you can start forgetting about the PDI right away."

Wheatley got to his feet automatically as the others left, but he couldn't bring himself to follow them immediately.

He'd just been fired. There'd be no transfer for him, no minor punishments. Buchan could dress it up however he liked with suggestions about "vacations" and "retirement," but Wheatley was finished in Washington. His career was over.

But Wheatley knew who to blame for his downfall.

Aerune mac Audelaine. And Ria Llewellyn.

And he'd have his revenge, on both of them.

It was only a matter of time.

∽

Eric Banyon will return in *Music to My Sorrow*

(available in December 2005 from Baen Books)